It's time to work her cri

Kailyn Wilde enjoys running her shop, Abracadabra, in the quaint New York hamlet of New Camel, where she lives with her six cats. Her family's been here for centuries, and she'd like to keep up the tradition. But the place may never be the same if a big hotel gets built, so she does her civic duty and attends a town meeting along with her aunt Tilly . . . and Merlin. Yes, that Merlin—though he gets introduced to folks as her "distant English cousin." The wizard is pretty grumpy about being transported here, but there are things about the modern world he doesn't mind—like pizza.

Kailyn was prepared for a heated debate about the hotel, but she wasn't expecting murder. When Tilly finds the body of a board member outside the schoolhouse, Kailyn doesn't want any suspicion cast on the wrong person. She plans to crack this case, even if she has to talk to every living soul in town—plus a few departed ones . . .

Visit us at www.kensingtonbooks.com

Books by Sharon Pape

Magick & Mayhem
Sketcher in the Rye
Alibis and Amethysts
Sketch a Falling Star
To Sketch a Thief
Sketch Me if You Can

Published by Kensington Publishing Corporation

That Olde White Magick

An Abracadabra Mystery

Sharon Pape

LYRICAL PRESS
Kensington Publishing Corp.
www.kensingtonbooks.com

First Electronic Edition: November 2017
eISBN-13: 978-1-5161-0057-6
eISBN-10: 1-5161-0057-3

First Print Edition: November 2017
ISBN-13: 978-1-5161-0058-3
ISBN-10: 1-5161-0058-1

Printed in the United States of America

To my mom—until I see you again.

Thanks for the ducks.

Acknowledgment

A special thank you to my editor, Michaela Hamilton, for her wise guidance and support. It's so much easier to create magick with an editor like her

Chapter 1

"Every living soul in this town must be here tonight," my aunt Tilly remarked as I pulled into the last parking spot at the New Camel Elementary School. It was the school I attended as a child, the school my aunt, my mother, and my grandmother had attended, as well as generations of Wildes before them. It had started out as a one-room schoolhouse and had been expanded over the years to accommodate fourteen classrooms, kindergarten through sixth grade. It still sat on the crest of Johnson's Hill at the eastern end of town. I loved the tradition and continuity it represented, the warmth of hometown I felt whenever I passed by.

"I'm not surprised," I said, turning off the engine. "Everyone I talk to has an opinion on the matter, a very definite opinion."

"We'd better hustle our bustles and get in there before all the seats are taken."

Tilly took off her seat belt, opened the car door, and nearly slid right out courtesy of her silk muumuu-clad bottom. I reached for her arm to stop her, but I still had my seat belt on, and she was too far away. At the last moment, she grabbed the doorjamb to stop herself.

"Whoops," she said with a gasp and a giggle. "That was like a carnival ride. I need to stop wearing such slippery fabrics, or you'll be scooping me off the pavement one day."

Merlin emerged from the back seat, grousing. "I cannot fathom why I am being compelled to attend a meeting, in which I have neither interest nor purpose. I am not a citizen of this town or, for that matter, of this state, this country, or this particular period in time."

My aunt and I let him grumble on without comment. It wasn't the first time he'd serenaded us with that particular tune. We joined the stream of people entering the school and heading down the hallway to the gymnasium. People were calling out hellos or stopping to share quick hugs, which caused everyone else to detour around them like water around a jetty. As a result, the normally short walk to the gym was taking far longer than it should have, but I had no right to complain. I was as guilty as everyone else. That's what happens when the residents of a small town congregate in one place. Merlin, on the other hand, griped enough for both of us. He knew only a few people, and he regarded the traffic snarl as a plot to keep him from his TV shows.

In spite of all the open windows, the building had a stale, musty odor from being closed most of the summer, and the late August heat wave was making matters worse. At least there was some decent cross ventilation going when we reached the gym. Rusty Higgins, the sum total of the school's custodial staff, had propped open the two large emergency exit doors in the back.

The gym had always been big enough to host the town board meetings, but tonight it was overcrowded, the walls bulging with people. The air vibrated with tension, and the loud droning of all their voices made me feel like I was walking into a massive beehive. In hindsight, not the best place to have brought Merlin, who was twitchy and out of his element under the best of circumstances. Tilly and I had debated for days about whether to take him. Despite the jeans and shirt we bullied him into wearing, his raging white hair and beard set him apart from the local population. There was no way around it. He was already drawing blatant stares of curiosity. On the other hand, leaving him home alone, where the deadly combination of boredom and magick might lead him astray again, wasn't a comfortable option either. In the end, keeping an eye on him had won handily.

"Let the gawkers gawk," I said. If anyone asked nosy questions, they'd get our now standard reply. Merlin was a distant English cousin from the eccentric side of the family, here on an extended visit. "Extended" barely covered it. He'd be staying until I figured out how to send him back to his own time and place. Although he'd been with us for two months, I was no closer to reaching that goal than I had been the day he crash-landed in the storeroom of my magick shop.

Apparently no one had told Rusty to expect a larger than usual turnout because there were fewer than two dozen folding chairs set up facing the mobile podium. By the time we arrived, they were all taken. I spied a few empty spots in the bleachers, but I knew my aunt would have trouble reaching them. I had visions of her stepping on the hem of her silk muumuu and either pitching forward onto her face or tumbling backward to the floor, taking others with her like a human avalanche. The safer option was to remain standing in the empty area behind the chairs with everyone else who found themselves seatless. There were plenty of disgruntled comments about the situation, but I didn't see one person leave.

This was my first town board meeting. According to Tilly, neither she nor my late mother nor my grandmother had ever attended one. But she knew that the town's charter, which had originally called for monthly meetings, had been changed to quarterly meetings decades before I was born, once it became clear that there was nothing the board needed to address that couldn't wait a few months—until now. Our mayor, Lester Tompkins, had called this meeting as a special session.

At precisely seven o'clock, three of the five board members, including the mayor, trooped into the gym from the adjoining supply room and stepped onto the podium. They took their seats behind a cafeteria table, grandly draped with the town's insignia, a camel on a verdant field.

"A camel," Merlin muttered when he noticed it. "And yet I am not permitted to tell these people the true name of their town. I should think they would welcome the knowledge."

"Some people don't deal well with change," I explained for the twentieth time. "We have to wait for the right moment." I didn't harbor much hope it would happen anytime soon.

"I disagree. This is the perfect time, given that the whole town is here."

"Everyone is too divided over the hotel. I can't imagine a worse time to throw another change at them."

He glowered at me but stopped arguing.

"I'm surprised the board members aren't down here, glad-handing the crowd, banking votes for the next election," Tilly whispered loudly enough for people within twenty feet of us to hear. As if on cue, Beverly Ruppert, the newest member of the board, swept into the gym with the aplomb of a Broadway star making her grand entrance. She was dressed for the part in a sleeveless beige sheath that was strained across her hips and stiletto heels that caused her to walk like a novice on stilts. Tilly rolled her eyes at me as Beverly threaded her way through the crowd, stopping to greet everyone with a handshake or an air kiss. It looked like she would miss us on her current trajectory to the podium, but at the last moment she spied us and changed direction. Tilly groaned.

"Well, look who's here." Beverly flashed her broadest political smile for us. "We finally got you two to attend a meeting."

Since she'd been on the town board for all of four months, I was tempted to ask how many meetings she'd attended before discovering her political calling. But I held my tongue. We needed Beverly on our side, at least until the Waverly proposal was decided. She was against it as much as

Tilly and I were.

"Hi, Bev," I said.

Tilly gave her a nod of acknowledgment.

Beverly homed in on her. "I guess there's no point in asking you which way the vote will go tonight, is there, Tilly, dear?" she said with syrupy condescension. "Everyone knows your track record has been abysmal lately."

I felt Tilly's anger flare and wished that telepathy was one of my stronger suits. Then I could have talked her down and urged her not to take the bait.

"My aunt is too ethical to try to influence the outcome with a prediction," I said before my ethical aunt could come up with a more caustic response. As I spoke those words, I realized it wasn't Tilly's reaction I should have been worried about. Merlin was glaring at Beverly, mumbling something unintelligible, his lips grim and all but hidden in the bird's nest of his beard. He was too far away for me to stop him with a discreet jab to the ribs, and Tilly, who stood between us, seemed content to allow him free rein for the moment.

"Don't they need you up there so they can start the meeting?" I asked Beverly in a last-ditch effort to get her away from Merlin. She'd still be within reach of his powers on the other side of the gym, but if I could break his concentration on her, it might buy me the few seconds I needed to talk some sense into him.

Beverly gave me a dismissive wave of her hand. "Amanda's not here yet any—"

Her voice cracked and was gone. When she opened her mouth, no sound emerged—not a croak, not a rasp, not a whine. Her hand flew to her throat, and her eyes widened with dismay and bewilderment. The harder she tried to speak, the more frustrated she became. She was opening and closing her mouth like the goldfish I'd had as a child. I turned to Merlin. He was wearing a beatific smile, as if all was right with the world. Tilly didn't seem troubled by Beverly's predicament either or by the fact that the wizard had gone rogue right under our noses. Of course, as apt punishments go, I had to admit that Merlin nailed it.

Panic was rising in Beverly's eyes, the corded muscles in her neck standing out with the prolonged strain of trying to make her vocal cords work.

I had to do something before she had a stroke or a heart attack. I slipped behind Tilly, grabbed Merlin's arm and squeezed. "Stop it!" I yelled into his ear to be sure he heard me. I threw in the worst threat I could imagine. "Or no pizza for a month."

In a matter of seconds, a blood-curdling scream rocked the gym. It ricocheted off the walls, the floor, the ceiling, and the wooden bleachers.

Conversations stopped dead. All eyes turned to Beverly. Merlin had released her from the spell once he understood his pizza would be forfeit, but he'd timed it to coincide with her effort to force sound through her vocal cords. Even she seemed stunned by the horrific noise she produced. Her cheeks turned crimson.

"Sorry, sorry—everything's okay," she called out, scowling at the three of us as if she suspected we were to blame for the fiasco. Muttering that she needed fresh air, she turned on her wobbly heels and stalked out of the gym with far less composure than when she had arrived. I locked eyes with Merlin. If steam had been shooting out of my ears it wouldn't have surprised me.

"Yes, I know," he said, preempting me in the sullen, world-weary tone of a teenager. "We need to talk—again."

"Well, we do," I said, my thunder stolen. We'd been letting him watch way too much TV. More important, although we made it clear that he must not go about randomly casting spells, he'd done just that. He was an old man with the abilities of a master sorcerer and the attitude of a teenage rebel. Disaster was always on the agenda.

Tilly pulled a tissue from her purse and dabbed at her forehead and upper lip. "It's sweltering in here. I'm going outside to cool off." When she caught the hitch of my eyebrow, she added, "Don't worry, I'm not chasing after Beverly to give her my two cents, even if she deserves it and more. I'll go out the back way. I won't be long."

I watched her shuffle through the crowd and disappear through the emergency doors. She couldn't have been gone more than a minute or two when another scream pierced the air. I knew that scream. It was Tilly's. But it sounded like part of a duet, or how I imagined a duet of screams would sound. Grabbing Merlin's hand, I ran for the rear doors. Having been closer to the gym's entrance, we were among the last to make it outside. By then, sirens were blaring in the distance

Once we made it outside, all I could see were people's backs. I elbowed my way through the crowd, pulling Merlin along with me and excusing ourselves as we charged ahead. I fielded a lot of dirty looks, but that wasn't going to stop me. Tilly had screamed, and the situation was serious enough to bring the local emergency squad. I had to find out why.

Merlin and I broke through the ring of onlookers and found ourselves directly across from Tilly. Her eyes were wide, her face bleached white. Beverly, who was standing a few feet away, didn't look much better. They were both focused on a woman's body lying prone on the grass between us. So many people were standing and kneeling around her that I couldn't venture a guess about her identity. Dr. Bronson, Tilly's rheumatologist, was at her side, along with an off-duty EMT and a nurse who looked familiar. They must have all been in the gym when the screaming erupted.

Dusk was already descending, courtesy of the mountains to the west. It was becoming harder to see by the minute. The interior lights in the school didn't reach around to this side of the school grounds. People were calling for flashlights; two men ran to find Rusty. Although it seemed like forever, it couldn't have been more than a couple minutes before the exterior floodlights flashed on, instantly turning twilight back into day.

With the help of the EMT, Bronson turned the woman over. Wasn't he supposed to wait for the ambulance to bring a spine board? I wondered. As they lay her on her back, the answer was easy to see. There was no need to stabilize her. Her neck had been slashed from ear to ear. She was probably dead before anyone got to her. Gasps and cries rose as those in the front passed this information to those behind them. The victim was Amanda Boswell, the missing board member.

Chapter 2

The ambulance left quietly. No lights, no sirens. No need for haste. Paul Curtis, who'd arrived in his patrol car at the same time as the emergency vehicle, remained. I hadn't seen him since Jim Harkens's murder was solved in the early days of the summer. Curtis was wearing his official business face as he escorted the EMTs with their gurney, but when he spotted me, he broke into a hi-how-you-doin' smile for a second. I was pretty sure he had what my grandmother Bronwen used to call "a sweet tooth" for me. I gave him a half-hearted smile in return. Although I didn't really know Amanda, it felt wrong to flirt or smile with her body still there. Besides, I didn't want to encourage him when I was in limbo about my relationship with Travis Anderson.

After the ambulance took Amanda away, Curtis secured the area where she died with stakes and crime scene tape. Merlin and I gave it a wide berth as we made our way over to stand with Tilly. We each put an arm around her, though she was no longer unsteady on her feet. To be honest, I was finding the contact comforting. Maybe Merlin did too. Beverly was nearby, telling anyone who would listen about the horror of discovering "poor Amanda." With each retelling, the story became more dramatic and her relationship with Amanda more intimate.

"Give her another ten minutes, and she'll be Amanda's long-lost sister," Tilly said with dry distaste.

"Are we waiting for a polite time to leave?" Merlin wanted to know. "I find so many of your social conventions vexing."

I tried to explain it was actually a matter of the law. "The police will want to speak to Tilly, because she was one of the people who found the body."

"I don't like being grilled," she mumbled.

I gave her shoulder a squeeze. "Come on now. It's not like they dragged you down to the police station and browbeat you under the glare of a naked light bulb the last time."

"It was very unpleasant all the same."

I wasn't looking forward to another round of interviews by Detective Duggan either, but I didn't want to stoke her distress. "We made it through then and we'll make it through now," I said. "Let's leave the theatrics to Beverly."

You have to know your audience. Comparisons to her nemesis enough to shore up her courage, Tilly squared her shoulders and lifted her chin. I was glad my friend Elise hadn't been able to attend the meeting. She had wanted to come, but with Jim gone, she was a single parent, and no one was available to keep an eye on her boys. The last thing she needed was to be party to another homicide. Two short months ago, she had been arrested for killing her husband. She had been placed in a squad car and taken away. Her children, already traumatized by the loss of their father, had watched it all from their front porch. It's not the kind of experience you can simply shrug off, when the police let you go with an "oops, our bad" apology. Her kids were still waking up with nightmares.

Curtis's voice interrupted my thoughts. He was calling for quiet, not an easy endeavor. The crowd, which had been silent and respectful while Amanda was placed in a black body bag, loaded into the ambulance, and carried away, was now venting its collective shock and fear. When it came to the issue of motive, there were all kinds of theories being floated. But it was pure conjecture. All we knew for certain was that we had another killer on the loose in our once-safe town, and until he or she was caught, we were all potential targets.

"Ladies and gentlemen," Curtis said once he finally had everyone's attention, "this is an active crime scene, and you will all have to remain here until Detective Duggan arrives and we can sort things out." His words were met by a chorus of groans and complaints. He had to raise his voice and outshout them. "I'm sorry for any inconvenience, but if you leave the premises before being cleared to do so, you will be held to account. This is not a block party. This is now a murder investigation. I know you want us to catch the killer as soon as possible. To do that we can't take shortcuts or give anyone a free pass because we happen to know them. I need everyone to go back inside through the emergency doors in an orderly fashion. This crime scene has been trampled enough."

"We didn't know it was a crime scene until they found Amanda," one man boomed.

"I understand that, sir," Curtis replied. "I'm not assigning blame. I just want to protect any evidence that might still be viable. So if you'll return to the gym, I'll get the process underway while we wait for the detective. Thank you."

In spite of his instructions, the crowd surged forward, rounding the building toward the back doors, no doubt recalling how few chairs were to be had. Bleachers might be bearable for an entertaining sports event, but sitting on backless wooden slats while waiting to be questioned didn't have the same appeal.

"Why are we standing here?" Merlin bristled when I didn't lead him and Aunt Tilly in a dash to the doors. "If we are among the last to enter the building, we may well be here all night."

My nerves were as frayed as everyone else's, so I took a deep breath to settle myself before replying. "First of all, that's not how this process works. The police have their own system. I'm pretty sure it isn't first come, first served. And second, I don't want Tilly to be pushed and shoved trying to get in there. You saw how wobbly she was." But even as I was explaining things to Merlin, I was wondering how to find her someplace decent to sit.

Curtis had taken up a position at the emergency doors. He used the small pad of paper he carried for notes to write down the names of everyone as they filed past him into the gym. As I expected, all the folding chairs were occupied before we made our way back inside. One became available when the young man sitting there left to join a woman in the bleachers.

The chair quickly became the subject of a heated argument between two men who apparently reached it at the same time. They each had a death grip on the back of it. I debated the use of magick to wrest it from them, but it was the sort of magick Merlin was handier at. How could I ask him to do what I'd forbidden him to do earlier in the evening? The implications for dealing with him in the future made my head spin. I was still weighing my limited options when Tilly squeezed past me and plopped down on the contested chair.

"Thank you, gentlemen," she said, smiling up at them. "You're lifesavers. I don't know how I would have managed, what with my arthritis and all." She could make disingenuous look downright sincere.

The men stood there with their mouths hanging open, unable to come up with a response. They shared a glance of bewilderment as if they were cohorts and not rivals. For a moment, I was worried they might join forces to dump her out of the chair. Tilly must have sensed it too because she added another stanza to her praise.

"These men have restored my faith in humanity," she said to everyone within hearing distance. "They deserve recognition for their selflessness."

She started clapping, and others soon joined in.

Caught up in the spirit, Merlin let out with a rousing "Huzzah! Huzzah!" The men knew they were beaten. They let go of the chair and stalked off in different directions, no doubt wondering how they'd lost control of the situation.

"I, too, should like a seat," Merlin announced when things quieted down. He and I were standing along the side at Tilly's row. "I could easily encourage one or two people to vacate theirs," he added. "It would be no bother."

"No magick," I warned him.

"Then you would have no objection were I to yell, 'Mouse'? Women on the TV are always running from the furry little creatures. We would have our choice of seats in no time at all."

Before I could answer him, Rusty entered the gym, pushing a hand truck loaded with chairs. Curtis must have urged him into action. It had been years since I'd seen Rusty around town. Or maybe I simply hadn't recognized him. He'd aged a lot since my childhood. Most of his distinctive red hair was gone, and his once-round cheeks were sinking into bloodhound jowls. People who greeted him received a quick bob of his head, but his lips stayed compressed in a grim line. Back when I was in school, my mother used to say he was the youngest curmudgeon she'd ever known. He'd apparently grown into his personality.

He got right down to business. As fast as he was unfolding the chairs, people were claiming them. It was like watching a game of musical chairs, minus the music and fun. One woman sat before Rusty could snatch his hand away. He yowled like a cat and treated her to some words I'd never heard him use when I attended the school. Another woman slid onto a chair at the same time a man was sitting so that he wound up in her lap. After those kerfuffles, Curtis came over to supervise the rest of the chair setup. I would have expected Amanda's murder to foster more civility among the citizens of New Camel, but tensions, which had already been running high in anticipation of the board meeting, had warped into something uglier after her death.

Lolly Donovan chose that moment to rush into the gym, her face all pink and shiny and wisps of dark hair that had escaped her barrette stuck to her cheeks and forehead. She stopped dead in her tracks, clearly confused by the scene before her. She'd expected to find the town board meeting in full swing, not a bunch of grim-faced townies milling restlessly around the room or talking in tight clusters. I told Merlin not to move, and I made my way across the floor to her.

"Kailyn, what's going on here?" she asked, latching onto my arm as soon as I reached her. "What happened?"

I explained about Amanda, trying to break the news gently. She'd known Amanda much better than I had. They'd lived on the same street for years. Lolly fell back a step. I grabbed her arm, afraid she was about to faint.

"No, that's...that's not...possible," she sputtered, her eyes welling up with tears. "I just saw her this morning as I was leaving for work. First Jim and now Amanda? How did we go from never having a murder in this town to having two in as many months? It makes no sense."

I let her go on for a while, trying to wrap her mind around this latest tragedy.

"Why is everyone still here?" she asked, finally running out of steam. "What are they waiting for?"

"Detective Duggan. We can't go until he's cleared everyone. Curtis is holding down the fort until he arrives. I'm sorry, Lolly," I said. "I should have called and told you not to come. With all the turmoil, I didn't think of it."

I'd known she was going to be late. She had one of her fudge-making classes after closing. The date had been booked weeks before by a women's club from Watkins Glen. As important as the town board meeting was, business considerations trumped it. And now that Lolly was in the building, Curtis would never let her leave. In fact, her late arrival might be seen as incriminating. Duggan would want to know where she'd been at the time of Amanda's death.

"It's okay," Lolly said, "I probably would have forgotten my name under these circumstances." Biting her lip, she glanced around the gym. "Maybe I'll just scoot back out before anyone realizes I'm here."

"Too many people have already seen you. You don't want to give Duggan any reason to think you're evading him. The best thing you can do is cooperate. You have nothing to worry about. The women in your fudge-making class will vouch for you."

"You're right. What was I thinking? Can you see me as a suspect on the lam?"

I would have laughed if I weren't so worried about my aunt's situation. Merlin and I might be the only ones who saw her go outside and knew she wasn't out there long enough to kill anyone. But how much weight would our statements carry, being family and all? Then again, who would seriously consider Tilly capable of murder? I had to remind her not to say too much. Lawyers are always telling their clients to answer questions succinctly. The more you embellish, the more likely you are to hang yourself, even if you aren't guilty. Tilly had done all right the last time, but that was no guarantee. She had a tendency to ramble, especially when she was nervous. My thoughts were tripping over each other, pinging around my brain like balls in an old-fashioned pinball machine.

"Where are you sitting?" Lolly asked.

"Tilly is over there on a chair," I said, pointing in her direction. "Merlin and I don't have seats yet. He's waiting on the sidelines near her."

And judging by the empty hand truck, we weren't going to have seats anytime soon. Lolly spotted Merlin and waved. He waved back enthusiastically, possibly hoping she'd brought along some of her wares. To no one's surprise, Merlin had embraced her chocolate with as much gusto as he had pizza. One evening he polished off an entire pound of the candy while waiting for Tilly to finish preparing dinner. After that, she started hiding her personal chocolate stash at my house.

Lolly and I were still talking when Duggan arrived. He marched into the gym, a man on a mission. His craggy face was set in an attitude that didn't invite greetings. Curtis met him halfway across the floor and led him the rest of the way to the podium, where they put their heads together to confer privately. I saw him give the detective the list of names he compiled. After a couple minutes, Curtis stepped down to the gym floor, appropriated two chairs, to the chagrin of the men already in them, and dragged them to an unoccupied corner of the room. Apparently Duggan deemed him competent enough to handle some of the interviews. Or he realized that without the younger man's help, we could all be holed up in the school for days.

Given the options, I would have preferred Curtis talk with my aunt. He was younger, more affable, less threatening, and therefore less likely to give Tilly a stroke. But I had no illusions. Duggan, himself, would be questioning Beverly and her. Lolly excused herself to find a seat in the bleachers. We hugged and wished each other an easy time of it.

Duggan settled himself in one of the chairs originally meant for the board members and glanced at Curtis's list again. I could only imagine what he was thinking when he saw Tilly's name there.

"Matilda Wilde," he said in that clipped, military tone meant to strike fear into the hearts of miscreants.

I knew from experience that it did a fine job of rattling innocent people too. She rose from her seat and sidestepped out of the narrow row, trying not to stomp on anyone's toes. With surprising agility and grace, Merlin swooped in and took possession of the vacated chair. I gave my aunt the crook of my arm to hold and escorted her up the few steps to the podium.

The detective scowled at me. "You can't remain here with her."

Tilly's arm tightened on mine like a toddler on the first day of preschool. I felt a tremor move through her as I helped her into the chair next to him.

"It's been a really hard night for her, Detective," I said in what I considered a deferential tone. "Maybe I could sit somewhere behind her for a bit of emotional support, you know, somewhere I wouldn't be able to influence her responses?"

"Good try, Ms. Wilde. You're going to have to step down—now."

There was no wiggle room in his tone or in the hard set of his jaw. I left the podium, feeling Tilly's eyes following my retreat. While I'd been preoccupied, Rusty had set up a portable table at the front of the gym. I watched him lift a large coffee urn off a cart and place it at one end. He pulled a handkerchief from the pocket of his work pants to mop his forehead and stuffed it back in. He wasn't a young man anymore, and his job was largely physical. Unfortunately, his second in command had given one day's notice before setting off in search of greener pastures, a path well trodden by his predecessors. The word around town was that Rusty wasn't an easy man to work with.

He left the gym with the cart, and when he returned minutes later from the direction of the cafeteria, the cart was holding plastic coffee cups, spoons, plates, napkins, and fixings for the coffee. I ambled in that general direction. After Rusty's third trip, the cart carried three platters piled high with donuts, the refreshments promised in the email about the meeting. The moment he stepped away from the table, everyone who'd been watching his progress made a beeline for the food. Nerves, boredom, and discomfort made for a bad case of the nibbles.

I was among the first to reach the table. I took two paper plates and put a chocolate donut on one for Merlin and a jelly donut on the other for Tilly. I had to do a slalom run around the people still trying to reach the table, protecting the donuts from the jostling and bumping on every side. While we were stuck in there, they were a commodity as valuable as gold.

When I reached Merlin's row, he was the only one still in his seat. The others had decided they needed coffee and donuts more than a comfortable chair. The few who had brought a sweater or jacket left the clothing behind in hopes of saving their seats. I didn't put the odds in their favor. Without feet or knees to navigate around, I slipped easily into the row and handed Merlin his donut before heading to the podium. I wasn't looking forward to Duggan's reaction, but I knew a donut would go a long way to improving my aunt's emotional state.

The detective was too focused on my aunt to notice my approach. Since surprising him didn't seem like a good strategy, I cleared my throat to let him know I was there. He was not happy to see me, but Tilly's eyes lit up when she saw the donut.

"This isn't some little meet and greet we're conducting," he growled at me. "If you continue to interfere, I'll have Officer Curtis haul you down to the holding cell and lock you up until morning."

"My niece is worried about me, Detective," Tilly said, finding her mettle now that the donut and I had been threatened. "I have a problem with low blood sugar. You don't want me passing out on you, do you?"

Duggan chewed on that for a moment before turning back to me. "Give your aunt the damned donut, but I don't want to see you up here again until I call you. Got that?"

I thanked him and reached up to put the plate in her outstretched hand. "It's okay, dear girl," she said, making the most of her new role as a woman with a condition. "Not to worry. I'll be just fine."

Two hours later we piled back into my car. It was easy to find, being one of the last cars in the lot. After Tilly was excused, the detective had called Beverly and then Merlin. At that point, I hadn't worked out if I should tell the wizard to stick to the truth. If he took that advice too far, he might end up in the psyche ward of the nearest hospital. Instead, I went with "answer every question with as few words as possible." His interview was mercifully short, but judging by Duggan's confused expression, I was afraid to ask Merlin for details. I hoped to be called next, but Duggan kept me waiting and waiting, until the end. My comeuppance for irritating him? Or maybe his nose was still out of joint because I captured Jim's killer before he could.

By the time he'd finally called my name, I'd gone from feeling anxious to not caring to just wanting to go home. Duggan had sounded tired too and bored. He had me account for my time that day, describe my relationship with the deceased, and rate her performance as a board member. He also wanted to know which side of the Waverly controversy I supported. Although I was staunchly opposed to the large hotel and what it would mean for the charming, provincial character of our town, I didn't know what Amanda's position had been. And I definitely didn't want to sound like I was at odds with her. I'd learned that it doesn't take much to become a person of interest in our town. Instead, I said that I wanted to keep an open mind until I heard the give and take at the now aborted meeting. I could only hope that my aunt had had enough presence of mind not to commit herself either. She was uncharacteristically reticent after her interview, deflecting my questions with a shake of her head.

"I refuse to attend any more of your meetings," Merlin announced once we were underway. "Meetings are an insufferable waste of time. Apparently it matters not if it's the Knights of the Round Table or your backwater town board meeting."

"I'll keep that in mind," I replied. I could have told him that our meetings don't usually include a murder and a police investigation, but I didn't bother.

Experience had taught me that arguing with Merlin was more frustrating for me than it was educational for him. Better to save my breath for more important matters. Besides, now that we were away from the detective, I wanted to hear about what my aunt called her "grilling."

"Did Detective Duggan warn you not to talk to anyone about the interview?" I asked her.

"Not exactly."

"Meaning?"

"He said if I discussed the interview with anyone and influenced their answers, I'd be charged with interfering with the investigation." The words flew out of her mouth like pent-up lava from a dormant volcano.

Although my knowledge of the law was limited to what I'd read in books or seen on TV and in the movies, it sounded like an empty threat. It wasn't hard to understand why Duggan used it. He wanted to keep people from coaching each other to avoid contradictory statements. Even the innocent worry about saying the wrong thing. I know because I'd been worried about undermining Tilly with my responses.

"I don't think there's any law that says you can't talk about a police interview," I said as I swung my car into her driveway and brought it to a stop. "Duggan never mentioned that when he questioned me about Gary. Did he warn you about it back then?"

"No," she said indignantly. "You're right! The nerve of that man! What do you want to know, Kailyn? Ask me anything. I'll sing like a bird." Without waiting for a question, Tilly gave me a complete rundown of her interview. The questions were basically the same ones he asked me but more detailed.

"Did he ask where you stand on the Waverly hotel?" I asked.

"I told him I haven't decided yet. Only a fool would have grabbed that noose and looped it around her own neck."

I heaved a quiet sigh of relief and then chastised myself for thinking she wouldn't know how to handle herself. "That was it?"

"No, now that I think about it. He wanted to know who reached Amanda's body first."

"Who did?" I asked, annoyed I hadn't thought of that earlier. Talk about an important piece of information. Rest easy, Nancy Drew. I still have a lot to learn.

"Beverly did. She was standing over the body when I got there."

"But she didn't scream until you screamed."

"Maybe she was in shock, and when she saw me, she snapped out of it."

"Howsoever that may be," Merlin piped up from the back seat, "we are not going to solve this crime tonight regardless of how long we remain in this vehicle. I beg of you, ladies, let us go inside."

"When he's right, he's right," Tilly said. "Besides, I could do with something to eat."

"Ice cream," Merlin proposed in a more jovial tone. "Is there more hot fudge to be had?"

"I'm not sure, but there is whipped cream."

I wished them good night, and they got out of the car debating the relative merits of hot fudge to whipped cream, if one had to choose. On the short drive to my house, it hit me how exhausted I was. I didn't need ice cream. All I needed was my pillow and a good eight hours of sleep. But when I turned onto my street and saw Travis's car parked at the curb in front of my house, those were the last things on my mind.

Chapter 3

Travis met me in the driveway as I emerged from my car. He was dressed in chinos and a blue button-down, a leather messenger bag slung across his chest. His hair looked like he'd been raking his fingers through it, a habit he had when he was frustrated. He looked good but tired. I must have looked worse after the ordeal at the gym. But tired or not, my heart did its little jig for him. I made a point of not letting it show. The way things were between us lately, Travis didn't need any added pressure about our relationship.

"Hey, Kailyn," he said. "How are you doing?"

The words were right, but the tone and delivery were perfunctory, as if he felt obligated to say them before he broached the real reason for being there.

"Good, I'm good," I said, aiming for carefree nonchalance and missing by a mile. Neither of us was on our A game tonight. I shut the car door and set the alarm. The proverbial ball was in his court, but he was studying his Docksiders, presumably working out what he wanted to say. It was unusual for a reporter who normally had his patter honed down to an art. I gave him another twenty seconds to say something, before I headed for the house.

"Listen," he said with five seconds to spare, "I'm sorry to drop by like this, but I'm here to run down the story about the woman...the one found dead behind the elementary school? When I got there, the cops had the school grounds roped off. I couldn't get two words out of any of them."

"I know," I said. "I was there." I needed to get off my feet, so I started up the slate walk to the old Victorian my family had called home for almost a hundred fifty years. The land itself had been owned by the Wildes for closer to four hundred. Travis fell in beside me. We took the steps up to the wraparound porch in tandem. I stopped at the door to root around in my purse for the keys.

"Was the victim a close friend?" he inquired, clearly trying not to make the same foot-in-mouth mistake he made shortly after we met.

I gave up on the Braille method of finding the keys, and I peered into the depths of my purse. "An acquaintance," I said, finally locating them inside the wrong compartment. I really had to get a smaller purse.

"In that case, maybe you can help me out?"

He kept his voice low as if he were in a funeral home to pay his respects to the deceased. I could tell by the twinkle in his eyes, though, that I was the answer to his prayers. Not long ago I could have elicited the same response by just being home if he happened to stop by. A sigh ambushed me, but I covered it by faking a yawn. "Give him time," I heard my mother say. "Give him time." I glanced around to make sure I'd only heard her in my head and she wasn't actually there with us. The last thing I needed was for Travis to meet my dearly departed. Although he seemed to take the proof of my paranormal abilities in stride that night two months ago, things hadn't been the same between us since then.

I opened the front door. It shuddered inward, the wood swollen by the August humidity. I'd been meaning to find a spell to return it to its proper dimensions or hire a repairman. I turned to Travis. "Would you like to come in?" Talk about a ridiculous question. The man had been waiting for me to come home and followed me up to the front door like a lost puppy. Unless he was there to sell me Girl Scout cookies, he wanted to come in and talk.

"If you're not too tired?"

I toyed with the idea of telling him I was too tired, but our current problems were not entirely his fault. He and I had both had a rough time that day in June. Tilly, Merlin and I, facing a killer who intended to add us to his list of victims and Travis racing back to us, afraid he would find all of us dead. In retrospect, it wasn't the best time to have further complicated matters by proving I wasn't the woman he thought I was. Since then, the easiness between us was gone, replaced by a wariness I could almost smell. It radiated from him like a pungent new cologne. But I didn't blame him. If the situation were reversed, I would probably have run for the hills. Life was hard enough without a sorcerer in it—my own included.

"It's okay," I said, holding the door open for him. "Just shake me if I fall asleep." I left my purse on the table in the foyer and led the way into the living room where Sashkatu was stretched out along the top of the couch. He'd always been an "up" cat, preferring to survey his domain from above. His eyes blinked open when Travis dropped heavily onto the couch, but after determining there was no imminent danger, he promptly fell back to sleep. The five other cats were probably bedded down for the night.

Travis set his messenger bag beside him on the couch, in the space where

I would have been sitting in the pre-revelation days of our relationship. I tried not to take it personally and made do with sitting on the wing chair across from him. He pulled out his mini laptop and asked me to begin.

I laid out the sequence of events as I remembered them, which is harder than it sounds after witnessing a traumatic event. I kept to the facts I knew for certain: Amanda's name, where she was found, and the sharp, bloody line across her neck. Travis kept his head down, taking notes without a word. He didn't look up until I stopped speaking.

"Can you tell me more about this Waverly Hotel deal?" he asked.

"The chain wants to build a hotel where the marsh is at the entrance to town."

He thought about that for a moment. "They'd have to dam the stream that feeds it and drain the land, a pricey proposition before you even calculate normal building costs. Is there any opposition to it?"

"Plenty, but Waverly is also asking for a change in the zoning laws. They claim the hotel has to have at least ten stories, a hundred rooms, for it to turn a profit."

"Folks are divided on that?"

"Well, it would change the look of the town, the quaint atmosphere that tourists find so appealing. As things are now, there's no building over two stories."

"And once the zoning is changed, they're worried it will snowball."

"Exactly, but that's still not the whole story. If you ask ten people, you'll get ten different reasons why they're in favor of the hotel or against it. I've never seen anything raise people's hackles like this before. That's why the board called the special session."

"Do you know where Amanda stood on the project?"

"No. I went to the meeting because I wanted to hear what everyone had to say."

"Any thoughts about who might have killed her?"

"I've been asking myself that question ever since I saw her lying there. Maybe the killer wanted to eliminate a vote that conflicted with his or her agenda. It shouldn't be too hard to find someone who knows which way Amanda was leaning." Someone like Beverly, who was also a board member. I could feel the Nancy Drew juices stirring in me. Another investigation might be the perfect way to distract myself from the issues between Travis and me.

"Kailyn?"

Travis's voice dragged me out of my thoughts.

"You're not thinking of going after another killer, are you? Because this time it's different. It's not a matter of trying to keep your best friend out of prison. There's no good reason for you to take the risk."

I couldn't decide if I was pleased with his apparent concern or irritated that he still felt entitled to have a say in my life now that we were barely a couple anymore. Travis seemed to be waiting for me to say something. "You don't have to worry about me," I told him, satisfied that my reply was vague enough to give me some leeway.

He wasn't buying it. "Have you forgotten how close you came to being killed the last time? And not just you. Your aunt Tilly and that peculiar cousin of yours might have been victims too, even poor old Sashkatu."

He was really pushing all my buttons. "I appreciate your input," I said. There was more I wanted to say, a lot more, but I don't believe in burning bridges I might want to cross again one day.

Judging by his furrowed brow, Travis had a lot more to say too. Maybe he shared my philosophy, because he dropped the debate. "We're both tired. Why don't we call it a night?" he said, closing his laptop and sliding it back into the bag. "I'll get out of your way. I appreciate your help."

I was annoyed with him, but now that he was on the verge of leaving, I wanted him to stay. "Can I get you coffee or anything?"

"Another time? I've got to write this up." He rose, messenger bag tucked under his arm, making it pointless for me to pursue the invitation. Just as well, I hate to sound needy.

"Give him time," my mother's voice came again, this time with my grandmother Bronwen providing backup vocals. It was one of those rare instances they were in agreement.

I walked Travis to the door. "I'll let you know if I hear anything else," I said, stepping on his attempt to request that very thing. We both stopped and simultaneously began again. Back before everything went haywire between us, we would have enjoyed a good laugh about being on the same wavelength. "Will do," I said quickly to put an end to our bumbling.

"Terrific, thanks. I'll be in touch." And he was out the door.

I don't know how long I was standing there staring at the closed door when my mother popped up in front of me. Her little white cloud of energy glowing a cheerful pink. "You need to relax and give him time," she said, getting straight to the point. Death hadn't changed her much.

"Yes, Mom, I got that loud and clear the first two times."

Bronwen popped up beside her in much the same mood. It had taken a while, but I finally had a handle on reading their moods from the state of their clouds.

"What your mother means to say, Kailyn, is that we've both been through relationships ourselves and have some expertise in the matter, should you want to avail yourself of it."

Morgana's cloud was turning a worrisome shade of red. "I'm quite capable of telling my own daughter what I mean," she said tightly.

"Of course, you have the floor," Bronwen responded in a look-what-I-have-to-put-with tone.

I took a couple of slow, deep breaths and reminded myself that the conversation would be over faster if I kept to the high road and didn't take sides.

"All right then," Morgana said.

I pictured her lifting her chin the way she always did when she felt vindicated, as though her victory had elevated her physical stature as well.

"Here's the hard truth. Every man I dated thought he was capable of handling the magick. The weakest of them didn't last a day after finding out the true extent of my abilities. The only one who stuck around for years was your father. And I believe he stayed as long as he did because it was hard for him to leave you. But in the end, he also took off to find less complicated women."

"Ditto with your grandfather," Bronwen added, "although if memory serves, he didn't last quite as long, possibly because your mother was a rather strident, difficult child. No offense, Morgana, dear."

"Why would I take offense?" she snapped. "Why would anyone take offense at such a lovely characterization?"

"Ladies," I said, hoping to keep the contretemps from escalating into a full-fledged battle, "thank you for your wisdom and guidance. I can take it from here."

"I'm pleased to hear that," Bronwen said. "Travis is a fine young man. He deserves a chance to adjust to this new paradigm."

"On that we agree," my mother said, setting aside her pique. "It's a good sign that he's still hanging in there. Be patient."

She vanished with a little pop of energy, followed immediately by Bronwen. If I were a betting woman, I'd lay odds they were continuing their argument on the other side of the veil. I had to admit that I felt more hopeful as a result of our chat, but I wasn't convinced that Travis was "still hanging in there" because of his feelings for me. It was possible he didn't want to lose me as a local resource. He called from time to time to ask how I was doing. The conversations were brief and awkward. The one time we met for coffee was even worse.

As much as I needed sleep, I was too wired, and my stomach was grumbling loudly about being ignored. I surveyed my options in the refrigerator and freezer and opted for a pint of banana fudge ice cream. One of the best perks of being an adult had to be eating what I wanted, when I wanted it. I took a dish from the cabinet, then put it back. Who was I kidding? I grabbed a spoon and took the container into the living room. I turned on the TV and clicked through the channels until I found a rerun of Charmed. The show was so far removed from the truth that it was always good for a chuckle.

I was down to the last dregs of ice cream when the phone rang, making me jump. Who would be calling so late? I was relieved to see that it wasn't Tilly's or Elise's number on the caller ID. Probably a solicitor trying to reach a quota. I answered it, intending to hang up if I was right.

"Is this Kailyn? Kailyn Wilde?" the man on the other end asked in a raspy voice. He didn't sound like a solicitor. He didn't have the rehearsed patter. There was none of the background noise you hear from a call center either. But I couldn't place the voice.

"This is Kailyn," I said. "Who's calling?"

"Rusty Higgins—you know, from the school?"

That reminded me of how some of the kids used to call him Rusty Hinges. But that aside, I couldn't imagine why he was calling me. "Hi, Rusty," I said. "What can I do for you?"

"It's about that poor woman who was killed tonight, you know, Amanda?"

My gut reaction was to ask him what he knew, but I made myself slow down "Rusty, if you have information about the killer, you really need to go to the police." I wasn't exactly Duggan's favorite citizen, and I didn't want to be charged with obstruction of justice. Unfortunately, I was too curious about what Rusty knew to let it go. I straddled that fence for another few seconds before taking the plunge. "How about this, Rusty? Tell me what you know, and if I think it's worthwhile, I'll go down to the precinct house with you in the morning." That way I'd be the one who encouraged him to come forward.

"I suppose that's all right. When can you be here?"

"Can't you tell me over the phone?"

"Nope, I'm not saying anything on the phone." He sounded determined to stand his ground, and I was just as determined to stay put.

"How is tomorrow morning?" I asked.

"It'll do. Seven o'clock and don't be late. I've got to finish getting the school gussied up for the new term."

I took down his address. "Seven sharp, I'll be there."

Chapter 4

Rusty lived ten minutes west of New Camel in a small Cape Cod with a steeply pitched roof. The other houses on his street were a mixture of Capes and small ranches, all bearing signs of neglect from lack of money, lack of interest, or a combination of the two. Rusty's house looked tidier and better cared for than its neighbors. The lawn was mowed, and the red salvia and white impatiens beneath the living room window abloom. I parked at the curb at two minutes to seven and walked up the cement path to the house.

On closer inspection, I could see that the cement was cracked, the paint was peeling on the front door, and the window frames and weeds were winning their battle for supremacy over the grass. An old black pickup truck sat in the driveway along with a shiny new snowplow. Rusty probably picked up some extra cash plowing out driveways during the winter months. He was clearly not lazy. It struck me that although I'd known the man for decades, I knew nothing about him beyond the fact that he was the school's custodian. I had no idea if he was an ethical person or if he treated animals kindly. He could be a liar, even a sociopath. I rang the doorbell, wondering how much faith I could put in the information he wanted to impart.

Rusty opened the door while it was still chiming. "C'mon in. Glad to see there are still folks who agree to a time and place and don't keep you waitin'."

I stepped inside. It was easy to see that a single man lived there, a single man with no interest in interior décor. He led me into a shabby living room dominated by a large flat screen TV on one wall. Facing it was an old recliner, the plaid fabric worn away on the armrests and the cushion back where he rested his head. Rusty had his priorities.

"Have yourself a seat," he said, nodding in the direction of a sofa that was catty-corner to the chair. "Mind if I call you Kailyn? It's how I knew you as a kid."

"Kailyn is fine," I said, perching on the edge of the sofa. It didn't look as distressed as the chair, but I had no desire to lean back and be enveloped in its oversized cushions.

"You can call me Rusty," he said, dropping into the recliner.

"Okay, Rusty. When you called you said you had information about Amanda."

He leaned forward with his elbows on his knees and lowered his voice as if he suspected his house was bugged. "Yup, that's right. I was cleanin' up last night when I overheard Beverly talkin' to some folks. I wasn't eavesdroppin', mind you. That woman was never taught to use her inside voice."

I couldn't help smiling. "What did she say?"

"That she knew for a fact Amanda was all for granting the Waverly's rezoning request. She believed the hotel would bring in more tourists and lower everyone's taxes."

Since the information came from Beverly, I made a mental note to check it out. She had a reputation for embellishing on the truth. If she knew part of a story, she didn't see anything wrong with filling in the missing pieces, using her own brand of logic. "Was there anything else?"

"Yup, I'll bet you dollars to donuts Hugh Fletcher hired the killer."

"Fletcher?" The name was vaguely familiar, but I couldn't quite place it.

"He owns Winterland, the ski resort outside of town," Rusty explained.

"I thought the owner was Eric Ingersoll."

"Ingersoll is the manager. Fletcher spends most of his time in Manhattan. The resort is just one of his businesses. He's what you call an entrepreneur."

"So you're a skier?" I asked. "Is that how you know all this?"

"Nope, never seen the point in paying to ride to the top of a hill in order to slide down it. I just keep my ears open."

"But why would Fletcher want to kill Amanda?" I asked.

"Easy. If the town grants Waverly's rezonin' request, there'll be competition for his hotel. As things stand now, the only other hotel is almost an hour away. Winterland's been pullin' in a fortune, chargin' sky-high prices for rooms." Rusty leaned back in the chair with his arms crossed over his chest and a grim but triumphant expression on his face. "There you have it."

I didn't want to reject his theory out of hand, but it made no sense for Fletcher to risk killing off a board member while negotiations were still ongoing. Besides, he had no guarantee that Amanda's replacement would be against the deal. I pointed this out to Rusty, trying my best to let him down gently

"I get what you're sayin', but I have this here feelin' in my gut about it."

"I think we're going to need some evidence before we can take that feeling to the police. Can I ask you something, Rusty?"

"Shoot."

"Why did you call me and not someone else? We hardly know each other."

"I know all I need to know about you. You're the one who caught Jim Harkens's killer."

"That's not entirely true. I poked around in the right places until he came after me."

"And that's when you nabbed him." Rusty was clearly not willing to let go of his over-inflated opinion of me.

"Yes, I guess you could say that." Although there were some scary moments when it could have gone very differently. "I'd rather if you didn't repeat that to anyone else," I added.

"You got it. But just so you know, it's been all over town since the day it went down." Great. I was sure Duggan enjoyed hearing that little refrain over and over again. "I appreciate the information," I said, rising from the couch. "Thank you."

* * * *

I stopped home long enough to take Sashkatu with me to the shop. He'd accompanied Morgana every day until her passing and did not take kindly to being left behind with the five new interlopers. I found out the hard way. The first day I left him at home, the six of them must have had quite a tussle because when I got back that evening, the house was topsy-turvy. Anything not nailed down was on the floor. The curtains in the living room were half off their rods, and someone had peed in my split-leaf philodendron.

When the culprits slinked from their hidey-holes for dinner, they were all missing tufts of fur. I could only assume that Sashkatu had vented his foul mood on his brethren, and they didn't take it lying down. That was the first and last time I left him home for an entire day. Besides, walking across the street to the back of my shop was the most exercise he got anymore. That and using his custom-built steps to ascend to perches he could no longer reach on his own.

We walked into the shop, and I turned off the alarm. In spite of his arthritis, Sashki made it up the steps to his down cushion in the front window before I could turn on the computer. Although it was more than an hour before opening, I had to pay bills, order more of the complimentary tote bags, and check my inventory for other items that might be running low.

The computer had made all of those chores so much easier. It was still a sore point with Morgana and Bronwen, though. When I'd tried to show them how it worked, their white energy clouds had contracted into angry red fists, and they'd zipped off with a crackle and a snap.

I should have known better. They never liked being proved wrong, another thing that hadn't changed after they shuffled off their mortal coils. I still didn't have a good handle on where they resided now, and it seemed they weren't permitted to tell me. Left to imagine my own theory, I thought of it as a transitional plane, a death-lite, until they were willing to relinquish their ties to this world and continue on their journey.

I was logging off the computer when two elderly women toddled into the shop, arms linked as if they were holding each other up. "Good Morning, ladies," I said, standing. "Welcome to Abracadabra. What can I do for you today?"

At first I didn't think they heard me because they didn't speak or look at me. They appeared transfixed by the merchandise arrayed before them. I was on the verge of welcoming them again when the taller of the women turned to me.

"Hello, dearie," she said. "Please excuse us, but we've never set foot in a magick shop before."

I came around the counter to them. "In that case, I'm twice as pleased that Abracadabra is your first. I'm Kailyn."

They unlinked arms to introduce themselves and shake my hand. "I'm Flora," said the taller one, "and this is my sister, Daisy."

Daisy bobbed her head. "Our mother, rest her soul, loved flowers. She would have named all her children for them, but the boys posed a bit of a problem." They smiled simultaneously.

"I imagine they would. Is there anything specific you're looking for today?"

"We need a memory spell," Daisy said. "We've been spending so much time searching for things we could have written the great American novel."

"Well maybe not the great one," Flora put in with a chuckle.

"I have just the thing." I wanted to offer them a seat, but I had just the one chair. My desk chair was too large to fit in the space beside the one already there. I really should keep an extra one in the storeroom for times like this. Maybe Tilly could spare one for a little while. "Flora, Daisy, please have a look around while I run next door for a moment."

"Take your time, dearie," Flora replied. "We love to browse."

"So many interesting things to see," Daisy murmured.

The sisters linked arms again and wobbled down the first aisle, exclaiming over the products like children in a toy store. I headed to the back of the shop and through the connecting door to Tea and Empathy. My aunt's shop had the same square footage as mine, but the spaces were divided differently. The back of my shop was a storeroom; the back of hers, a kitchen. The front of my shop was larger because I needed to display my entire line of products, whereas the front of hers only needed to accommodate a few small tables and chairs. She conducted her psychic readings at one of the tables. The others were elegantly set for an authentic English tea, which most of her clients opted for after their readings. Tilly did all the baking herself but imported the clotted cream straight from the finest English dairy.

That morning I found her bustling around in the kitchen. As usual, Merlin was perched on his stool in the doorway awaiting samples. He was back in the burlap pants and dingy shirt he was wearing when he arrived in the twenty-first century. The shirt had improved somewhat after Tilly put it through several washings, but it couldn't rightly be called white. In any case, Merlin had made it clear that these were his garments of choice, and he would wreak vengeance on anyone who disposed of them.

I greeted Merlin and poked my head into the kitchen to ask about borrowing the chair.

"Sure, sure. You're welcome to it," Tilly said, kneading dough. "My first client isn't until eleven."

"Linzer tarts?" I guessed when I passed the kitchen again carrying the chair.

"Hardly a brilliant guess," Merlin said, "when one can plainly see the smudges of raspberry jam on her apron."

"I'll save one for you," Tilly called after me. She always does. The day she forgets, I'll know her memory is fading.

On the way back to my shop, I crossed paths with Sashkatu, who was heading over to visit them. For reasons I couldn't fathom, Merlin was like human catnip to all the felines. They simply couldn't get enough of him. On the other hand, it was no mystery why they adored Tilly. She was not only a devout cat lover but also the Santa Claus of fresh-baked goodies.

I found the sisters in the last of my three jam-packed aisles. They followed me and the chair up to the counter as if I were the Pied Piper.

"How thoughtful of you," Daisy said, lowering herself onto the seat as soon as I set it down.

Flora gave an appreciative sigh as she took the other one. "Thank you. At our age, our energy tends to run out before our curiosity."

I leaned over the counter, grabbed a pad and pencil, and held them out to Flora, who was closer to me.

"Oh good," she said. "I misplaced my pad a few days ago and I was afraid we might have to memorize the spell."

Daisy laughed. "Talk about a wasted trip." Her laughter was as honest as a child's; I couldn't help laughing along with her.

"I'm a great believer in backup," I said, "especially when it comes to memory spells. This is an easy one, but it should serve your purposes. Ready?"

Flora nodded.

"You'll need to have a mirror, a piece of paper and a pencil. A pen won't do." I paused to let Flora finish writing. "Begin by thinking about what you've lost, write it down on the paper, and then lay the paper facedown on the mirror. Leave it there until you find the object."

"How long does it take to work?" Daisy piped up.

"It differs from person to person, but it shouldn't take long."

"What if it doesn't work?"

"After half an hour, try it again. There's no limit to the number of times you can use it."

"That's the whole shebang?" Flora sounded deflated.

"Except to stress that magick works best with the active participation of the practitioner. You can't just sit back and wait for the object to fall into your lap. You have to continue looking for it throughout the process."

"I guess I expected there to be some mumbo jumbo involved," she said.

"I'll tell you what—I'll give you another spell free of charge, one that involves words. You can alternate using the two, until you decide which works best for you."

Daisy beamed. "What a lovely thing to do. Isn't it, Flora?"

"It most certainly is." Flora had the pencil poised over the paper again.

"Okay, for this one, you need to find something that reminds you of the lost item. Set it down in front of you. Then chant the following three times:

'Lead me to what I must find,

'Restoring it and peace of mind.'

Flora didn't seem any more convinced of the spells' ability to work.

"I know the spells seem too simple," I said, "but magick is what you make of it. It helps you to focus your attention and connect with the universe."

Flora tore off the paper with the spells and returned the pad and pencil. "Thank you for explaining that. It puts one in the proper frame of mind to succeed."

"We'll dig deep and give it our all," Daisy promised.

"I wonder how much of our 'all' we still have at our age?" Flora said, causing both of them to dissolve into giggles.

In spite of their age and physical frailties, they managed to be as lighthearted as a couple of kids. If anyone had the right attitude to make the spells work, they did. They thanked me again, and I told them to come back soon. I often say those words but rarely mean them the way I did with Flora and Daisy. I'd been tense and stressed since the events of the previous night, but they'd lifted my spirits with their own brand of magic. A good thing, because they weren't gone five minutes when Merlin ambled up to the counter with Sashkatu for a shadow.

"Tilly has exiled me while she conducts business," he informed me.

I'd completely forgotten I was wizard-sitting. I tried to come up with some chores to keep him busy, but I couldn't think of anything that didn't carry the risk of disaster in his hands. "Do you want to use my computer?" I proposed. He loved modern technology almost as much as he loved pizza and chocolate. After being introduced to Tilly's computer, he proclaimed it to be the most magickal object he had ever encountered.

"I would be most appreciative," he said with an adventurous twinkle in his eyes.

"Don't you dare buy anything," I warned him.

Tilly had made the mistake of giving him her username and password to log on, never anticipating where that might lead. He happened upon one of the home-shopping websites where he clicked his way to a gold-and-diamond bangle bracelet for her. Although his intentions were fine, he didn't understand the modern concept of money. He should have been stymied at the checkout, but Tilly had bought some bedding on the site in the past, and it had her credit card on file. All Merlin had to do was click again, and the bracelet was on its way to her. For the better part of a week, my aunt and I couldn't figure out why he was so unbearably full of himself. The mystery was solved when the bracelet arrived, followed closely by the credit card statement. If the numbers on the statement didn't give Tilly a heart attack, perhaps nothing ever will.

"You have naught to fear," he told me. "Your aunt has instructed me in the usage of credit cards, debit cards, and the like. If you ask me, barter was a much simpler system. You either had a goat to trade for a laying hen or made do without the hen."

"Just remember—nothing is free. Even if it says it's free, it's not."

"Baffling times," he mumbled, installing himself at the computer. "I don't know how anyone can be expected to keep it all straight." With some difficulty, Sashki managed to climb into his lap and curl up for a snooze. I picked up my pad and a pen and got to work on the list of potential candidates for the role of Amanda's killer.

I've heard there's no such thing as bad publicity, but I disagree. Crime isn't the kind of advertising that attracts tourists to a quaint, family-friendly destination like New Camel. Although no one could undo what had happened, capturing the killer as quickly as possible would be the best way for the town to move forward. The sooner the story stopped making headlines, the sooner it would fade from the public's memory. It seemed wrong to think that way, as though I were also trying to erase Amanda from our minds. But she was well beyond anyone's help. Pursuing justice on her behalf was the best I could do.

Chapter 5

Beverly occupied first place on my list of suspects. It was more a formality than any real suspicion I had. She didn't strike me as a killer, but then I didn't know her very well. Like an extra in films, she'd inhabited the background of my life as far back as I could remember.

But even if I were better acquainted with her and knew her to be of sterling character, I couldn't dismiss her out of hand. The fact remained that she had discovered Amanda's body. Of course, Tilly had supposedly arrived at the scene of the crime at the same time, the difference being that she was my aunt and I knew her as well as one person can know another. She had trouble killing any living being, with the exception of spiders. Even then she had to enlist someone else to do the dirty work while she stood screaming a safe distance away. What's more, the spider killer had to swear on all things sacred that the beast was dead. Tilly was certain that if the spider was captured and released outside, it would find its way back in and would lie in wait for her, plotting eight-legged revenge.

I had no idea how Beverly felt about spiders or killing, in general, but talking to her seemed to be a logical way to start my investigation. And the sooner, the better. I didn't want to give her a chance to regroup and regain her equilibrium. The more vulnerable she was, the more easily I could catch her in a lie. When I called to ask if I could stop by, she was wary.

"I want to hear what it was like for you when you found Amanda's body." I tried to sound like someone on the gossip hotline.

Beverly went for the bait. "I bet you're helping that handsome reporter of yours?" she said. "Did he ask you to get some points of view and local color for his report?"

"Am I that transparent?" I said, all innocence. It wasn't actually a lie, I told myself, more like a bit of harmless misdirection, but I felt a twinge of conscience anyway.

"When do you want to stop by?" she asked. "I'll be home all day."

That's what I was counting on. The woman loved the sound of her own voice. Add a pinch of gossip to it, and the possibility of her name being mentioned on TV and you were in like Flynn. I had no idea where the expression came from, but I'd heard Morgana and Bronwen use it often enough that it was a part of the family lexicon.

I waited for Tilly to finish with her client so I could return Merlin into her keeping; then I set the hands on the I'll Be Back sign to two o'clock and put it in the front window. With my business not fully back on track, I couldn't afford to be gone longer than a traditional lunch hour. Even so, I risked missing potential customers. On my way out, I grabbed a bottle of our best-selling skin rejuvenator to pave my way into Beverly's good graces. She didn't sound like she still blamed us for her vocal distress, but it couldn't hurt to bring along a peace offering.

Beverly answered the door, wearing red capris and a red-and-white-striped T-shirt, her blond hair pulled back into a sleek ponytail with just the right bit of curl at the end. There were plenty of negative things you could say about her, but her skill as a hair stylist wasn't one of them. She had a half-eaten chocolate cupcake in her hand and a ring of chocolate icing around her mouth that she tried unsuccessfully to lick off as we exchanged pleasantries.

I presented her with the skin cream, saying I hoped it would cheer her up after her ordeal the previous evening. Her eyes lit up when she realized it was one of her favorite products from my shop. Reaching for it, she lost the cupcake to the floor. She thanked me a number of times as she scooped up the fallen cupcake. She pulled a tissue from her pocket and wiped the chocolate off the floor. It was all so efficient I wondered how often she did it.

"I was having a cup of tea," she said, turning the cupcake over in her hand as if trying to decide if it was clean enough to eat. "Can I make you a cup?"

"That would be great," I said. I wasn't actually in the mood for tea, especially what my aunt disparagingly called "teabag tea," but it was the sociable thing to do, and my relationship with Beverly needed all the social niceties at hand.

She led the way into the kitchen, running on about how she hadn't slept a wink all night what with grieving for Amanda and fearing that every creak in the house signaled an intruder sneaking up the stairs to kill her too.

I took a seat at the glass-and-chrome table in the corner of her newly renovated kitchen and watched her put the fallen cupcake on the counter. I suspected she was saving it for after I left. She filled the teakettle and set it on the gas range to boil. There was a six-pack box of cupcakes on the table beside her teacup. Half the box was empty. Anxiety eating was something I could understand, but my food of choice was usually ice cream.

"Did you have trouble sleeping last night too?" she asked once we were settled with our tea.

"Actually, I was so tired I fell asleep when my head hit the pillow."

"You're not at all worried the killer could still be around here?" Her words had an edge to them, as if she begrudged me my peace of mind.

"Of course I'm concerned. I just don't think worrying or running around like Chicken Little is going to keep me any safer. I'd rather focus on trying to solve the case. Then we'll all be able to sleep better."

Beverly sat up straighter and squared her shoulders. "Under the circumstances, a healthy amount of fear is nothing to be ashamed of."

"I wasn't calling you Chicken Little," I said. "I was using it as a figure of speech." I'd forgotten how touchy Beverly could be. She gave a little nod that I took as forgiveness. "What I meant to say is that I assumed from the get-go the killer is from New Camel and is most likely still here. Who else would be invested enough to kill over such a local issue? The killer may be at home right now, lying low in hopes of getting away with his crime."

"That's precisely the reason I'm worried. If I thought the killer was on the run, I'd be a lot calmer about the situation. Beverly turned the box of cupcakes around to face me. "I'm not big on store-bought, but these aren't bad."

"Thanks, maybe later? I'm interested in hearing about what you went through last night." With the clock ticking on my lunch hour, I had to steer her in the right direction, or I'd be leaving without a single bit of useful information.

"Well, after that trouble with my voice..." she paused, her brow wrinkling.

Was she remembering her suspicion that the Wilde clan was to blame? I wondered if I was about to be shown the door. She must have decided she didn't want to lose my good will or the prospect of more free merchandise because she picked up where she'd left off.

"I went out front to get some fresh air. I thought a quiet stroll around the school grounds would help me restore my composure. As it turned out, walking on grass is not easy in three-inch spikes, especially when the grass is damp. I guess the sprinklers were on earlier. Anyway, I cut the walk short and headed to the emergency doors. It was a good thing I was looking down, or I might have stepped right on Amanda with my spikes. Of course I didn't know it was Amanda at the time."

Beverly quaked at the thought. If she wasn't innocent, she was doing a convincing job of pretending to be. "How long was it before Tilly showed up?" I asked.

Beverly reached into the box and helped herself to another cupcake, a vanilla one with strawberry frosting. She peeled off the paper holder. "She must have gotten there at that very moment because we screamed at the same time."

I realized that estimating the time Beverly came upon the body based on the scream wasn't necessarily accurate. Some people coming upon a body might start to scream instantly, whereas others might be momentarily frozen by the discovery, unable to issue a sound. More important, if Beverly were the killer, she wouldn't have screamed unless someone else came along. Why call attention to the crime you've just committed? Maybe Tilly could shed more light on the timing.

"When you were walking around that side of the building, did you pass anyone?" I asked. "Did you see anyone in the area?"

The cupcake was halfway to Beverly's mouth when her hand stopped. "Wait. You think I might have seen the killer leaving?"

"It's a possibility. Didn't Detective Duggan ask you about that?"

"Maybe." She lowered her hand to the table, frowning. "He asked me so many questions...one after the other, so fast, and my head was already spinning...."

"Did you see anyone else?" I repeated to nudge her back on track.

"I suppose there could have been other people walking around. It was a warm night. I was focused on trying not to snap off a heel." She stopped to sip her tea, the cupcake still in her other hand. Before the cup reached her mouth, she set it down abruptly, causing the tea to slosh over the rim. "Oh good Lord, if I'd been there a minute earlier, I could have been killed instead of Amanda." Her voice was hollow with dread.

"I doubt it," I said. "I don't think this was a random act. Whoever killed Amanda had an agenda. They were after her, specifically."

Beverly heaved a shaky sigh. "Do you really think so?"

I assured her I did.

"I suppose that does make more sense." She remembered she was holding the cupcake and nibbled on it distractedly. "Do you think the killer wanted to get rid of Amanda because of her position on the hotel?"

"I wouldn't rule it out." It was my first thought when I saw her lying there with her neck slashed open. But I also knew it would be shoddy investigating to start out with my mind closed to other possibilities. The killer's motive might not have had any connection to the hotel at all. He or she could have chosen the high-profile venue to hide their true motive.

"That means anyone who feels like she did about the hotel could also be in danger," Beverly said.

"Do you know if she was for the hotel or against it?" I asked. No harm in making sure Rusty had heard her correctly. Although Beverly was hardly the most reliable source, at the moment she was the only game in town.

"Oh yes, she was gung ho for it, and she wasn't shy about making her opinion known."

"Do you share that opinion?"

"I'll be keeping my opinion to myself from now on, thank you very much, and I plan to talk to the mayor about having a secret ballot when the time comes for the board to vote. If he refuses, he can find himself two replacements instead of one."

It was a pretty good bet that Beverly was in favor of the hotel. I had one more question for her before I excused myself to get back to work. "Any thoughts about who the killer might be?"

She appeared taken aback by the question. "How would I know?"

"Don't worry," I said. "Whatever you say stays with me. I'm not going to broadcast it. And you never know—if you're right, you may help catch the killer."

She chewed on her lower lip. "If I'm right, would I get credit for it in the news? Or money like a reward?"

Ah, there was the Beverly I knew and disliked. "I could put in a good word for you with Detective Duggan." As if he would ever listen to me.

"Well okay," she relented. "I have been wondering if it was Amanda's almost ex, Alan Boswell. The second time he cheated on Amanda, she threw him out and filed for divorce. But she couldn't bring herself to sign the divorce decree and sever all her ties to him. She still loved him and felt sorry for him yada yada yada."

"What kind of ties?"

"If you ask me, it was mostly him coming around to grub money from her. The guy's a sleaze, a parasite."

"She told you all that?"

"And more. Bartenders and hairdressers—we know more secrets than the CIA," Beverly said with a sly smile.

"Did she usually give him the money he wanted?"

"Yeah, when she couldn't stand his whining anymore."

"Then why on earth would he kill his golden goose?"

"Maybe he found out his goose was about to sign the divorce papers and cut him off."

"Was she?" I wished Beverly would stop the teasers and flat out tell me the rest of what she knew.

"Yes, I finally talked her into signing it and changing her will and the beneficiary of her life insurance policy." Her chest puffed up with pride over her powers of persuasion.

"Did he know his time was running out?"

"That I don't know. Amanda had an appointment to come in for a cut and blow-dry this Friday. I was going to ask her then. That reminds me. I have to take her name out of the book."

After politely chatting for another minute, I left Beverly to her cupcakes and drove back to Abracadabra. The trip had been worthwhile. I had Beverly's account of finding Amanda, which I could compare to Tilly's, as well as a possible lead to the killer.

Chapter 6

I spent a good part of that night debating whether to call Travis and tell him about the leads I'd gotten. My head told me the information was too vague to pass on. At the very least, I should wait until I followed up on it. My heart told me I shouldn't squander a chance to speak to Travis and possibly see him. This time my mind won out. If he needed space, as my matriarchs seemed to think, I was going to let him have all he needed. I never mooned over any guy, not even in my teens; I sure wasn't going to start now. Having made that decision, I awoke the next morning feeling lighter and more energized. I fed the cats, showered, and slipped on a cotton sundress and sandals. It had been a hot summer, and the heat wasn't showing any signs of letting up. Don't get me wrong. I love the summer, but I was tired of my summer wardrobe. And this late in August, all the stores were showing winter coats, fur-lined boots, and bulky sweaters.

In spite of the heat, when Sashkatu followed me over to the shop he had more bounce in his step too. He was starting to key into my moods as the months went by without Morgana. The thought warmed my heart but also brought tears to my eyes. It took effort to shut down the waterworks. I couldn't very well greet customers with red eyes and mascara tracks down my cheeks. After I turned off the security system, Sashki and I walked through to the front of the shop. He hopped up the steps to his window seat and settled in with a little grumble of pleasure. Both of us in place and ready for the day, I slapped on a determined smile and opened the front door.

Since no one bowled me over in a mad rush to get inside, I used the lull to dust the shelves and the myriad products on them. It wasn't a job I enjoyed, but customers tend to be put off by dust and spider webs. I stopped at the halfway point. There was a finite amount of tedium I could stand. I promised myself I'd tackle the other half later. Besides, I had other work that required my attention.

My grandmother had been urging me to work on my telekinetic ability with the eventual goal of mastering teleportation—moving my body through space with the power of my mind. And although Bronwen no longer possessed a corporeal body, it was never wise to ignore her. Besides, growing up I had bemoaned the fact that I lacked a specialty, a unique magickal skill that set me apart from the other members of my family. My mother had been amazing at developing new spells, Tilly was a preeminent psychic, and Bronwen had been a wiz at creating potions to address nearly any problem you threw at her.

Trying to come up with a game plan, I leaned back against the counter. In the past, I'd experimented with telekinesis in a muddled way. As a result, I could never depend on it to work. One day I could slide a piece of furniture across the floor, but the next I couldn't budge a paper clip. I told myself it was because of our recent overall problems with magick, but that was just taking the easy way out, and I knew it.

After fifteen minutes of pondering my options, I had only one idea spring to mind, but one was all I needed. I'd handle it like any bodybuilding program at the gym. In essence, it wasn't all that different; I'd be building my telekinetic muscle. I'd start off with smaller, lighter objects and work my way up to larger, heavier ones. Then I'd add in the variable of distance.

I made myself comfortable in what I thought of as "the customer chair" and set my sights on The Beginners Book of Spells displayed on a table six feet away. I concentrated on lifting it off the two other books there without disturbing them. To my delight, the book wobbled in midair for a moment and then sailed easily into my hand. It wasn't the first time I'd used telekinesis successfully. Travis could attest to that fact. But it was now a step completed in my training program.

Feeling a little cocky, I snagged an ornate canister filled with Tilly's special blend of tea leaves. But instead of becoming airborne, it bumped along the table, scattering everything in its path. So much for patting myself on the back. I needed to stay focused. I cleared my mind and tried again. This time the tea tin lifted cleanly off the table and flew straight to me. Lesson learned. If I wanted telekinesis to work reliably, I had to give it my full attention regardless of the size of the object I was trying to move.

For my next test, I tried picking up the items I'd knocked onto the floor and putting them back on the table. Instead of moving them to me, I'd be moving them from one place to another, a slightly different skill. But before I could start, the phone rang.

"You need to get over here ASAP." It was Tilly in full crisis mode.

"What's wrong?" I asked, assorted disasters flashing through my mind. "Are you and Merlin okay?"

"We're not in danger—yet, but you have to get over here."

I told her I'd be there in five minutes. I made sure Sashki had water, set the alarm, and would have beat my estimate, but there were so many cars and people congregated at the intersection with her street that I couldn't make any headway. I pulled to the curb, ignoring the No Parking signs posted every few feet, and jumped out to hoof it through the crowd.

I was getting close to her corner again when some of the people ahead of me started shrieking and running in my direction. I didn't know what had caused their panic until I spotted a little red fox trotting after them. It looked more lost and confused than any animal I'd ever seen. Stranger still were the two cottontail bunnies hopping along in the fox's wake. All was not right in the animal kingdom when rabbits chose to follow foxes and foxes had no interest in their favorite meal.

I picked up my pace. Turning onto Tilly's block, I finally understood what had prompted her distress and had attracted the throngs of people. Under different circumstances, I might have had myself a good, long laugh, but although it was funny, it was even more sobering. I had no idea how I was going to explain it to the police.

Everywhere I looked there were furred and feathered woodland creatures. I felt as though I'd made a wrong turn onto the set of a Disney movie. Troops of squirrels, mice, rabbits, fox, deer, porcupine, and skunks roamed across the lawns and driveways of the homes. Raccoons, possums, and other nocturnal critters stood squinting in the sunlight, looking as bewildered as the fox that had crossed my path. I watched chickadees, robins, blackbirds, cardinals, hawks and dozens of other birds I couldn't identify wheeling around the sky before settling in trees, on rooftops, and cars. Owls populated the fir trees. And dogs from miles around provided a deafening soundtrack to the craziness. It came as no surprise to find that Tilly's house was ground zero.

Her neighbors were all out watching the spectacle, the bravest wandering among the animals, taking pictures, and petting furry heads. The less daring stayed on their porches or behind screen doors. Tilly and Merlin were conspicuous by their very absence. Although there was no police presence yet, I spied a van from the county's animal-control unit parked haphazardly in the middle of the street. Whoever had alerted the unit must have failed to mention the scope of the animal invasion or a need for the police, an oversight for which I was grateful.

The driver was standing next to his vehicle, talking on a cell phone and gesticulating wildly with his free arm as if the person on the other end could see him. Even if he'd had enough equipment and men to round up the multitude of different creatures, he would have needed another hundred vans to cart them away. The most troubling part of the whole scene was that in the couple minutes I was standing there, the number of animals had grown. I had to get to my aunt's house and try to rectify the situation, though I had no idea how to go about it. I ran through the crowds, dodging people and animals, especially the skunks.

Tilly must have been looking out the window because the front door swung open before I could ring the bell. She yanked me inside, shut the door, and double locked it.

"Thank goodness you're here," she said, her voice an octave higher than normal. Her forehead was shiny with perspiration, and her short red curls limp around her face. "You have to do something to stop it or...or...I don't know what will happen."

"Where's Merlin?" I asked. She pointed in the direction of the living room. "Okay, Aunt Tilly. I want you to go make us a nice pot of tea."

"Yes, that's what I'll do," Tilly said, grabbing onto the idea as though it were a lifeline. She headed full throttle toward the kitchen. "A pot of tea is always helpful. I should bake something to go with it."

I found Merlin pacing in the living room. Isenbale, my aunt's big Maine Coon, was walking in and out of his legs so that the two of them look like a well-rehearsed dance team. For his part, Merlin seemed completely unaware the cat was there. He was muttering to himself, most of the words garbled or in another language. I walked right up to him so that he had no choice but to stop or crash into me. At the last possible moment, he came to such a sudden stop that Isenbale was caught between his legs. The cat yowled in protest, wriggled free of his prison, and fled.

"I was not aware you were expected," Merlin said, sounding equally irritated.

"I'm here to help," I said. "What happened? What went wrong?"

"I was lonely for the creatures that populate the woods near my home, so I cast a simple spell to summon a few of them. The spell appears to have become stuck in an open-ended position, and I can't remember how to reverse the bloody thing."

"What were you thinking? You know we've been having trouble with our magick here. How about your wand? Would that help?" I asked. I hadn't seen him with it since the day he found the wood for it.

"I gave up on it," he said. "It appears I am every bit as talented without it. Perhaps it is a necessity for lesser practitioners of the magickal arts."

"Okay," I said, unable to debate the fact since I'd never found a wand to be helpful either. "But you must have a failsafe spell for emergencies."

"I've never needed such a thing," he snapped. "What is wrong with this cursed era of yours?"

"If you had listened to me and not cast any spells, we wouldn't be having this problem, would we? And in case you've forgotten, pizza and computers are also products of this era."

I took a deep breath. Arguing and assigning blame were not going to fix the problem. I vaguely recalled Bronwen teaching me an incantation to stop and reverse spells. I couldn't have been more than five at the time. She had insisted I learn it by heart before she would teach me how to cast my first spell. But what was it? My mind was racing helter-skelter, skimming the surface of my memory. I was on the verge of giving up when I heard a familiar voice say,

"A spell was cast
Now make it past.
Remove it here
And everywhere."

I was in such a state that for a moment I thought the words had finally popped into my head, but then Bronwen's white energy cloud materialized.

"Say it with me, Kailyn. Say it ten times."

As we began, I noticed that Merlin was staring at the cloud, clearly mesmerized by it. I realized he'd never been with me when my mother or grandmother dropped by for a visit. Before I could stop him, he reached out his hand to touch the cloud. He was rewarded with a shock that threw him back against the wall with a resounding and sickening thud. How many times had Tilly and I warned him about the dangers of electricity? He clearly hadn't taken us seriously enough. By the time I got to him, he was sitting up, cradling his injured hand, and spitting a string of expletives that sounded enough like modern English for me to get the gist of them. I hunkered down beside him to look at his hand, but he pulled away from me.

"Merlin, I have to see how bad it is." I prayed he didn't require medical attention. Without ID or health insurance, he would be treated and then incarcerated. We'd be mired in enough red tape to tie a ribbon around the globe.

"I am capable of tending to it myself, I assure you. I will prepare a decoction for burns and add a bit of magick. I'll be good as new in no time."

More magick? It was the last thing we needed, but I bit my tongue. It couldn't be worse than taking him to the emergency room. "Didn't we tell you that electricity can kill you?" I don't know why I was beating this particular dead horse, but my brain seemed determined to vent.

"Yes," he replied, "you made a point of it. I believe you said, 'It can kill just like a lightning bolt.'"

"Then why did you—"

"Curiosity," he said. "I had never encountered a cloud within a building. Now if you wish to be useful, I am in need of some help to rise."

After I got him on his feet, he went off to the kitchen in search of Tilly and the ingredients he needed to treat his hand. "If there's anything you need from my shop, let me know," I called after him. Bronwen had been silent while I dealt with Merlin, but once he left the room, she spoke to me.

"Clear your mind, my child, and let's start over."

We finished the ten repetitions without further interruption. When I ran to the window to look outside, I breathed a shaky sigh of relief. The animals were leaving. I didn't know where they were going, but then I didn't know where they'd come from either. I prayed no harm would come to them. I was still standing there when I heard the sirens. The cavalry was coming. Although Merlin was to blame, he was a man without a country or identity, technically a man who didn't exist in the twenty-first century. I couldn't let Tilly handle it. She might panic and say something that would doom all three of us. The responsibility fell to me alone, and I was no closer to an explanation the police or onlookers were likely to believe. If I wasn't careful, I could be responsible for ushering in a new age of witch trials. Quite a day—and it wasn't yet noon.

Chapter 7

I stood at the screen door, watching the animals disperse. Their numbers had dwindled by a third as the police rolled into town. Two patrol cars led the way, followed by Detective Duggan's unmarked car. I recognized Curtis in one of the patrol cars, but I didn't know the officer in the second car. Maybe it was close to the shift change, so both men had heeded the alert. Or maybe Duggan had requested more muscle. They stopped near the animal-control van. The driver, who'd been waiting in the van, emerged and met the police in the middle of the street to provide what I assumed was an update.

Tilly shuffled over to me in her slippers, her preferred footwear at home. Soft and unstructured, they were kindest to her feet. Her time in the kitchen seemed to have restored her to an even keel, but I could tell by the way her gaze was flitting around that panic was hanging out just beneath the surface.

"Kailyn, what are you doing?" she asked. "Don't stand there like we're expecting the cops."

"But we are expecting them. Let's face it, Aunt Tilly. We're the only sorcerers around here, and as far as we know, this bizarre migration of animals has occurred only on your block. In fact, most of the creatures were encamped on your lawn."

"I still think we should play it cool, like we've been busy inside and didn't notice what was happening out there." As she was speaking a large raccoon ambled up to us from the direction of the stairs. Tilly flattened herself against the wall in the narrow foyer.

"Right," I said, "we have no idea what's going on. And this fellow just happens to be our pet."

"Merlin!" Tilly shrilled, causing the hissing and growling animal to turn its masked eyes to her. She clamped her mouth shut.

The wizard came out of the bathroom, wrapping a poultice around his injured hand. He stopped short when he saw the raccoon. "Egad. Who thought it wise to let that creature in?"

"Exactly what we want to know," I whispered.

"Ah," Merlin said, lowering his voice too. "Mayhap it climbed in when I opened the bedroom window earlier to freshen the air."

My aunt's eyes bulged with disbelief. "Mayhap?" she said, nearly losing control of her voice. "Close it this instant."

"I'll be of more use getting rid of this chap," he countered.

This was no time for an argument. "Aunt Tilly, go close the window," I said, hoping nothing else had climbed in.

She bobbed her head, apparently relieved that I'd taken charge. She slid along the wall until she was a safe distance from her uninvited guest; then she hobbled toward the stairs. I backed out of the foyer to watch Merlin deal with the raccoon from a safer distance. He fixed his eyes on the creature, who seemed unable to turn away. They remained locked together like that for a minute or so, communing or communicating in some way I didn't understand. When Merlin looked away, I could tell the connection was broken. The raccoon seemed to lose its balance from the abrupt release. It swayed on wobbly legs before finding its equilibrium again and shaking its head as if it had been roused from sleep.

Merlin opened the screen door. The animal lifted its snout to the air wafting in and, after a moment's hesitation, headed outside to join a group of its brethren in their retreat. Merlin appeared altogether pleased with himself as he passed me on his way to the kitchen. He'd clearly forgotten about the greater havoc he'd created outside. Or the fact that I would have to answer to the police for it.

Duggan appeared on the other side of the screen door, as if I'd conjured him up with my thoughts. "Hello again, Ms. Wilde," he said too amiably for my comfort. "I'd like to speak to you and your aunt. May I come in?" He reminded me of a junkyard dog whose wagging, come-hither tail was all a ruse to lure you closer so it could sink its teeth into you.

"I suppose so," I replied. "Come on in, and I'll get her."

I could have flat out refused. No judge was going to grant a search warrant based on the suspicion that we were behind the sudden influx of animals, but I didn't need any additional demerits in Duggan's mind. I considered asking him to have a seat in the living room, but the more comfortable he was, the longer he might stay. I left him in the foyer and went after Tilly. She was in the kitchen removing a blueberry pie from the oven. Merlin was watching from the table, a plate in front of him and a fork in his hand.

Since he'd been living the modern American lifestyle, he'd gained enough weight to make his burlap pants split their seams multiple times. Tilly always stitched them up again because he refused to wear twenty-first-century clothing at home.

She set the pie on a cooling rack, wiped her hands on a dishtowel, and turned to me. "I know. I've been summoned. That man has a voice that rattles the timbers. It's a good thing I baked. At least we'll have some comfort food to restore us after our grilling."

"I think it's best if we keep Merlin out of this," I murmured.

She nodded, leaning down to whisper in his ear. "Don't touch the pie; it has to cool. Just stay here and be quiet and you'll get the first piece. Will you do that for us?"

"I shall be as quiet as a mouse," he whispered. "You won't know I'm here."

If only, I said to myself. I hooked my arm in my aunt's and told her to follow my lead with Duggan.

He was standing where I'd left him. "All right, Detective, now that we're here, what can we do for you?" I can do sociable as well as anyone.

"As you're both aware, I have a murder case to investigate. The folks in this town are scared; they want the killer behind bars. I don't have the time or patience for nonsense like this...this animal thing." His upper lip started to curl, but he quickly shut it down. I wondered if there had been complaints about his attitude and if Police Chief Gimble had taken him to task about it.

"I understand," I said. Tilly echoed me.

"Good. Let's try to make this quick then. Do either of you know how all those animals came to be congregated on your street?" Although his tone was polite, it had a peculiar undercurrent, as if he'd actually said, "I dare you to explain away this one."

"I've been wondering that myself," I replied. I'd decided our best defense would be to answer his questions with some of our own. I was waiting for the right moment.

He looked from me to Tilly and back again. "You mean to tell me that neither of you did anything that might have lured those animals here?"

I gave him a beats-me shrug. "I'm sorry it's not what you want to hear, but that's exactly what I'm saying."

"Then how do you explain it?"

He was studying us like he was trying to detect the lie in our eyes. Time to turn the tables. "Seriously, Detective," I said with a smile, "are you saying my aunt and I have magickal powers? That we're some kind of animal whisperers?"

Duggan opened his mouth to answer me, but his brain didn't seem to have come up with a response, so he let it fall closed again.

"Maybe what happened here should be chalked up to a mystery of nature," I continued. "For all we know, it will happen again this time next year. We may be witnesses to a new pattern of animal migration." I stopped myself short before I became too fanciful and overplayed my hand.

Duggan's eyes narrowed. I imagined the debate raging in his head. How hard could he come down on me without being chewed out again by his boss?

"I'm going to let it go this time," he grumbled, turning his failure into a magnanimous gesture, "but remember, I've got my eyes on you— on both of you."

"Good to know," I said, holding the screen door open for him. He hadn't asked about Merlin, and I certainly wasn't going to remind him. But it might not have been an oversight on his part. When he first met the wizard, he made a snap judgment about him. I'd seen it written plain as day on his face. He believed Merlin was the addled and eccentric black sheep in my family. And I had no plans to disabuse him of that notion anytime soon.

The last of the wild animals were heading away, probably wondering why they'd come here in the first place. After closing and locking the front door, Tilly fell back against it, looking weak with relief. After a few seconds, she straightened up. "Let's go see if that pie is cool enough to slice!"

I glanced at my watch. It seemed like I'd been away from my shop for the entire day, but in reality it had been less than two hours. I made an executive decision. There was time for a quick piece of pie before I headed back to work. Tilly deemed the pie ready to eat, even though it was still venting steam and didn't hold together properly when she put the knife into it. None of us cared about the aesthetics. I think we would have sucked it up through a straw if we had to.

The day's events had made two things crystal clear to me: life was unpredictable enough without the added stress and craziness Merlin brought to it, and it was up to me to figure out a way to send him home, whether or not he wanted to go.

* * * *

I wasn't back at work for long when Paul Curtis stopped in. I almost didn't recognize him out of uniform. He looked younger, like the boy next door, in jeans, a polo, and sneakers.

"Hey, I just wanted to see how well you weathered Duggan. He can be tough when he's stressed, and right now there's a lot of pressure on him to catch Amanda's killer, not that I'm trying to defend the guy, you know, though it probably sounds that way." He was rambling like an awkward teenager.

"Thanks for checking on me," I said, "but as you can see, I'm none the worse for my talk with Duggan. He did try to bite my head off, but I guess it was just too hard."

Curtis laughed. "Listen, I was wondering if you'd like to go to lunch sometime. With me, I mean."

I wasn't surprised by his invitation. It had been a long time coming. But I hadn't worked out how to respond. I couldn't cite my relationship with Travis as a means of letting him down gently because I didn't know if Travis and I still had a relationship. Then there was the more central issue—sure Curtis was nice enough, but I wasn't particularly attracted to him. I hadn't even worked out what I should call him. Until then I'd thought of him as Officer Curtis, but in his civvies, talking about a potential date, it had to be Paul.

"Here's the thing, Paul," I said, trying out his name, "I'm just coming out of a relationship, and I'd hate to ruin our chances by starting over when my head and heart aren't in the right place. May I have a rain check?"

He looked disappointed but not crushed. "Yeah, sure, whenever you're ready, just give me a call." He took one of my business cards from the counter, asked for a pen, and wrote his number on the back for me. He asked if my aunt had recovered from the shock of finding Amanda. I asked how he liked working with Duggan, and we shared a couple of laughs at the detective's expense. I felt like we'd left things between us at a good place.

A steady parade of customers kept me from dwelling too long on my love life or my lack of one. Toward the end of the day, Nancy Clemens walked in. She and Clifford, her husband of sixty years, were the "mom and pop" owners of The Soda Jerk. The diminutive couple had moved to New Camel and opened the café/soda fountain more than thirty years ago. As a kid, I remember always seeing Nancy behind the counter, making her extravagant ice cream concoctions. Clifford preferred socializing with the customers but was quick to roll up his sleeves if they were short-handed. It had become a rite of passage for teenagers in New Camel to wait tables there. The summer I did my stint, I walked my feet off and still managed to gain seven pounds.

"Hi, Mrs. Clemens," I said, coming around the counter to give her a hug. I didn't see her or her husband much anymore. Their son and daughter-in-law had taken over the day-to-day operation of the café around the time they'd turned eighty.

"How many times have I told you to call me Nancy?" she scolded me, her blue eyes twinkling with good humor. "Mrs. Clemens was fine when you were a kid, but you're an adult yourself now."

"Okay, Nancy," I said, "but my grandmother would have had a meltdown if I'd done that when she was alive." For all I knew, she was having one at that very moment.

"Bronwen was a fine woman but a little behind the times. Informality is the order of the day. I firmly believe that if you don't adjust, you go the way of the dinosaurs."

"What brings you in today?" I asked.

"Goodness," she said with a chuckle, "I almost forgot. Clifford has a cold and all the cough medicines he's tried upset his stomach. So I said to myself, Nancy, you need to take yourself over to Abracadabra, and Kailyn will know what to give him."

"Colt's Foot should do it," I said. "Have a seat here while I grab it for you."

"You've put in a chair. What a grand idea."

It took me a full five minutes to locate the right jar. Whenever Merlin helped around the shop, I had trouble locating things. I finally found the Colt's Foot on the shelf with jars of Bearberry and Lion's Mane. He must have decided to group together all the herbs with animal names.

"Sorry that took so long," I said, putting the jar down on the counter. "I have a new helper who gets creative when he restocks the shelves." Nancy started to push herself up from the chair. "No hurry, sit a while longer" I told her. "I'll ring this up whenever you're ready."

"Thank you. It does feel good to get off my feet. Don't get me wrong, Cliff is a wonderful man, but when he's not feeling well, he keeps me hopping."

"Hopefully this will do the trick. It acts like an expectorant and a cough suppressant. Just make a tea with it."

. "It's not actually made from a horse's hoof, is it?" she asked hesitantly.

"No, not at all. It got the name from the shape of its leaf. Someone thought it looked like a colt's foot, I guess."

"That's a relief. Tell me, has there been anything more about Amanda's tragic death?"

"Not that I know of, but everyone I speak to seems to have their own theory on the killer's identity."

"Interesting," Nancy said. "I believe I know pretty much everyone in this town, but I can't imagine any one of them doing such a terrible thing. Of course Clifford says I'm the same naive kid I was when we met."

"Does he have a suspect in mind?"

"Well, to be honest, he's never much liked our mayor."

"Do you know why?" I'd never heard anyone speak badly of Lester. He was a bit smarmy for my taste, a typical glad-hander who had sailed into the mayor's position because no one else wanted the job. To his credit, during seven years in office, he'd held onto the good will of the majority of the electorate.

"Cliff is sure he's on the take."

"Does he have evidence?" I asked.

Nancy giggled. "He claims he has a sixth sense, but I've known the man for over sixty years, and I've never once seen it in action." She glanced at her watch and sighed. "As lovely as it is to sit and chat, I need to be getting back to him."

I rang up her purchase and put it in one of our reusable mini totes. "Let me know if the Colt's Foot does the trick," I said, handing it to her, "and give your husband my best wishes for a speedy recovery."

After she left, I sat in the chair she'd vacated. I had to get busy interviewing possible suspects. We had to find the killer before tourists chose another quaint town to visit, one that didn't have murder victims cropping up on a regular basis. First thing in the morning, I would go over to Winterland. The manager of a ski resort shouldn't be too busy to see me on a hot day in August.

Chapter 8

I made an appointment to see Eric Ingersoll over my lunch hour. I don't know why I still called it a lunch hour when most days I downed a PB and J between customers. I drove into the ski resort expecting a ghost town at that time of year. Instead, I found a whirlwind of activity. Construction vehicles and electrical and plumbing trucks and vans from virtually every aspect of interior design were chaotically parked wherever there was space. The resort was apparently in the last stages of a major renovation. Ginger, Ingersoll's secretary, hadn't mentioned a thing about it. She told me to use the resort's main entrance, to make the second right, and that the one-story administration building would be on my left.

Driving in, I could see that the walkways were covered with dirt, the roads hidden beneath a thick coat of mud from the heavy vehicles that must have been parading through there for months. Although Ginger's directions proved accurate, I would have appreciated a heads-up about the conditions I would face. Boots or sneakers would have been much more appropriate than the delicate strappy sandals I was wearing. I squeezed my SUV in this nook. between two trucks, hoping they would notice it was there and not demolish it.

When I opened the car door and looked down, I knew my sandals were not going to fare well. A spell might help mitigate the damage, but I needed one that relied only on words because I didn't generally keep candles, herbs, and other magickal elements in my purse or glove compartment. I settled on a clothing protection spell. Although it was meant to protect the person wearing the clothes, I figured I could tweak it to shield my shoes. I'd never tried to ad lib with a spell before, but I had nothing to lose. I ran through the spell in my head until it sounded more or less the way I remembered it. Then it was just a matter of changing a few words to make them fit the situation. When I was ready, I closed the windows. No need to serenade any workmen walking by.

"A spell of safety here I cast
A word of might to hold me fast.
A shield before me and beneath,
All around protection seek.
To these sandals no harm come,
Dirt and mire keep them from.

I repeated the spell three times, committing my will and energy to help it succeed. I stepped from the car and carefully weighed each step before I took it. I made my way around the worst of the muck, but just before I reached the curb, I miscalculated, and my left foot sank ankle deep into a thick puddle that sucked at my foot like a living creature trying to drag me under. Balancing on my right foot, I pulled the other one out. To my delight, the mud slid off the sandal as though it were covered in Teflon-coated fabric. It was as pristine as the day I bought it. I don't know if I was more thrilled about the state of my sandal or the fact that the hastily reworded spell had actually done its job.

I made it the rest of the way to the building without further mishap. When I walked into the lobby, I found Ginger at her desk. She was about my age with ginger-colored hair that made me wonder if she was born that way or felt constrained to dye her hair to match her name. She looked up when she heard me come in, a smile already in place.

"Good afternoon, how may I help you?" she asked.

"I'm Kailyn Wilde. I have an appointment to see Mr. Ingersoll."

Her smile widened into a grin, and she pointed at me. It took me a second to realize she was actually pointing past me. I turned and came face-to-face with a man who looked way too Hollywood to be the manager of a ski resort in nowhere New York. He was tall and blond, with aviator sunglasses that hid his eyes and a T-shirt that celebrated his biceps. He whipped off the glasses and gave me a smile that could have caused snow blindness. If Ken dolls were your thing, he was a great specimen, but like Ken, he was too waxy perfect for me.

I held out my hand. "Kailyn Wilde."

He took it and held it for a beat too long for my comfort. I didn't try to draw it free, though, because he was more apt to let down his guard with someone he liked. "Nice to meet you, Ms. Wilde, I'm Eric Ingersoll. Come join me in my office and we'll talk."

As we walked, he kept up the patter, apologizing for being late, which he wasn't, because he had to troubleshoot a problem with the "reno."

"I think I've seen you around town...wait...give me a sec." He snapped his fingers. "I've got it. You're the girl from the magick shop."

"I don't recall seeing you there," I said.

"I never came in. Saw you through the window. The one with the cat. Is he your familiar?" he asked with a wink. We had stopped at an open door with the name Dwayne Davies stenciled on it.

"As a matter of fact, he is," I replied as if it was a perfectly normal question he might have asked anyone. Ingersoll studied me, probably trying to decide if I was serious or just teasing him back. He gave up after a few seconds and led the way into Dwayne Davies's office, flipping the switch for the overhead lighting panels. The room was large and awash in paper. There were piles of it everywhere: on the desk, on the floor, and on the two chairs in front of the desk. He relocated the paper from one chair to the floor and invited me to have a seat. He dropped onto the chair behind the desk, making it squeak in protest.

"Now what can I do for you?"

"I'm planning a family reunion for next summer, and I've been checking out venues in the area."

Ingersoll was busy rooting around in the papers on the desk with no apparent regard for the dozens of pages he was pushing over the edge and onto the floor. He unearthed a yellow legal pad with a flourish and found a pen in the top drawer. "Okay, how many people do you need to accommodate?"

Great. I hadn't thought of that. Way to go, Nancy Drew. "Between twenty and forty."

He raised an eyebrow. "That's a lot of 'between.'"

"I have a big family, and they're hard to pin down. I guess I just need to know if you can accommodate up to forty."

"Forty? That won't be a problem." He dropped the pad and pen back onto the desk. He must have decided I didn't have enough of my ducks in a row for him to bother taking down specifics.

"I guess what I really need is a schedule of room prices, meal options, and a rundown of your summer activities," I said. At least that sounded more organized.

He opened one desk drawer and then another. In the third one he found what he was after. He leaned across the desk to hand me a brochure and a breakdown of their package deals with a price list. "Our summer rates are a considerable savings over the winter ones," he said. "Take a look through the material. If you have any questions give me a call. Word of advice—we get a lot of family groups in the summer, so if you're interested in having your reunion here, get everyone to agree on a couple of different dates in case one isn't available."

"Thanks, I will." I was trying to figure out how to shift the conversation away from reunions to Amanda's murder without being too obvious and before he ran off to tackle another reno crisis. "So, is Dwayne Davies your alter ego?" I asked lightly, grabbing the only arrow in my quiver.

Ingersoll gave a hoot. "Hardly. Dwayne the Dweeb was the manager until he left work one day about a month ago and never came back. No heads-up, no take this job and shove it. Fletch was a raving lunatic when he found out; he's lost a couple of other people recently."

"You mean Hugh Fletcher?" From what little I'd heard about the billionaire, I wasn't surprised that he had trouble keeping people on his payroll.

"Yeah, he owns this place. He asked me to cover things here until he can hire another manager. It's not exactly my dream job, but I don't have much going on this time of year, and he made it worth my while."

That explained Ingersoll's lack of proprietorship about the position, the office, and its contents. "So when you're not wearing the manager's hat, what do you do around here?" I asked.

He leaned back in the chair, making it groan. "Actually, I'm in charge of the entire ski operation. I hire the instructors and make all the critical decisions about safety conditions on the slopes. I decide when to shut things down and when to open them" He was clearly taken with the power he held—a big egocentric fish in a piddling pond.

"Then you're not a ski instructor?"

"I teach advanced classes, from time to time." He sat up straight again. "Why, you a skier?"

"I've never been on skis."

"I can fix that."

I finally had my opening. "I guess skiing can't be any more dangerous than living in New Camel these days."

"You're talking about that lady who was murdered?"

"There are a lot of ways to die, but I didn't think that going to a town meeting was one of them. Maybe that kind of thing happens in big cities, but not here, not in this town."

"Everything changes," he said with a philosophical shrug. "Probably has to do with that Waverly hotel business."

"I know, but come on. Who commits murder over a zoning issue?" I pretended to be appalled by the idea, which wasn't a stretch. "I don't want that hotel here, but it would never occur to me to kill someone to stop it."

"You dig deeper, and you'll find the real reason she was killed comes down to money or sex," Ingersoll said. He sounded like he knew from experience.

"How do you feel about another hotel in the area?"

"Me, I don't much care how it's resolved. As long as there are people who want to ski and old Mother Nature keeps the snow coming, I'm good. Now Fletch, he's another story. He doesn't like competition. It's bad for the bottom line."

Did Ingersoll realize he was saying his boss had a motive for killing Amanda? Or did he do it as a ploy meant to deflect suspicion from himself? I wondered if his job description included getting rid of obstacles in his boss's way. "Were you at the meeting that night?" I asked. "It was so awful. Everyone was in shock."

He grinned. "Can you really see me at a town board meeting? No way. I was having dinner with my girlfriend over in the Glen."

"Someplace you'd recommend?"

"You've never been to the Grotto? For Italian, it's as good as it gets around here. You have to get out more."

"I probably should," I said rising. "I'll call when I have the possible dates for the reunion."

* * * *

Before heading home, I stopped for a prewrapped turkey and Swiss on whole wheat at the Grab and Go Mart outside of town. I was eating it at my desk when Lolly came in. I was so preoccupied thinking about my meeting with Ingersoll I'd momentarily forgotten that she and I had planned to talk after she got back from Amanda's funeral. I came around to the front of the counter and hiked myself up on it, sandwich in hand. I offered Lolly the other half. She took it and collapsed into the customer's chair.

"You're a lifesaver. I'm starving." She took a big bite of the sandwich. "Funerals always leave me exhausted and hungry," she said after swallowing. "A shrink would have a field day figuring out what it means." We ate in companionable silence for another couple minutes. "Dessert is on me," she said and popped the last bit of sandwich into her mouth. "I made a big tray of chocolate-dipped fruit for the Boswells, and I brought the leftovers to my shop for us."

"How was the funeral?" I asked. She'd agreed to be my ears and eyes there. I'd stopped in at Amanda's wake the previous night to pay my respects to her family. Her elderly parents were there, standing beside their nineteen-year-old granddaughter, Kate. Alan Boswell, Amanda's almost ex, was on Kate's other side. The tension between her father and grandparents was palpable, riding just beneath the grief. And Kate was literally in the middle of it.

Although I'd never met the family, I needed to go as much for myself as for them to acknowledge their loss as well as the second loss to our town. I had skipped the funeral itself because the service was to be held in the small church Amanda had attended, and I didn't want to take a spot away from someone closer to the family.

"It was heartbreaking," Lolly said, shaking her head. "Nineteen is too young to lose your mother. Those two were so close. What a pointless, unnecessary death."

"Except someone thought it was necessary."

"You did the right thing by not going. The church was jammed. I made sure I was there early enough to find a seat in the pews, but we were packed in tight as a tin of sardines. They had a sound system rigged up so people who weren't able to get into the church could listen to the service from outside. A lot of people from the school were there. Even Rusty Hinges. That's what my grandson used to call him, but I don't think I ever knew his real name. Isn't that awful?"

"Higgins," I said. "Rusty Higgins."

"Oh, now I get it," Lolly said, brightening for a moment. "Anyway, I felt so sorry for him. He was standing in a back corner alone, weeping. I don't think he ever got married, so I guess the faculty and the kids are kind of like his family." She took a deep breath and twitched her shoulders as if to shake off the lingering gloom of the funeral. "I did my best to stay alert, but I'm afraid I didn't catch any useful leads for you."

"Wishful thinking on my part. How did her husband seem?"

"He was front and center, playing the grieving widower."

We were quiet for a while, thinking our own thoughts. Lolly finally broke the silence. "Kailyn, if you're determined to find the killer, I'd like to help out in some way."

"And by 'help,'" I said, "you mean doing more than keeping me supplied with chocolate?"

Lolly laughed, her body vibrating. "Thanks. I needed that."

"Seriously, though, you already have a lot on your plate. You're up at all hours of the night making candy. You work all day. You babysit your grandkids. I don't know how you do it."

"That's how I stay young," she said. "Seriously, though, tell me what I can do to help."

"Continue what you were doing at the funeral. Listen to what people are saying, who they think the killer is, and why. But I don't want you to question anyone unless it's in the normal course of conversation. If you're too obvious, you could catch the attention of the killer, and that might become dangerous fast."

Lolly blanched, but she recovered quickly. "Don't you worry," she said, "I know how to play it cool. I wasn't the star of my high school drama club for nothing."

I had to admire her. She had a lot of pluck for a seventy-something grandmother of five. I just hoped she wouldn't put herself in harm's way.

"I don't know about you," she said, "but I'm ready for dessert."

"One quick question before I forget—do you happen to know what Alan Boswell does for a living?"

"He's a plumber. I've actually used him a couple of times. Are you having a problem?"

"I'm planning on it."

Lolly frowned. "What am I missing here?"

"I want to question him without his knowing it. If he's a plumber, all I need is a clogged drain, and he'll come right to my door."

Chapter 9

A week after Amanda's funeral, I set my plumber plan in motion. Although a week isn't nearly enough time to mourn a supposed loved one, the man worked for himself and had to pay his bills, at least until Amanda's will was probated and he inherited all of her assets. If he was indeed her killer, once the estate was settled, he'd most likely take off for parts unknown. I had to find out what I could about him before that happened. After dinner, I spent the better part of an hour trying to catch and brush my cats, except for Sashkatu, whose age and infirmities bought him an exemption. I wound up with nothing for my efforts, but a bunch of scratches and a lot of feline ill will. I finally gave up and called Merlin.

"To what end are you trying to wrangle the critters?" he asked, his speech already showing evidence of his most recent TV obsession—old westerns from the fifties.

"I need their fur, and they're not cooperating. If anyone can help, it's you."

"Should I take it you've found a use for the pesky stuff?"

"A very limited use, but I'll explain later. Ask Tilly if I can borrow you." I heard them talking in the background; then Tilly got on the line.

"I'll drive him right over," she said. "I'm intrigued. I'd love to find a use for all the fur my Isenbale sheds. He's an eating, walking fur factory."

The moment they stepped into my house, the five cats came from their low or lofty perches and congregated around Merlin like kids around an ice cream truck. I swear they gave me nasty glances as they passed me on their way to him. Sashkatu remained a safe distance away. He'd seen me chasing his kin around the house and was probably wary of this new development.

"Howdy," Merlin said with a twang.

"Thanks for coming over," I said, wondering how long it would be before he "wrangled" Tilly into buying him a ten-gallon hat and cowboy boots.

"Is it mandatory that I brush them by hand?" he asked. "Because one quick spell and they'll shed that lose fur in less time than you can skin a skunk."

"No spells, Merlin!" Tilly said, "Not. A. Single. One!"

I couldn't remember the last time I'd heard my aunt sound that menacing. I agreed with her. We had to provide a united front if we expected him to take us seriously. Besides, if the magick went awry, I could wind up with five bald cats.

I led the way into the living room followed by Tilly, Merlin, and the cats. It was a slow procession because the cats kept getting under the wizard's feet as they tried to outmaneuver each other to get closer to him. I had spread a sheet on the living room floor, beside one of the arm chairs, and placed the cats' brush and a plastic bag on it. I asked Merlin to sit in the chair, and once the cats were settled around him, I sat on the sheet close to his legs. Tilly chose the couch for the best viewing angle, and Sashkatu watched the proceedings from the back of the couch. In his younger, sprier days, he would have headed for a seat in the bleachers—on top of the china cabinet.

I handed Merlin the brush and asked him to start with the two long-haired cats and work his way down to the one with the shortest hair, in case they mutinied in spite of his charm. When he reached down for the first cat, there was a mad scramble to be chosen, punctuated by hissing and yowling. I have no idea how he restored order, but in no time the cats were once again minding their manners.

He picked up the Persian-Himalayan mix, and the fur was soon flying. I managed to stuff most of it into the plastic bag, but bits escaped, floating off like dandelion fluff. If they reached Sashkatu, he swatted them back in our direction. One cat done, we were all picking the errant fur out of our mouths. By the time Merlin was finished with the five of them, I had a bagful of fur and the bonus of a well-groomed clowder of cats.

"Okay, we've been patient," Tilly piped up. "What on earth are you going to do with the fur?"

"Clog up a drain or two," I said, enjoying the confusion on her face. "Don't worry. I haven't lost my mind." I explained my plan to speak to Alan Boswell.

"Add some honey to the fur and that will do the trick," Tilly suggested with the authority of one who's had experience in the matter.

I decided not to ask for details. My aunt can be longwinded at times, and I was tired. I still had drains to clog and a plumber to call bright and early the next morning.

* * * *

Alan Boswell was polite, but his voice was lifeless on the phone. He sounded like someone in mourning, which begged the question of whether he was truly suffering or pretending. My cynicism was based to a large degree on what Beverly had told me about him and the fact that Amanda had decided to finalize the divorce right before her untimely death. Even so, the law of the land stipulated that a person be considered innocent until proved guilty, and I wanted to afford Alan the benefit of the doubt. Making that determination was uppermost on my agenda. Well, that and having my drains unclogged. I'd done a dandy job of clogging them.

I was up before the sun and immediately made my way downstairs to take the emergency coffee cake out of the freezer to defrost. It was one of Tilly's magnificent creations, irresistible to anyone with a sense of smell and working taste buds. If Alan didn't open up to me over cake and coffee, he never would.

The grandmother clock in the living room was chiming eight o'clock when I tucked the cake into the oven to warm. Five minutes later the doorbell rang. When I opened the door, I was looking at a stocky man of medium height with hair the unlikely color of black shoe polish. I thanked him for being prompt and expressed my condolences once more. His eyes were sunken in dark circles, and it was clear he hadn't shaved in days. He was carrying a toolbox, and there was a motorized machine beside him, which he said was for snaking deeper in the pipes than handheld snakes could go. He followed me to clog number one, the sink in the laundry room, sniffing the air that was redolent of cinnamon and sugar.

"Something smells good," he said. "You baking?"

"It's coffee cake," I said. "It'll be ready in fifteen minutes. If you're not in a hurry, I hope you'll stay and have a slice."

"That's mighty nice of you," he said, his tone a little brighter. "I might just take you up on that." He set his toolbox on top of the drier and pulled out a simple telescoping snake that I recognized from other plumbers' visits over the years. He rooted around with it for a bit, and when he pulled it out, he studied the tip, where a bit of the clogging material was hanging. "Fur and honey?"

"I was bathing my cats."

"Cats don't like to be wet."

"That's why I was using honey to bribe them."

"How many cats do you have, if you don't mind me asking?"

"Six, but I was only bathing five of them." Why had I felt the need to explain that? If I was worried about becoming known as the crazy cat lady, I wasn't doing myself any favors.

"I'm afraid this is going to take the big guns," he said, wheeling the machine into place. "It's going to be noisy; you may want to wait in another room."

He turned it on for a second to demonstrate. It was a deep, grinding noise, like a dentist's drill on steroids. It vibrated in every bone, muscle, and sinew of my body. Since there was no way to have a conversation over the noise, I took his advice and retreated to the kitchen where the noise wasn't as much of an assault. The coffee was ready; the oven timer had five minutes to go. I set out coffee mugs, plates, utensils, napkins, and fixings for the coffee. When Alan finally turned off the machine, the silence was like a gentle blessing, so deep it seemed as if a giant blanket had been thrown over the house, smothering all sound.

After he unclogged the second sink in the main-floor powder room, I invited him into the kitchen. I poured the coffee into the mugs on the counter and carried them to the table where Alan was already seated. I cut the cake and set a hefty slice on his plate.

"This is amazing," Alan said around his first mouthful.

"Thanks. I'll tell my aunt you enjoyed it; she's the baker in the family." Since Alan was busy eating, I took the opportunity to dive right in with my questions "How is your daughter doing?"

He licked crumbs from his lips. "She's holding up okay. But it's hard, you know. She acts like she's grown up, being in college and all, but she has a little girl's heart, and she misses her mom. I can tell." There was a little quaver in his voice. Nicely played, if it wasn't genuine.

"How about your in-laws?"

Alan poured cream into his coffee and watched it swirl around the surface before stirring it in. "To be honest," he said without looking up, "they've never liked me. They always thought Amanda could have done better. They were probably right. Anyhow, now that she's gone, they're trying to turn Kate against me."

Although the whole point of clogging the drains was to give me a chance to find out more about him and his relationship with Amanda, the quick admission caught me by surprise. I didn't know how to respond. I'd expected at least some resistance to my questions. Why was he so eager to air the family's dirty laundry to a complete stranger like me? Either he desperately needed to vent to somebody or he'd heard I was investigating Amanda's death and wanted to get me into his corner by playing the loving, but misunderstood, husband. He might have succeeded, had I not been aware of the impending divorce and his frequent money problems.

"Your in-laws have lost their daughter, and everyone's nerves are raw after such a tragedy," I said. "Given time, they may come around." I was apparently full of useless platitudes.

Alan sniffled. "You really think so?" I swore I saw a glimmer of hope in his eyes. "I can't bear the thought of losing my little girl too. You have nothing in life if you don't have family."

I had to admit he was making headway in winning me over or at least in making me less sure of what I thought I knew. His words alone hadn't done it; they were more trite than eloquent, but it was increasingly difficult to believe he was faking his emotions. I found myself weighing what Beverly had said about Alan against the man across the table from me. Given her propensity to exaggerate and indulge in malicious gossip, I couldn't dismiss the possibility that she had her own reasons to vilify Alan or to send me on a wild-goose chase. I was sorry I hadn't asked Tilly to be there for another opinion. Then again, she was hardly neutral about her dislike of all things Beverly.

After forking the last of his cake into his mouth, Alan asked if he could have more. I was happy to oblige, as long as our little barter system of "cake for information" continued. I gave him another wedge.

"I heard you and Amanda were thinking of getting a divorce," I said.

I'd heard a lot more than that, but I thought a vague approach would be less likely to antagonize him. He looked up at me from his plate as if trying to decide if he could trust me. I wanted my face to show compassion rather than nosiness, but without a mirror it was hard to assess how well I was pulling it off.

"Yeah, you know how it is. Like most couples, we've had our ups and downs. But I think we were at a point where things were going better. The sad part is that the last time I talked to Amanda, she wanted me to move back in and give it another go. Now we'll never have that chance." He blinked rapidly as if he were trying to hold back tears.

"Life isn't always fair," I said.

Alan glanced at his watch, immediately pushed back from the table, and got to his feet. "Sorry, I wasn't paying attention to the time. I'm going to be late for my next appointment. Thanks for the coffee and cake. You've been very kind to listen to my tale of woe."

"Not at all," I assured him. "Everyone needs a shoulder now and then." I could write a whole book of clichés. I paid him for his work and sent him on his way with the remainder of the cake, feeling like I'd come away with a bargain.

I was forty minutes late arriving at Abracadabra. When I opened the front door, Travis literally fell on me, shoulder first and we both went down in a heap. He apologized as he helped me up.

"Are you okay? I was leaning on the door, waiting for you."

It was a riff on our first meeting when I'd also been late. This time was considerably more awkward though and left me wishing we could go back to that other day and start off fresh.

"Are you all right?" he asked again.

"I think so. Everything feels like it's still connected to everything else."

"You know your door isn't up to code, right?"

Was he seriously trying to lay the blame on me? "What are you talking about?"

"Buildings that serve the public are required to have doors that open outward." By the look on his face, I could tell he regretted bringing it up when things between us were rocky enough. "It's actually a fire safety regulation," he added lamely.

"Well, I've never been fined or told I had to fix it." Of course that didn't mean he was wrong. The shop may have somehow slipped through the bureaucratic cracks.

"It could be your shop was granted status as a historic landmark, making it exempt."

"Sounds good to me," I said, happy to change the subject. "But if you've come for information on Amanda's killer, I'm afraid I'm not that far along in my investigation. Things are still very sketchy."

"Actually, this time I came to pass some on to you."

"Come sit down." I started walking toward the chair, but when I glanced back, Travis hadn't budged from the spot near the door. "What's wrong?" I asked, pretty sure I knew the answer. I wanted to hear what he'd say. This was his first time back in the shop since he'd taken flight, and he was clearly uncomfortable.

"So, all the stuff in here"—he waved his arm in a wide arc encompassing everything in the store—"is magickal in some way?"

"To varying degrees, but yes."

He walked over to me hesitantly, like he was crossing a shaky bridge over a moat of starving crocodiles. Or maybe he was worried the merchandise might spring to life with one command from me. I offered him the chair and took my usual seat on the counter. He seemed undecided about whether to sit and stay a while or pass on the info and hit the road. I was glad when he committed himself to the chair.

"You know you moved the ground from under my feet that night and not in a good way," he said wryly.

"I got that. It would have been hard to miss." At least he was finally opening up and talking about it. That was progress in my book.

"Yeah, I guess so. Here's the thing, my whole life has been based on facts, hard facts. I've never spent a second considering anything remotely paranormal or fantastical."

"And I've grown up believing all things are possible and hard facts may be softer than they seem."

He didn't say anything, but that was okay, I told myself. Better than if he had said, "That's the end of it. The two of us will never work." I still had hope he'd come to accept who I was. I didn't want to set a deadline. I'd know when enough was enough. Wouldn't I?

"So," I said in a lighter tone, "are you waiting until I beg for that information you have?"

"That could be interesting." He gave me one of his real smiles, not the kind he pulled up on-demand for TV. "Okay, here it is. I was talking to a buddy of mine last night. Turns out he's been working on the Winterland renovation. He had a lot to say about the owner, Hugh Fletcher, and none of it was kind."

"You don't need to build dramatic tension," I reminded him. "This isn't a newscast."

He laughed. "Okay, I'm getting to it. He told me Fletcher is always trying to shave construction costs. He tried to bully my friend into doing things on the cheap, using materials that weren't up to code. He's got a reputation for it in the construction industry."

"But how does the work pass inspection?"

"According to my friend, Fletcher just pads a few of the right pockets. He's been lucky so far. Nothing's come back to bite him. But I did some digging into his past, and there have been a lot of complaints over the years about shoddy construction and safety issues."

"So he fills some more pockets and keeps getting away with it."

"Essentially."

"Did your friend mention Ingersoll? He's the ski pro and interim manager at Winterland."

"No, but if Fletcher trusts him, he can't be a saint."

"Do you think Fletcher would stoop to murder to keep the Waverly hotel from being built?"

"He takes chances with peoples' lives every time he ignores safety regulations. But if you're asking me if I think Fletcher stuck the knife in Amanda, I'd have to say no. I doubt he would do his own dirty work. Having said all that, I have no solid evidence he was involved in her murder in any way."

"I think I'd like it better if the killer was an outsider like him instead of someone who lives right here in New Camel. It wouldn't feel quite so personal."

"Understandable. This is a great little town. You don't want to be suspicious of everyone you know or pass on the street." Travis stood and stretched his arms over his head. "I've got to drive back down to the city, but I'll let you know if I hear anything else."

"Same here." I stayed on the counter. If I hopped down and walked him the short distance to the door, we'd have to deal with the awkward moment of good-bye again. This way was easier.

Travis paused at the door and looked back at me with a crooked smile. "Don't worry. We'll get this figured out."

Get what figured out? I wanted to run after him and ask if he meant Amanda's killer or the two of us. What kept me up on there on the counter was the fear that I'd be disappointed by his answer.

Chapter 10

When I opened my eyes, I didn't know where I was or how I'd gotten there. My heart was racing, my blood pounding in my ears. My body throbbed like a bad tooth, making it hard to think. I reached back to the last thing I could remember. I was in my shop. There was a powerful blast of wind or energy that felt like it would suck the air out of my lungs and the skin right off my body. That memory brought it all back to me with a jolt. I was attempting to teleport myself. But I was still in the dark about where I had wound up. My intended goal was Tea and Empathy, but I could have been anywhere on the planet. And I had nothing with me, no ID, no phone, no money.

I levered myself up to take stock of my condition. The movement ignited a searing pain in my back and side. I'd probably bruised or broken ribs. I choked off the scream rising in my throat, so all that emerged was a whimper. I didn't want to give myself away until I knew more about my circumstances.

Below the hemline of my sundress, I could see that my left knee was swelling and turning angry shades of red and purple. My upper lip felt like it was swelling too. I ran my tongue over my front teeth, afraid I'd chipped them or knocked them out. They seemed to be intact. When I reached up to assess the pain in the back of my head, my fingers came away with blood, a scary amount of it. But I knew small scalp wounds are notorious bleeders. All in all, my injuries didn't appear to be critical. I could patch myself up when I got home. But to do that, I first had to figure out where I was.

There was one grimy window set high in the wall that provided enough light for me to check out my surroundings. At least there were no bars on the window. Aside from that, the place wasn't much better than a cell. The floor beneath me was badly scratched and gouged hardwood. It accounted

Sharon Pape

for the splinter I'd felt digging into my left palm since the wind spat me out there. The walls were a dingy, yellowed white and were festooned with spider webs. Whoever owned this place wasn't much of a housekeeper. The only furniture, if you could call it that, was an aluminum shelving unit, holding a dozen or so damaged and empty plastic bins. By my best guess, I'd landed in a storeroom no longer in use.

For my purposes, the most important feature of the room was the door to my right. It took a ridiculous amount of time to drag myself off the floor and onto my feet. Tears sprang to my eyes from the pain that exploded all over my body. My stomach lurched and churned with nausea. I waited for it to settle down before limping over to the door. I told myself not to worry. If it was locked, I'd simply use a spell. I shut my mind against the possibility of failure, but some negativity squeaked through anyway. What if I hadn't correctly remembered the spell Morgana had created when I was little? What if it didn;t work because I wasn't in the right frame of mind and spirit?

When the knob turned easily in my hand, my heart lifted like a balloon. But I wasn't ready to open the door just yet. I put my ear to it and held my breath, listening for evidence of someone in the room beyond. I wasn't in any shape to defend myself for breaking and entering, which is how it would surely seem to the property owner. If I explained my presence as the result of teleportation run amok, who would believe me? I'd be carted away to a very padded cell and medicated with antipsychotics. So I waited until I was reasonably sure I was alone in the building before I opened the door a crack and peered out.

Relief spread through me like a warm bath. I was in the old candle shop two blocks down from Abracadabra. The sickly sweet smell of scented candles lingered in the shop, though it had been closed for two years. Mrs. Kowalski had decided it was time to hang up the candle-making business and join her sister on the west coast of Florida. The shop had remained empty since then. Quaint shops in little towns aren't everyone's cup of tea in this brave new age of technology.

I hobbled through the musty shop to the front door and found it locked. Two open doors would have been asking too much of the universe, I thought grudgingly. I eased myself down on the ledge of the plate glass window that once bore the stenciled name of the shop. Now only bits of each letter remained, looking like an alien alphabet. There was nothing in the shop with which I could break a window, but that would have been a last resort anyway since it meant involving the police and the property owner.

I could try to attract the attention of a passerby, but the person would have to call the police to open the lock. Either way, it wouldn't look good for me. I had no business being in the shop—a locked shop, no less. My best option was a spell. Morgana had created one to open locks after she'd locked herself out of the house, the shop, and the car on a half-dozen occasions. I was seven at the time and kept a marble notebook where I wrote down spells I deemed worth keeping. Other children learned nursery rhymes; I stockpiled spells. Now all I had to do was remember it after twenty years. Unfortunately, the worst time to access a memory is under stress, and I wasn't likely to be stress-free until I was out of the candle shop.

I did what I could to slow my breathing and heart rate, while I waited for my brain to locate the right spell. One line immediately popped into my head. "Release your hold." I said it over and over, hoping to prime the pump.

A frustrating hour later, I gave up on my memory and tried to ad lib my own version. Given my worsening frame of mind, I knew it was a long shot and I was proved right. I was thoroughly exhausted. I never knew that pain could drain you to such a degree. Even my brain had slowed like a computer compromised by malware.

I needed to rest for a little while. I curled up on the hard, dusty floor and closed my eyes. I must have fallen asleep, because the next time I looked at my watch, half an hour had passed. I sat up and waited for the fog of sleep and pain to dissipate. As it did, my mother's spell sprang to my tongue. I recited it as I got to my feet, afraid to lose it again. My battered body hurt more than it had earlier, but I was so grateful to finally have the spell that I was able to shove the pain out of my head long enough to focus on the doorknob and recite the spell three times:

"Let go your bonds,
"Release your hold.
"You're too loose now
"To stay closed.
"May good of heart
"Pass through untold."

When I took hold of the knob again, it turned and the door opened without so much as a scrape or shudder. I said a silent thank-you to my mother. She'd never created a locking spell, though, so I couldn't relock the door. But the spell itself contained a line of protection. Besides, there wasn't anything worth stealing in the shop. I checked to be sure no one was nearby to see me exit. I walked out, closed the door behind me, and slowly made my way to Abracadabra.

Every step brought with it another wave of agony, starting in my head and traveling the length and width of my body. The two blocks were an endless marathon. At least it was a slow business day. I didn't bump into anyone I knew, and there were no shocked stares from tourists.

Back in my shop, I immediately checked on Sashkatu. I needn't have worried. He was still sleeping soundly on his windowsill. The cat could sleep away an entire day. I collapsed into the customer's chair. The padded desk chair behind the counter was more than I could manage at that moment.

"Heavens to Betsy!" My aunt Tilly exclaimed. "What happened to you?"

I hadn't heard her come into my shop through the adjoining door. She padded over to me as quickly as her arthritis and bunions could carry her.

"I know, I look like a mess," I said as calmly as possible, "but it's almost all cosmetic. I'm perfectly fine. I just had a little accident."

She gasped. "A car crash?" Ever since my mother and grandmother had perished at the hands of a drunk driver, my aunt's anxiety level went from zero to sixty in a split second if anyone mentioned an accident. To be honest, I wasn't much better about it.

I dragged myself out of the chair and put my arm around her shoulders. "No, no, I...I fell down the stairs at home," I said reaching for a quick answer. I intended to tell her the truth but not until she was calmer. I didn't want to scare her into a heart attack or stroke. I had no intentions of losing the last of my family that way.

"Maybe you should go to the ER." Tilly hated hospitals, so her remark was a good gauge of how upset she was.

"I'll be fine. Absolutely fine. One of your healing teas is all I need." Giving her something to do would help her, if not me.

"Right. Of course. Let me think. I'll need yarrow and comfrey, lavender and—"

"What you need is calendula," Merlin said as he ambled up to us. "Do you have it amongst your herbs?"

"Second aisle on your left," I said. I'd forgotten how well calendula can heal as both a poultice and weak tea. Merlin went off to find it, muttering about amateurs.

"Somebody needs to learn some manners," Tilly called after him.

One moment they were soul mates, and the next they were sniping at each other like an old married couple. I took the role of Switzerland whenever things got dicey between them.

Merlin came out of the aisle holding the jar of ground calendula leaves. "Make haste woman," he said, gesturing to Tilly. "You shall fix the tea whilst I prepare the poultice."

"Once we have you squared away, I'm going to set that wizard straight," my aunt whispered to me through clenched teeth. Sashkatu had awakened from his deep sleep when Merlin came in. He descended his stairs, stretched languidly, and followed the two of them back to Tea and Empathy. "We'll let you know when we're ready for you," Tilly called over her shoulder.

I sat in the chair again and tried to figure out how my first conscious attempt at teleportation went wrong. I thought I was ready. I had worked hard to max out my telekinetic skills before moving on. Of course there was no way to be sure I'd reached 100 percent of that ability since our magick was often subpar these days. But I had to assume part of the blame for my failure.

The allure of teleportation was irresistible. The ability to leap through space from point A to point B would be "Beam me up, Scotty" without the technology or the machine. It would certainly herald a major step forward in my powers. I'd finally have a special talent like everyone else in my family. It would make me unique among my kind. If my mother and my grandmother had their history right, only one other sorcerer in our line had ever accomplished that feat, and she had lived centuries ago. When they first mentioned it to me, I had dragged out the family scrolls to see for myself.

I had pored over the documents, but the writing back then was Old English, much of it using the runic alphabet. Between that and the flowery script faded by time, the writing was virtually incomprehensible. After hours of straining my eyes and getting nowhere, I gave up and stowed the scrolls back under the floorboards in the living room. Finding corroboration in the past was a waste of time anyway. I already knew I had the intrinsic talent to perform teleportation because I'd done it by accident. It didn't matter if no one else in our family had ever mastered the skill. I had. I just needed to figure out how to do it again and by design.

When my aunt called me into her shop, I was no closer to pinpointing the reason I'd landed in the candle store, nearly killing myself in the process. I found Tilly and Merlin waiting for me in the tiny bathroom she had to install before opening for business. Apparently there was a county ordinance requiring establishments that served food to have a working bathroom. Over the years, it had come in mighty handy for us as well. No more sloughing through the snow to use the bathroom at home.

Tilly had me sit on the lid of the toilet to sip the tea while Merlin dressed my injuries. The tea was awful. It tasted like hot water and bitter grass, but under my aunt's watchful eye, I managed to finish it. As bad as it was, arguing about it would have been worse.

On the way back to my shop, I bumped into Elise at the connecting door.

"There you are," she said about to pull me into a hug. She stopped short when she registered my physical state. "Oh my Lord, what happened? Are you okay? Listen to me," she chided herself. "Any fool can see you're not okay. You're extremely not okay." She wound her arm through mine and helped me back to the customer chair, where she insisted on hearing in detail what I'd been through.

"Teleportation sounds awfully risky," she said, her brows pinched over her nose. "Maybe you should consider taking up something safe like stock-car racing or alligator wrestling."

"Please, don't make me laugh," I begged, bracing my injured ribs with my arms. "Seriously, though, if I don't try to reach my potential, it would be like turning my back on my family tree, on my genetic identity, on who I am, and on who I'm supposed to be." I was surprised by the gush of words that had poured from my mouth. I'd never thought about it in those terms, but I guess my subconscious had been moonlighting.

Elise seemed equally amazed. It took her a moment to recover. "Well, as long as you don't feel strongly about it," she said, cracking us both up, my laughter laced with groans of pain. "Sorry," she said, wiping away tears of laughter.

"Can we stop talking about me now?" I said. "It feels like months since I've seen you." After solving her husband's murder, we'd both been sucked back into our own demanding lives. Elise was busy learning how to be a father as well as a mother to her sons, and I was busy trying to keep my business going and keep a certain wizard out of trouble. Thus far, I'd been more successful at the former than the latter. Although Elise and I had talked on the phone and exchanged daily e-mails, nothing could replace a live face-to-face for my state of mind.

She glanced at her watch. "I'm afraid I'm out of time. Noah has a checkup date with his doctor, followed by a trip to buy new sneakers. He's already outgrown the pair I bought him at the end of school. If he doesn't have a growth spurt to even things out, he's going to look like he has clown feet."

"Judging by Zach, that growth spurt is right around the corner. ."

She pressed her cheek to mine and headed to the door. "I promise we'll get lunch or dinner soon."

"I'd love to see the boys. How about I bring pizza for all of us? Name the night."

She paused in the doorway. "Thursday."

"With mushrooms?"

"And sausage."

Chapter 11

Thursday morning Mayor Tompkins breezed into my shop with Patrick Griffin, the owner of Remember When, in tow. My grandmother loved browsing through the antiques and memorabilia in his store. I knew Patrick too but not well. All I could say about him with any confidence was that he was married, had one son, and lived in the same general area I did.

"Hey, Kailyn," Tompkins said, sounding strangely jaunty and sober at the same time. "Patrick and I are making the rounds. We're letting folks know he's agreed to take Amanda's place on the board until we can have a proper election." Patrick gave me a sheepish smile that said he'd rather be anywhere else. "I don't know if you recall," the mayor said, "but Pat here was on the board for five years; he knows the ropes. So when he walked into my office and offered to help out, I couldn't have been more pleased."

"I'm sure you were, Lester," I said, trying to sort out my thoughts about his pronouncement. "But I can't help wondering if everyone is going to be okay with an unelected board member voting on a heated issue like the zoning code—no offense, Patrick."

He nodded.

"I took that into account," Lester said, bulldozing on, "and that's why Pat is the perfect man for the job. He's always demonstrated a willingness to listen to both sides of any issue before arriving at a well thought out decision."

"Then I guess he really is the perfect candidate," I said dryly. There was nothing to be gained by arguing the point in front of Patrick, who seemed ready to bolt. I wanted to ask around and get a sense of how the community reacted to the news. I was about to thank them for stopping in when the Star Wars theme rang out from the mayor's phone, startling all of us. He excused himself and stepped outside to take the call. Patrick and I were left standing there smiling awkwardly at each other.

"Patrick," I said, "do you mind if I ask you a question?"

"Not at all."

"Did you go to the mayor and offer to step in, or did he come to you to talk you into 'volunteering'?"

He laughed. "You don't pull your punches. I'm afraid I'll have to take the fifth, though."

"Enough said. That's what I thought." I would have liked to ask him more, but Lester walked back in.

"Sorry about that," he said. "A mayor's job is never done. Good talking to you, Kailyn. We're off to continue our rounds. Look forward to seeing you at the next town meeting. I'll send an e-mail blast once we firm up the date."

* * * *

"Pizza delivery," I called out when Noah asked who was there. I heard him disengage the lock and pull the door open. He was standing in the open doorway beaming at me and the pizza.

"Ma," he yelled over his shoulder, "Kailyn's here."

He plucked the boxes from my hands and was off with them to the kitchen. I could see Elise at the sink. I was on my way to her when Zach came charging down the stairs, making a last-second course correction to avoid crashing into me. I could swear he'd grown another foot since I'd last seen him. He gave me a quick peck on the cheek and trotted into the kitchen.

"Welcome to the crazy Harkens house," Elise said, hugging me. "There's salad on the table, so please join my two hooligans, and I'll be right there." She opened the boxes and touched the crust. "It's still warmish, but it'll be better hot and crisp." Zach and Noah groaned in unison. "You'll survive for another five minutes," she told them. "Patience is a virtue, though I'm not altogether sure why." She pulled a large griddle out of a lower cupboard and set it over two of the stove's gas burners. I scooched into the kitchen nook beside Zach, leaving Elise the side near Noah.

We ate salad with oil and vinegar, and I chatted with the boys about the upcoming school year. Zach was looking forward to basketball and track. Noah was baseball all the way, though he thought he might also try fencing during the winter. Both of them were eager to connect with friends again. The learning part of school came in a distant third. I was surprised because they'd always done so well academically. Thinking back to my own school days, I realized I'd felt the same way they did.

Elise served up the pizza, oozing cheese and smelling like heaven, on paper plates. "I put more slices on to heat, so yell when you want seconds."

She'd barely slid into her seat when Zach was ready for more. She laughed. "I should probably just put a whole pie in front of him from the get-go."

When the kids couldn't eat another bite, they left to play with the new game station Noah had received for his birthday. After I helped Elise clean up, we sat back down at the table with coffee.

"How are they doing?" I asked her.

"Better. Definitely better. Getting back to school and all their activities should help too. But I'm dreading the holiday season."

"Maybe it would be good to shake things up this year. Instead of staying home, you could spend some time with your sister's family. The kids love being with their cousins."

"I might. My sister has been harping on it. But we're not done with summer yet. I can't plan that far ahead right now."

I didn't want to push her about it, so I switched topics and told her about the unexpected visit from the mayor and Patrick.

"You cannot be serious," she said, putting down her coffee cup with a clatter. "It sounds like Lester is trying to rig the zoning vote."

"Can he do that? Appoint whoever he wants just like that?"

"Not really, but he can sure try. If anyone protests and cites the town's charter, he'll have to back down. He's made it clear from the beginning he wants that hotel to be built. I wonder how big a kickback he's been promised."

"Wait," I said, reminded of Nancy Clemens remark, "am I the only one who isn't aware he's been on the take?"

"No, I doubt many people are aware of it. I know because Jim was his attorney. Of course Jim shouldn't have told me, confidential information and all, but he was never great at keeping his pants zipped or his mouth shut."

"That buys Lester a pass off my suspect list," I said with a sigh. "Since Amanda was in favor of the hotel, Lester didn't have that motive for murdering her. Too bad, I could have wrapped up the case in no time and swept another sleaze out of office in the process."

Elise chuckled. "Don't lose hope; he might have killed her for a different reason."

"Your optimism is one of the things I love most about you," I said.

"I imagine he picked Patrick to fill the seat because he's also pro-hotel," she mused. "Otherwise, why take the chance of alienating his electorate?"

"That's my guess too. I intend to pay Patrick a return visit, just to be neighborly, and see what I can find out." I paused to drink my coffee. "I've been meaning to ask you about the other two members on the board. How well do you know Corinne DeFalco and Eddie Hermann?"

"We're acquaintances. They both have kids who've been in classes with

Zach and Noah. If I remember correctly, Eddie works for a cable company in Watkins Glen, and Corinne works part-time in a doctor's office."

"Do you know which way they lean on the hotel issue?"

"We've never gotten much further than 'Hello, how are you?' or the occasional comment about school-related stuff. Why? Do you think either of them could have killed Amanda?"

"No, but I'd be remiss if I didn't check them out."

"I'll see what I can dig up for you," Elise said. "I could use a little intrigue to spice up my life."

* * * *

The tour bus scheduled to arrive the next morning pulled into town on time. Within five minutes my shop was humming with activity. Advertised as a Last Fling of Summer tour out of Brooklyn, it had attracted a diverse group of people. There were seniors, young families, a couple of self-proclaimed witches and a group of singles who thought they'd signed on for a tasting tour of the Upstate wineries. They kept me on my toes explaining products, answering questions and ringing up sales. Tilly was fully booked for the day too, so I couldn't ask her for help, and we'd decided it would be best to leave Merlin home to watch the Cowboy Network.

Toward the end of the morning, the crowd thinned out until the two pseudowitches were the only people remaining in the shop. I'd noticed them earlier, smug and smirking as they went through the aisles and listened to my conversations with other customers. I'd heard snippets of what they were saying to each other: "What a crock.... Do you believe her...? This place is pathetic...."

I didn't say a word, but when they passed the counter giggling, I sent some of our brochures flying over to them. They batted them away, their giggles replaced by nervous mutterings. They stepped up their pace and headed for the door. I used a quick spell to make the door swell in its frame. The spell wasn't exactly for that purpose, but I saw no harm in trying it.

First one, then the other, tried turning the knob. When it didn't budge, they tugged at it to no avail. Their growing anxiety was evident on their faces. When they finally looked over at me, I smiled graciously and made a big show of reducing the size of the door and swinging it wide open for them. "Come back soon," I called out cheerfully as they bolted for the street.

Once I was through congratulating myself, I had a stroke of conscience. I was no better than Merlin. I couldn't even call what I did gray magick, because there was no benefit to balance out my use of power. Scaring them was an act of vengeance. I did it because I could, and that was unacceptable.

"Fifty lashes with a limp noodle," my mother said, startling me. Her little energy cloud was behind me, bobbing up and down like a skiff at anchor. "Good morning, Kailyn."

"If you're here to lecture me, get on with it."

"Oh that—no, no, you're only human, and they were asking for it. Had it been me, they would have fared a whole lot worse."

"That's hardly the way to instruct your daughter," Bronwen said, her cloud appearing out of the ether.

"Can you swear that you never once used your powers inappropriately, Mother?" Morgana asked her.

Bronwen didn't immediately answer. I could tell she was arguing with herself because her cloud had turned a bilious shade of green.

"Fine," she said. "I suppose there was a time or two when I was younger that I might have disobeyed the rules to indulge in some questionable acts. Nonetheless, that doesn't make it right."

"Ladies, I understand. I'll try not to let it happen again." I turned to my mother. "Are you here for a visit, or is there something else on your agenda?"

"I want to know how your teleportation efforts are going."

"Kind of hard to say. I did manage to teleport myself but not to the place where I intended and not in the best of shape." I spent a minute elaborating. "Hopefully I'll improve with practice."

"I knew you had it in you!" Bronwen exclaimed. "I have absolute faith that in due time you'll master the skill."

My mother was far less enthusiastic. "Excuse me," she said to her mother, "I'm not sure we should be encouraging her to continue. The potential risk may well be too great."

"Courage was never your forte," Bronwen said dryly.

"There's an important distinction between courage and folly, Mother," Morgana snapped. "I'll never forget the time you were sure that with the right spell you'd be able to fly."

"What happened?" I asked, though I knew better than to insinuate myself into their dramas. But since I'd never heard a whisper about this, I couldn't let it go by.

"I was only five years old, but I remember the incident vividly. Tilly and I watched our mother climb to the top of Dinkman's Hill, jump off and nearly fall to her death."

"You're making it sound much worse than it was," Bronwen said indignantly.

"Why don't we let Kailyn judge that for herself? All I need to add is that Tilly and I had to be placed in foster care for three months while you recuperated and went through rehab. What do you say to that, Kailyn?"

"It probably wasn't the smartest thing to attempt, especially with two little kids looking on, but I have to acknowledge my grandmother's courage in trying." I had to offer a split decision or risk making a worse mess of our family dynamics.

"Is it any wonder that Tilly and I grew up to be more cautious?"

Morgana was clearly not going to let the issue go. I had to do something. "Excuse me," I said, "but I have to see a man about a hotel."

They weren't even listening to me. Their clouds had turned red and were sparking from their anger. I stuck the I'll Be Back clock sign in the window, grabbed my purse from behind the counter, and left them to their argument. With any luck, they'd be gone when I returned.

* * * *

Patrick Griffin was eating a hero on the front porch of his antique shop. "Hi, how are you doing?" he asked when I stopped near the steps.

"I'm good. I didn't mean to intrude on your lunch hour. I can come back later."

He wiped his mouth with a napkin. "Not at all. Come sit down. Eating alone is boring. That's why I sit out here and watch the world go by. Please join me." He pulled another foil-wrapped sandwich out of the insulated bag near his feet. "Meatball hero made from scratch by my wife." When I hesitated, he said, "I never eat the second one, but she insists on sending two just in case. Like I might starve here in the middle of town. With The Soda Jerk across the street."

The sandwich did smell delicious. "You talked me into it," I said, hopping up the steps to the porch. I thanked him and took the sandwich, installing myself in the wicker chair beside his. The hero was even better than it smelled. One bite made me realize I was hungrier than I thought. "This is amazing. Please thank your wife for me. She ought to open a restaurant in town."

"I've suggested that a dozen times over the years. She's not interested."

"Nice tour group today," I said to keep the conversation going."

"Best kind. They had money and weren't afraid to part with it. I sold more this morning than I did all of last week."

"By the way," I said after swallowing another mouthful, "how did the rest of your campaign stops with Lester go?"

"Let's just say I didn't expect everyone to be thrilled with the idea, and I wasn't disappointed." He laughed. "Luckily I have a day job to fall back on if the town wants to wait for another election. Of course, the delay could make the Waverly people decide to bail altogether. Between you and me, I'm not sure how I got roped into this anyway."

Sharing a meal seemed to be loosening Pat's tongue. Or maybe it had elevated my status from acquaintance to friend. "Everyone figures you're in favor of the hotel or Lester wouldn't have asked you to come aboard," I said and took another hearty bite as though I was more interested in the sandwich than in his answer.

"I am for it," he said. "I know a lot of people feel strongly against it. Where do you come down on the subject?"

I shrugged. "Still undecided." I wasn't, but I figured he would be freer with his words if he didn't see me as an opponent. "May I ask why you want the hotel to be built here?"

Pat finished his last bite of sandwich before answering. "Antiques are not everyone's thing. So the more people who visit our town, the higher the number of prospective buyers. It's a flat-out business decision. I care about maintaining the charm of our town as much as the next person, but I also want to earn enough to put my son through college."

I bobbed my head. I couldn't deny it made sense. "Does it look like Lester can get you seated on the board without starting a town-wide civil war?" I absently licked the sauce off my fingers.

Pat passed me a napkin. "Good to the last drop," he said with a wink. "We'll find out soon enough. He's going to call for another town meeting. He claims if we don't change the zoning law soon, they may walk away from the project."

"I'm still wondering if Amanda was killed to keep the zoning law from being passed."

"Why else?" he said. "The fact that she was murdered at the meeting can't be just a coincidence. There are a dozen other places where she could have been killed more easily and with a lot less risk to the killer."

That was the consensus from everyone I'd asked, including Travis. It seemed logical enough, but I couldn't dismiss the nagging little voice in my head playing the what-if game. What if the killer had chosen the time and place precisely to make everyone think Amanda was killed because of the zoning issue and not something else?

Chapter 12

Business was slow but steady the next morning. A string of locals came in for remedies to treat a range of problems from athlete's foot to the side effects of chemo. Every one of them was unhappy with the mayor's efforts to seat a board member of his own choosing. Yet no one had the time or energy to run against Patrick Griffin. A few people admitted to being afraid of meeting the same fate as Amanda. But unless someone stepped up, Patrick would automatically become our new, albeit temporary, board member. I wondered if this was how democracies started slip-sliding away.

One customer suggested Tilly for the position, but my aunt didn't have the right temperament for campaigning or sitting on the board. She was too easily upset and flustered. Besides, she, too, had a business to run. And although no one was aware of it, she was the other half of our Merlin security program. Keeping the legendary wizard out of trouble and off the grid required more woman hours than you might think. With all this talk swirling around me, I felt a twinge of guilt about not tossing my own hat into the proverbial ring. But between Merlin, my magick shop, and trying to find a killer, there were not enough hours in the day. Judging by the way the media kept recycling the old news, I had to assume that Detective Duggan hadn't made any progress in his investigation, meaning I needed to stay focused on the case too.

When I was trying to decide on my next move, Hugh Fletcher came to mind. Travis had said the man would never do his own dirty work. Could that mean Eric Ingersoll did it for him? He'd told me he was wining and dining his girlfriend at the time Amanda was murdered. Verifying his alibi shouldn't be too difficult. I found the Grotto's website with its phone number and hours of operation. They opened for dinner at five o'clock.

I called as soon as I got home from the shop. The earlier in the evening, the more likely it wouldn't be too busy. I took the precaution of blocking my number. The woman who answered the phone was upbeat and friendly until I asked to speak to the manager. At that point, I was told in a more officious and wary tone that I was speaking to her. Maybe she was expecting a complaint because after I explained that I was writing an article for the e-magazine, The New York Palate, and that it would highlight the best places to eat in Schuyler County, her tone quickly warmed up again. She introduced herself as Sherry Atwood and assured me she was "tickled pink" to have the Grotto included in my article.

"May I inquire how you chose us?" she asked.

Although she was clearly trying to remain professional, I had the sense she was doing a happy dance in her head. "Eric Ingersoll is one of our freelance food critics. He's eaten in the Grotto on a number of occasions. The last time would have been August fifteenth. You can probably find him on your reservation list for that date. He has nothing but praise for your establishment."

"Would you excuse me a minute?" When she returned to the phone she was pleased to confirm that she did indeed find his reservation for two at seven o'clock on the night in question. "Now I can picture exactly where they were seated. I'm so glad he enjoyed his meal."

I hadn't said Ingersoll was there with a date. By mentioning the reservation was for two, Sherry confirmed his alibi. I felt a little guilty about conning her, but I couldn't think of any other way to verify it. If Fletcher hired a hit man to kill Amanda, it was not Eric Ingersoll. Speaking to the business mogul in person moved up my to-do list. The problem was that he lived and worked in Manhattan. It would mean having Tilly tend my shop on a day when she didn't have any appointments in hers. And she'd have to take full responsibility for Merlin. It wouldn't have been an issue if I'd perfected my teleportation skills, but that was wishful thinking and a long way off.

* * * *

I didn't sleep well that night. I was awakened by troubling dreams. In one I was running from an angry mob, and when I looked over my shoulder, I recognized their faces. They were the faces of my friends and neighbors, people I had known all my life. But as I watched, their features morphed into vicious caricatures.

In another dream, they were pelting me with rocks. I was crouched on the ground against a wall, a dead end, with nowhere to run. I tucked my head down, trying to protect myself with my hands and forearms. The smaller stones pinged off me, stinging like insect bites. The larger rocks slammed into me, eventually knocking me over. I felt blood running from my head into my eyes and down my cheeks. It was getting harder and harder to breathe, to expand my diaphragm enough to draw in the air. Mercifully the barrage stopped. I was in a pocket of quiet where the only noise was the thudding of my heart. Then I heard Travis saying, "Don't worry. We'll figure this out."

I opened my eyes, surprised to find myself in bed. All the cats were arrayed around me sleeping, except Sashkatu. He was sitting on my chest staring at me. I really had to put him on a diet. It was his weight on me that was making it hard to breathe. At least that part of the dream made sense. I felt for blood on my face but found none. My nightgown was damp with sweat, though, as if I'd actually been running from my attackers. I didn't have to look at the clock on the bedside table to know it was still the dead of night.

I've never been afraid of the night, not even as a child. But something about this night was different. Whatever had disturbed my sleep was still lying in wait. Sashkatu must have sensed it too. He'd been known to sleep through thunderstorms that shook the house to its foundations, through hurricane-force winds that mangled patio furniture, through minor earthquakes, and through breakfast smells that awoke all his brethren and stray dogs from miles away. But here he was, wide awake, sitting on me. He must have come to warn me about some approaching menace, the same way the dreams had.

"Good boy," I whispered to him, "I'm going to make sure the wards are still working." I set Sashki on his pillow and got up without disturbing the others. I didn't want to turn on lights, thinking that would alert an intruder that he'd been found out. I opened the top drawer of the nightstand and fumbled around until my fingers closed around a flashlight. I picked my way slowly down the stairs, flinching at each squeaking floorboard. Everything seemed to be as it was when I'd gone up to bed. No one lurked behind the living room drapes or in the hulking shadow of the china closet. I was about to attribute Sashkatu's distress to old age creeping into his brain when I heard a truck's engine roar to life.

Late-night traffic, especially on the side roads of New Camel, was rare and limited to the beeping of snowplows in the wake of a big storm and the infrequent shrill of emergency vehicles. I unlocked the front door and stepped onto the porch. Whatever truck I'd heard was gone. The night was still and calm. The street lamp closest to my house cast a dim yellow halo that didn't reach beyond the perimeter of my property. I ducked back inside and switched on the exterior lights, a sconce on the wall next to the door, and a lamppost that illuminated the steps and walkway.

I padded halfway down the walk and turned back to look at the house. The front windows were intact. There was no egg stuck to the clapboards or toilet paper laced through the trees. The protection wards I'd placed during the Harkens's case seemed to be holding. But as I turned to go inside, the wind lifted, billowing my thin nightgown and carrying with it the unmistakable smell of paint.

The wards extended to the edges of my property, including the fence, but it was possible that something as innocuous as paint could slip past them. I followed the smell the rest of the way into the street where it was strongest and looked back at the fence. My breath caught in my throat, and a chill slithered wormlike through my heart.

* * * *

I had to wait for morning before I could do anything about the hateful message on the fence. Heart racing, I lay in bed, sleep a hopeless wish. I was dressed and ready when the sun rose. But once I was outside my resolve faltered. I gave myself a no-nonsense pep talk and, jaw clenched, marched down the flagstone path and out into the street. In daylight it was worse than I had realized. The message was scrawled in red, the excess paint dripping from each of the letters making it look like the cover of a horror novel. There was no mistaking the words and sentiment: We Hang Witches! It was accompanied by the crude drawing of a woman hanging from a noose.

I'd encountered similar threats during the Harkens case. But what if this was not just to scare me into dropping my investigation? What if there had always been an undercurrent of bias against my family? I didn't want to believe that. No, I couldn't. Our friends were truly friends. How could I entertain doubts about Elise, who was like an older sister, or Lolly, who always had my back? Or any of the others who greeted me with a smile whenever our paths crossed? Yet it takes a lot of hatred to fuel an act like this.

I was still standing there trying to make sense of the senseless when Tilly's car pulled to the curb beside me. She and Merlin jumped out, or came as close to jumping as a woman with bad feet and an elderly man could. Tilly grabbed me in a smothery hug, the thin layers of her muumuu pressing against my face and suffocating me. I had to pull back enough to breathe.

"Poor, dear girl," she said, choking on emotion as she released me.

"Your aunt woke up screamin'," Merlin said, sounding a touch irritated. "A cowpoke could die of a heart attack."

Tilly had gone quiet, staring at the fence. "The work of a spineless coward," she hissed. "And if I ever catch him, I'll have Merlin turn him into a slug. Permanently."

Maybe it was the product of my tension and distress, but her statement struck me as hysterically funny, like a kid siccing his older brother on a bully. I burst out in laughter, great belly-aching peals. My eyes filled with tears, causing my aunt to regard me with startled concern. Merlin joined in the laughter, having a grand time, though I doubt he understood why. Only Tilly remained sober and perplexed. Once the laughter ebbed, I wiped the tears from my face and embraced her.

"What would I do without you?" I said, meaning it with every fiber of my being.

"I'll have your fence fixed up proper before you can whistle 'Dixie,'" Merlin said, still invested in cowboy lingo.

"Oh no you don't," I warned him. "No spells."

"Can't we make an exception for this, this..." Tilly threw her hands up, unable to find a word adequate to the situation.

I wanted to say yes, but I couldn't be a hypocrite and let Merlin cast a spell simply because it suited me, especially out here in public. "No spells means no spells," I said. "I don't want to stoke the suspicions or misgivings people may already have about us."

"But people come into your shop asking for spells all the time," Tilly protested. "It's part of your merchandise."

"That's different. Those people want spells. There are plenty of others who want nothing to do with spells or anything I sell. They're afraid. And every time they see us using sorcery, that fear grows darker. You know how fierce Bronwen was about obeying that rule," I reminded her.

"I suppose."

"Dagnabbit! Then how are you fixin' to remedy this?" Merlin asked.

I really had to find a different TV channel for him to get hooked on. One with more contemporary language. He attracted too much attention as it was, without sounding like a refuge from the Old West. "If it's washable, we'll wash it," I said. "If not, we'll use primer and paint."

"And a passel of elbow grease," he muttered.

He proved to be right about that. I spent the morning trying five different products to erase the red paint, without success. Tilly, who didn't own appropriate garments for painting, supervised and cheered me on. To his credit, Merlin took a turn at scrubbing the fence, though he nattered endlessly about the unnecessary work.

We adjourned for lunch. Too tired to try painting over the mess, I chose the easier, though more expensive, solution. I'd buy a new piece of fencing.

I was heading upstairs to change out of my painting clothes and head to the store when Merlin came up with an idea that seemed both practical and not likely to go wrong—a winning combination. Or maybe fatigue had left me in a weakened state.

While we were inside, he would cast a spell over a bucket of soap and water, giving the simple mixture the ability to remove paint of any kind. We would scrub the fence again, using the magickal water. To anyone passing by, it would seem like we were using manual labor and not sorcery.

"Brilliant," I said, glad to have a reason to praise him because all too often I was lecturing him.

"At your service, ma'am," he said, with a sweeping bow from the waist that went too low, nearly sending him face-first onto the hardwood. Arms wind-milling like crazy, he caught himself at the last moment, and the three of us heaved sighs of relief.

I should have felt better now that we had settled on a plan, but I still felt like a hypocrite. So I came up with an idea to fix that. "I'd like to loosen the rule against Merlin casting spells," I said, which instantly caught my cohort's attention. "From now on, Merlin can present his case for casting a spell, and if we all agree, he may proceed with it."

Tilly looked dubious, but Merlin was gleeful enough for both of them. The new rule was completely dependent on the wizard's discipline not to rush into anything before getting our permission. Only time would tell if I'd made a wise decision or opened a Pandora's box chock-full of disasters.

We trooped outside again to test the charmed water. It proved so potent that I only had to touch my brush to the paint to see it dissolve. The only downside was that I had to go slowly and pretend to put my back into it, or I would have been finished in eyebrow-raising seconds.

Doris Steinmetz, from down the block, came by with her Lab mix, Maggie. "I can't imagine who would do such a despicable thing," she said, shaking her head. "I hope you know that most folks in New Camel are fond of you and your family and always have been. I, for one, truly miss Morgana and Bronwen. They were women of substance and wisdom. There's a scarcity of that these days."

Tilly and I thanked her. Merlin went on pretending to scrub the fence, which was fine with me since I never knew what might come out of his mouth.

"Do you have any idea who's responsible for doing this?" Doris asked.

"I didn't get outside in time."

"You should get yourself a dog," she said. "Both you and Tilly. Maggie here gives me such wonderful peace of mind. If she doesn't hear something, there's nothing to be heard. Cats are lovely companions, but a dog is better for protection."

I assured her I'd think about it. She spent another few minutes chatting with us until Maggie started to whine and strain at her leash. "Excuse us," Doris said, "I think she needs to relieve herself. I hope the police catch the culprit," she called as Maggie pulled her away.

For that to happen, I would first have to report the incident to the police, and I wasn't planning to go that route. I'd already decided to buy a high-resolution video camera to record the perpetrator should he or she ever come back.

Chapter 13

After another night of little sleep, I showered, dressed, and downed a cup of coffee before rushing out of the house. I promised Sashkatu I'd be back for him soon. He regarded me from atop the couch with a skeptical look in his eyes.

"Sorry, Your Highness," I said, "but I have to go."

I was a woman on a mission. If I'd installed a video camera two months ago, it might have captured the miscreant who'd painted the message on my fence and possibly his or her vehicle and license plate as well. No more procrastination.

I was headed for one of the big-box stores with no charm whatsoever. But who needs charm when the price is right? As soon as I walked in, a gangly young salesman swooped down on me. I told him I was looking for a video camera. He led me over to the display and tried to sell me the most expensive one there. I selected one he grudgingly declared "okay," although it didn't have all the bells and whistles he himself might have wanted. Having lost that battle, he did his utmost to convince me it would be foolish not to purchase the extended warranty. I stood my ground, though. I had my own kind of warranty that didn't cost a penny.

I pulled back into my driveway a scant hour after I'd left; scooped up a huffy Sashkatu, who acted like I'd abandoned him in a back alley somewhere; and off we went to open my shop. I planned to install the camera after work. How hard could it be? I could have had the security company, Third Eye, take care of the whole thing, but then someone would be monitoring the feed and alert the police of any questionable activity. I didn't want the police involved. I figured I had the right to make that decision.

My first customers of the day were three middle-aged women who hailed from Buffalo. They'd heard about Abracadabra from a friend who'd been here with a tour group earlier in the summer. I watched their eyes pop as they walked in. They weren't stingy with their praise. They loved everything about the shop, from the arched door to the wicker shopping baskets. They especially loved Sashkatu basking in the sunlight, as if this were a mini Disneyland and I'd installed the sleeping cat on the window ledge for their pleasure. They asked dozens of questions about the products that crammed the shelves and wanted my help in choosing the best skin creams for the harsh winters they faced at the edge of Lake Erie.

The petite one was finished shopping first. She came up to the counter to pay. "Are you an actual practicing witch?" she whispered as if she feared I'd find her question too impertinent.

I didn't know why she felt whispering the words would make them more acceptable. If I minded, it wouldn't have mattered if she'd whispered or shouted from the hilltops. I gave her a reassuring smile. "I prefer to be called a sorcerer."

"Why is that?" the loud one asked, joining us at the counter with her basket.

"A lot of today's so-called witches are just playing around the edges of magick, which can be dangerous if they don't know what they're doing. My family comes from a long, long line of sorcerers who trace their roots back to a time before England was the country it is today."

The petite one was hanging on my every word with obvious delight, a little frisson making her shoulders twitch. The loud one sighed. "It's a pity we live so far from here. This place is so enchanting," she said and chuckled at her pun.

The mother hen of the three set two baskets on the counter with a thud. "What?" she said in response to the astonishment on her friends' faces. "You know my daughter. If I don't buy two of everything, she'll steal mine, and I'll be left empty-handed."

"I'm glad I only have sons," the loud one said.

The petite one turned back to me. "Do you also sell spells?"

"I do. Is there something specific you have in mind?"

"I'd love to have a wellness spell, if there is such a thing."

Her two companions echoed her sentiment.

"There certainly is, and because you're all buying so much today, the spell is my treat." It was a good business decision since I didn't have a soundproof chamber and they would have shared the spell in any case. This way I seemed generous.

"It's like getting a bonus," the petite one declared. "I love bonuses."

I handed them each a paper and pencil and apologized for not having enough chairs. They worked it out quickly, the mother hen saying that the loud one should sit due to her bad back. She and the petite one would lean on the counter to write.

"You'll need a glass of pure apple juice, preferably organic; a cinnamon stick; and a white candle," I said, allowing time for them to write it all down. "Stir the apple juice four times clockwise with the cinnamon stick. Light the candle, drink a few sips of juice, and say these words:

"Bless my body
"Bless my soul,
"Health and wellness
"Is my goal.

"Then finish the juice and snuff out the candle. You should use the spell whenever you feel an illness coming on or every morning to remain healthy."

"That's almost the same as the old saying 'an apple a day keeps the doctor away,'" the loud one said skeptically.

"Where do you think that saying originated?" I asked her.

She thought about it for a second and chuckled. "Touché."

It wasn't the first time one of our spells had been challenged. But as Bronwen used to say, the truth always rings true.

I was totaling up the mother hen's order when an older woman walked in. She looked somewhat familiar to me, but I couldn't quite place her. She didn't start browsing like most customers would have but stood off to the side as if she was waiting to speak to me. I thanked the three women, and they promised to be back in a few months or as soon as lake-effect snow allowed.

After they left, I came from behind the counter as the newcomer approached. "Hi," I said. "May I help you?"

"Hi, Kailyn. It's been a long time, and you probably don't remember me—Estelle Gingold." She put out her hand.

The name and face instantly connected in my brain. My hand flew to my mouth. "I'm so sorry I didn't recognize you, Mrs. Gingold." I took her hand that was gnarled from the ravages of arthritis and held it gently in mine. Her hair had gone snow white and looked like a halo around her face. When she smiled, it was the same smile I remembered. It still twinkled in her eyes.

"No apologies necessary," she said. "You've been busy growing up, and I've been just as busy growing old."

"Third grade," I murmured, the memories flooding back into my mind as fresh and detailed as if it were only yesterday that I sat in her classroom.

"First seat on the right, second row."

"How on earth do you remember where I sat? You must have taught hundreds of kids since then."

"You remember the good ones," she said, adding wryly, "and the awful ones."

"You were the one teacher who made me love school. I always meant to tell you that."

"Thank you, dear. It sounds just as sweet hearing it now."

I offered her the chair, which she accepted. "Are you still teaching?" I asked.

"No, I retired almost seven years ago. But I keep up with everyone at the school. Not a week goes by that I don't meet one or two of my friends for lunch or dinner, especially Amanda. We were very..."

She trailed off, and I could see her jaw tensing to staunch a flood of emotion.

"I'm told you're looking into Amanda's death," she went on. "I guess you found a second calling in those mysteries you were always reading," she said with a weak smile. "It's the reason I came to see you today."

"You have information related to her death?" I asked.

"Yes, but it's possible I'm an old fool tilting at windmills. I'll let you be the judge." She took a deep, shaky breath before beginning. "Amanda Boswell was one of my closest friends at the school in spite of our age difference. Maybe I was a mother figure to her, and she was the daughter I never had. Anyway, she confided in me over the years, and now that she's been murdered, I need to betray her trust in this one instance."

"Under these circumstances, I'm sure she would understand."

"Maybe so."

"Are you sure you don't want to speak to the detective on the case?" I asked, hoping she didn't.

Estelle shook her head. "Telling you doesn't feel like as much of a betrayal somehow...unless it would put you in a bad position with the police?"

"I'm afraid it's too late for that," I said dryly.

"Has my perfect student gone over to the dark side?"

"Maybe just the dark side of Detective Duggan."

"If you're sure then?"

"Full speed ahead."

"Thank you. Ever since Amanda moved here and started teaching, she's had a not-so-secret admirer."

"You mean like a stalker?" I asked.

"Not to my knowledge. It never reached that level. In fact, for the first few years Amanda thought the attention was sweet. But when word got around that she and Alan were separating, things changed. Her admirer started asking her out. She turned him down in the kindest of terms, saying that she and Alan were separated but working on their marriage. That explanation worked for a while, but as time passed, the admirer became more insistent, and she realized she had to do something about it. She told him that as wonderful as he was, she thought of him as a good friend and that would never change. She hoped he would understand. Well, he didn't. He screamed at her, said he'd been so patient all these years, how could she just cast him aside, et cetera. I'm sure you get the gist."

"Wow," I said. "Now I see why you felt you had to tell someone. Who is he?"

She sighed heavily, clearly reluctant to say the name. "Rusty Higgins. I've known the man since the day he started working at the school. He's always been a grumbler, but I never saw anything aggressive or murderous in his character. He was always kind to the kids, no matter how much they teased him. I guess it's a good thing I didn't go into police work or profiling."

"Wow," I repeated. It seemed to be the only word left in my vocabulary.

"I know. Now would be a great time for you to tell me you've figured out who killed her and it wasn't Rusty."

"I wish I could. Would it help if I told you I'm looking at a few suspects who also seem to have good motives?"

"I'll take what I can get," she said. "Will you let me know if you turn up anything else about Rusty or, even better, if you're able to cross him off as a suspect?"

"I will. In spite of the reason for your visit, I'm glad you came. How does someone win a place on that list of friends you lunch with?" I asked.

"I always keep a slot open for the right kind of person," she said. "Give me a ring when you're in the mood for Mexican. The rest of my buddies are wimps when it comes to anything spicy."

We hugged good-bye, and she went on her way, leaving me with topsy-turvy emotions. I was glad to have her back in my life and for the chance to get to know her as more than a teacher. But I was also in a state of shock over what she'd told me about Rusty. Was it possible for so many educated, supposedly intelligent people to have so badly misjudged him? Although I hadn't wanted to point it out to Estelle, Rusty had both motive and opportunity. In fact, if he was innocent, he might have a hard time proving it.

Chapter 14

My family has always kept tools and related equipment in the detached garage behind the house. It originally served as a carriage house, but these days it easily accommodates two cars. However, its location made it less than ideal for that purpose. It was easier to park halfway up the driveway where the flagstone path led right to the front door. I could remember the first and last time my mother decided to put the car in the garage before an impending blizzard.

"This way we won't have to dig the car out of the snow," she'd said, delighted with her epiphany. What she hadn't taken into account was that instead of digging out the car, we would have to clear the entire length of the driveway to even reach the car. I'd thought for sure it would take us until the summer. In the end, Bronwen broke her own rule and went outside in the dead of night to use a spell to melt the snow. Luckily no one was witness to the magickally vanishing snow, although a few people with raised eyebrows did remark about the exceptional job we women had done in clearing the driveway.

After getting home from my shop and feeding my household, I changed into jeans, a T-shirt, and sneakers. It was too light out to chance using telekinesis to carry the aluminum stepladder out of the garage and around to the front of the house. I'd been practicing the skill in every spare moment, and I'd become stronger at it. The ladder would not have posed any problem. However, given the circumstances, I had no choice but to actually carry it.

Once it was in place, I spent a ridiculous amount of time looking for a screwdriver. For projects inside the house, my family rarely resorted to using tools if a quick spell would do the trick. As a result, years went by without needing the tools, so none of us could recall where we last stowed them. I finally found the screwdriver in the basement with the dubious help of the cats, who were climbing all over me. They were understandably curious. I rarely invaded their sanctum sanctorum because I had a deep and abiding aversion to spiders. I searched for the screwdriver, prepared to flee if I felt anything smaller than a cat brush my skin. I finally found the tool on a pegboard near the furnace and scooted back upstairs.

By the time I was ready to start the installation, daylight was waning, the sun playing hide and seek with me through the trees as it drifted toward the horizon. I had maybe an hour of decent light left. I refused to put it off for another day in case my tormentor was planning to strike again.

Fortunately, when I purchased the camera, I had the foresight to buy a mounting kit too. I decided to attach the camera to the fascia of the porch roof, a term I discovered by doing some online research. With the screwdriver in the pocket of my jeans and the mounting kit in one hand, I started up the ladder. While I was on the second rung, it occurred to me that I had little to no experience with ladders and that I'd never been particularly comfortable with heights. Well, I told myself, this was as good a time as any to remedy the situation. I wasn't going to get experience by staying rooted to the ground.

I made it onto the last rung, feeling pretty good about myself until I realized I couldn't quite reach the fascia. "Seriously?" I demanded of the universe. So much for installing the camera then and there. I'd have to wait until I bought or borrowed a taller ladder.

"Someone call for a handyman?"

Travis's voice startled me. My heart tripped like a racehorse stumbling out of the gate. I pressed myself against the ladder, grasping the poles with both hands to anchor myself there. The mounting kit fell out of my hand and onto the grass.

"Don't you know better than to sneak up behind someone on a ladder?" I sputtered once my heart subsided from my throat.

"Sorry," he said, coming to where I could see him. "Here, I'll hold it steady for you."

I took my time climbing down, trying to catch my breath in the process. "I'd be happy to give you a hand with whatever you're trying to do up there," Travis offered once I was back on the ground.

"I could have done it myself if I'd had the right size ladder," I said, not sure why I felt the need to justify my failure to him.

"I have no doubt about it, but under the circumstances, maybe I can help?"

Part of me wanted to say no thanks. Unfortunately, that wouldn't get the camera installed. "Sure," I said instead. "I'd appreciate it." I picked up the mounting kit that had landed a few feet away and told him where I wanted the camera placed.

He skimmed the instructions in the kit. "No problem. I worked for my uncle's construction company over a couple of summers. This should be child's play."

"Assuming said child isn't afraid of heights," I murmured.

"What's that?"

"Nothing," I said, pulling the screwdriver out of my pocket and handing it to him.

He winced. "It's not a great idea to carry a tool like that in your pocket when you're up on a ladder, you know, in case you slip and fall."

I felt my face redden. "I guess it's pretty obvious I don't have an uncle in construction."

"How come you didn't just wiggle your nose or something to install the camera?" he asked with a grin.

"Not funny," I said. "I don't like being mocked."

He held up his hands. "Hey, I'm sorry. I didn't mean anything by it." He sounded genuinely contrite.

I knew I should let the remark go and accept it as simple teasing, the way he'd surely meant it. If I wanted to nurture our relationship, I had to develop a thicker skin. But I was tired of having to be super careful not to spook him again. He could do his share by trying to be more sensitive about my feelings too. "Are you surprised I don't like being compared to a ridiculous TV sitcom?" I asked.

"It was only a joke," he said lamely. "I didn't realize you'd take it that way."

He seemed so lost; I felt sorry for him. "Try to think of my magick the way you would musical or artistic ability. Magick has been in my family's genes forever, like hair or eye color."

"Okay, I'll do my best," he said. "I'd better get your camera mounted before it's pitch black out here."

I couldn't tell if he'd given up trying to understand me or actually realized how little sunlight remained.

By the time he was done screwing in the bracket and setting the camera at the proper angle, all that was left of the sun was a golden afterglow. I showed him where to store the ladder in the garage.

"Do you want me to program the video feed to play on your computer?" he asked.

I'd forgotten all about that part, and I had no idea how to go about it. "That would be super," I said, "but only if you'll stay for a potluck dinner."

"I don't think I've ever had one."

"Don't get too excited. In this case, it's grilled cheese sandwiches or omelets."

"Grilled cheese is one of my favorites."

While he tinkered with the computer, I got dinner started. He came down to the kitchen as I was taking the sandwiches off the stovetop. I set our plates down across from each other. I'd already put glasses, lemonade, and iced tea out.

"You're all hooked up and ready to go," he said taking a seat. He poured himself iced tea and took a big bite of the sandwich.

"Were you just passing by or did you have a premonition I needed help?" I asked.

"I can safely say I have no psychic ability whatsoever," he said after swallowing. "This is great grilled cheese by the way. And the answer to your question is none of the above. I came to tell you the good news, but when I saw you up on that ladder it knocked everything else out of my head."

"Good news? I could use some of that."

"I'm going to interview the elusive Hugh Fletcher."

I set my glass down so hard I almost broke it. "How did you wangle that?"

"I played on his ego, said I wanted to write an article that would do him and his achievements justice. I didn't mention what kind of justice I have in mind. I was as floored as you are when he said okay."

"What an opportunity. He is definitely not your average suspect. I have to admit I'm more than a little envious."

"No need to be. We're partners in this investigation. Besides," he added with a grin, "Fletcher agreed to let me bring along the intern I've been mentoring."

"Me? You're kidding! You seem to have your own brand of magick. When is the auspicious occasion?"

"Nine a.m., Thursday morning. We'll drive down on Wednesday, do the interview the next morning, and drive back here afterward."

Wednesday was all I heard. Wednesday, as in the day after tomorrow. My brain went into overdrive, spinning with the logistics of leaving the shop and my cats.

Travis was regarding me over his glass. "Why so quiet? A second ago you were thrilled."

"It's such short notice. I have to see if my aunt can cover for me," I said, thinking aloud. "I know there aren't any bus tours due in until Saturday, so I suppose it won't be the end of the world if I needed to close for a couple of days."

"You deserve some time off, Kailyn. Don't you ever take a vacation?"

"Since my mother and grandmother died, I'm my whole staff. Unlike you, I don't get paid vacation time. If I don't work, I don't get paid. Too bad I can't just wiggle my nose and sneeze up a clone," I added, hoping he'd take my words as the olive branch I meant them to be.

Travis smiled and gave me a wink that was as good as a thank-you. "You took the words right out of my mouth."

I swear I could hear the sound of a barrier between us shattering.

* * * *

The next morning, I went through the connecting door between my shop and Tilly's. My aunt was singing "Eleanor Rigby" at the top of her lungs while she dusted her tearoom. Although she had numerous talents, singing wasn't one of them. She couldn't carry a tune in a bucket as Bronwen used to say, and the high, squeaky register of her voice made small animals burrow into the ground seeking refuge. Merlin was either more tolerant or blissfully going deaf.

Although Tilly's voice was an assault on the ears, the aroma of her baking was a fair enough trade-off. That day the air was so dense with the scent of warm apples, sugar and cinnamon, it could have formed into clouds and rained the heavenly mixture.

"Where is Merlin the Magnificent?" I asked after wishing her a good morning.

"Guarding the oven," Tilly said. "He can sit there peering into the window like it's the television." She glanced at her watch. "You're in early today. Something up?"

"Travis and I have an opportunity to interview Hugh Fletcher. But it means driving down to Manhattan and being away overnight. Do you think—"

"Yes" she said, interrupting me, "I believe I'm available to cat- and shop-sit if that's what you're leading up to. Let me check." She set down the feather duster and went to look at her appointment book. "No one until the tour on Saturday." She looked up at me. "I'm free to tend your shop, and I'll bring Sashkatu along with me. Would he do better in your house overnight or in mine?"

I had to think about that. He was used to my bed since he'd slept there with Morgana from the time he was little. On the other hand, he might enjoy a sleepover that involved Merlin. On yet another hand, Sashki and Isenbale, Tilly's big Maine Coon, had never liked each other. I didn't want to return and find my aunt looking like a battlefield of scratches from having to separate them. Merlin might be able to make peace between the felines, but they might fight over him as well.

"He'll be happier in my house," I said finally. Or at least I'd be happier not having to worry about it.

"It's settled then. It'll be good for you to get away. You're too young to be spending all your time working and tending cats. Morgana and Bronwen have been concerned about you too."

"So the three of you get together to talk about me? A secret cabal—who could have imagined?" I said and laughed. "Maybe I'm the one who should be worried."

"I'll expect a detailed account of the interview," Tilly said, neatly changing the subject.

"From what I've read, Hugh Fletcher is practically a recluse. He guards his privacy like a piranha. I wish I were going with you. I wouldn't mind being a fly on that wall." A timer rang in the kitchen, followed closely by Merlin bellowing that the pie was done.

Chapter 15

My eyes blinked open at 2 a.m., which is when it dawned on me that I had no idea where Travis and I would be staying overnight. I'd been focused on the shop and my cats to the exclusion of everything else. Travis must have booked a hotel or a motel, I told myself. He was always on the road; surely he wouldn't have forgotten such an important detail. In fact, he was probably wondering why I hadn't brought it up. Maybe he thought I expected him to pay for me as well as for him. I had to make it clear I preferred to pay my own way. I wasn't a charity case or a gold digger. I sat up abruptly, dislodging a couple irritated cats in the process. I was reaching for the phone when I remembered it was too late to call him. If I did, he'd be within his rights to add clueless to my already off-putting résumé.

I don't know what time I finally fell back to sleep, but the alarm I'd set for seven o'clock woke me. I was groggy and anxious about getting the arrangements worked out with Travis. I didn't want to sound neurotic, though, so I forced myself to wait until eight to call him.

"Hi there," he said, sounding as though he'd slept well and without a care in the world.

I dove right in. "Hi. You must be wondering why I didn't ask about our accommodations for tonight, and I wanted to let you to know that I intend to pay for myself." I immediately wished I could have a do-over, so I could slow down and speak with some composure.

"I appreciate the sentiment, but I wouldn't know what to charge you." There was no mistaking the amusement in his voice.

"Excuse me?"

"I have an apartment in Brooklyn. It's a small one bedroom, but it should do us for the night."

Given the current state of our relationship, if he expected me to sleep with him, he was sadly mistaken. "No, no," I said. "I don't want to put you out of your bed." That should get my point across.

"It's no big deal. I do it whenever women stay over."

That was hardly the response I'd expected. Words failed me.

Travis laughed. "Relax, I'm talking about my mother and sister. When they're in town I always give them the bedroom, and I bunk on the sleeper sofa in the living room."

"Oh, good," I said, "because I'm not interested in joining a harem."

"That's a pity; I hear there's a lot to be said for them."

* * * *

Tilly came by at eight thirty in the morning to take Sashkatu with her to open my shop. When I plucked him off the top of the couch and placed him in Tilly's arms, he looked from her to me with questions he didn't know how to ask. Not for the first time, I wished I could explain things to him and the other cats. I gave him a reassuring smile. See, everything is normal and fine. He narrowed his eyes as if to say, "I'll be the judge of that."

He'd never been fond of car rides, but that was rarely a problem for me. Walking from my front door to the back door of my shop took less time than getting in the car and driving around the corner to it. But walking can often be so difficult for Tilly that she preferred to always have her car at her disposal. I walked out to Tilly's car with them, anticipating a rebellion. Sure enough, when she tried to put him into her car, he took a stand. A mêlée ensued, with feline and human limbs flying in all directions. It was by no means a foregone conclusion that Tilly and I would prevail. I stopped it before anyone could be injured, but there were still enough bad feelings to go around. In the end, I walked Sashkatu into the shop while Tilly drove herself there. She called me fifteen minutes later to report that after I left, Sashki made his way onto his windowsill and promptly fell asleep. I was as relieved as a mother whose three-year-old was finally adjusting to preschool.

* * * *

Travis pulled into my driveway at exactly ten o'clock. He tossed my overnight case into the trunk beside his. Seeing the two bags bumped up against each other was a strangely intimate sight. It spoke of shared vacations and joined lives. I chided myself for letting my imagination run away with me. Bronwen always said I had too fanciful a bent, but neither she nor my mother could teach me how to rein it in.

The five-hour drive passed quickly since we were never at a loss for conversation, one of the benefits of a still-new relationship. I leaned on the normal parts of my history and skimmed over the parts that involved magick and therefore marked me as different in his eyes. I knew it wasn't the smartest way to proceed if I expected him to take me as I am. But for these two days I wanted Travis to look at me as he had before I'd shown him the kind of magick he couldn't ignore or explain away.

Our first stop was his apartment, which was as small as advertised and decorated in an early bachelor, man-on-the-go style. Wherever there was a doorknob, there were shirts hanging from it. In the ancient bathroom, towels bedecked the shower rod. The dining room table had been co-opted by a computer that rose like a cliff from a chaotic sea of papers.

"Excuse the mess," Travis said, kicking a pair of Nikes out of our way. "I meant to straighten up for you, but I was stuck in the Glen chasing down a story."

"It's fine. I assumed this is how single men live." At least they had back in college and in TV sitcoms.

"Good, then you won't judge me too harshly. But in spite of the way it looks, I can promise you it's clean. My mother insists on sending her cleaning lady, Hilda the Hun, here every Friday.

"You don't sound properly grateful," I said and laughed at the image of him doing battle with a female Attila.

"Well, it was touch and go for a couple of months until Hilda and I worked out a détente. As long as she doesn't touch my papers or try to rearrange my stuff, she can sanitize to her heart's content."

"I think I'd like your mom and Hilda."

"I'm sure they'd like you...too." His words ran out of steam when he no doubt remembered that I'm more than meets the eye. "Let's get you installed in the bedroom," he said, compensating with too much enthusiasm.

Once I'd had a chance to wash and pull a comb through my hair, Travis took me on a walking tour of his neighborhood, ending at his favorite "pizza joint." "What passes for pizza in your neck of the woods can't rightly be compared to these culinary works of art," he said.

I tried to defend New Camel's reputation, but after one crisp, oozing bite, I became a convert. "Now you've ruined me for pizza anywhere else," I lamented on our way back to his apartment.

"Here are a couple of tips to remember: a pizza joint should never be named O'Leary's, and it should never offer a topping of Spam."

* * * *

We were ushered into Hugh Fletcher's inner sanctum at precisely 9 a.m., after spending fifteen minutes in the reception area under the scrutiny of his secretary, Ms. Robbins.She looked like she'd been purchased along with the rest of the high-end décor. She was sleek and polished in a dove-gray suit that had clearly been tailored to her precise measurements. Her blond hair was swept up in a lacquered French twist, her eyes a shade of green I'd only seen in Persian cats and ads for contact lenses. And her mouth seemed permanently curved into the barest of smiles, as if she knew things beyond our ken and was merely tolerating riffraff like us.

By comparison, Fletcher proved to be warm and gracious, not at all the man I expected from his bio, Ingersoll's words, or his sumptuous surroundings. Travis's expression told me he was experiencing the same sense of whiplash. Was this slightly paunchy, fifty-something with a balding pate the real Hugh Fletcher, or had he stuck us with an underling?

He came around his desk to greet us, dismissing Ms. Robbins with a nod. "Please, make yourselves comfortable," he said, gesturing to the armchairs in front of the desk. He didn't speak again until he resumed his seat. "I understand you're here to interview me and learn about my meteoric rise to greatness," he said with a self-deprecating chuckle. "I usually let my nephew, Rebel, handle this kind of thing. He leaned across his desk to whisper, "Rebel. What's with the crazy names these days? Eh"—he shook his head and sat up straight—"my sister's always been a little out there, if you know what I mean. But I digress."

"If you'll excuse me," Travis said, "why did you agree to talk to us?"

Fletcher shrugged. "You know, I'm not entirely certain. I haven't done an interview in a long time, so maybe I needed to take a break from big business for an hour." He laughed. "Or maybe the universe whispered your name in my ear. Do you believe in that stuff? My sister believes in a lot of that bologna. She never gets tired of trying to expand my mind. I ask you," he said, looking from Travis to me, "do I look like someone who needs advice on how to live? I'd say I'm doing just fine," he answered himself. "So, you've got questions. Let's give this thing a whirl."

If Fletcher's goal was to throw us off balance, he'd done an admirable job. I was glad that Travis was the point man and that I was the lowly intern.

I listened closely to his questions and more closely to his answers. I watched the older man's body language, trying to catch any tells. Travis took him from his childhood through his college years to his first small-business venture. Like most successful people, Fletcher clearly enjoyed talking about himself. He went off on tangents, provided amusing anecdotes; in short, he was the perfect subject. But the more he talked, the less I was taken with him.

He was too perfect a subject. I couldn't tell if Travis had come to the same conclusion, but he was far too astute to have missed it. Something Fletcher had said earlier came to mind: "Maybe I needed to take a break from big business for an hour." He was using up the hour with his rambling answers, his good-ol'-boy demeanor. Maybe it wasn't the universe that had whispered Travis's name in his ear. Maybe it was one of his minions advising a goodwill gesture, because there were inklings, rumors of rumors that his name was being raised in connection to Amanda's death.

I looked at my watch. We were never going to find out anything of import unless Travis switched tracks on the runaway train that was Hugh Fletcher. But he couldn't very well interrupt the man mid-story. That's when I saw the fly. It was perched on the wall closest to Fletcher's desk. No, it couldn't possibly be...could it? Had Tilly convinced Merlin to turn her into a fly so she actually could tag along for the interview? I found myself staring at the insect, searching for a telltale bit of muumuu that might have survived the metamorphosis.

"Kailyn?" Travis said. He was looking at me, his brow furrowed.

"Is something wrong, Ms. Wilde?" Fletcher asked.

"Sorry, I just...I don't like flies," I said with a phony shiver of repulsion.

Before I knew what was happening, Fletcher had pulled a fly swatter from a desk drawer and was on his feet.

"No, don't kill it," I yelled as he got ready to wield the swatter. "Please," I added, remembering belatedly that I was a guest in his office. "I don't want any creature killed on my behalf."

"Would you prefer I offered it a drink?" he asked dryly.

"I'm sorry. Please just let it be. It probably flew in with us. Maybe it will follow us out when we leave." If he took one more step in the fly's direction, I was prepared to jump out of my chair and take him down.

Fletcher shook his head. "You'd get along great with my sister," he said, taking his seat again. "Now, where were we?"

Whoever the fly was, it had served to interrupt the interview long enough for me to hijack the conversation and redirect it. "I noticed that Winterland is undergoing a major renovation," I said. "I'll be interested in how it turns out."

"You're an aficionado of winter sports?" Fletcher asked.

"I'm thinking of taking up skiing. In fact I discussed it with Mr. Ingersoll recently."

"Eric's a fine instructor. You won't find better five hundred miles in any direction."

"He's a busy man too. He told me he's been interim manager since the last manager walked out." From the corner of my eye I could see that Travis was trying to catch my attention. His eyebrows were working overtime like Groucho Marx in the old movies he loved. I pretended not to notice. One of us had to make waves, or we'd never lure the real Hugh Fletcher out of hiding. "Why on earth would anyone walk away from such a good job?" I mused aloud.

"Well, if you run into him, you can ask him for me. One day everything was fine and dandy, and the next he was gone. No notice, no reason. You give someone a chance to improve their lot, and that's the thanks you get," Fletcher said with blatant disgust.

Ingersoll had told me the same story about Davies' disappearance. Either they were both telling the truth or Ingersoll was parroting the party line.

Travis had finally figured out where I was going with the subject and dropped the Groucho routine. "Does human resources have an emergency contact number for him?" he asked, getting into the game.

"No," he replied, the word clipped and testy. "And I don't see how this is any of your business."

Travis didn't respond. As a journalist, maybe he was trying not to burn his bridges. I harbored no such concern. I had to get what I could out of Fletcher because I was never going to get another opportunity. "It's possible he was injured and lost his memory," I said, picking up the standard.

"I'll consider that right after I go back to believing in Santa and the Tooth Fairy," Fletcher said, a sneer tugging at his upper lip.

I was at a crossroads. I'd originally intended to ask him how he felt about the Waverly proposal and if he was worried about the competition. But something told me he'd be well prepared to answer such an obvious question. I decided to go with Robert Frost down the road less traveled. "It's so much easier to locate people these days," I said. "I'd be happy to see what I can find out for you about your missing manager."

Fletcher smoothed back the nonexistent hair on top of his head. "Very generous of you, Ms. Wilde, but I don't need your help. Locating him isn't important. People don't get second chances around here." He made a point of checking his watch and turned his gaze on Travis. "I have a meeting in a couple minutes, Anderson, do you have a last question to wrap this up?"

"If I may, sir. Where do you see yourself in ten years, both personally and professionally?"

Serving a life sentence for taking out a hit on Amanda, I hoped.

"In ten years, my business will have grown tenfold, although that's probably low-balling it. Personally?" He produced a laugh that was more like a grunt. "Did you really think you could slide that one under my radar? You know I don't talk about my personal life."

"Hey, you can't blame a guy for trying," Travis said, clearly hoping some boyish, aw-shucks charm could win him points with the billionaire.

"That's where you're wrong, my friend," Fletcher replied darkly.

He hit a button on his phone. Ms. Robbins opened the door so quickly that she must have been waiting outside with her hand on the knob, ready to rescue her boss at a moment's notice. As Travis and I stood and headed out, I looked for the fly. It hadn't moved from its spot on the wall. "Tilly," I said, reaching out to her with my mind, "you have to come with us, or he may kill you. Tilly, please." I was so preoccupied that I walked straight into Ms. Robbins. I apologized, but she looked over the top of my head as if I wasn't there.

"Anderson," Fletcher called out as we left, "ditch the girl. She'll only hold you back."

Chapter 16

I called my aunt the second we were out of Fletcher's building. I sweated out four rings, panicked that she had been the fly on the wall. Just before her voice mail kicked in, she picked up. "Thank goodness." I exhaled the words, relief making my knees give way. Travis grabbed me around the waist in time to keep me upright.

"Thank goodness to you too," Tilly said. "Is that some new kind of greeting? I'm falling hopelessly behind with social customs."

I explained about the fly, which sent us both into gales of laughter that left her gasping for air and me with a sore belly. When we'd recovered enough to speak, I asked how she was faring in my absence.

"Everything is under control," she said in a way that told me everything had not been under control at some point.

"We'll talk when I get home," I said. The crisis, whatever it had been, was apparently over, and I couldn't have done a thing about it in any case. Travis and I still had a five-hour drive ahead of us.

Traffic in and around Manhattan was a nightmare of snarls and gridlock. I wanted to discuss our interview with Fletcher, but I didn't want to distract him from the job at hand. An hour later we were finally on the highway, where fifty-five miles an hour felt like we were flying.

"Did you catch the change in Fletcher's demeanor when I brought up Davies and asked if he knew what happened to the man?"

Travis, who'd been singing tunelessly along with Celine Dion, stopped. "It was hard not to. He nearly dropped his mask."

"Exactly. He thought he was home safe until I started poking him on the subject."

"Which is probably why he told me to dump you."

"Sure, he's worried about me," I said, grinning.

"Just don't let it go to your head, though I suspect I'm already too late with that advice."

"Very funny," I said. "Getting back to Fletcher, if he ordered the hit on Amanda, and Ingersoll wasn't the henchman, Davies becomes a likely contender for the job and best employee ever. In fact, he's probably enjoying his ill-gotten gains on a tropical island as we speak."

"I'm not so sure about that," Travis said. "Fletcher wouldn't take the chance on Davies getting drunk one night and running his mouth about it."

"You think Fletcher planned to have him killed too?" As awful as it was, it made sense. If Fletcher had no scruples about targeting a woman because of a zoning vote, why would he lose any sleep over eliminating her killer? Maybe in his warped mind he even considered it a kind of justice. "So if Davies turns up dead, he was probably Amanda's killer. But what about his killer?" My head was spinning. How many deaths would it take to make Fletcher feel safe?

"Let's not jump the gun," Travis said. "It's worth keeping in mind that we have other suspects with equally strong motives."

"You're right," I said, feeling a bit silly. Travis was kind enough not to press the point. Instead, he regaled me with funny stories from earlier in his career when he'd been an overeager rookie reporter.

We were hours late arriving in New Camel, thanks to roadwork on the highways and the eventual need to stop for food and drinks. On the last leg of the trip, I was having a hard time keeping my eyes open. Travis's bed had been comfortable enough, but the very fact that I was in his bed made me think about how it would be to have him there with me. That led me to reexamine our relationship and its chances for survival over the long haul. If that hadn't been enough to keep me staring at the ceiling, I was also amped up about the morning meeting with Fletcher.

When we pulled to the curb in front of my house, Tilly's red Mustang was parked in the driveway. I invited Travis inside, but he begged off, claiming exhaustion—a reasonable excuse, given the endless drive back. I hated the doubt that immediately pricked at my mind. Was his reluctance fueled in part by the prospect of being in the company of not one but three sorcerers? I wondered if there would ever come a time when I wouldn't question his mindset.

I walked into the house and dropped my overnight bag in the foyer. A welcoming committee was assembled at the entrance to the living room. Tilly, Merlin, and Sashkatu were there along with the other cats. Although they were crowded around Merlin, when they saw me, they came right over to take turns, winding their way between my legs and purring contentedly. It was lovely for the minute it lasted before they sprinted back to the wizard. Sashki alone remained at my side with a haughty look on his face as if to say, "What fools are the young."

Tilly embraced me, and Merlin took my hand and kissed it. "It's so wonderful to have you back here," Tilly said, beaming at me. "Did you have a good time? What did you find out about Hugh Fletcher? I'm dying to hear all of it."

Before I could open my mouth, Merlin jabbed her in the ribs, making her yelp. "Keep those pointy elbows to yourself, old man, or you won't even get a taste of my pie." She turned to me, her irritation melting into a smile. "I made you that mixed-berry pie you adore."

"But it was I who insisted we procure the vanilla ice cream to accompany it," Merlin added with the modified bow dictated by his faltering equilibrium. As expected, he dealt with this new indignity of aging with little grace and an abundance of grumbling.

"Thank you both," I said, glad to be home. "Let's dig into that pie and ice cream before I fall asleep standing here." While we ate, I filled my aunt in on the meeting with Fletcher and managed to pry out of her what happened while I was away.

Apparently Merlin had decided to try his hand at baking while she was at my shop. He claimed he wanted to surprise her with a treat the way she did for others. Unfortunately, he'd always been more focused on the results of her baking than on the details of the process itself. He set out to make a blueberry pie, working under the assumption that if some sugar was good, twice the amount was better. Ditto for the blueberries, which Tilly had purchased for an upcoming tea at her shop. She arrived home to a blueberry pie that made her teeth ache and an oven overflowing with dripping blueberry goo. Of course, it had leaked onto the floor, and of course, both Merlin and Isenbale had stepped in it and trailed it all over the house, including the beige carpeting in her bedroom. Listening to her describe the mess and how long it took to clean up made my own fatigue worse. I thanked them again for the warm homecoming and saw them out the door, thinking I might never be able leave home again.

Chapter 17

As tired as I was, it was too early to go to bed. I tried to get interested in a TV show, and when that failed, I sat down at my computer and searched the Internet for an address or a phone number for Dwayne Davies. When I came up empty, I Googled his name and found thirty men in the state of New York sporting that moniker. Narrowing the search parameters to Schuyler County, I whittled the number down to a more manageable four. The one who lived closest to the Winterland Resort was the Dwayne Davies of Hassetville. But even Hassetville wasn't around the corner. Davies would have had a forty-minute drive to and from Winterland, certainly doable but not an easy trip in snow, sleet, and ice. He'd either been desperate for a job at the time or loved the work. People don't usually walk away from a job they need or love unless they come into enough money to make working no longer necessary. A winning lottery ticket or an inheritance came to mind, as well as a hefty bonus from Fletcher for removing the Amanda thorn from his side. There hadn't been any million-dollar lottery winners in Schuyler County for a long time, so I lopped that one off my list.

I logged onto my e-news subscription and scoured the death notices going back two months. If Davies had come into a life-changing sum of money from a relative's passing, he hadn't paid for even the most basic death notice to honor his benefactor. Maybe he wished to keep other relatives from sniffing around for a piece of the pie. In the end, all of this was supposition on my part. I couldn't even be sure I had the right Dwayne Davies. For that I needed a phone number, a street address, and a road trip. I could try sweet-talking Ingersoll into giving me the manager's info or ask Travis to use his connections. I pushed back from the computer, too tired to make even that simple decision. It would have to wait until morning.

* * * *

I was awakened by a chorus of off-key cat vocals and the tickle of whiskers on my face. The clock on the nightstand read eight fifteen. I'd forgotten to set the alarm. I dragged my sleep-logged body out of bed. I had cats to feed and a shop to open.

Sashkatu was stationed at the top of the stairs. I followed him down to the kitchen, the other cats hard on my heels. The house had gotten chilly overnight, and my light cotton nightgown wasn't up to the challenge. But I didn't want to waste time going back to the bedroom for a robe.

When my bare feet hit the cold tile floor in the kitchen, I instantly went from cold to freezing. Morgana should never have changed out the old hardwood. If I ever had the time and money, I was going to change it back, or maybe I'd have radiant heat installed to keep the floors toasty all winter. The cats would surely love sleeping on a warm floor, but then I'd have a hard time navigating the kitchen without stepping on anyone.

I fixed their breakfasts in record time, my freezing feet and goose-bumped arms proving to be good motivators. I couldn't wait to get into a warm shower. The hot water felt wonderful, but it slowed me down. It was hard shutting it off and harder still leaving the steamy warmth of the bathroom. With my terry robe tied snugly around me, I rummaged through my closet until I found jeans and a long-sleeved shirt. I stuffed my feet into sneakers, ran a comb through my hair, and grabbed my denim jacket. Not a land speed record but impressive nonetheless.

Then I spent five minutes looking for Sashkatu. I'd decided to come back for him later when I stumbled over him. He was asleep on the braided doormat at the front door. He clearly didn't want to be forgotten in my mad dash to work. It was a plan he may have regretted when I woke him with a shriek as I fell onto my side to avoid stepping on him. He gave me a look that said, "Stupid human." It was a look he'd perfected over time. He yawned and stretched each arthritic leg as if he were in no hurry. I suspected he knew that I was.

The two of us went off to the shop, at least one of us grateful for the ten-second commute. Sashki was installed on his windowsill and I on the chair behind the desk when the clock chimed nine and Lolly came through the door.

"Welcome back," she said. "I have to talk to you."

I came out from behind the counter to exchange quick pecks on the cheek. "That sounds mysterious."

Lolly planted herself in the customer chair. "Alan Boswell came in for candy while you were away. Today's his daughter Kate's birthday, and he was really down in the dumps. You know, it's been two years since I lost

Martin, and I still get blue at birthdays and holidays. Would you listen to me preaching to the choir," she chastised herself. "I am so sorry, dear. Morgana and Bronwen are barely gone three months. Martin always told me to spend more time thinking and less time talking."

"That's okay," I said, though Martin was right to some degree. But Lolly was all heart and no harm. "Sometimes it feels like their passing was a lot longer ago than three months." Then there are the times it doesn't feel like they're gone at all, I thought dryly. But the truth was that I did miss their company and advice. I missed the way we laughed at ourselves and each other. The way we stood together, closing ranks if one of us was threatened or troubled. The stuff of families. I was surprised by the tears that sprang to my eyes. It didn't happen as often anymore.

Lolly reached into the pocket of her skirt and produced a little packet of tissues and a purple foil-wrapped candy I recognized as one of her raspberry truffles. She pulled out a tissue and offered it to me along with the candy. "You can tell I'm a grandma," she said, chuckling. "I always have tissues and goodies in my pockets." She had such an infectious laugh that it was hard not to laugh along with her. "Now where was I?" she muttered.

"You were saying that today is Kate Boswell's birthday."

"Right, right—Alan's taking her and her best friends to the Grotto for dinner. He even arranged to have them present her with a birthday cake. And he's giving her five hundred dollars to spend on clothes or whatever she wants."

"Don't forget about the candy he bought for her."

"That's just what I said to him, which is when he mumbled that it wasn't for her."

"The candy wasn't for her? Who was it for then?"

"A new lady friend," Lolly said. "He wouldn't say much about her, not that I didn't try to worm it out of him. I've dragged information out of better, smarter men than Alan Boswell. I guess he had his guard up, worried about the old rumor mill."

"He should be," I said, jarred by her revelation. "He didn't waste any time." So much for the grief-stricken husband who unclogged my drains and poured his heart out to me. Would the real Alan Boswell please stand up?

"Pardon the comparison, but money is a lot like magic," she said. "One moment Alan is a past-his-prime average Joe, and the next he flashes some serious cash, and presto change-o, he can have any girl he wants. Some pretty heady stuff for a loser like him. But then, I've never had a high opinion of the man, a natural result of having been Amanda's friend."

"Poor Kate," I said. "First her mother is murdered, and now her father's idea of mourning is partying like a teenager."

Lolly sighed. "I imagine she'll be hanging out with her grandparents as much as he'll let her."

"He's probably too busy to care," I said, my stomach turning in disgust as I thought about his phony performance at my kitchen table. "You should have heard him whining about how his in-laws are always bad-mouthing him, trying to turn Kate against him."

"He's doing more damage to his relationship with her than they could ever do. Uh-oh," she said, pulling herself up from the chair with some effort. "I just saw a couple of kids run into my shop without their parents. And I left a whole tray of candy cooling on a countertop," she called over her shoulder as she hustled out the door.

* * * *

I wanted to call Eric Ingersoll, but I didn't want our conversation to be interrupted by customers. Tilly was busy baking for two readings, one of which was staying for a tea. I considered asking Merlin to cover for me. After all, the call shouldn't take longer than a few minutes. How much mischief could he get into in such a short time? I threw caution to the wind and asked him. He seemed pleased by the request and promised he wouldn't do or say anything to cause a problem. He'd be as mute as a monk under a vow of silence.

"I'll be in the storeroom, but don't come for me unless the shop is on fire." I closed the door to the storeroom and dialed Winterland. The secretary put me right through to Ingersoll.

"The reunion lady. You have those numbers firmed up for the event?"

I'd forgotten about the ruse I used to get in to see him. "Not yet, but that's not the reason I called."

"What can I do for you?"

"I guess I should start at the beginning."

"Generally a good place to start."

"I was talking to my aunt from Albany," I said, picking the first place that popped into my head, "about having the reunion at Winterland. She asked me if Dwayne Davies was still the manager. They met in college, kept in touch for years after graduating, but eventually lost track of each other. She begged me to get his phone number or address so she could catch up with him. To tell you the truth, I think she had a crush on him back then."

"Hey, I wouldn't mind helping you and Cupid, but like I told you, Davies flew the coop with no forwarding address. If you call his landline, his elderly mother answers, and she swears she has no idea where he went or why. In fact, she filed a missing persons report with the police after he didn't come home from work that first night."

"How awful," I said. "My aunt knew the whole family. I'm sure she'll want to contact Mrs. Davies to offer whatever support she can."

"I guess there's no harm in that," he said, followed by an enthusiastic "All right!"

"Excuse me?"

"Sorry," he said with a laugh. "I'm throwing paper balls into the trash basket across the room, and I made another basket. It's not as easy as it sounds."

I could picture him leaning back in the padded chair, feet hefted onto the desk, playing the makeshift game. "Congratulations," I said trying not to sound snide about it. "So you'll find the address and number for me?"

"Sure, why not."

I gave him my number and clicked off, figuring I had a fifty–fifty shot of hearing from him.

I relieved Merlin, who was disgruntled because no one had come into the shop during my brief absence. "We'll have to try this again sometime," I told him, which seemed to brighten his mood.

An hour later, Ingersoll kept his promise and called with Davies's information. I thanked him, and he reminded me that ski season was only a few months off. If I was serious about taking lessons, I should make an appointment soon because his schedule filled up quickly.

It turned out I was right about the manager living in Hassetville. Visiting his mother would take too long for a lunch hour, though. I'd have to go after work, but first I needed to call the woman and convince her she wanted to see me.

Chapter 18

"I don't want to upset Mrs. Davies," I said to Tilly. "She's elderly, and she already had to go through the whole thing when she filed the missing persons report." We were seated at her kitchen table with cups of tea after having stuffed ourselves with her legendary shepherd's pie. She'd decided I was looking a little pale and in need of some home cooking. And she knew shepherd's pie was one of my childhood favorites. Morgana had tried to make it for me on several occasions, but Tilly's always won hands down.

"Do you know of a spell that will prevent my words from hurting her? From making her grieve all over again?"

"You're operating under the wrong premise," Tilly said. "Talking to you couldn't make her grieve again unless she'd somehow managed to forget about him, let alone his mysterious disappearance. Trust me when I tell you that she has not forgotten, that the pain has not receded, though she might have learned to hide it better. Her son is with her every minute of every hour whether she's awake or asleep. I wasn't fortunate enough to have a child of my own, but I know in the deepest level of my soul that losing a child is a wound that never heals. Talking about him may be the only real pleasure left in her life. Friends, even relatives, reach their saturation point. It's natural for them to want to put the sadness behind them and move on with their lives. Your being there to listen to her will be a gift."

Every now and then, my often-silly aunt surprised me with her wisdom, and this was one of those times. What her words told me was that a spell wasn't necessary and probably wouldn't work even if I found one. There are some things beyond the ability of even the most accomplished sorcerer.

"I'm hankerin' for some dessert," Merlin said, coming into the kitchen. "How much longer are you hens gonna be jabberin'? A fella could starve to death around here."

"Why don't you nibble on the mashed potatoes stuck in your beard?" Tilly said, trying not to laugh but not entirely successful.

Merlin was too fixated on dessert to care if he was the subject of her mirth. "What are we havin' anyway?"

Tilly pushed back from the table. "Fresh peach tarts. Probably the last ones of the season."

* * * *

It was eight o'clock when I got back home, not too late to call Mrs. Davies. She answered the phone on the first ring as if she still sat by the phone waiting for her son's call. I explained who I was and why I was interested in hearing more about her son's disappearance. I asked if she could spare me a few minutes.

"I have more time on my hands these days than I know what to do with," she said. "You're more than welcome to come by." We settled on four the following day. It meant closing the shop early, but weekdays in the late afternoon in August were notoriously slow for business—my business anyway. Magick isn't quite the staple groceries, pharmaceuticals, or chocolates are. Lolly never seemed to lack for customers. The forecast of a blizzard brought people to her door in droves. Chocolate can make the unpleasant a lot easier to bear.

Before going off to bed, I went online to pay some bills and check my e-mail. A notice from the mayor's office caught my attention. The rescheduled town board meeting would be held in two days. Less than forty-eight hours! I checked the date of the e-mail, thinking I must have overlooked it days ago, but the notice had been sent while I was having dinner at Tilly's. Mayor Tompkins waited until the last minute, no doubt hoping fewer people would show up to attack the zoning issue and further prolong the process. Not only had he pushed a like-minded ringer onto us in the form of Patrick Griffin; he also failed to notify us about the rescheduled meeting in a timely manner! I, for one, had no intention of missing that meeting. I put it on my calendar in the slot next to my visit with Mrs. Davies. My evenings were getting busy. I was a real jet-setter.

* * * *

Travis called to touch base when I was on my way to Hassetville. We'd agreed to talk every day, even if it was only to say we had nothing new to report. With several suspects, his busy schedule, and my day job, it was the best way to keep each other in the loop. Forgetting to relay one detail might not mean much, or it might mean a delay in putting the pieces of the puzzle together. As Travis had reminded me, it could also mean the difference between life and death.

"On your way to see Mrs. Davies?" he asked.

"If I didn't know better, I'd think you were stalking me," I said.

"It's all in the name of efficiency and safety."

"Let's not go another round on the safety issue," I said. Travis had brought it up for the first time when we were investigating the death of Jim Harkens. "I've already proved I'm capable of taking care of myself." Before he could squeeze in another word on the subject, I told him about the email notice I received from Tompkins.

"The man's really overstepping. The Waverly people must be dangling a big chunk of cash over him to get the zoning passed right away. I'll have to get over there for a follow-up on my initial report. I guess I'll see you there?"

"You couldn't keep me away."

* * * *

Jane Davies lived in a tidy white Cape Cod with black shutters and a red door. The only thing that hinted at neglect was the Boxwood hedge that ran along the perimeter of the front yard. I could tell by the height of the new growth that the bushes hadn't been trimmed for the past few months. Dwayne must have been his mom's gardener and maintenance man, a good son.

Mrs. Davies opened the door and welcomed me in with a tremulous smile that seemed ready to break down at a moment's notice. I put her to be in her seventies, and I could tell she was used to keeping up her appearance. She'd applied brown liner to her eyelids, but the lines had been drawn with a shaky hand. And the blush on her cheeks was too round and rosy against the pallor of her skin. The most telling sign of her stress was the thick line of gray rising from the roots of her otherwise brown hair. Like the hedge, it hadn't been touched up in months. Things like that stop mattering when your life has fallen apart.

She brought me into her small living room. The furniture was fussy, the fabrics faded. A glass-front cabinet against one wall was filled to the brim with a collection of small owls. Owls of every shape and material. Dozens more resided on every flat surface in the room. For all I knew, the birds had colonized the other rooms as well. Dusting had to be a nightmare.

We sat on armchairs a few feet apart. I expressed my condolences again and thanked her for seeing me.

"Forgive me," she said, "my mind isn't what it once was. Why do you want to know about my son?"

"I'm a private investigator," I told her. "I became interested in your son's disappearance while I was investigating another case in New Camel."

Her eyes brightened. "Dwayne works at the ski resort..." Her voice trailed off.

"Winterland," I supplied.

"Yes, that's right. May I ask what sort of case you were working on?" She probably wanted to grab me, turn me upside and shake me, until everything I knew about her son fell out like loose change. But she maintained the polite restraint that was a hallmark of past generations when the social graces were observed regardless of the circumstances.

"A woman by the name of Amanda Boswell was recently killed in New Camel," I said. I'd wrestled with how to present this subject to her if she asked. Apparently there was no tactful way to speak about murder when her own son was MIA.

"I heard something about that on the news," she said. "Horrible. Just horrible." I watched her expression start to crumble as she made the inevitable connection. "You don't think the killer may have also—"

"No, no," I said, interrupting before she could get the difficult words out. Did I really believe that if I stopped her from verbalizing them, she would also stop thinking them? Had Tilly been there she would have rolled her eyes at me and given me a demerit. "That's not what I meant. I'm simply trying to locate anyone who may have known the woman or witnessed the murder."

Jane didn't say anything. She searched my face for reassurance I couldn't give her. Although I'd tried to do right by her, I'd made a muddle of it. Since I was the one who scared her into thinking about a serial killer, it was up to me to turn down the fire under that possibility. Not an easy thing to do when the purpose of my visit was Amanda's death and her son's disappearance.

"Keep in mind that Amanda and Dwayne traveled in very different circles," I pointed out. "There is nothing about them that is even vaguely similar. A dating service would never have matched them," I added, hoping to elicit a smile from her and failing. "The odds are they weren't even acquainted."

"I don't recall hearing Dwayne mention the name Amanda," Jane said, latching onto the fact like it was a life vest I'd thrown her. "But then New Camel isn't around the corner from here. I can count the number of people I know there on one hand and still have fingers left over. But Dwayne did work there, so their paths may have crossed. Of course, Dwayne has always been painfully shy around women—pretty women especially." She paused and seemed to gather herself before going on. "Do you think my son could have been murdered?"

"Did he have any enemies?" I asked. "Did he ever say he was worried about his safety?"

"He was bullied by two boys ages ago in high school. I don't know if that counts. They both moved away after graduation. He never mentioned having safety concerns since then. Miss Wilde, my son is a gentle soul."

"How did he feel about his boss?"

"Fletcher?" Her lips compressed into a tight line. "I don't think anyone likes that man. I've never met him, but from what Dwayne has told me, he's cold and calculating without a scintilla of compassion for anyone. A tightwad, too, if my son's salary is any example. You know what he gave him for a Christmas bonus last year?"

I shook my head.

"A hundred dollars. That might have been generous back in the thirties, but with today's prices? It's more like an insult."

"Did Fletcher ever ask him to do any work on the side?"

"On the side?" She repeated, frowning. "I don't think I know what you mean."

"Did Dwayne run errands for him, attend events, anything beyond his job description?"

"If he did, Dwayne never mentioned it to me. But if Fletcher had asked him to do other things, Dwayne probably would have obliged. He was always worried about losing his job."

"Why is that?"

"Fletcher doesn't give his employees a feeling of job security. He likes to keep them guessing, keep them on their toes. Personally, I don't think being under a constant threat of dismissal builds loyalty in an employee." She gave a sharp bark of a laugh. "Then again, he's the one sitting on billions, and I'm the one wondering how she's going to pay her taxes this year." Her eyes filled with tears that she tried to blink away. One escaped and spilled down her cheek. She dashed it away with the palm of her hand. "I'm sorry."

I pulled my chair closer and reached out to put my hand on hers. "Don't apologize. You're entitled to your tears with all you've been going through."

"Thank you." She sniffled, covering my hand with her other one. It was becoming a weird game of patty-cake. She probably felt the awkwardness, too, because she quickly released my hand to draw a tissue from her shirt pocket.

"Mrs. Davies," I said, "do you have any idea, even a far-fetched one, about where your son might have gone?"

She shook her head.

"Does he like traveling? Does he visit friends out of town?"

Again she shook her head.

"Does he ever go on fishing trips or camping?"

"No. He goes to work, and he comes home to me. Don't get me wrong, I love his company, but a man of his age should have more of a life than watching television with his old mother."

"Does he have friends who might know where he is?"

"A couple, but I called them when he didn't come home from work that day. The police spoke to them too. They're as much in the dark as I—" Her throat seemed to constrict with emotion, cutting off her words. "This is so unlike him," she continued. "That's why I'm so scared. He's all I have. I keep holding onto the hope that he's okay."

"Did you notice anything different about your son's behavior, his attitude, in the days before he went missing?"

Jane seemed about to say no but changed her mind. "Now that you mention it, he was acting a little off for days: short tempered with me, not sleeping well, fidgety. When I asked him what was wrong, he blamed it on stress at work. I didn't pursue it because I didn't want to make it worse."

I couldn't help thinking that his stress level might have included a little after-hours job of doing away with Amanda, followed quickly by a trip to a place in the sun with fake ID and a hefty bonus in his pocket. Maybe Dwayne wasn't the angelic son Jane imagined him to be.

"If you're not too tired, I'd like to hear about Dwayne," I said, remembering Tilly's advice.

"I'm sure you have more important things to do than sit here and listen to me babble," she said, though without much conviction.

"Actually, I don't have anything to do right now, and I like getting to know the people I meet in the course of my investigations."

The muscles in her face relaxed, and I caught a twinkle in her eyes. "That's my Dwayne," she said, pointing to a framed photograph presiding over the owls on the coffee table. "It was taken for his college graduation." The serious young man in the picture was average-looking, interchangeable with any number of others across the country, except in his mother's eyes. The photographer had posed him at an angle to the camera, looking off into the distance as if he were trying to peer into his future. "Can you believe he weighed ten pounds when he was born?" Jane said as if the fact still amazed her. "I was in labor for twenty hours before they decided to take him by Caesarean."

"How was he as a little boy?" I asked. And without further encouragement, she was off and running. Half an hour later, she pressed me into staying for a light dinner of egg salad sandwiches with potato chips and iced tea. She was clearly eager for the company, and with Tilly on tap to feed the cats, I couldn't find it in my heart to say no.

Chapter 19

This time the parking lot wasn't full when Tilly and I arrived at the elementary school for the board meeting. We'd left Merlin home on his own recognizance with strict orders not to use any appliance in the kitchen. He was so delighted to skip the meeting that we dared to think he'd stay out of trouble.

As soon as we walked into the school, we both felt the difference. The air was tense and somber. The last time the town gathered here, Amanda had been murdered. From the snippets of conversation I overheard on our way to the gym, I could tell that the tension was due, in no small part, to the mayor's move to stack the deck in favor of the rezoning. Human nature being what it is, the people in favor of the hotel were silent about his conniving, but those opposed were making their displeasure known. Unfortunately they were all bluster and no action. And I was as guilty in that respect. If no one was willing to challenge Patrick's appointment and throw their hat in the ring, we had no one to blame but ourselves.

The gym, like the parking lot, was only three-quarters full. If Tompkins's goal in sending out the late e-mail was to cut down on naysayers who might influence the board, it may have worked, which rankled more than I wanted to admit. The portable podium was once again at the rear of the gym, but this time the emergency exit doors were closed in deference to the nippier temperatures that had finally given summer the boot. There wasn't a tank top or sundress in evidence, though there were a few hardy souls wearing flip-flops with their jeans and flannel shirts. People had dug their warmer clothing out of their closets and storage bins, where they'd been since the end of winter.

Rusty must have expected the same huge turnout as before because he'd set up the school's entire complement of folding chairs in advance.

When Tilly saw that they were nearly all taken, she made a beeline for two of the remaining ones. Aching feet or not, my aunt can move when she's motivated. All we lacked for the meeting were the board members.

I looked around us, but the only one I saw was Beverly, deep in conversation with several women on the far side of the gym. She was as toned down in dress and behavior as everyone else. Even my aunt had opted to wear a more sedate muumuu in earth tones. Her only nod to the autumnal weather was the brown shawl around her shoulders.

It turned out that the woman seated on Tilly's right was a good friend she hadn't seen in months. I wanted to let her know I was going to take a walk around, but the two women were so busy catching up that I couldn't get a word in edgewise. I gave up, hung my denim jacket on the seat back and went in search of the missing board members, Amanda's death weighing heavily on my mind.

I found Eddie exiting the men's room and Corinne on her phone at the front entrance. She clicked off her call and hurried past me to the gym. Three accounted for; two to go. I was passing the darkened cafeteria when I heard two men arguing in the dimly lit food-prep area in the back.

They couldn't see me from where they stood, and I didn't need to see them. I instantly recognized their voices. Although Patrick and the mayor were making an effort to keep the volume down, I could tell by the fury in their hushed tones that they wanted to shout. I don't normally eavesdrop, but I wasn't going anywhere until I learned why the mayor and his anointed one had had a falling-out at so critical a juncture.

The men had clearly chosen to have their showdown in the cafeteria because the hallway from the front door led to the gym first. There was no reason for anyone to be this far down, except for Rusty, and I suspected he was ensconced at his desk in the basement watching baseball.

". . . nothing but a traitor," Tompkins snarled. "Admit it—you were plotting to take advantage of me all along."

"Plotting?" Patrick's tone was more bemused than angry. "You're the one with schemes and plots, Lester. You've always been focused on your own agenda. Have you forgotten that you're the one who came and begged me to return to the board or that I declined the offer? Does that sound like someone who's trying to play you?"

"You have a convenient memory," Tompkins said.

"Same old, same old. You attack anyone who gets in your way. Well, there are some things in this world more important than building another hotel."

There was a pause, during which Tompkins must have been searching for a scathing rejoinder. When he finally lurched on, it was with far less conviction. "You should have come to me as soon as you realized you were having second thoughts."

"I did," Patrick said, anger finally sharpening his words. "If you have anything else to say to me, you can do it in front of the board and your constituents."

I heard his footsteps crossing the cafeteria, so I double-timed it back to the gym more curious than ever. When I slipped into my seat, Tilly was still chatting with her friend. She probably didn't realize I'd ever left. The three other board members had taken their seats on the podium during my absence. I noticed two of them checking their watches. The meeting was ten minutes late in starting. Patrick entered the gym right behind me. There was nothing about his body language or expression to indicate he'd been in a heated dialogue moments earlier. He greeted the other board members and sat down, leaving the center chair for the mayor.

Tompkins hadn't regrouped as well. He marched in, eyes straight ahead, ignoring the people who called out greetings. He had more on his mind than good will and the next election. His mouth was compressed into a grim line, his fair skin mottled with the anger raging through him. I wouldn't have been surprised to see steam coming out of his ears. He mounted the podium, nodding stiffly at the board members as he took his seat.

Once the room quieted, he opened the meeting by saying that the evening's purpose was to afford residents an opportunity to ask questions and voice their opinions about the Waverly Corporation's proposal to build a hotel in New Camel.

"I'll be acting as moderator. The meeting is scheduled for two hours, and I intend to shut it down at that point. Let me tell you ahead of time that I will not brook any interruptions, foul language, or any effort to disrupt this meeting. If you get it into your head to disregard the rules, you will be spending the night in the Watkins Glen lockup as a guest of the county."

A buzz of reactions swept across the gym. Even the board members were looking at one another in disbelief. I was probably the only one there who realized Tompkins was flexing his mayoral muscle to intimidate Patrick Griffin into returning to his fold. If I were Patrick, I'd be laughing at the threat. What could Tompkins actually do to make him rethink his change of heart? I doubted there was anything in his arsenal with real teeth. Anything that couldn't also come back to bite him one day. Tompkins had to thump his gavel several times to restore silence.

"Let's get started. Raise your hand if you wish to speak and wait your turn."

As the meeting dragged on toward the two-hour mark, I was increasingly glad we hadn't brought Merlin with us. Of course, that feeling might change once we got back home. We heard the opinion of every soul in the gym. Some more than once. Those who were against changing the zoning laws were every bit as passionate and eloquent as those who were in favor of it. By my estimate, the audience was split fifty–fifty. Nothing I heard made me change my mind. I suspected that was also true of everyone else there. But at least the board members now had a better idea of how the people felt. Whether any of it would have an impact on their vote remained to be seen.

Tompkins ended the meeting within minutes of the scheduled time. He should have been pleased by how polite and respectful everyone was. But I could tell his anger was still simmering below the surface. On the other hand, Patrick appeared to be on an even keel. Maybe he was just a better actor. I had to find out what had really gone down. What had caused Patrick to spin such a one eighty?

* * * *

I had one stop to make before driving Tilly home. She'd run out of vanilla and needed it for the morning's baking. The only store that sold vanilla and stayed open late was Bigbee's, on the road to the Glen. There wasn't much traffic at that hour. I was driving and listening to Tilly fill me in on her friend's life. She'd recently become a grandmother for the fifth time, her brother had passed from a heart attack, her daughter had made partner at her law firm, and her daughter-in-law had left her son and their two little ones to run away with another man. Between trying to pay attention to her narrative and keeping an eye out for possums, raccoons, and other nocturnal creatures, I didn't immediately realize we were being followed. Driving out of the school's lot, there were a dozen or more cars, SUVs, and vans headed in the same direction we were. The pack thinned as the cars turned down side roads until there was only one set of headlights in my rearview mirror.

I pulled into Bigbee's parking lot; the other vehicle pulled in right after me. I assumed it was someone else who needed a few late-night items. There were five other cars in the lot, a few owned by the grocery store's skeleton night staff. I pulled into a spot close to the door. The other vehicle parked at the far end of the lot. It was a dark-colored pickup truck, most likely black. I watched it for a minute. The driver shut the lights and the engine but didn't emerge, which struck me as odd. It was probably the mom or dad of a kid working late at the store, I told myself. But why park so far away? It sure seemed as if the driver didn't want to be seen.

"What are we waiting for?" Tilly asked when I didn't get out.

I lied. "I'm trying to remember if I need anything while we're here."

"You'll figure it out sooner in the store than you will sitting here like a bump on a log." She opened her door and started to get out. "Come on. We've already left Merlin alone for too long."

That got me moving. I followed her into the store, glancing back at the truck. I wanted to believe that if there was danger lurking, Tilly would have felt it in her bones. But I knew better. My aunt, the brilliant psychic, was often inept when it came to herself and her nearest and dearest. Neither Bronwen nor Morgana had ever figured out the dynamics of her huge blind spot or any way to correct it. My theory was that it must be a survival mechanism to keep her sane. Constantly being aware of every threat, large or small, to herself and her loved ones would have driven her mad by now.

Tilly found the vanilla and decided she needed a few overripe bananas for banana bread. I took two green ones that I realized I needed after all. We were back in the car in fifteen minutes. The truck hadn't moved. I debated going into the store again and reporting it or calling 911, but it seemed like an overreaction. In the morning, I'd probably be laughing at my bout of paranoia.

But just in case I was wrong, I started the engine and threw the gearshift into Drive as soon as I heard my aunt's seat belt click in. We sped toward the driveway, Tilly exclaiming about pulling Gs. She must have been watching the SYFY network again. I heard the truck's engine turn over and saw its headlights blink on as I took the driveway fast enough that we were lucky to be belted in.

"Kailyn," Tilly yelled. "Take it easy before you make Merlin an orphan."

"Sorry," I mumbled as I swung right to head home. The truck followed. Adrenaline kick in. "We're being followed," I said. I didn't like scaring her, but I thought she deserved to know. "I'm going to try to lose him, so hang on." Tilly grabbed the armrest with one hand and the edge of her seat with the other.

I waited until the last second and swung a hard right onto the next side street, nearly doing a stunt driver's wheelie. I didn't realize I was holding my breath until the car stabilized and a whoosh of relief escaped my mouth. I snuck a peek at Tilly who was uncharacteristically quiet. Her eyes wide, she gaped as if she wanted to scream but was temporarily rendered mute.

I checked my rearview mirror. The pickup had been too close to execute such a sharp turn without flipping, which had been my goal. The driver must have come to the same conclusion because he shot past the street. We weren't home free, though.

"Call 911," I said as I wove in and out of streets I'd never traveled, hoping to lose our pursuer.

Tilly rummaged around in her huge tote of a purse for a while before coming up with the phone. "Where are we?"

I realized I had no idea, and I didn't dare slow down at cross streets to read the signs. The truck could be waiting to intercept us at any moment. "Tell them we're on the outskirts of New Camel"—I glanced at the dashboard—"going mostly north." I was still making rights and lefts all over the place.

Before Tilly could punch in the numbers, she fumbled the phone, juggling it between her hands until she lost it to the floor. "Oh no," she cried, leaning down to see. "I think it went under the seat. I have to take off my belt to try to reach it."

"Absolutely not!" I shouted. "What if I have to slam on the brakes or make a sudden turn?"

"Where's your phone?"

"In my purse in the back somewhere." It was probably a bad idea to call for help anyway. An additional car racing through the streets might wind up killing us instead of saving us. It wouldn't be the first incident to end with that kind of irony. Fate had a grim sense of humor. But we couldn't ride around all night. I needed a plan, a destination. If I tried to make it home, I could be leading our enemy there as well. We'd be too vulnerable getting from the car into the house. "Do you have any sense of who's in that truck?" I asked her.

"I've been trying to pin it down," she said, "but you know how it is when I'm this nervous."

I was afraid of that. Adrenaline could act like interference, blocking her ability to read another person's mind. "It's okay," I said. "We'll be fine." The words were barely out of my mouth when a screech of tires made us both jump in our seats. The pickup flew around the corner we'd just passed and came up so close to our tail that I could barely see its headlights in the rearview mirror. I didn't dare slow down, or he'd been in my back seat. My attempt to lose him had apparently only served to make him more aggressive.

"Wait, I know...what to do," Tilly said, her breathing erratic. "Turn around...head for the police station...in New Camel."

"You're brilliant," I said, wishing I could hug her.

"I learned that... at the safety...class at the...Y."

I was worried that her struggle to breathe might be a sign of an impending heart attack. I asked if she had pain in her arm, her chest, her jaw. Was she nauseated?

Before she could reply, the pickup hit us hard enough to jolt our heads back then forward to the headrests. I had to fight the steering wheel to stay on the right side of the road. The driver was making it clear this wasn't just a beer-fueled lark to scare some witches.

"You okay?" I asked Tilly, still worried about her heart.

"Don't...worry about...me."

"I'm getting you to an ER," I said, with no idea where we were or how to get to the closest one. "Hang in there for me."

"No ER. Get us to the...police station." Her breathing was getting better, probably through sheer determination.

I looked in the rearview mirror. The truck was closing in again. "The phone," Tilly said, leaning over as far as she could in the seat belt. "The jolt must have pushed it out." She sat up, already punching in the emergency numbers.

"The police can't get here in time to help us," I said.

"I want whoever's on duty to be watching for us."

She was talking to Officer Justin Hobart when the pickup hit us again. Harder this time. We were thrown toward the curb on the right where I missed a row of parked cars by inches. I dragged the wheel in the opposite direction. With tires squealing, I hooked a left onto the next cross street. Our trajectory sent us in a wide arc bumping along the far curb until I wrestled the wheel under control. When I looked back, the truck hadn't made the turn yet.

Tilly and I saw the traffic light at the same moment. It was maybe six blocks ahead of us. If we reached it on the green and the truck missed it, we had a chance to make it back to the police station. On the smaller side roads at that hour, there hadn't been other traffic. Now, for better or worse, there was. Maybe our pursuer would give up the chase for fear of involving other vehicles and being caught. Or maybe he didn't care whom he injured. But I did.

"He's coming," Tilly said, looking in her side mirror. In spite of her fear, her voice was steady. She was holding it together.

We were two blocks from the light when it turned green. I gunned the engine, swinging a left at the end of the yellow. We'd finally caught a break. Not only were we headed south to the police station, but I also recognized the stores we were passing. This road would end at the loop onto Main Street. But we had at least a mile yet to go.

"He's still coming," Tilly reported.

The other cars on the road were turning off onto side streets. We were alone again, except for the pickup and it was gaining on us. There was one more light ahead of us. We made it through the yellow again. Our pursuer was stopped by the red, but only for the seconds it took for him to check for cross traffic. Getting a ticket was small stuff when vehicular assault topped your list of priorities.

We were coming to the loop. Without decelerating, I turned right, grateful there were no other cars to worry about. The pickup flew onto the loop after us. In the rearview mirror I saw the driver lose control. He sideswiped a parked car but quickly recovered.

The loop curved onto Main Street, where Hobart was hopefully ready and waiting to assist us. I was checking the mirror again when the pickup hit us for the third time. The force of the impact made my hands fly off the steering wheel and threw our heads back and forth again as if we were ragdolls. My car veered across the center line into what would have been oncoming traffic in a larger town. I grabbed the wheel and slammed the brake pedal down to the floorboard. But there wasn't enough time or space to avoid a van parked at the curb across from the police station. We hit it with a glancing blow before coming to a stop on the wrong side of the street.

Hobart was at my door in an instant. I opened my window with a shaky hand, and he leaned down to ask if we were okay. I turned to Tilly, who looked as though she'd been on a roller-coaster ride through a tunnel of horrors, but she wasn't clutching her chest, and her color was returning to normal. I had no idea how I looked, but I was pretty sure I'd aged a couple of years in the past hour.

"That was quite a hit you took. I'm calling for an ambulance." He pulled his phone from his utility belt.

"No, we're fine. We're absolutely fine," I said with all the strength I could dredge up.

He seemed reluctant to take my word for it. "You're sure?"

"We're both absolutely fine, Officer," Tilly chimed in with cheerful vigor to back me up.

"All right then," he said, putting his phone away. "I'm going to need you to make a U-turn and park across the street. Or would you prefer me to hop in and do it?"

I told him I could do it, but I didn't realize how shaken I was until I parked and got out of the car. My knees threatened to give way, but I drew myself upright before Hobart could grab his phone again and have us carted off to the hospital. I walked around the front of my car to check on the damage. The driver's side fender needed some work, but I'd been pretty lucky about that too. Things could have been far worse.

"Please come inside for a minute, Ms. Wilde. I need to write up a report, and you and your aunt need a little time to decompress before you drive home."

If I was unsteady, Tilly was a jellyfish. Hobart and I had to help her out of the car and into the station house. He pulled a second chair over to the one in front of his desk and gave us each a bottle of water from a small fridge in the corner of the office. Once he was seated behind the desk, he asked me to begin. I explained what happened, with Tilly filling in details here and there. I would have sworn I recalled every second of the incident, but she brought up things I'd missed or already forgotten. It was a scary lesson in how stress affects your memory.

I asked him about the paperwork for the insurance company, and he told me I could download the forms on the DMV site. "Were you able to get a look at the driver or his license plate?" I asked.

Hobart shook his head. "It was dark, and he was moving too fast. My first concern was to make sure you were both all right. Don't worry. We're going to catch the creep. I've sent out an APB for a black pickup with front-end damage. If you ladies are ready to head home, I'm going to follow you and make sure you get there safely. Lock your doors and windows, and if you have a security system, use it."

Chapter 20

"You and your aunt could have been killed," Travis said. His brows were tightly knit as if pulled by a needle. His voice was even, but the muscles in his neck were standing out from tension. It was the next night, and we were sitting in my living room—at least I was. He'd gotten up and started pacing while I told him about the assault. That's what I'd decided to call the incident. It wasn't a fender bender, although my fender had suffered considerable damage. And it wasn't an accident. It was a premeditated vehicular assault. And the only reason it ended the way it did was because we'd made it to the police station in time.

"I know, and I swear I didn't enjoy it one bit," I said, hoping to lighten the tenor of the conversation.

He stopped in front of me. "This isn't a joking matter."

I sighed. "Look, last night was pretty awful, but I can't keep dwelling on it. I need to move on. I promise you I'm not shrugging it off or trying to forget what happened. I doubt I ever will. Tilly's life was in my hands, Merlin's too, in a way."

"Not to mention your own life."

I wanted to say that I didn't mention my own life, but it was clear he wasn't going to be jollied out of his sober mood. Instead, I said, "I didn't do anything to provoke the assault."

"You're investigating Amanda's death. That may be all the provocation that driver needed. You have to let the case go."

"I don't recall asking for your opinion," I said. If I'd been an animal, my hackles would have been standing at attention. I've never liked being told what I can and cannot do. My mother and grandmother could attest to the fact. So could Tilly.

Travis looked at me as if I'd struck him. He dropped down on the couch across from me. "I'm sure you realize that what this guy did last night isn't normal, no matter what his beef is."

"Yes, I get that, but I'm not a quitter. As you may have noticed, I don't give up at the first sign of trouble." If he took that as a reference to the way he'd withdrawn from our relationship, so be it. Maybe I'd subconsciously chosen those words for that exact purpose. I must have struck a sensitive chord because he didn't have an immediate comeback. When he did speak, he dialed down the bossy rhetoric.

"Isn't there some kind of magick you can use to protect yourself?"

If I'd been standing, his suggestion would have knocked me off my feet. He actually wanted me to use magick. I felt as if one wrong word or move on my part could send him running for cover like a skittish cat. "I placed wards, protection spells, around my house and shop. Since my car was in the driveway, I thought it would be covered too. Apparently I was wrong. I learned that the hard way. I'll have to place separate wards around the car."

"I guess it's not something you can do while you're being chased."

"No, it's not a matter of saying, 'Bibbidi-bobbidi-boo,' or waving a wand. I didn't have the necessary materials with me. But even if I had them, you're right—I couldn't have focused well enough while we were being chased."

"Promise me you'll put those ward things on it tomorrow?"

"First thing in the morning. I promise."

"Okay, good. Have you checked the footage from your security camera?" He sounded relieved to change the subject.

"Why? The pickup followed me from the school."

"Indulge me. It's possible he came by your house first to make sure you went to the meeting. It would have been a simple thing to do. Your car is in the driveway whenever you're home."

"I didn't think of that," I said, already out of the chair and on my way to the stairs. Travis was right behind me. I switched on the light in the study, startling one of the cats asleep on the computer keyboard. He jumped up and scooted off to find a more private place to nap. I tucked myself into the chair. With Travis peering over my shoulder, I brought up the link to the video camera. We'd programmed the system to dump old footage after twenty-four hours, assuming we would check it at least that often. We were on the cusp of that period. I rewound back to the beginning and switched to fast-forward mode. Even so, the footage could have put an insomniac to sleep. But at eight seventeen last night, by the camera's time stamp, that all changed.

"Stop," Travis said as we both saw something black flash by.

I rewound and hit play. There it was: a black pickup rolling past my house. Unfortunately, the angle of the license plate was too oblique to read. Travis swore under his breath. Then the truck pulled into my driveway to make a U-turn. It seemed to pose for the camera while the driver changed gears, giving us a perfect view of the front plate.

"Gotcha," I said, grabbing a pen. I jotted the letters and numbers on the pad beside the computer, tore off the paper, and swiveled around to face Travis. "Do you think you can impose on your cop buddy to run down the owner's name?"

If he refused or said he couldn't keep asking his contact for favors, I'd have to give the plate number to Duggan and pray he was feeling charitable enough to share with me what he learned. I didn't hold out much hope for that. But in the end it could lead to Amanda's killer, and that was the goal, even if I wasn't the one who took him down.

"I'll ask him," Travis said after a moment's hesitation. He took the paper from me and slipped it into his shirt pocket. "If I'm able to get you the name of the truck's owner, do you promise to let the cops make the arrest?" He was looking me straight in the eye.

"I don't even own a pair of handcuffs."

"That's not what I asked you."

"Yes, of course," I said. Later when he was leaving, he took my hand and held it tightly. "Don't forget about those ward things."

"I won't forget." Even if last night's ordeal hadn't made a lasting impression, knowing that Travis wanted me to use magick surely had.

"I'll call if and when I get the DMV info. This is a good time for you to lie low. Let the killer think he scared you into giving up detective work."

"You're right," I said, not willing to make any promises I might renege on. He seemed to have forgotten he was still holding onto my hand because he looked a little startled when I withdrew it under the pretext of brushing hair out of my eye.

"Sorry," he said, a tinge of pink rising in his cheeks. "I don't generally do weird things like that. Believe it or not, I'm a lot more suave."

I grinned. "I suppose I'll have to take your word for it."

* * * *

I set the alarm clock for a half hour earlier than usual so I'd have enough time to take care of the wards before opening my shop. Maybe it was a throwback to my school years, but I hated having to wake up extra early on a Saturday. The cats must have sensed my irritation because they were surlier than usual too.

After a strong cup of coffee, I was ready to take on the day. I pulled Bronwen's magickal satchel down from the shelf in the bedroom that was once hers and took out the bell and the symbols of the four elements. Sand stood for earth, seawater for water, and a candle that when lit represented both air and fire. Although I'd chafed against having to be up early, I knew I was lucky it was the weekend. None of my neighbors were up and about yet. Even so, I went through the ritual as inconspicuously as possible. I didn't want to have to explain what I was doing should anyone see me. To the casual observer, I might have been checking my tires or looking for dents and dings. When I was finished, Sashkatu and I walked over to Abracadabra.

Barely an hour later, Travis called. His contact had come through with the pickup's owner. When he told me the name, I dropped the phone. It landed on the hardwood floor of the shop with a thud loud enough to wake Sashki, who was a master at ignoring the usual sounds of the day.

"Sorry," I said, fumbling the phone as I retrieved it. "Are you sure the information is accurate?"

"Absolutely, why?"

"I'm surprised, but I probably shouldn't be. I don't really know him all that well."

"He's on your list of suspects."

"But down at the bottom."

"Unrequited love and rejection have caused any number of people to come unhinged over the ages. And he had the opportunity. He was at the school the night Amanda.... Hey, gotta go," he said, interrupting himself. "I'm on the air in five. We'll talk later."

Chapter 21

Rusty Higgins occupied my mind throughout the busy morning, whether I was helping a customer select the best product for a particular health issue or teaching someone a spell. I couldn't wrap my brain around the idea that he'd tried to run me off the road. And although the license plate alone wasn't proof that he'd killed Amanda or defaced my fence, in my mind, the three things were linked.

Although I had a steady stream of customers, I closed for one of my lunch-hour errand runs. I decided to check out Rusty's truck for myself. I had no intention of confronting the man. I merely wanted to get a quick peek at his truck. Maybe if I saw the license plate on it and saw the front-end damage, I'd be able to accept that he was the man who came after Tilly and me.

I put the I'll Be Back clock sign in the window as soon as there was a lull in the day's foot traffic. It was approaching one o'clock. I walked back home to get my car. Sashkatu would be fine until I returned. In fact, he was probably happier when there was no one in the shop to disturb him.

Rusty's block was like a snapshot of Americana. Two adolescent girls were playing their own version of street tennis down near the dead end. A young man was tinkering with a car's engine in his driveway. A woman was walking a small dog with a scruffy face and ears that bounced as he trotted along. It was a perfectly ordinary afternoon in late summer.

I was hoping that Rusty's black pickup was facing the street, so I could drive by without needing to stop and get out. Although I could verify the plate from either end, I wanted to check front-end damage. But, of course, it was facing the house as it had been the first time I was there. I pulled to the curb at the end of his driveway where my car was partially blocked by the truck if Rusty happened to look out his living-room window. I left the engine running for a fast getaway, just in case.

I walked around the far side of the truck to the front end. The proof was plain to see. The bumper and grill were badly dented, the paint scratched and scraped off in places. The damage matched up well with the damage my car had sustained. The insurance company would be happy to have another party to sue for restitution. Maybe they wouldn't even raise my rates. Sometimes I can be a cockeyed optimist.

"Hey...what's going on here?" Rusty boomed from the other side of the truck.

My heart thudded hard, missing a beat and making me briefly lightheaded. I hadn't heard him come outside. I told myself I'd be fine as long as I didn't faint on the spot or go into the house with him. Instinctively, I glanced around to make sure there were still people outside who would hear me if I screamed, not that I didn't have certain defensive skills of my own. I just preferred not to use them in public.

I could hear his footsteps moving down his side of the truck toward the street while I scooted back down my side. I had to reach my car before he reached me. But he cut me off as I crossed behind the pickup. I was puzzled that Rusty didn't look the least bit angry. In fact, once he saw it was me, he smiled. It wasn't a villainous now-I've-got-you smile. It was an oh-hi smile. It didn't make sense, given what I knew. And what he knew I knew. I was close enough to my car that I could certainly outrun him if it came to that, but I decided to leave the option on the table for the moment to satisfy my curiosity.

"Is there something you wanted?" he asked, all nice and neighborly.

"Yes," I said calmly. "I'd like to know why you were trying to run me off the road last night."

"It wasn't me. I would never do anything like that. I've known you since you were a little kid." He seemed hurt that I could think that of him. I wondered if he took acting lessons on the side because his denial was so convincing. "Come on inside, and I'll explain everything," he offered.

Warning sirens blared in my head. "You can tell me out here," I said firmly.

"Yeah, okay. My truck was stolen a couple of weeks back. The police know all about it. I reported it missing right away. I had to take the bus to the school and back home again during that time. I don't like public transportation," he added with disgust. "In all the years you've known me, have you ever seen me take the bus?"

I'd never seen him get on or off the bus that made a loop around the town, but that was mostly because I'd never looked for him at the bus stop. He wasn't exactly on my radar until I found out it was his truck that had tried to kill Tilly and me. "So it just turned up in your driveway today?"

"Officer Curtis called a couple days ago to tell me they found the truck parked over by the entrance to Winterland. They said I couldn't have it back until forensics went over it because it was used in the commission of a crime. They didn't mention it involved you and your aunt. I'm awful sorry to hear that."

I believed him. No one would make up a story that could be checked out with one call to the police. "Thank you," I said. "But you don't have anything to be sorry about." I started to turn away but turned back. "Did the police say they found paint or a brush in the truck?"

"They wouldn't say, but I found a few splatters of paint here and there."

I thanked him again and got back in my car. I was glad I'd come, glad to know Rusty wasn't the one who painted that hateful message on my fence and then tried to kill me or scare me to death. But whoever had stolen the pickup was still out there somewhere, and I wouldn't be safe until he was caught. I wasn't any closer to finding Amanda's killer either.

* * * *

"You promised not to do anything dangerous," Travis said when he called that night, and I told him about my talk with Rusty. His voice was even, but I had a hunch he was struggling to keep it that way.

"That's not technically true," I replied. "I promised not to try to arrest him on my own. Besides, I was outside the whole time, and there were plenty of other people around. I was never in danger."

He was silent for so long that I thought he'd hung up on me. "Travis...hello?"

"I'm here. I had this thought. Will you hear me out before you say anything?"

"That's cryptic and ominous, but go ahead. I won't interrupt."

"What if Rusty staged the whole stolen-truck scenario? It would have been pretty easy. He parks it in a garage somewhere for those two weeks, reports it stolen, and only takes it out to do his dirty work. Then he leaves it near Winterland in the middle of the night and waits for the police to find it."

"He would have been taking a big chance. What if somebody recognized the truck when he took it out those times? I don't know. Rusty doesn't strike me as the type who'd come up with such a convoluted scheme."

"I'm just throwing it out there. When you're dealing with a killer, you've got to figure every angle."

"I suppose."

"Have you had a chance to ask Patrick Griffin about his sudden change of heart on the zoning issue?"

"I'll get to it later today or tomorrow. I wish I had a spell to squeeze more hours into a day," I said.

"If you ever come up with one, count me in, as long as it doesn't involve newts' eyes or bats' wings."

Not too long ago, I would have thought he was deriding magick, but from my evolving perspective, he was getting comfortable enough with the idea of magick to make jokes about it.

* * * *

My life had been so hectic lately that I hadn't had an opportunity to work on my teleportation skills. If I waited for the perfect time, I would never get around to it. I decided the cats wouldn't starve if they ate half an hour late while I worked on teleporting an object. Until I perfected that feat, I couldn't risk trying to teleport myself again. I was lucky I survived the first attempt. After closing for the night, I walked around my shop, considering a variety of objects for the trial run. I selected a small ceramic bowl. It weighed less than a pound, and I knew it might break if I didn't land it carefully. I'd chosen it partially for that reason. I had to learn how to teleport with finesse, a difficult goal. Beyond the actual act of teleportation, the hardest part was figuring out the amount of force necessary to send the object or the person to its intended destination in one piece. Cheap ceramics could be replaced; living beings were not so expendable.

I placed the bowl on the counter and made myself comfortable in the customer's chair. I did some deep breathing to clear and center my mind. I imagined my psychic energy as a force erupting from my mind and body, and I focused it on the ceramic bowl. The bowl was suddenly hurtling at me. I snatched it out of the air inches from my face. Telekinesis on steroids. But I'd intended to teleport the bowl into Tilly's shop. I probably needed to dig deeper, way down into my core, to reach the energy threshold for teleportation.

I started over. Deep breathing centered me. I marshaled the energy from the mitochondria of every cell in my body. I focused on the bowl with singular attention. The bowl vanished, winking out like it had never been there. It didn't leave a trace. The air around it didn't wobble or cleave from its passage. Before I could congratulate myself, I heard a muted thump from Tilly's shop, followed immediately by a howl of pain that could have only come from one person. I jumped out of the chair and raced through the door to my aunt's shop. I found Merlin on the floor holding his head, the bowl in pieces around him. Tilly was in the kitchen, grabbing an ice pack.

"Oh, Merlin, I am so sorry," I said. "I thought you two had gone home. You never stay this late."

"Mayhaps one should be more cautious in future endeavors of such a nature." The smack in the head seemed to have knocked his western accent out of commission.

"You played a part in this accident too, your lordship," Tilly said, leaning down to put the ice pack against the rising bump on his forehead. "If you hadn't eaten half the mini scones for tomorrow's teas while I was paying bills, I wouldn't have needed to bake more of them, and you would have been home an hour ago, enjoying dinner. Put your hand up and hold the ice. I can't stand here holding it for you."

"Those scones are not worthy of the name," Merlin said indignantly. "They couldn't satisfy the appetite of a child, much less a man." He was clearly a proponent of the saying that a good offense is the best defense.

"Good job on the teleportation," Tilly said to me. "Of course the landing could use a bit of work."

Chapter 22

Patrick Griffin didn't earn a spot on my list of suspects until he changed sides on the zoning issue. When he was in favor of the new hotel, he had no reason to have wanted Amanda off the board. But in turning against it, he instantly acquired a motive and rated another visit from me.

I decided that my best chance of getting him to open up would be to stage another impromptu chat—fellow shopkeepers hanging out, shooting the breeze. Luckily, he was a man of routines. Over time, I noted that unless he was delayed by a customer, he ate lunch at one o'clock. And if the weather was temperate, he preferred eating it outside. So I wasn't surprised to see him sitting on the front porch of his antique shop when I strolled down that way the first sunny day to come along.

I was hoping he would initiate the chat; that way he wouldn't think I had an agenda. With that in mind, I waved from the sidewalk as if I were merely passing by.

"Hello there," he called to me. "Good timing, I have a sandwich with your name on it." I stopped and pretended to consider the invitation. "My wife's Yankee pot roast," he coaxed. "Of all the great meals she makes, this one's my favorite." What he didn't know was that I would have accepted his offer even if maggot stew was on the menu, the thought enough to make my stomach lurch.

"How can I refuse?" I said, grateful his wife stuck to traditional fare. I climbed the steps to the porch and sat in the other wicker chair. "I can't believe how good that smells," I said, immediately famished.

"I guarantee it tastes a hundred times better." He wiped his mouth and hands on a napkin before digging into the thermal bag at his feet. "However," he went on, handing me the foil-wrapped sandwich, "I must warn you that it comes with a disclaimer."

"Oh, what's that?"

"It's the messiest thing to eat." He pointed out the brown dots that ran down the front of his blue polo shirt. "On pot roast days I always bring an extra shirt. I've tried aprons and lobster bibs, but I manage to get gravy on me anyway. For that reason, I won't be held responsible for any dry-cleaning expenses you incur."

"Got it," I said with a grin. "I'll take my chances."

"Smart girl."

We ate and talked about the things people talk about when they don't know each other very well: the weather, the well-being of our families, the state of business. At one point, Patrick excused himself and returned with two bottles of cold water from his mini fridge. It was such a pleasant lunch I had to remind myself to get to the subject of my visit before I missed the opportunity. There are only so many times you can arrange "impromptu" meetings without blowing your strategy.

"I guess you've heard the talk going around," I said at the first lull in our conversation.

Patrick took a swig of his water. "What is it this week?"

I hated to wreck his day with made-up gossip, but I was pretty sure I wasn't the only one questioning his motives. "Someone overheard you and the mayor arguing about your change of heart on the zoning issue. Now people think you lied about wanting the new hotel to trick the mayor into putting you on the board." I watched Patrick's expression turn sour as I spoke.

He wagged his head. "Little-town rumor mills," he said with disgust. "I can't say I'm surprised."

"May I ask what made you change your mind?"

"Why not?" he said. "In fact, maybe I should call a press conference to set the story straight before the good people of New Camel decide to lock me in a stockade and pelt me with tomatoes." He paused and took a deep breath. "Sorry, Kailyn. I shouldn't be attacking the messenger. If you want to know the truth, my political flip-flop was sort of my son's fault."

I was having trouble keeping my face neutral when my eyebrows were poised for flight.

"You're shocked I'd blame my kid, right?"

"It was...unexpected," I admitted.

"Before you judge me, let me explain. The last time we talked, I told you I wanted the new hotel because it would bring in more business."

I nodded. If a customer interrupted us before he answered that riddle, I might be tempted to turn the offender into a frog. I've never messed around with transmutation, but there was no time like the present to give it a shot.

"But my son Chris has been against it from the start. He's become quite the advocate of environmental protection. He even joined the high school HOP club last year."

"HOP?" I repeated, after washing a bite of my sandwich down with water.

"It's an acronym for Help Our Planet."

"Oh, cute."

"They're a pretty committed group of kids. When he joined, my wife and I thought maybe there was a girl in the club he wanted to get closer to. It wouldn't have been the first time. Turned out he'd found a subject he was passionate about."

"You should be proud of him," I said, down to my last bite of pot roast heaven.

"Sure we are," he said with a chuckle, "but I'm talking about a kid who can't keep his own little slice of the world clean. That's a teenager for you."

A drop of gravy had oozed out of his sandwich while he was talking and landed in the center of his shirt. He made a half-hearted attempt to wipe it with his napkin before giving up with a why-bother shrug. He had the standby shirt inside. "HOP arranged to have a speaker from the EPA do a presentation for the whole community. Summer was the best time to hold it in the high school auditorium. Once the school year starts up it's much harder to hold an outside event there."

I remembered finding a flyer about something to do with the EPA tucked under my windshield wiper. I must have thrown it away without reading it. "Did you attend?" I asked.

"I'm embarrassed to say I didn't. I could make up all kinds of excuses, but the plain truth is that I just wasn't interested."

"I'm sure you weren't the only one," I said, hoping to make him feel he could tell me anything.

"In any case, Chris went up to the woman and talked her into stopping by my shop before she left town. He was hoping she'd help change my mind about the rezoning."

"Did she?"

"Not entirely, but she laid the groundwork for Chris to win me over a few days later. The kid's sly. He waited until after dinner when I was relaxed and watching TV—tired and vulnerable, as he put it. He hit me with a one-two punch to the conscience that I never saw coming. He said if I wanted to be a role model for him, I couldn't be a hypocrite. Destroying wetlands in the hope of cashing in doesn't fly when you get right down to it. Besides, didn't I want to save the environment for my future grandchildren?"

"Low blow," I said.

"You don't have kids yet, Kailyn, but any father who says he doesn't care about being a hero in his child's eyes is straight out lying. Then the grandkid thing finished me off."

"Don't beat yourself up, you're a good dad and your son is growing up to be a good man," I said, meaning it.

He laughed. "Thanks, but I still wish he'd clean his room."

* * * *

That night I took Sashkatu home, fed everyone, and met Elise at The Soda Jerk. She'd called a few hours earlier in desperate need of some quality friend time and a BLT with a chocolate shake. Since Zach was old enough to resent having a babysitter, she'd been letting him babysit Noah. In theory, Noah liked the idea of hanging out with his brother instead of having adult supervision. In practice he hated it. He complained that Zach was stricter than the sitter was and "just mean for no reason." As a result, Elise didn't often leave them home alone. So when I got one of her save-my-sanity phone calls, I dropped everything that could be dropped and changed whatever could be changed to spend some quality time with her.

When I arrived at The Jerk, she was already seated in a booth, sipping a shake with a blissful expression on her face. The restaurant was busy for a weekday evening before the ski season. I recognized all the patrons, but they were only acquaintances, for whom a quick hello was adequate as I passed their tables. Just as well. Elise didn't like to leave the boys for too long, and I didn't want to cut into our limited time together.

I slid in across from her. "Hey there," I said, "I see I have some catching up to do."

She let go of the straw and came up for air. "This is definitely my addiction of choice. I could sit here all night long sipping shakes until I explode."

"Not a bad way to go, all things considered."

"How are my girls?" It was the gravelly voice of Margie McAndrews. She'd waited tables at The Jerk for as long as I could remember. She was tall and buxom, with tomato-red hair and earlobes that had stretched to triple their length because of her long-running devotion to chandelier earrings. We spent a couple minutes asking after each other.

"Two BLTs, extra crispy on the bacon, and a chocolate shake for you, Kailyn?" Margie asked once the schmoozing wound down.

"It's pathetic how predictable we are," I groaned.

"Make that two shakes," Elise put in.

Margie's sharply penciled eyebrows popped up. "So it's a two-shake night, is it?"

"I'm afraid so."

"You know I'll have to cut you off after that."

Elise laughed. "Well somebody sure has to. This one," she said, using her chin to point in my direction, "she's an enabler."

Margie went off to attend to another table and place our order. "Something beastly happen at work?" I asked Elise when we were alone.

"No, some days it just gets to me—this feeling that I'm on an endless treadmill of sameness. And I have to jump off for a little while or lose my sanity."

"You're such a rebel," I said, rolling my eyes. "You're lucky Duggan doesn't haul your butt off to jail for abandoning your children so you can sneak out to have not one but two shakes. What on earth are you thinking?" I was having trouble keeping a straight face.

Drunk on dairy and giddy with freedom, Elise cracked up. "Oh, I almost forgot," she said after catching her breath. "I saw Corinne DeFalco today. It seems our kids go to the same orthodontist. I bent the conversation around to the town board, and I got an earful. She's in our corner, worried the hotel rezoning will be just the beginning and before long we won't recognize our quaint little town anymore."

"Does she happen to know which side Eddie is on?"

"No, she said he's been tight-lipped about it from the beginning. If you ask his opinion, he says he hasn't made up his mind yet."

Margie came by with our shakes and a promise the BLTs were on their way.

"If Eddie is on the on the mayor's side, they should have the votes to win," I said. "Eddie is the linchpin; the outcome is in his hands."

"Not necessarily. I wouldn't put it past Tompkins to bribe someone over to his side with cold, hard cash. I just hope no one else winds up dead over this. We've had more than our fair share of murder lately."

"Amen to that." I winced at the pain knifing through my head. When would I learn not to drink cold liquids too fast?

"Where are you and Travis on finding the killer?"

"Sometimes I think we're chasing our tails." The busboy arrived with our sandwiches. I waited for him to leave before continuing. "Suspects keep popping on and off my list. Every time I think I have proof of motive and opportunity, I have the rug pulled out from under me."

"Any idea if Duggan is having more success?"

"It's not like he has me on speed dial."

"But you are the apple of a certain cop's eye," Elise said with a sly smile.

"You mean Paul Curtis?" She nodded as she bit into her sandwich. "If

I go to see him, he'll think I'm interested in him. I can't do that after I turned him down once before."

"You could go to report a missing cat," she suggested.

"I'll think about it," I said, "but I'm not making any promises."

We spent the remainder of our precious time together talking about her boys, my aunt, and Merlin, who was always a good source of comic relief. Elise was describing Zach's new girlfriend when it struck me that both he and Chris Griffin were both high school age. "Did a woman from the EPA do a presentation at the high school recently?" I asked once we'd moved on from the girlfriend. "I think it was open to the community."

"Yes. In fact, Zach went with his girlfriend. She's in that HOP club. He said the presentation was excellent. Although, in the spirit of full disclosure, I should point out that he also thinks every superhero movie is excellent. Likewise, my mac and cheese and a hundred other things."

I laughed. "Thanks for the heads up. It's great that the kids today care about saving the planet. Would Zach know if Chris Griffin is in HOP too?"

Elise wiped some mayonnaise off her chin. "I can answer that. Zach and Chris have been friends since they were little kids. Chris has been trying to persuade my son to join ever since he did. I think his girlfriend has a better chance of success. Why the sudden interest in Chris and the goings-on at the high school?"

"Just following up on something I heard today. I'll fill you in on the details when we have more time."

"I'll also expect a full account of your visit to Officer Curtis," she said as we slid out of the booth.

"I haven't decided if I'm up for that."

"Oh, you'll go to report your missing kitty. Have you forgotten how long I've known you?"

Chapter 23

Filing a report that one of my cats was missing was going to take some serious acting on my part. I was lucky to have never been in that unenviable position. I did my best to imagine how I would react and managed to work myself into a nearly hysterical state, fretting over where the poor thing would find food or shelter, survive the traffic, stray dogs and potentially rabid raccoons. If I could tap into those feelings when I went to report the cat missing, I'd be golden. In this instance, it turned out to be a good thing my mother had gone on her familiar-gathering spree before she died. Although she'd done it in a misguided effort to fix the problems with her magick, having six cats would come in handy now. Curtis had met Sashkatu in my shop, but he had no idea how many other felines I had at home or what they looked like.

He was sitting behind the desk when I walked into the small precinct house at eight o'clock in the morning. His smile turned to concern once he saw my agitated state. It was clear I wasn't there on a social call. "What's wrong?" he asked, jumping up and helping me to a seat.

"Rosanthum is missing," I said. I perched on the edge of the chair as though prepared to run if I heard a plaintive "meow" outside.

"I'm sorry to hear that. Can you give me a description?"

"She's an American short hair, black, gray and white."

Curtis typed the description into the computer. "I'd catch hell if I put out an APB for a cat, but what I can do is send e-mail requests to the local fire department and any cops from the Glen passing through this area to keep an eye peeled for her. You should tell your family and friends, everyone you know, and put up photos around town with your phone number, in case anyone spots her. When I'm off duty, I'll cruise around looking for her too."

"That's what I've been doing since I woke up hours ago and realized she was gone. It must have happened when I took out the garbage last night. She's never shown any interest in leaving the house. I don't know what came over her."

"Don't torture yourself. We'll find her."

"Thank you." But I wasn't ready to leave yet. Looking around for a reason to stay, I spotted the coffee machine. "Do you mind if I have a cup of coffee before I go? I'm so bleary-eyed I can hardly see straight."

"Sure...of course," he said, already on his feet. "I should have offered you some. How do you take it?" He was already pouring coffee into a throwaway cup.

"A little cream or milk would be great."

He brought it to me and took his seat again. I sipped the coffee until the silence in the room grew awkward. Curtis was fidgety, picking up papers on the desk and putting them down again, Stretching a rubber band that flew out of his fingers and across the room. He was probably searching for the right topic with which to break the silence. It was time to put him out of his discomfort.

"How's the hunt for Amanda's killer going?" I asked distractedly as if I were trying to make polite conversation, despite my Rosanthum being front and center in my mind.

Curtis pounced on the question like a starving man on a T-bone. "It could be better. Between you and me, I thought Duggan would have the case nailed down by now."

"No suspects, huh?

"Actually, too many."

It sounded like Duggan was having the same problem Travis and I were facing. "He must be leaning in someone's direction," I prodded gently.

"He doesn't confide in me much, and to be honest I don't like to ask."

"I can empathize," I said. "I've had more dealings with him than anyone could possibly want or deserve."

Curtis laughed, and I felt our connection strengthen. He must have felt it as well because he leaned over the desktop and whispered, "He's had Alan Boswell in for questioning at least twice that I'm aware of, not that it's surprising. The Boswell house has been party central since Amanda was killed. It's only a matter of time before he's busted for drug possession."

"He certainly doesn't sound like the grieving husband," I said, "but maybe that's because he's innocent and isn't worried about how it looks."

"If you ask me, he's one of those sociopaths you hear about. You know, the type with no conscience at all. My mom went to elementary school with him. She told me he had a pet snake and he just loved feeding it live mice."

A chill flashed along my spine and took my stomach for a spin. It seemed that all my suspects were as multilayered as Russian nesting dolls. "Thanks so much for your help," I said, getting to my feet and tossing my cup in the wastebasket beside the coffee machine.

Curtis jumped up as well "You bet. And if anyone finds Rosan...your cat, I'll let you know ASAP."

* * * *

The first customer of the morning was newlywed Dana Whitcomb, who came through the door with a white mountain of a dog she called Louie. He was gently mannered and looked like a huge furry cloud with a face. He and I were instant pals. I can't say as much for Sashkatu. He opened one eye enough to evaluate the newcomers and came fully awake in a flash. He leaped to his feet on the ledge as spry as a cat half his age. He arched, his ears flattened against his head, and his hackles stood at attention. There was no misunderstanding how he felt about Louie. But when he started hissing, Louie responded by barking. Had Sashkatu been any closer, the force of the bark would have bowled him over. On the plus side, if a thief tried to break into the Whitcomb house, one of Louie's barks would surely send him on to another less-threatening abode.

"Maybe I should leave," Dana said without much conviction. From the moment she walked in, her gaze had been flitting around the shop with unconcealed curiosity. "I can come back another day without him."

"Don't be silly. If I were Louie, I would have barked too. My shop welcomes customers of all species." I turned to Sashkatu, who was still in combat mode. "Go to Aunt Tilly," I said sternly. "Go get a cookie."

He jumped from the ledge to my chair without the benefit of his steps. Maybe he didn't want to appear weak in front of the enemy. But I saw him wince when he landed. My heart ached for him—and for me. I didn't like to think about how old he was getting.

"I've never seen a cat that obedient," Dana marveled.

"He's obedient when it serves his purpose, and he loves my aunt's baking."

Dana introduced herself while I petted Louie. She told me that she and her husband, Gavin, had moved to New Camel in time for the beginning of the new school year. She'd accepted a teaching position in the elementary school. He'd be teaching math in the high school. I welcomed her to the town and asked if there was anything in particular she was looking for or if she'd prefer to browse.

"I was hoping you might have an herbal cure for Louie's itchy skin," she said.

"As it happens, I do."

It was a lotion my mother had whipped up for one of her newer familiars who also suffered from allergies. We had found that it worked wonders on dogs as well. Dana and Louie trailed after me to the aisle where I kept skin products but didn't follow me in.

"We'll wait here," she said when I motioned for her to join me. "One wag of his tail would knock everything off the shelves."

I hadn't thought of that, but she was probably right. I brought the jar of salve to her. "It's composed of natural herbs and plants like coconut, peppermint, and chamomile—and a wee bit of magick," I added with a wink.

I'd found that a well-timed wink gave customers the freedom to believe it was magick or not, as they wished. In the salve, as in most of our products, a magick spell was an intrinsic part of the recipe. It's what set them apart from the more common and less effective competition sold elsewhere. "If you give me half a minute, I'd like to see if I have a fresher jar in the storeroom."

I try not to lie to customers unless it's in their best interests. I'd made the salve just days ago, but I wanted a minute out of sight to give it a booster shot of magick. Given our recent inadequacies, the booster shot seemed to increase the potency of the products. Better for the customers; better for business, in general.

I closed the door to the storeroom. I didn't have all the necessary items for an advanced healing spell, and I couldn't ask Dana to wait while I gathered them, so I used a spell that didn't rely on props but had served me well in the past.

Let illness be purged
And good health flow forth.
Let nothing coerce
Or make matters worse.
Hear my humble plea,
And let it so be.

I repeated the spell three times. When I returned to the front of the shop, I found Dana in the customer chair with Louie lying beside her on the floor. "Here we go," I said, handing her the salve. There are larger jars, but you should start with the small one to see if it works for him."

Dana came out of the chair, but Louie seemed content to remain where he was. "Thank you so much," she said. "Now I have the daunting task of looking through his mounds of fur for the hot spots. If I decide to adopt another dog one day, I think I'll go with a shorter-haired one."

Louie lifted his big bear head and grumbled as though he'd taken umbrage at her remark. He stood up and gave his coat a vigorous shake.

"Just teasing," Dana said, rubbing his ear. "I wouldn't change a single tuft of your fur." She turned to me, smiling. "I swear he understands every word I say." As if to prove her right, he wagged his long, plumed tail with fervor.

After she paid, I handed her a canvas mini tote with her purchase and asked her to let me know if the salve helped. She promised she would, adding that she'd be back soon to explore the shop without the wrecking ball otherwise known as Louie.

* * * *

Travis called later that morning to ask me out to dinner. "Why don't I cook dinner?" I suggested. I wanted to see if he was comfortable enough to eat my cooking and hang out in my house for more than an hour at a time.

"Sure," he said after a brief hesitation that may have been due to my unexpected invitation. "I'll bring the wine. Red or white?"

"I've got a couple of steaks in the freezer. How are you with grilling outdoors?"

"I'm a master of the grill. Prepare to be dazzled."

"Then let's go with the red."

It was a good thing my whole commute was just around the corner because a woman I'd never seen before walked into my shop five minutes before closing. She wandered around and asked a lot of questions. I thought she was one of the looky-loos I get now and then, the ones who monopolize my time and leave without buying anything. But she proved me wrong to the tune of two hundred dollars and said she'd be back once she decided what spells she wanted to try. She even took a handful of my business cards to distribute to her family and friends. So much for judging people too quickly or by some arbitrary standard.

Back home I fed the felines, tidied up the house, and defrosted the steaks before running upstairs to comb my hair and slap on some lipstick. Travis was at my door at six on the dot, one of the perks of dating a reporter. At least it was a perk when he wasn't working. Sashkatu joined me at the door to greet him. I wondered if that meant he'd given his royal approval. The other cats fled to their hidey-holes, clearly reserving judgment.

Travis handed me the bottle of wine and a bakery box tied closed with string. I'd completely forgotten about dessert. If he'd brought pie, I had a pint of vanilla ice cream that had been calling to me all week. He followed me to the kitchen.

"What's in here?" I asked, hoping Tilly didn't drop by. Whenever someone brought bakery fare, she always found it necessary to point out its deficiencies.

"Blueberry crumb pie," he said.

Uh-oh. She would have plenty to say about that. By the age of five, I'd learned that she preferred mixed-berry pie for its more complex blend of flavors. In her opinion, for blueberry pie to shine, the crust had to be above reproach. Of course, the only crust to ever attain that status was hers. My aunt had few faults, but a lack of humility about her baking prowess could easily have counted for two.

"I turned on the grill fifteen minutes ago," I said, taking the steaks from the refrigerator. "It should be ready to go."

Travis took the plate from me and headed outside through the French doors that connected the kitchen and patio. While he did his outdoorsman thing, I set the kitchen table, made a salad, and baked a couple of potatoes in the microwave, feeling very domestic. I always think it's a small miracle when all the components of a dinner are ready at the same time, especially when there's no magick involved.

During dinner, I brought Travis up to date on the reason for Patrick's reversal and told him that Elise had confirmed that there was an EPA program at the high school recently.

"Okay, that corroborates what Patrick told you, right?"

"Yes, except for the part about the spokeswoman stopping off to speak to him."

"If that's nagging at you," Travis said, "it's easy enough to find out the truth. Call the EPA and speak to the woman who did the presentation."

I groaned. "Talk about not seeing the forest for the trees."

"Well to be fair, there are an awful lot of trees in this case. By the way, I heard that the board is going to meet tomorrow night to vote on the zoning. I understand it's going to be a closed-door secret ballot."

I had a mouthful of salad to finish chewing, but after I swallowed, the words burst out of me. "Can they do that?"

"The town charter says they can if there are safety concerns. And you can't invent a better concern than a murder committed at the site of a previous meeting." He cut a chunk off the New York strip and forked it into his mouth. I swear I heard a groan of pleasure.

"It doesn't sound like the democratic way to handle things," I muttered.

"Cool your engine," Travis said with a chuckle. "I know you're curious about how each of them votes, but all that really matters is the outcome. If the mayor was going to do any arm twisting or bribing, that wouldn't have happened in public anyway."

"Just because he didn't kill Amanda doesn't mean we can trust him."

"You're preaching to the choir, lady. I haven't liked the guy from the day he was sworn in."

"You're a reporter. You should be busy digging up all his secrets instead of calmly advising me to be patient."

"Don't worry. I've been investigating him about a number of other matters. But I've learned it's not a good idea to jump the gun unless you want to be sued for libel."

"It sounds like that wisdom comes from personal experience," I said.

"Yes, but luckily the plaintiff settled with the network before the trial. The crappy part was that I had to make an on-air apology."

"You never said anything about it."

"It's generally not what I lead with when I'm getting to know someone. You probably don't introduce yourself as a sorcerer when you first meet people, although I guess your shop kind of does that for you."

"You'd think so, but most people don't take magick seriously. Being in my shop is fun, but they don't want to believe I'm the real deal. That would take the fun train too far down the track to Scaryville. It's why my family's policy has always been not to show off with our magick."

"Then what was the little demonstration of telekinesis you treated me to on my first visit?"

"You were such a smug disbeliever; it was like teasing a bull with a red cape. No self-respecting bull would have ignored the challenge. And in my defense, no one else was in the shop when I did that."

We were enjoying the blueberry pie and vanilla ice cream when the phone rang. Jane Davies was on the other end. She sounded agitated. "I'm sorry to bother you, Ms. Wilde, but something happened today, and I don't know what to do about it. Could you possibly stop by tomorrow? Anytime is fine. I'd be ever so grateful. I don't have anywhere else to turn."

"Why don't you tell me right now?" I asked, not eager to make another trip to Hassetville.

"I don't trust phones. You never know who else might be listening."

"Okay, how about going down to the police station?"

"Oh no," she shot back so quickly that she must have already considered and rejected the idea. "Not the police," she said vehemently. There was no mistaking the fear in her tone.

"Okay, I can be there after work tomorrow."

"Bless you," she said with obvious relief. "I'll make a roast chicken."

I told her it wasn't necessary, but she couldn't be talked out of it. After I hung up, I told Travis what she'd said and, perhaps more important, how she said it. We dissected her words down to the bone, but the only conclusion we could reach was that it had to involve her son, Dwayne.

"Or maybe she's just desperately lonely and wants a companion for dinner," Travis said.

"No, her fear was real," I said, taking another scoop of ice cream. "I'd bet my life on it."

Chapter 24

Travis offered to come with me to Hassetville. As much as I would have enjoyed the company, I worried that bringing a stranger along might keep Jane from being forthright with me. It would be even worse if she were to recognize him as a TV reporter. If she didn't trust the police, she surely had no welcome mat for nosy journalists.

With Tilly once again on cat duty, I locked up the shop and headed straight out to see Jane. She must have been sitting near the window watching for me because she opened the door before I rang the bell. I stepped inside to the fragrant embrace of roasted chicken, a homey smell if ever there was one. It reminded me how hungry I was. Lunch had been a slice of pizza I'd gobbled in the ten minutes between when the morning bus tour left and the afternoon one arrived. Hunger and comfort food were a match made in heaven. But first I wanted to let Jane unburden herself and hopefully enlighten me.

We sat in her cozy living room again, she on the sofa and I in a wing chair. She appeared less dazed but more anxious than at my last visit. Her makeup had suffered in the transition. She'd given up on eyeliner and made do with mascara, which didn't rely as much on a steady hand, and her gray roots had marched farther across her head.

"I'm so happy to see you, Kailyn," she said for the third time since my arrival. Travis may have been partially right about loneliness prompting her call, but there was something else, something bigger, going on too.

I assured her it was my pleasure to be there. "What happened?"

Her shoulders twitched. Whatever it was, merely thinking about it seemed to rattle her. She looked down at her brown skirt and smoothed it over her lap several times, though it wasn't wrinkled.

"A man came to see me yesterday," she began, her voice so soft I had to lean forward to hear her. "I never saw him before in my life. He was wearing suit pants that were too short, a T-shirt, and dirty old sneakers. His face was clean shaven, but his hair needed a good washing. I could smell the greasiness through the screen door. He looked so disreputable I was sorry I hadn't looked through the peephole before opening the door. He said he was looking for Mrs. Jane Davies. It scared me that he knew my name, like he'd Googled me or something. On the news they're always talking about scams that target the elderly. So before he could say another word, I told him I wasn't interested and was about to shut the door when he said, 'Dwayne sent me.'"

I waited for her to continue, but she looked like she was straining to swallow. I asked if she was okay.

"I could use a glass of water, if you don't mind fetching it?"

Having been in her kitchen, I knew where she kept the glasses, and I was back with the water in seconds. She drank it all before setting the empty glass on the side table.

"At my age I get dehydrated very easily," she said. "I guess I forget to drink enough during the day. My mouth gets so dry I don't have enough spit to swallow. The doctor keeps telling me I'll wind up in the hospital if I don't drink more."

"Do you want me to refill it?" I asked.

"Not just now, thank you. That glass should hold me till dinner. I left the chicken and potatoes in the oven keeping warm," she added. "Now where was I?"

"The man said he was sent by your son."

"Well, when he said that I couldn't shut the door on him, could I? Of course not," she answered her own question. "But I kept my wits about me. He asked if he could come in. I told him in no uncertain terms that wasn't going to happen. I made him talk to me through the locked screen door. He said Dwayne paid him to bring me a letter. He had to go through all his pockets before he found it. I wasn't surprised the envelope was crumpled and had stains on it. Lord only knows what they were from."

She shuddered. "I opened the screen door just enough for him to slip the letter through. My hands were shaking terribly by then. I was afraid to believe Dwayne was alive after all these weeks without a word from him. I mean how awful would it be to get my hopes up just to have them dashed again? I asked him where Dwayne was. He swore he didn't know. He'd answered an ad for a messenger. He said Dwayne sent him half the money up front and wouldn't send the rest until he received my signature in return. He pulled a pen and a little pad out of his pants pocket and asked me to sign my name on it. I did that and handed it back to him. He stood there, shifting his weight from one foot to the other, like he was waiting for a tip. My son was paying him. If he wanted a tip from me, he should have cleaned up some. I just thanked him and shut the door. I double locked it too, like I do before I go to sleep at night."

"What did the letter say?"

"I have it right here."

She reached for the envelope on the side table. I hadn't noticed it. So much for my observational skills. Oh, Nancy, I still have a lot to learn.

"I want you to read it for yourself," Jane said, holding it out to me. "In case I missed something subtle in the meaning. I think they call it a 'subtext.'"

I took the letter out of the envelope. It was written in pen on the kind of white ruled paper students use.

> *Dear Mom,*
> *I hope you're okay. I'm sorry if I made you worry, but I had to leave town in a hurry. I didn't tell you I was going because I was afraid the police or certain other parties would stake out your house or tap your phone. I'm some place safe for now. This is important—I leased a safety deposit box in your name at the Sentinel Bank branch you use. There's a good deal of money in there for your future. Don't be afraid to use it. Please shred this letter after you read it—just in case.*
> *I'll write to you again when I can.*
> *Love,*
> *Dwayne*

I didn't find any subtext in the letter. It was straightforward, except for the reason he had to leave town quickly. I had a pretty good idea why, but it wasn't because of hidden meaning in the letter. It was because of Amanda's death.

Jane's eyes were riveted on me, waiting for my take on the letter. I saw no reason to burden her with dire speculation. I preferred to leave her with something positive, something that would buoy her spirits. "The letter is mysterious," I said, handing it back to her. "Was there a key with it?"

"Yes, I've hidden it away. I should tell you where," she added as if the thought had just occurred to her. When I started to protest, she said there was no one else she trusted and her memory was not that reliable lately. What would she do if she forgot the hiding place? I finally agreed.

"It's at the bottom of my sewing kit in the closet of the spare bedroom," she said.

"Got it," I said. "No more need to worry about it."

"Now tell me what you think of the letter."

"I think you should focus on the good news in it. You know your son is safe."

"True," she said. "I'm incredibly relieved he's okay, although the words for now trouble me."

"No one has a guarantee about tomorrow or ten minutes from now," I pointed out.

"I never thought of it that way," Jane marveled as if she were seeing the world from a new perspective.

"And don't forget about the money in the safety deposit box. Dwayne has secured your future for you. He's a devoted son." And possibly a killer for hire, but I left out that part. It would be cruel to torture Jane with maybes.

"How do you think he came by that money?" she said, pressing me, apparently determined to wring every last bit of worry from his words.

I'd been wondering the same thing. In deference to her, I went for the nicest answer I could think of. "You told me he worked a lot of overtime. He must have been stashing it away as a surprise for you."

"Or he won a lottery," she said, joining in the game. "Not the one with the billions; those people have to come forward, and I would have heard about it. A scratch-off million or two would be fabulous enough."

"There you go."

"You're so good for my spirits," Jane said with a smile. "Now we'd better eat that chicken before it dries out, or you'll leave here thinking I'm a terrible cook."

* * * *

On my drive home, I called Travis to report on my evening with Jane. "What do you think?" I asked him when I'd finished

"I think the money in that safety deposit box is dirty."

"Murder dirty?"

"What do you think? If Dwayne was barely making ends meet on his salary and Christmas bonus, how else could he have made enough money that his mother wouldn't have to worry about her future?"

We were both quiet, thinking our own thoughts. "There's a problem with this case," I said, finally giving voice to something that had been troubling me for a while.

"There are too many suspects with perfect motives," Travis said for me. "It's been bothering me too."

"Some pearls of wisdom would be good at this point. Have any?"

"If we keep our noses to the grindstone, we'll eventually catch a break. How's that hit you?"

I laughed. "That's awful. But as pathetic as it is, I can't think of anything better."

Chapter 25

The following night, I think every resident of New Camel was glued to his or her TV, computer, tablet, or phone, awaiting the results of the town board vote. I was no exception. Tilly had asked me to join her and Merlin for the "big reveal," as she put it. She'd made strawberry ice cream sandwiches on her version of jumbo Oreos. Depending on which way the vote went, we'd be celebrating with them or using the sugar rush to raise our deflated spirits. The three of us were lined up on her sofa, watching for the breaking-news banner to flash across the screen and interrupt a rerun of NCIS. By the time it finally happened, Merlin had become engrossed in the program and complained bitterly about the interruption. Tilly told him he could have a preemptive ice cream sandwich, and off he went.

The banner gave way to a view of Phil Phillips, our local news anchor, sitting behind his desk, looking somber. Since I didn't know how he felt about the zoning issue, it was hard to guess the result from his face. I imagine neutrality was his goal anyway. He introduced himself and the subject of the breaking news before passing the baton to the reporter in the field, stretching out the process to build tension. This is what passed for big news in our little town.

The reporter thanked the anchor for the handoff and started his spiel with some background every viewer already knew. "The town board convened here at the New Camel Elementary School a short time ago for an up-or-down vote about changing the zoning laws. As you may recall, the Waverly Group's proposal to build a hotel in the freshwater marsh on the eastern end of town depends on that zoning change." He touched his ear piece. "Okay, folks, I've just been told the result is in." He paused for a dramatic beat. "The proposal has squeaked by with a three to two vote. The board has voted to change the zoning laws. Back to you in the studio, Phil."

Tilly and I looked at each other, our mouths hanging open. "How on earth did that happen?" she said once she found her words.

"The way a lot of things seem to happen around here," I said grimly. "Tompkins may have bribed one or more of the board members." I was thoroughly disgusted.

"Which one of you is the traitor?" Tilly demanded as the camera showed the board members filing out of the building and walking to their cars. Police were stationed along their route in case anyone took exception to the results.

"In the end, everyone has their price," I said, wrestling with my own anger and dismay. "It's just a matter of figuring out what it is."

Merlin wandered back into the room, licking his fingers where the melting cookie had stuck to his skin. There was also a ring of chocolate around his mouth. "Hasn't that galoot said which way the vote went yet?" he asked.

"It passed," Tilly told him.

The anchor wished the viewers a good evening and signed off. After a parade of commercials, NCIS resumed.

"My show's back on," Merlin said as he squeezed in between Tilly and me again, "Wait a gall-darned minute! They've gone and skipped over part of the show."

I thought about explaining syndicated reruns and places where the news bulletin hadn't preempted the show, but I just didn't have the patience for the Q and A that would inevitably follow. I took the cowardly way out and followed Tilly into the kitchen for our ice cream sandwiches.

* * * *

"I think I'm more disturbed by the way the vote was manipulated than by the fact that the tone of the town may be forever changed." I was sitting with Lolly in the kitchen of her shop. She'd invited me there for a three o'clock candy break. With school back in session and no scheduled bus tours, it had been a quiet day for both of us. I left a note on the door of my shop, telling any potential customers to look for me at Lolly's.

"I know what you mean," she said. "I'm so frustrated. Why do you think I was up at dawn making candy?"

"I can't honestly say I'm sorry about that part," I mumbled around a mouthful of caramel swaddled in a thick layer of dark chocolate. "I don't know how chocolate ever fell into the hands of mere mortals. It is the closest thing to pure magick."

"Considering it's my livelihood, this mere mortal is beyond grateful that it did. Here, try one of these," she said, passing me a dish of oddly shaped chocolates.

"Nuts?" I asked, taking one.

"You tell me."

"I took a bite. "Walnuts and raisins."

"Keep going."

"Um, pomegranate seeds. Oh, and peanut butter chips."

"My new kitchen-sink chocolates," she said, beaming like a new mother. "You're my beta tester."

"You've got a winner here. I predict you won't be able to keep up with the demand...from me alone."

"At least some good came from Tompkins's chicanery," Lolly said with a sigh. "Speaking of which, while I was lying in bed not sleeping, I was trying to figure out which board member caved."

"You and everyone else. I don't know Corinne or Eddie well enough to guess at their moral code," I said, "but I have been wondering about Patrick. First, he was for the zoning change because it would bring in more tourists and potentially increase his bottom line. He even mentioned his concerns about money to me. But then his son raised his consciousness about the environment, and just like that he changed his position. I can't shake the feeling that a substantial offer of money could have been behind that reversal."

"Hello. Anyone here?" Travis's voice boomed in the quiet shop, making us both jump.

"We're coming," Lolly and I sang out in unison as we covered the short distance from the kitchen into the shop proper.

Travis looked sharp in lean jeans and a crisp white polo. I'd already moved on to light winter gear with a cotton sweater and boots. The two of us appeared to be living in different climates.

"Were you back there planning revenge on Tompkins?" he asked.

"We've been stuffing our faces with chocolate," I confessed.

"And no one thought to invite me?"

"I would have," Lolly said, "if I'd known you were going to be around today." She looked pointedly at me.

I laughed. "Hey, not my fault. I had no idea either."

Lolly liked Travis and never missed an opportunity to tell me so. If I didn't know better, I'd think she was in cahoots with Bronwen and Morgana. "How can I make amends?" she asked him.

"One chocolate-covered strawberry should do the trick, thank you."

Lolly pulled out the entire tray of chocolate dipped fruit and let him choose the one he wanted. He plucked a huge strawberry off the tray and took a bite.

"The best," he said with a satisfied sigh. "When it comes to chocolate, you are without equal. In gratitude, I'll take Kailyn off your hands," he added gallantly.

"Have fun you two. All work and no play...."

* * * *

"What's up?" I asked Travis once we were in Abracadabra. Sashkatu raised a furry eyebrow at the sound of my voice, smacked his lips like the old man he was, and fell back to sleep. Having lived the majority of his life with women, he had minimal interest in men, with the notable exception of Merlin. Of course, that was like comparing apples to orangutans.

"I was going to call you, but then I decided to cheer you up in person," Travis said. "I didn't know Lolly had beaten me to the punch."

I hiked myself up on the countertop, and he did the same. We were sitting inches from each other, which made me ache to be closer. Not for the first time, I wondered why he wasn't feeling the same tug. Or if he was, why he was ignoring it. Had learning my strange lineage permanently destroyed his deepening feelings for me? My thoughts must have bled through to my face because Travis was looking at me with the bewilderment of a caveman trying to understand modern art.

"What's wrong?" he said. "I came here to make you happy, not more miserable."

I forced a smile. "Sorry, my mind wandered. But I'm ready now. Lay that happiness on me."

"I've been thinking about Rusty. Of all the suspects, he was the only one who would have needed to get back into the school building after killing Amanda. Anyone else could have immediately left the grounds. If Rusty had waltzed into the gym through the open emergency doors, an awful lot of people would have seen him. Now Duggan questioned everyone there and, to the best of my knowledge, didn't find a single person who'd seen Rusty outdoors at that time."

"Go on," I said, curious about where he was headed with this reasoning.

"Based on that, I nearly crossed him off our list. But being a journalist, due diligence was browbeaten into me. That would be Browbeating 101, if you're taking notes."

I was following his words so intently that the unexpected aside almost slipped past me. I chuckled a few beats late.

He winked at me and continued. "I wanted to be sure there was no other door Rusty could have used—where he wouldn't have been seen reentering the building. I went down to town hall and asked to see the blueprints for the elementary school."

"I'm surprised that didn't raise any eyebrows. School security is a huge deal these days. You're lucky they didn't call the cops and haul you in for questioning."

"It did get a little sticky. I showed them my personal ID and my network ID, but they weren't buying it until one of the women there recognized me from TV. Even then they would only show me the plans under supervision and for like half a minute. I couldn't take notes or pictures."

"And?"

"There is a door on the side of the building where Amanda was found."

"Did you go to the school to check it out?"

He shook his head. "I think you'll have better luck gaining access to the grounds than I would. You're an alumna, and everyone knows you and your family. Plus, you're a woman. You're less likely to be seen as a threat, especially if you go there after the kids have left for the day."

I looked at my watch. "I can go right now," I said. I was excited to have a new lead to follow, though I wasn't exactly happy that it might point to Rusty's guilt. I still had a bit of a soft spot for the guy.

"I'll wait for you at The Jerk," Travis said. "I never had time for lunch." He leaned closer and planted a kiss on my mouth before jumping down from the counter. "Be careful."

Frozen in place, I watched him walk out. I'd forgotten how good it was to be kissed by him. I sat there for another couple minutes trying to process what it meant, if this was the first step of a new beginning for us. I had to give myself a mental slap to break the heady trance I was falling under. It was time to get my show on the road before the school shut down for the night.

* * * *

Travis was right. I had no trouble getting permission to walk around the school grounds. I didn't mention I was looking for the door. I'd learned it was best to say as little as possible to as few people as possible. Most of the staff had heard I was investigating Amanda's death, so they didn't seem to find my request strange. The vice-principle's only caveat was that I not take photos. I had to leave my phone in his office.

I went out the front entrance and made my way around the building to the spot where Travis had seen the door on the blueprint. And there it was. I hadn't noticed it the night Amanda was killed because there didn't seem to be any exterior light to illuminate it. A coincidence or part of the killer's plan? I tried the door, expecting to find it locked. To my surprise, the knob turned easily in my hand. When I peered inside, it was dark, except for the light coming in behind me. I felt along the walls and located a light switch that turned on a weak fluorescent fixture in the ceiling. I walked in, hoping I didn't bump into Rusty. I shook the thought from my head. Think too much about the negative and the universe will comply. It was one of my grandmother's adages that was finally gaining acceptance with my generation.

The space I was standing in was small, no more than a ten-foot square, and windowless, with a cement floor and peeling green paint on the walls. It appeared to be some sort of anteroom, although it didn't lead to another room. Instead, directly in front of me was a staircase leading down into more darkness. I wanted to kick myself for not thinking to bring a flashlight or a light spell for that matter. Logic dictated that there should be another light switch unless the stairs were only used by nocturnal creatures like raccoons and vampires. I ran my palm over the wall near the stairs and found it. But when I flicked it on, nothing happened. The bulb must have burned out. I considered my options. I could turn around and leave. After all, I'd found the door and fulfilled my purpose in going there. Or I could walk down the stairs and see where they led. Who was I kidding? It wasn't a choice at all.

I estimated that I was halfway down when the spill of light from the anteroom petered out. It was slow going after that since I had no idea how many steps actually lay ahead of me. I made a deal with myself. If I reached the basement floor and found another switch wired to a working light bulb, I'd go on. Otherwise, I'd head back upstairs.

I came off the steps and did another Braille search for light. Once again the switch I found proved worthless. I was disappointed, but a deal was a deal. Besides, what if my soft spot for Rusty was a combination of nostalgia and poor judgment? He could have left the door open, figuring it was just a matter of time before I came snooping around. He could have removed those light bulbs too, putting me at a serious disadvantage in an unfamiliar place in the dark.

When I turned to start the climb back up, I heard the squish and squeak of a man's rubber soles in the anteroom above me. My heart skipped a beat or two, stealing my breath and rocketing my brain into overdrive. I had to find a place to hide. But with no light, no knowledge of the layout, and time rapidly running out, only one possibility came to mind. There might be space beneath the staircase.

I felt my way along the wall to where that space would be if it wasn't a walled-off dead end. Finally luck was with me. But my relief was short-lived. The man descending the stairs turned on a flashlight. Rusty. Who else would know the lights weren't working? I huddled in the darkest shadows at the back of the stairs, willing him not to look in my direction when he reached the basement floor. I knew the spell of invisibility and had used it with limited success in my last investigation. But it required such complete focus that it was difficult under the best conditions, useless with the anxiety and fear already filling my core.

The man moved away from the stairs. I dared to take a quick peek at him as he moved toward a hallway and in the backwash from his flashlight I could see he was roughly Rusty's size. I couldn't remain where I was, or he was bound to see me when he returned and was facing the staircase. I had an idea. If it worked, I might get out of there safely. I would wait until he was far enough away from the staircase to give me a decent lead, then I would race back up. I was young and quick on my feet. Rusty had grown slow with age. He will not catch me. Do you hear me, universe? He will not catch me.

My heart pounding in my ears, I monitored his progress by the glow of the flashlight. When he was far enough away, I came out from the underside of the staircase and sprinted for the steps. I grabbed the hand rail and swung myself in a tight arc onto the bottom step. I was a third of the way up when he shouted, "Don't move!"

I froze. It wasn't Rusty's voice. I held onto the banister to steady myself as I turned into the glare of the flashlight.

"What in hell are you doing here, Ms. Wilde?"

"I can explain, Detective," I said, hoping I could come up with a reason that would appease him.

"I can hardly wait to hear it," Duggan replied. "Here's how we're going to play this. You're going to take yourself down to the precinct, and I'll meet you there as soon as I'm finished here. If you're not there when I arrive, I'll find you and drag you down in handcuffs. Maybe even throw you in jail, so you'll have time to reflect on the benefits of life on the right side of the law."

"I'll be there," I said, refusing to let him intimidate me, "but I haven't done anything wrong." The school had given me permission to walk the grounds. It wasn't my fault if the door was unlocked and there was no sign warning people not to enter. No one in the office had said I couldn't go in. Of course no one had said I could, either. My innocent plea needed some work.

Chapter 26

I called Travis on my way to the precinct to tell him not to wait for me at The Soda Jerk. "I was wondering what was taking you this long," he said after hearing a condensed version of my misadventure. "Are you all right?"

"Yes, I'm fine, though I suspect when Duggan gets there, he's going to do his best to make things unpleasant for me."

"I'll be right there. He'll think twice about using the thumbscrews with a reporter present."

Travis was probably right. The New Camel station house was so small that even in the waiting area, he'd be able to hear everything that went on between Duggan and me. I also liked the idea that Duggan wouldn't be expecting an audience other than Curtis or Hobart, not that I actually expected to be tortured, but a verbal thrashing wasn't on my bucket list either.

I arrived at the station two minutes later and was happy to find Paul Curtis behind the desk. It never hurts to have as many allies as possible when it comes to legal matters. He seemed happy to see me too, but I was pretty sure it was for a different reason.

"I'm glad you found your cat," he said after we helloed.

Thank goodness I'd remembered to call and let him know that the missing feline was waiting at the door of my shop when I returned. Imaginary animals can be so accommodating. If I'd let him continue to search for her, this would have been a much more uncomfortable conversation.

"What brings you in today?" he asked.

"Detective Duggan and I had a little misunderstanding. He asked me to wait for him here to discuss it."

A gross exaggeration, but I didn't want to answer a lot of questions. He'd be treated to the whole sorry tale soon enough. He offered me a seat in the chair across the desk from him, the same one I occupied during my missing-cat report. It was beginning to feel like my seat. Before we could continue our conversation, Travis walked in. He was wearing his journalistic I'll-get-to-the-bottom-of-this face. He introduced himself to Curtis and said he was there as an interested party and to provide support for me. While Curtis was trying to assess exactly what that meant, Travis came to stand behind my chair. He put his hands on my shoulders in a sweet, protective way. I watched Curtis take in this little tableau and register the fact that Travis and I were "together."

"Excuse me, Mr. Anderson," he said, "you'll have to wait in the designated area." The designated area was a grand-sounding name for a small space near the door with a bench that could seat three, cheek to jowl.

I saw the way the two men were sizing each other up. In a bygone era, they might have resorted to dueling over me as if I were chattel and didn't have any say in the matter.

"No problem, Officer," Travis said. He gave my shoulders a squeeze before walking the ten feet back to the waiting area.

For the next five minutes, the three of us sat in an increasingly awkward silence to the point where I was almost relieved when Duggan arrived. He came through a back entrance and, a man on a mission, strode into the room where Curtis and I were sitting. Travis stood, at the ready to do battle for me. Given all the rampant testosterone in the building, I wondered if I might have fared better on my own.

Curtis vacated the padded chair behind the desk and stepped back, deferring to his superior. Without any acknowledgment, Duggan grabbed the arm of the chair and dropped into it at a peculiar angle and with such force that it tipped backward. There were a frenetic couple of seconds as he readjusted his position and wrestled the chair back down onto the floor. An unexpected giggle raced up my throat before I could abort it. I clamped my mouth shut and pretended the resulting noise was a cough. I would have paid good money to see him go tail over teakettle, as my grandmother used to say.

The embarrassing incident didn't help Duggan's mood. He spent a good thirty minutes questioning every why and wherefore of my visit to the school. When he was done, the interview had lasted three times longer than my sojourn there. I answered him truthfully since nothing short of the truth could explain my presence in the basement of the school. He threatened me with a charge of obstructing justice and made it clear that the next time he found me meddling in a police investigation, he'd "arrest my ass," as he put it. He tilted his head toward Travis, who was toeing the invisible line between the waiting area and the rest of the station house. "Your reporter boyfriend there is a witness. I gave you fair warning."

* * * *

"Let me take you to dinner," Travis said as we walked to our cars in the precinct lot. "Some wine, a good meal, a decadent dessert?"

"Are you planning to lecture me about ad-libbing when I was only supposed to be looking for a door? Because I have to tell you, it would not be well received."

Travis laughed. "How can I reproach you when I would have done the same thing?"

"Thank you. I really needed to hear that."

"So, is that a yes to dinner?"

I glanced at my watch. "Oh, wow, I didn't realize how late it is. I left Sashkatu in my shop. I have to pick him up and feed them all. I'm afraid I'll have to pass." I opened my car door and started to climb in.

"Chinese then? Tell me what you like, and I'll bring dinner to you."

"It's a deal."

* * * *

"What did we tell you?" my mother said brightly, her energy cloud popping up between me and the television screen. She was all white and fluffy, which I'd come to think of as a smile. My grandmother was also cheerful when she joined us a second later. I reached around them with the remote to pause the show I was watching.

"Excuse me?" I asked, completely lost.

"We told you to be patient with Travis," Bronwen said.

"Because he's a keeper," Morgana added.

"You may be right," I admitted since they seemed to be expecting an acknowledgment from me. My mother always loved a good I-told-you-so, except when she was the recipient.

"Let's not forget the other reason we stopped by," Bronwen said.

"I haven't. I simply didn't get to it yet." There was a slight dash of pique in Morgana's tone as though she'd been working on her relationship issues with Bronwen but hadn't nailed it yet.

"Sorry for jumping the gun," Bronwen responded, her words sounding like they were coming through a clenched jaw.

I wondered if their progress was being monitored. If they couldn't fool me, they didn't stand a chance of fooling whoever was evaluating them. Or maybe they didn't care if they failed. Maybe they weren't ready to close that final door and leave Tilly and me on our own.

"Kailyn," my mother said, "we've noticed that you're having difficulty teleporting objects to a safe landing, and we have a suggestion."

"I'll try anything." I'd already smashed half a dozen objects, although fortunately not on anyone else's head.

"There may be a solution to the problem right in our family scrolls," Bronwen said. "We were never able to properly decipher the sections written in Old English, but I'll bet Merlin can. He can be your Rosetta Stone."

I took the scrolls from their hiding place under the area rug and beneath the hardwood floor in the living room. They were rolled into dozens of protective tubes, a project Bronwen had undertaken in an effort to better conserve them. My grandmother was determined to pass them on to future generations of Wildes without entrusting them to "the cold clutches of a computer." She'd explained to me, "The contraption might succeed in preserving the words, but it could never capture the spirit of the women who wrote them." It's hard to argue with emotion, so I didn't try. I did, however, have a secret plan to transcribe them into my computer, just in case.

I told my aunt Tilly I was bringing the scrolls to her and why. At first she said it was a dandy idea, but by the time I loaded up my car and drove there, I found my aunt in calamity baking mode. She'd whipped up a batch of chocolate chip cookies, because the prospect of being responsible for such a treasure had made her a fidgety bundle of nerves. And the prospect of monitoring how Merlin used them had rendered her nearly apoplectic.

I did my best to address her concerns while she went on bustling about the kitchen. "We make Merlin wear cotton gloves when he reads the scrolls," I said. "We make him promise not to go near them unless you or I are in the room. We don't allow him to eat or drink in the room where they're being kept. And we threaten to send him out into the cold, cruel world on his own the very first time he breaks any of the rules." Not that we would, of course, but we needed some kind of leverage to make sure he complied. What else could we use against a legendary wizard who could, on one of his better days, turn us into maggots if he chose to?

The timer for the cookies rang, and I suggested she make tea for all of us. It was a measure of her anxiety that she didn't think to make it herself. We planned to sit in her cozy kitchen, soothed by the aroma of warm cookies, while I explained the mission and the rules to Merlin. If he had any objections, the chocolate chip cookies should help to sweeten the deal.

Chapter 27

The Waverly Corporation didn't waste any time breaking ground. The ink was barely dry on the revised zoning laws and the state and federal permits when they brought in heavy equipment to drain the marsh so construction could begin. The site attracted a lot of attention, slowing traffic in and out of New Camel to a crawl. Tour buses, businesspeople, and anyone who had an appointment to keep were outspoken in their disgust over the situation. Those who were in favor of the hotel, including the mayor, wisely kept their own counsel, avoiding the topic at all cost. More than once, I saw Tompkins cross to the other side of the street to avoid certain constituents.

Regardless of their feelings about the hotel, everyone appeared to be interested in what was happening at the marsh. I was no better than anyone else. I took advantage of the snail's pace crawl by the site to check things out. I'd never seen equipment of the kind being used there. According to the Watkins Glen Journal, one of the strange amphibious vehicles was a Marsh Buggy and the other, somewhat more conventional one, a Marsh Excavator. But nothing prepared me for the headline the next day, screaming that a body was found at the bottom of the marsh.

Work was halted while dredging equipment was brought in to look for evidence and other bodies. If traffic suffered before this discovery, it was at a virtual standstill now. Police were dispatched to keep things moving, but they met with only limited success. We were in for a long siege. There was, however, a silver lining in the situation, at least for me. Travis was spending nearly all his time in the area as point man on the evolving story. Once again the nation's eyes were focused on New Camel. Two murders in small-town America made for good copy "from sea to shining sea."

Without information to fuel the rumor mill, conjecture filled the vacuum. When someone speculated about the identity of the body, by the next morning the grapevine had turned it into fact. Gossip in our town was nothing new, but it now galloped from mouth to ear in record time. For that reason, I was super-careful about what I said and to whom I said it. My dear aunt Tilly didn't even make the cut because she often didn't think before she spoke. Although her intent was never malicious, she'd ruined a number of surprise parties over the years. Morgana and Bronwen had finally solved the problem by keeping her as much in the dark as the celebrant. That's why only two people on planet Earth made it onto my list: Elise and Travis. I didn't believe anything I heard, unless it came from Travis. And if he told me something on the QT, I didn't repeat it to Elise, much as I trusted her. It wasn't my decision to make.

My opinion was that the body in the marsh was one Dwayne Davies. He was a perfect candidate because he had gone missing so suddenly. In my scenario, Fletcher paid him to eliminate Amanda. After the deed was done, Dwayne was too much of a liability for Fletcher to let him live. So it was good-bye Dwayne as well.

In a press conference less than twenty-four hours after the body was discovered, Detective Duggan announced that no ID was found on the victim. "However," he said, "with the help of a sketch artist and computer technology, we now have an image we believe to be a reasonable representation of our John Doe. We're asking for the public's help in identifying him. Please take a good look at the picture and call us if you recognize this man. You have my personal assurance that you will remain anonymous."

The image that filled the TV screen was not, by any stretch of the imagination, Dwayne Davies. At least not the Dwayne Davies in his mother's photographs. I was enormously relieved for Jane Davies but disappointed in my instincts as a sleuth.

"Do you know how long the body was in the marsh?" a reporter called out as Duggan turned away from the microphone. He kept right on going, descending the podium without a backward glance.

I turned off the TV and reached for the phone. Too many unnecessary words. I stopped halfway through punching in Travis's number. Given the circumstances, I shouldn't be bothering him. He was probably up to his neck in work. Five minutes later he called me.

Forgoing hello, he asked, "Were you watching?"

"Yes. Where are you?"

"On my way back to New Camel," he said. "I had the day off, and I was taking care of some personal stuff in the city. I just saw the picture on my phone. Do you recognize the guy?"

"No, that would have made things too easy," I said. We hadn't yet solved

Amanda's death, and now we had another. "If John Doe isn't from around here, his death might not even be connected to the new hotel. If this keeps up, New Camel's claim to fame will be as the murder capital of the country."

"Let's not get ahead of ourselves. We'll have more to go on after the autopsy is completed. Here's a thought. Maybe the guy was following directions from his navigation system or his cell phone. He wouldn't be the first one who wound up in water."

"Nice try, except they didn't find a car in the marsh."

* * * *

It was hard to believe that five days had passed since Travis suggested I call the woman from the EPA to check out the rest of Patrick's story. So much had been happening that my head felt like it was in a perpetual spin. I couldn't let it go any longer. The next morning, as soon as the clock struck nine, I placed a call to the closest branch of the EPA. After doing battle with the automated system, I was routed to a person by the name of Devon. Instead of getting into a lengthy explanation, I told him I attended a wonderful EPA-sponsored program at New Camel high school and wanted to speak to Melanie Sharpe, the woman who conducted it.

Devon was polite but insistent that he was qualified to answer any questions I had. We sparred for a good few minutes, getting nowhere. "Okay, okay," I said, finally. "I would like to know if Ms. Sharpe also spoke to Patrick Griffin while she was in New Camel."

"I can check that for you," Devon said. He was back on the line in a minute "I have Ms. Sharpe's calendar up on my computer, and I see she was scheduled to make the presentation at the high school. Please hold for another moment." When he returned, he told me that she filed her report on the presentation but made no mention of any additional stops in the town.

"Thank you, Devon. I appreciate your help. But maybe I can leave a message on her voice mail too? That way she can decide if she wants to get back to me."

"If I helped you, I don't see why you need to leave her a message," he said with a surly edge to his words.

I'd been patient for long enough with Devon's little power trip. Although I rarely used it, I knew a spell that could make a person agreeable. It only worked for seconds at a time. Making someone behave in a way that went against their nature or their will was one of those spells that Merlin considered gray magick. Subverting someone's will for longer than that or for dark purposes crossed the dangerous line into black magick. It had been drummed into me at a young age that our family held no truck with the evil side of sorcery.

I murmured the words of the spell so softly that Devon could barely hear them.

"Listen to me
"And do as I bid thee
"As long as no harm
"To anyone be."

When he asked me to repeat what I said, I asked him to connect me to Ms. Sharpe's voice mail instead.

"No problem," he said. "Have a good day."

In my message, I said I had a question about her recent presentation in New Camel and would appreciate a call when she had a moment. I added my phone number and thanked her in advance. I'd done all I could.

The rest of the day flew by in a blur. The tour bus that was scheduled to arrive at ten was right on time. The one that arrived fifteen minutes later, was actually scheduled for the following week. There was a little dustup at the New Camel Tourism Bureau, which took care of scheduling tour groups, among other things. The bus company insisted that the scheduling office made the mistake. The scheduling coordinator, a lofty title for the single employee who ran the office, insisted the bus company was in error.

The passengers on the second bus had apparently become restless and decided to disembark while the problem was being ironed out. They milled around in the street outside the bureau, the more vocal venting their irritation loudly enough for everyone to hear. The passengers from the first bus were having trouble weaving their way through the crowd to reach the shops they wanted to visit. It took the mayor's intervention to settle the ruffled feathers by saying both groups were welcome to be there.

Lolly and I heard the hubbub because the bureau was just two doors down from Abracadabra and her shop. We stepped outside at the same time to see what was going on. Tilly, who was busy baking, either didn't hear the noise or wasn't curious about it. And if Tilly was baking, Merlin was a rapt audience.

Two busloads of tourists proved to be an embarrassment of riches. As people trooped into my shop nonstop and the volume of noise escalated, Sashkatu jumped ship for the calmer shores of Tea and Empathy. I heard him caterwauling at the closed connecting door until Tilly or Merlin let him in. Thirty minutes later, I was wishing I could have followed him.

All the people trying to pass each other in the narrow aisles kept knocking jars off shelves. I spent so much time cleaning up broken glass and the contents of the jars that I couldn't properly answer questions or ring up purchases in a timely fashion. Some would-be customers abandoned their full baskets and left in a huff. It was a no-win situation. If I ignored the mess, someone could slip on it, and then I'd be slapped with a lawsuit. They didn't seem to understand that no one had told the merchants to expect such a crowd.

When I heard people grumbling that I should hire more help or my business would go belly up, I knew how the camel felt when that final straw landed on him. The grumblers were awfully lucky I didn't dabble in black magick.

I've never been so happy to see buses heading out of town. I surveyed the mess around me. Too bad I couldn't just wiggle my nose to put things right. There was still breakage to clean up and merchandise to reshelve, but I flopped into the customer chair, done in. That's where Tilly found me an hour later. Compared to me, she looked fresh and perky.

"Good Lord," she said, clearly shocked by the condition of my shop. "What happened?"

"Too much of a good thing," I said. "You're lucky you work by appointment now."

"As soon as I saw the swarms of people, I locked my door and put a sign in the window that said No Available Appointments. I stationed Merlin at the door to let in the right folks at their assigned times. I had to pay him in baked goods, but it was worth every cookie and scone I had on hand, plus the promise of a tray of brownies in the future. He can drive a hard bargain."

When I didn't laugh or say anything, Tilly gave me an appraising look. "You are positively whipped, sweetheart. I'm a fool for not seeing that right off." She clucked her tongue. "Instead, I go babbling on about how clever I am and what an easy day I had."

"It's okay," I said.

"It most certainly is not. I'm going to roll up my sleeves and help you get this place back in shape."

"But you don't have sleeves," I said, tired to the point of silliness.

It wasn't all that funny, but maybe it was my solemn delivery that caused us both to start giggling like a couple of kids. Once we recovered, we set to work sweeping glass off the floors and reshelving the dozens of items that had been left wherever customers happened to be when they lost patience and walked out. Things were piled on display tables, in empty spaces on the wrong shelves, on the floor, and on the counter. I didn't need a calculator to tell me I lost a lot of revenue to the chaos. Perhaps more important, I'd lost the goodwill of many potential customers.

I was putting the last jar of skin softener back where it belonged when Tilly called to me from the front of the shop. She didn't sound happy. I hurried over to her, wondering what else this day had in store for me. I found her standing at the counter where one of the shopping baskets full of merchandise had been forsaken. She was holding a sheet of white paper and looking as grim as she'd sounded.

"What is that?" I asked.

She held the paper out to me. The message on it had been printed from a computer. There was no mistaking what it said: "If I can get in here, I can get in anywhere. You can't hide from me."

For my aunt's sake, I did my best not to react, but it wasn't easy. This message shook me more than the earlier one painted on my fence. It was less emotional but somehow more chilling. The wording was as well honed as the knife used to slit Amanda's throat. And now the killer had been here, in my shop, maybe mere inches away from me.

"This is serious," Tilly said. "How was he able to get inside? If the wards were working, they should have picked up on the darkness in him and kept him out."

"With all the people coming and going today, there might have been too much confusion for the wards to work properly." I had no other way to explain why the powerful spell of protection had failed me for the first time in my life.

"I know you were overwhelmed today, but humor me," Tilly said. "Close your eyes and think back. Are you sure you didn't catch a glimpse of a familiar face before you were distracted by something else?"

I had everything to gain and nothing to lose. I leaned back against the counter, closed my eyes, and tried to recall a familiar face among the shifting waves of strangers. It was no use. I looked at Tilly and shook my head, sure that Nancy Drew would have spotted the killer.

Chapter 28

We were getting nowhere fast hunting down Amanda's killer. Travis's coverage of her death was reduced to snippets of local color designed to keep the story in the public mind until real news came along. The case was always in my thoughts, regardless of what else I was doing. It didn't matter if I was busy with customers, the minutiae of running the business or the upkeep of a household that included six furries, it ran like a loop through my mind—motive and opportunity—over and over. I wanted to shout, "Will the real killer please stand up?"

Alan Boswell became a wealthy man when Amanda died before signing the divorce decree. All that money added up to a hell of a motive.

As for Rusty, unrequited love may have finally caused him to snap after Amanda's last rejection.

Dwayne Davies had been worried about losing his job and angry because Fletcher had undervalued him. A bonus and recognition by the boss may have been enough incentive for Dwayne to do his dirty work for him.

The fact that Patrick Griffin had changed his position on the hotel troubled me, but it didn't point to a motive for slashing Amanda's throat, especially since they were on the same side of the issue at the time of her murder. He claimed his change of heart was due to his son's efforts, plus a single conversation with the EPA representative, which still had to be verified.

In one of those strange coincidences that aren't coincidental, Ms. Sharpe from the EPA called as I was thinking about her. I asked her to hold while I finished up with a customer.

"I got your message, Ms. Wilde," she said when I picked up the phone again. "How may I help you?"

I thanked her for getting back to me. "I'm hoping you can answer a question that came up as part of an ongoing investigation in New Camel."

I was careful to avoid the words murder and killer. I didn't want her to think I was trying to implicate her in the crime.

"Are you talking about the murder of that woman on the town board," she asked, "or the John Doe they found in the marsh?"

"The town board murder," I said, feeling foolish for thinking that like Superman's glasses, clever wording could mask the obvious truth.

"I'll try to answer your question," she said after a brief hesitation.

I could hear the wariness in her tone and assured her that she had no cause for concern. "It has to do with a program you recently presented at the high school here," I said to provide her with some context.

"Okay."

"By the way," I interrupted myself, "you really reached a lot of people that day, most important, the kids who were there."

"Thank you for that," she said, her voice warming. "We don't usually find out how effective our programs are, though I understand there are surveys in the works."

"I'd just like to know if you stopped by Christopher Griffin's house to speak to his father after your presentation."

"As a matter of fact, I did," she said.

"Thank you. When I tried to reach you the other day, I spoke to Devon Crowley."

"Ah yes, Devon," she said, trying to swallow a groan but not quite succeeding. "He's very—how shall I put it—take-charge. I imagine he told you there was nothing about a visit to the Griffins in my report."

"He did."

"The answer is simple. My reports don't include what I do on my own time."

I asked myself if I believed her and decided I did. I was more than happy to dismiss the irritating Devon.

"Chris came up to me at the end of the program," she went on. "He was all fired up about the possibility of the marsh there being drained. He told me his dad's vote could stop it from happening. Then he all but begged me to stop by the house to speak to him directly."

"I was under the impression the Waverly Corporation acquired all the necessary permits," I said.

"Yes, they did. I checked into it myself. But just because they were granted the permits doesn't always mean it was the right call."

Although she stopped short of any outright accusations, her meaning was clear. Decisions at the agency were not immune to influence by interests with deep pockets. It didn't surprise me. It was the fodder of daily news reports—kickbacks, bribes, and influence peddling were part of doing business at all levels of the government.

I thanked her, hoping that if our conversation had been recorded "in an attempt to improve their service," she didn't get into trouble on my account.

* * * *

Later that day, Lolly escorted a young woman into my shop. When the door chimes jingled, I poked my head out of the aisle where I'd been restocking our best-selling depilatory cream. "Hi," I said, walking to the counter to greet them.

The young woman looked about my age, but there was a hardness to her, as if life had knocked her around some. Her hair was a brassy blonde, and she had on enough makeup to throw off her balance on the spiky-heeled boots she was wearing.

"This is Tammy," Lolly said without preamble. "Tammy, this is Kailyn. I would trust her with my life, which means you can too."

Tammy's expression said she was reserving judgment on that. She came up with an uncertain smile that quickly withered.

"I want you to tell Kailyn what you just told me," Lolly coaxed her.

Tammy looked from her to me and back again. When she spoke, her voice was hard too. "I changed my mind. I don't want to do this." She turned away from us and toward the door as if she were about to run.

Lolly grabbed her forearm. "This is not just about your relationship with Alan. This is about keeping anyone else from being killed," she said with what I'd dubbed her Iron Grandma expression. If any of her grandchildren misbehaved, that expression shut them down without the need of a single word. How such a sweet, rosy-cheeked face could morph into Iron Grandma ranked up there with the other great mysteries of the universe.

"I was wrong to tell you those things. I just wanted to badmouth him is all. Alan's not capable of that kind of violence."

"Don't kid yourself," Lolly said, "Everyone is capable of violence given the right circumstances."

Tammy was clearly more resistant than most to Lolly's alter ego, making me wonder if she'd known a lot more than a stern face in her childhood. Lolly must have arrived at the same conclusion. In the blink of an eye, she was a kindly grandma once more, purveyor of fine chocolates.

"Tammy, Tammy," she clucked, "I know you have a good heart. I know you want to do the right thing here. What if Alan is the killer? What if he decides he doesn't want you hanging around anymore?"

The possibility of her own demise seemed to reach Tammy. Her face gave away the battle being waged in her mind "All right," she said finally. "I'll tell her."

Lolly lowered herself into the customer chair with a small groan. She rarely complained, but once, after a particularly busy week, she told me the hardest part of her job was spending most of the day on her feet.

I hopped onto the counter. Tammy could have joined me, but she elected to remain upright, teetering slightly on her heels. "It's like this," she began, "I met Alan a few years back. He's old and not much to look at, but he treated me nice, made me feel special, you know?" I bobbed my head. "I'm no fool, though; I knew if his wife wiggled her pinky at him, he'd dump me and run back home, not because he loved her; it was just for the money. When she started really pushing for the divorce, he sort of came unglued. He was angry a lot of the time, especially if he drank too much. But he never hit me or nothing," she was quick to add, which made me think maybe he had.

"I understand," I said.

"Go on," Lolly urged like the trainer in a boxer's corner. "You're doing fine."

"Anyway, when Alan was in one of those moods, he paced around his apartment cursing and talking to himself but aloud. One night I heard him say he'd kill her. He'd kill her before he'd let her cheat him out of his rightful share."

"He said those exact words: 'I'll kill her'?"

"That's what I said. Are you calling me a liar?" She seemed genuinely insulted.

"Not at all, Tammy. But sometimes, in a stressful situation, a person's memory isn't completely reliable."

"My memory is just fine, thank you."

"I'm sorry if I gave you the impression I didn't believe you."

"Well, okay," she said grudgingly.

"You need to tell Kailyn what you told Detective Duggan too," Lolly reminded her.

"I said Alan was over at my place for dinner the night Amanda was killed."

"Was he?" I asked.

"Yeah, he just got there a little late," she said with a sudden interest in the floor. She clearly didn't want to look me in the eye. It would have been a perfect opportunity for me to point out that she had lied to Duggan, but I took the high road and let it pass.

"How late was Alan?" I asked.

"Thirty, maybe forty minutes." Her tone had lost some of its edge.

I wanted to believe it was because I'd won her respect by not calling her out on the lying issue.

"I was really angry because I'd made sloppy joes, one of his favorites."

"What time did you expect him there?"

"Six thirty," she said miserably.

A perfect window for killing Amanda. "What was his excuse for being late?"

"He said it was none of my business."

"Did he act strangely when he got there? Preoccupied or antsy?"

"I don't know. Like I told you, he'd been acting squirrelly for a while. Look, I gotta go," she said, turning abruptly and heading for the door as fast as her stilettos would allow.

"You did the right thing," Lolly called after her.

"Does she always come by to pour her heart out to you?" I asked after the door closed behind her.

"From time to time," Lolly said. "She comes for her chocolate fix, and if there's no one else in the shop, we get to talking. She's upset because ever since Alan inherited the money and the house, he doesn't call or come around much anymore. He flaunts his wealth and women flock to him, fawn over him. Tammy is yesterday's news. I can't help feeling sorry for her." Lolly hauled herself out of the chair, her joints popping and grinding with the music of advancing age.

"I guess when Tammy provided Alan with that alibi, things between them were still okay. She lied to protect the man she loved."

"Exactly," Lolly said. "She's not stupid. She realized that even if Alan didn't kill Amanda, circumstantial evidence might convict him anyway. He had a great motive, and he was unaccounted for during the critical period."

"I bet she's having second thoughts about lying for him now," I said. "The trouble is she's painted herself into a bad corner. If she goes back to Duggan and confesses, he can arrest her on charges of obstructing justice, aiding and abetting, and anything else he can think of.

"That's why parents teach their children not to lie," Lolly said. "It always comes back to bite you. It's a pity Tammy has to learn that the hard way. Now I'm going home to take a nice warm bath."

Chapter 29

The cats were in a tizzy. Merlin hadn't been in my house for several days. They knew from the moment Tilly's car pulled into the driveway that he was nearby. They came running from wherever they were to gather at the front door in two rows facing each other like a mini honor guard. Only Sashkatu took his regal time in joining them. He could afford to be blasé. Most days he saw Merlin at my aunt's shop.

I stayed on the sofa, watching the news. Tilly preferred to let herself in with her key. She claimed a family member shouldn't need to ring the bell or wait for someone to let her in like a common visitor. In the beginning, her unexpected appearances caused the rest of us some heart-hammering moments. Fortunately, we adjusted to them without a single emergency room visit. As the family matriarch, Bronwen could have put an end to the practice, but she never did. The family allowed Tilly some latitude in her behavior because, well, because she was dear, sweet Tilly. I saw no reason to change things now that my mother and grandmother were gone.

That evening, Tilly was fiddling with the key for a lot longer than usual. I could hear Merlin haranguing her, but I stayed where I was until one of them finally rang the bell. When I opened the door, Tilly walked in with a sheepish expression.

"I took the wrong key with me," she mumbled. "I'd appreciate it if you didn't tell Morgana and Bronwen. They'll never let me forget it."

I squelched the grin forming on my lips and gave her a hug instead. "It'll be our secret."

"How did my inflexible sister ever have a child like you?" she marveled, hugging me back.

"Make way, make way," Merlin said gruffly, trying to walk around us without stepping on one of his feline groupies.

"What happened to Tex?" I whispered to Tilly.

"I think he's so excited about finding what you need that he forgot about Tex for now."

Merlin had planted himself in the middle of the sofa, and the cats were stuck to him like barnacles on a ship. As usual, Sashki opted for the high ground on top of the sofa. Tilly and I took the two armchairs facing it. I waited for Merlin to tell me why he'd come, but he just sat there with a Mona Lisa smile on his face as if waiting for me to pry the news out of him.

"I understand you have a surprise for me," I said finally.

"That I do."

"I'll be ever so grateful if you tell me what it is."

His eyes twinkled. "Yes, I imagine you will be."

I had no idea how much longer he intended to tease me, but I can play games as well as anyone. "After you tell me, we can celebrate with ice cream," I said. Merlin's eyes widened, and he licked his chops like the golden retriever who lived next door. I'd clearly scored.

"What flavors?" he asked.

"Peach and vanilla."

"You win," he said, getting to his feet and shedding cats as he did. "I found you a spell to keep your crockery from smashing into my head again."

I put up my hand. "Wait a minute. Will this spell also insure a soft landing for anything or anyone being teleported?"

"Quite so," he replied, already on his way to the kitchen.

By the time Tilly and I trailed after him, he was ensconced in a chair awaiting service. I looked at him with my arms crossed over my chest. "The deal was for you to give me the spell and then we celebrate."

"Oh bother." He reached into the pocket of his gunny-sack pants and pulled out a crumpled piece of paper.

I took it from him and unfolded it. Reading his handwriting was almost as difficult as deciphering the Old English in the scrolls. I turned to my aunt. "Did you see this?"

"I did," she said, opening her tote, which she'd carried with her from the living room. She fished out a sheet of paper and handed it to me with a flourish. "I knew you'd need this."

"You were able to figure out what he wrote?"

"Of course not. I made him dictate it while I typed."

* * * *

Half a gallon of ice cream later, Tilly and Merlin were headed home. I sat back at the table with the spell Merlin had found. I'd read it quickly while they were there, but I wanted to read it again without distractions:

From here and now to there and then,
Attract not change, nor harm allow.
Safe passage guarantee all souls.
As well as lesser, mindless things.

It was succinct and covered my concerns. I liked it. If I hadn't been so tired, I might have given it a trial run. But I knew it would be better to wait until I was rested and my powers of concentration were optimal.

The phone rang as I was drifting off to sleep. I grudgingly reached for it. "Hello," I said, slurring the word, my tongue sluggish from my fatigue. If it was a solicitor, he was going to get an earful, if my tongue ever woke up.

"Hi," Travis responded, entirely too awake and upbeat. "Sorry if I woke you," he said, not sounding the least bit apologetic. "Guess what's scheduled for eight o'clock tomorrow morning?"

"Breakfast?" It was all I could think of, with half my brain still stuck in dreamland.

"The ME is issuing his report on John Doe."

It took another few seconds, but his words finally succeeded in penetrating my brain. I understood his elation. He finally had real news to report instead of just rehashing other cases in the area's history. "I assume you'll be there for it," I said.

"Front and center. Just wanted you to know. Go back to sleep; we'll talk tomorrow."

The next morning, I was up before my alarm rang. I saw to the cats, had coffee, showered, and dressed well before the morning news broke away for the ME's report. Travis appeared on the screen. He was explaining where he was and why. "They're about to get started," he said as his cameraman swung away to focus on Mayor Tompkins, Police Chief Gimble, Detective Duggan and ME Charlie Cuthburton filing onto the podium. They took their seats behind a table that was set up with a microphone for each of them.

"Good morning," Cuthburton said. "I'm here to present my findings on the deceased John Doe found in the marsh." The silence in the room deepened as if everyone there was literally holding their breath. "Based on the condition of the body, I estimate that the victim was in the marsh somewhere between two and three months. Decomposition was delayed to some degree because he was in the mud at the bottom of the marsh. Cause of death was a bullet fired from a forty-five-caliber handgun. From the bullet's trajectory after entering the body, we know that it entered the victim's back and tore through his lungs and heart, killing him instantly.

"Fortunately, for the purposes of the police investigation, the bullet became lodged in his sternum. I was able to retrieve it intact. I found no other evidence of trauma to the body." The moment he paused, every reporter in the room had his hand in the air. Some were already throwing out questions. "I only have time to answer a few of you," the ME said, pointing to a woman in the middle of the pack.

"Is there anything about the deceased or the way he died to suggest that he and Amanda Boswell might have been murdered by the same person?"

"Detective," the ME said, "do you want to take this one?"

Duggan cleared his throat. "From what we know at this point that doesn't seem likely. Given time to plan, most killers will stick with the same type of weapon, especially if it proved successful in the past. That was clearly not the case here. Amanda Boswell was killed with a knife and John Doe with a gun. In addition, the body of John Doe was disposed of in the marsh, presumably to avoid detection, while hers was left in plain sight, perhaps to send a message."

The ME scanned the audience and selected a man near the back. "Did the computer-generated picture of John Doe get any hits?"

"We ran it through NAMUS, the National Missing and Unidentified Persons System, but there was no match. Nor did it match anyone in the country with a criminal record. We even checked with the Doe Network, an international missing-persons database. Again nothing." He nodded at Travis, who'd worked his way up to the front.

"Were there enough remnants of his clothing that might help police track down where he bought them or where he came from?"

"A few, which we handed over to the police. I can't speak to whether or not they've been of any help. Detective?"

"I won't be discussing any specifics of the investigation while it's ongoing," Duggan said.

"Follow-up?" Travis said before Cuthburton could move on to someone else. The ME gave him a nod. "I'm sure the clothing was not in good shape after so many months in the water, but did you get any sense they were in rough shape before the victim was dumped there?"

"That's an interesting question," Cuthburton said. "It occurred to me as well. I've seen clothing on other bodies that spent significant time in water, but they didn't appear quite as ragged as the clothing on our John Doe. I want to make it clear that this is purely subjective and should not be confused with scientific data."

A low buzz of comments spread through the crowd.

"That's all we have for you today, folks," Gimble said, rising and leading the others off the stage. The press continued throwing questions at them until they were out of sight.

* * * *

"Why did you want to know about the clothing?" I asked Travis. We were eating a late dinner at the Caboose. Our burgers were parked in front of us, mine with cheddar and his with cheddar and bacon, each accompanied with a heap of crispy fries.

He popped a fry into his mouth before replying. "If he was a vagrant, it would help explain why nobody reported him missing. It's possible he didn't have any family or friends to care if he dropped out of sight."

"I'm impressed."

"Don't be. I'm sure the police considered the possibility from the get-go. But if you tell the public he was a hobo, they stop paying attention. They figure it can't be anyone they would know."

I was about to take a bite of my burger, but I put it back down. "That's so sad. To be all alone in the world without anyone to care if..." Tears welled up in my eyes. I tried to blink them back, but I wasn't entirely successful. "Sorry," I said, wiping away the couple that escaped.

"No need to be. Strong women with soft hearts have always been my weakness."

"Oh really?" I said, grateful for the banter. "And just how many of us have you known?"

He frowned in concentration as he counted silently on his fingers.

"Okay, okay," I said and laughed when he reached ten. "I've changed my mind. I don't need to know."

We attacked our burgers as though we hadn't eaten in a week. It was late for me to be eating, and I was famished.

"It's been months since I was last here," Travis said, coming up for air. "I always forget how great their food is."

"I never eat burgers anywhere else." I nibbled on my fries. "Now that the police know the bullet came from a forty-five, can't they just look at registration records and interview anyone who has that type of gun?"

"Sure they can. Everyone who buys a handgun in this state is legally obligated to register the weapon with the police. But people with criminal intent never do."

"So unless an average, law-abiding citizen turns to a life of crime and is stupid enough to use his registered handgun, knowing the caliber of the bullet isn't going to be a big help."

Travis nodded, too busy chewing to speak.

"Then I guess there's no point having your buddy check the records," I said.

He swallowed and took a swig of his beer. "I'll still ask him, but I'm not expecting to find a smoking gun. Pun intended."

I laughed. "I'm going to chalk that up to fatigue."

Chapter 30

I decided to open my shop an hour late the next morning. I wanted to try my ancestor's protection spell at home, where I was assured of peace and quiet—or as assured as I could be, factoring Tilly and Merlin into the equation. I rose at my usual time, but Sashkatu slept in, making me wonder if he'd read my brainwaves and knew he had time for some extra shut-eye.

Although I was tempted to try the spell on myself, the memory of that first disastrous attempt was enough to make me proceed with caution. I went downstairs and fed the other cats, who'd never shown any signs of psychic awareness with my mother or me. Then again, she'd died before she could work with them on that bond. And I simply hadn't had the time to do it now that I was the only one left to do the work previously done by three.

I thought about making coffee but decided against it since I didn't know what effect the caffeine might have on the spell. This first test of it should be as pure as I could make it. I sat down at the kitchen table, where I'd already placed a small glass bowl. I'd chosen the upstairs bathroom for its landing site. The room with the hardest surfaces should give me a definitive answer about the spell's protective qualities and my ability to use it. I began with meditation to focus my mind and establish its control over the magickal energy in my body. Once I felt fully engaged, I began:

"From here and now to there and then,
"Attract not change, nor harm allow.
"Safe passage guarantee all souls
"As well as lesser, mindless things."

I envisioned the words coupling with my energy and flowing from me toward the bowl, covering it with a fine fabric of light. I repeated the spell twice more. The bowl shimmered for an instant and then vanished. There was no reason to celebrate yet. This part of the teleportation I'd done a number of times. It was the landing of the bowl in the proper place and without damage that I was hoping for. I listened for the sound of breaking glass but heard only a thump. A promising sound.

I raced up the stairs to see for myself if the spell had worked. I'd left the bathroom door closed to prevent the cats from going in and getting hurt like Merlin had. I opened the door slowly, afraid to look in and be disappointed. The bowl was sitting on the tile floor as if I'd carefully set it down there, which I had in a sense. "Yes!" I shouted, forgetting I might startle Sashki out of a deep sleep. At his age, a heart attack didn't seem out of the question.

When I went down the hall to my bedroom to check on him, he was stretching his legs, a process that took longer with each advancing year. I sat down beside him on the bed to stroke his back. He twitched as if to be rid of my hand and padded to the end of the bed where he could climb down his stairs. It was a classic snub for waking him with my victory shout. At least I hadn't put him in cardiac arrest.

I followed him down to the kitchen like an obedient servant and fixed his breakfast. He dined in the privacy of the powder room to prevent any of his brethren from joining him for second helpings. The few times that had happened, a major brawl ensued with all six of them joining in the fray like a bench-clearing fight in baseball. After Sashki was settled for his first nap of the day, I practiced using the spell twice more with the same encouraging results.

I was pulling on jeans when Bronwen's cloud appeared before me. "Well done, my dear," she said with thunder applause.

I tugged up the zipper. "Thanks. How are you?"

"I can't complain," she said, though I suspected she could. "I popped in to give you a bit of advice."

"I'm always happy to see you," I said, determined not to let her get under my skin and ruin my morning's victory. I walked around her to open the armoire and take out my red cotton sweater that was a good weight for the fickle days of autumn. When I turned around, I almost smacked right into her. I jumped back. I'd had a preview of what can happen if flesh and bone came into contact with an energy cloud, courtesy of Merlin. I wasn't eager to try it for myself. With fuller contact, electrocution seemed like a distinct possibility.

"Are you paying attention?" Bronwen asked.

I detoured carefully around her. "A hundred percent," I said. If I hadn't been before, I certainly was now. Maybe that's why she came close enough to scare me. Everything my grandmother did had a purpose.

"You did a beautiful job with the bowl, and I'm sure you're going to try it on yourself as soon as you have time. I know I would. Just promise me one thing. You'll take into account the fact that our magick has not been consistently reliable of late. Each and every time you try it on yourself, test it first by teleporting an object. If that goes well, by all means, proceed. If not, let it go for another day."

It seemed like reasonable advice. "I promise," I said.

"Each and every time?" she said, pressing me.

"Each and every time. And please tell my mother about my promise so I don't have to go through this again with her."

"As soon as we're on speaking terms," she said and was gone before I could ask any questions.

* * * *

I was busy showing a new customer around the store that afternoon when the door chimes jingled. I was in the last aisle with Lorna, explaining which night cream would be best for her skin. I excused myself to see who'd come in. The three murders that summer were taking their toll on me. I jumped at the smallest noises and imagined killers behind every door. I was surprised and relieved to find Jane Davies standing on the threshold, holding the door open as if she were prepared to escape at a moment's notice. When she saw me, her face relaxed, and she stepped inside, letting the door close behind her.

"There you are," she said. "For a moment, I thought I was in the wrong shop." She was looking around as she spoke, and I could tell she was unsettled by the idea of magick, or at least the kind of magick I was selling. Like a lot of people, she was probably comfortable with the old sawing-a-woman-in-half trick because she knew it was only a trick. The very atmosphere of my shop spoke of the ancient and the arcane: lotions and potions, brews and spells.

"It's good to see you, Jane," I said, quickly covering the distance between us before she could decide her trip to New Camel was a bad idea. "I should have told you about my day job."

"It's an adorable little shop," she said politely.

"I want you to know that everything in here is for the practice of white magick."

Jane mulled that over. "You mean all this stuff actually works?"

"Yes, but it's only purpose is to help people."

"I see."

I could tell that she didn't and my explanations were only making matters worse.

At that moment, Lorna brought her basket up to the counter, smiling. "I was told by a couple of people that your products are amazing. I want to buy everything, but if I do, my husband will file for divorce. We're saving up to have a baby."

"That's wonderful," I said, excusing myself from Jane to take care of her. Lorna paid by credit card, and I packed her purchase in a mini tote. "Enjoy," I said. "And remember, you can bring back anything that doesn't perform to your expectations."

When she left, I flipped the Open sign to Closed. It was less than an hour until closing time anyway, and I didn't want to rush Jane after she drove all the way from Hassettville. I offered her the chair and took my usual spot on the counter. She seemed a little calmer. Maybe having seen normal-looking Lorna buy my products and pay with a normal credit card helped ease her mind about my shop and me.

"You didn't have to drive all this way to see me," I said. "I would have come up to you if you'd asked."

"You've been very kind to come up twice already to listen to an old woman's tale of woe. I wanted to do my part."

"Did something happen since I last saw you?"

"I had another visit from the man who brought me Dwayne's letter."

Questions immediately flooded my head, but I shut my mouth on them and let her continue at her own pace.

"He told me Dwayne never sent him the second half of the money he was promised on completing the job. Kailyn, you don't know my son, but he would never cheat anyone." Her voice cracked on the last word. She took a moment to compose herself before she went on. "The only possible explanation is that he's dead."

"Not necessarily," I said, hopping off the counter to hunker down beside her. I took her hand. She looked at me with hope in her eyes. "Your son may have paid this guy, but he decided to hit you up for more. He knew Dwayne set up a bank account in your name. Scam artists are everywhere these days."

Jane's eyes widened. "I didn't think of that. And you're right about him asking me for the money."

"You didn't give it to him, did you?"

She shook her head.

"How did you get him to leave?"

"I threatened to call the police. I even got the phone and hit 911 in front of him. That's when he took off."

We chatted for a little while about how she was managing on her own and if I could help in any way. Meanwhile, my conscience was nagging at me for withholding the other, less attractive prospect about her son's circumstances. How could I tell her that Dwayne, who never cheated anyone, might be a cold-blooded killer as well as the target of a hit? I told myself I wanted to shield Jane until we knew for sure if Dwayne was alive or dead. My overactive conscience contended that I was just trying to shield myself from how she would react or how on earth I'd be able to console her. My inner debate ended in a stalemate, so I decided to follow my heart and wait for definitive proof before I helped Jane plan a funeral for her only child.

It was five o'clock when Jane checked her watch and abruptly stood up. "I'm so sorry," she said, picking up her purse. "I didn't intend to occupy this much of your time. I want to get on the road while it's still light out."

I rose with her. "You're welcome to spend the night with me and my six cats," I said.

"I do love cats," she murmured as if she was considering the offer. My Saucy passed away three years ago, and I still miss her so." She glanced around the shop again before coming to a decision. "I appreciate the invitation, Kailyn, but I prefer to go home. I sleep best in my own bed."

Her unspoken words were just as clear to me. She wouldn't be able to sleep a wink in my house now that she knew about this side of me.

Chapter 31

Sunday was one of those rare September gifts: cloudless blue skies and eighty degrees. My mother used to say, "It's a crime to stay indoors when Mother Nature bestows such a day on us."

No matter what else had been planned for that day, she packed up the picnic hamper and off we'd go. It was in that spirit that Elise invited me to join her and the boys for a last barbecue that afternoon. Sundays are generally busy days for the New Camel shops, and you can multiply that by a factor of ten when the weather cooperates. Work versus fun, the eternal yin–yang of life. I decided I could manage to have both. When I mentioned my conundrum to Elise, she was immediately onboard with starting the festivities an hour later. I'd keep the shop open until three and then hightail it over to her house. Hightail it? The phrase must have slipped into my vocabulary now that Merlin was back in old-west mode.

Elise's menu called for burgers and hot dogs with coleslaw, potato salad, and the last of the season's corn. I was in charge of dessert. On my way to the barbecue, I stopped at Pie in the Sky, where I picked up an open-faced Italian plum pie. It was only available in August and September and happened to be Elise's favorite. We had an agreement never to mention that to my aunt Tilly. The shop's owner had been shrewd enough to install a freezer full of ice cream because who doesn't want ice cream with their pie? I bought a half gallon of vanilla and made it to Elise's at three fifteen.

I waved to Zach and Noah, who were playing a noisy game of hoops on the driveway with neighborhood kids. Elise always left the front door unlocked when the boys were outside. I let myself in, stowed the ice cream in the freezer, and left the pie on the counter. I could see Elise through the sliding glass doors. She was on the deck with the grill already fired up. I went to join her. With a long-handled spatula occupying one hand, she used the other to pull me into a clumsy, one-armed hug.

"One of each?" she asked me as she started throwing meat on the fire.

"Absolutely," I said. "In fact, it might be mandatory on a day like this." I looked around to see if there was anything I could do to help, but she'd already set the redwood table with paper plates, utensils, and cups, as well as ketchup, mustard, pickle relish, and chopped onion. "I'll call the boys in," I said, seizing on the one thing left to do.

Less than ten minutes later we were all seated at the table, mouths too full to say a word. Once the eating slowed down, Elise asked Zach to repeat what he told her that morning.

He wiped a smear of ketchup off his chin. "So, Aunt K," he said, having recently dropped the rest of my name, "you know I'm friends with Chris Griffin, right?" I nodded, my Nancy Drew antennae quivering with interest.

"Well, I mentioned to Mom I'd like to learn to shoot trap or skeet."

"Shooting clay pigeons at an outdoor range," Elise explained when she saw I was lost.

"Yeah, and it's completely safe," Zach said, pleading his case. "Chris has gone dozens of times with his dad."

"What kind of gun do you use for that?" I asked.

"A shotgun," Zach said eagerly, perhaps hoping to find an ally in me. "Virtually accident proof."

What he didn't realize was that I would never countermand one of Elise's decisions. Besides, I had a very different agenda in mind with my questions. "What other things do he and his dad do together?"

"Lotsa stuff. They go to the batting cage and camping, sometimes bowling or shooting billiards. I know my dad never liked that stuff, but it sounds like a lot of fun."

"Do they like fencing or archery or martial arts with knives?" I asked, thinking about the knife that killed Amanda.

Zach thought for a moment before responding. "I never heard Chris talk about any of that, but they do go to an indoor range to target shoot with a pistol. The place monitors everyone very carefully." He added, "No one's ever gotten hurt there." He cast a sideways glance at his mother, no doubt to see if she was warming to the idea of letting him try it.

"Forget it," she told him bluntly. "Isn't it enough that your dad was killed with a gun?"

Zach knew when he was beaten. He sighed as only a teenager can sigh under the yoke of a tyrannical parent and consoled himself with another hotdog.

"Zach," I said, "do you happen to know the caliber of the pistol Chris and his dad use?"

"I don't think he ever said." He'd clearly lost interest in my questions, now that his mom had shut him down.

Over the years, Elise and I had become fluent in eye messaging. The one she was sending me at that moment said, "Do you believe my kid?" My eyes replied, "Oh yeah."

Zach mounted a sneak attack to steal the half piece of corn on Noah's plate. A minor scuffle ensued until Elise called a truce. She leaned into me and whispered, "He'll be off to college before we know it, but once in a while he still loves to torment his brother. Gets me a little crazy."

"Ma, I'm right here," Zach said, waving his hand in front of her. "You do realize I can hear every word you're saying. You want to know your problem? You need to lighten up. Besides, tormenting your little brother is a sacred responsibility. It's like the eleventh commandment." He smiled a broad, mischievous smile. "And FYI, I'm never going to outgrow it."

"Hey, no fair," Noah whined. "I don't have a little brother."

Before Elise and I went inside to get the dessert, she gave the boys a warning about keeping the peace. Noah gave his brother a defiant chin thrust. Zach responded by running his finger across his throat like a knife. Elise looked up at the sky, probably pleading for an extra helping of strength and patience.

Once we were inside, I made her sit down on a kitchen chair and do some deep breathing.

"Remember what great kids you have," I said. I waited two beats and added, "Most of the time." My last words struck her as hysterically funny.

"Thank you," she said, out of breath. "One day I will literally die laughing, and it will be your fault."

"Isn't that what friends are for?"

Zach opened the sliding door and poked his head in. "Seriously, what's taking so long?"

"Some much-needed laughter therapy," I said. "Dessert is on its way."

Elise took the small paper plates and more utensils, including a scooper, and I followed her with the pie and ice cream. By the time we finished dessert, she and I had gone from being pleasantly full to feeling like we might explode if we moved. The boys, who showed no signs of similar discomfort, jumped up and ran around to the driveway to see if the basketball game was still ongoing.

Elise leaned back in her chair and opened the button on her jeans with a groan. "Believe it or not, they'll be asking for more pie and ice cream in half an hour. Proof positive that growing boys are a species unto themselves."

We sat outside until a cool wind sprang up, tossing the tree limbs around, blowing the plates and napkins off the table, and sending the eighty degrees packing. We ran down the paper goods and dumped them in the garbage can Elise had stationed nearby. Gathering up what was left of dessert, we ran inside. Once everything was put away, Elise made tea, and we settled in the family room with big mugs, hoping the hot beverage would banish the sudden chill in our bones.

* * * *

I was getting into my car to head home when my cell rang and Travis's picture popped up on the screen.

"Hey where are you?" he asked, sounding frustrated.

"Just leaving Elise's. She had me over for a last barbecue. Why? Where are you?"

"At your house, waiting for you."

Had I forgotten we had a date? No, I was pretty sure we didn't. "Did we get our signals crossed?" I asked.

He chuckled. "No, I'm messing with you. You're usually at work or at home, so I didn't bother calling ahead."

"I guess I shouldn't be so predictable," I said, wryly. "I'm making it way too easy for any crazies who might be stalking me."

"Well hurry home; this crazy has some interesting news to impart, plus I really need a bathroom."

When I pulled into my driveway, Travis was sitting on the rattan rocker on the porch. He met me at the top of the steps and planted a light kiss on my mouth. Had I made a wrong turn and driven into an alternate universe, one in which he'd never freaked out about my magick and withdrawn from our relationship? I decided not to over think it. "So, what's this interesting news you used to lure me home?"

"Bathroom first; then news."

I opened the door and let him in ahead of me—directly into what appeared to be a mob of unionized felines. All six of them were congregated in the foyer to demand their dinner the second I walked in. I looked at my watch and saw that I was an unforgivable ten minutes late. Sashkatu was leading the chorus of plaintive vocals with all the aplomb of a starring tenor. Travis, who must have expected clear sailing to the powder room, stumbled over and around the cats until he made his way past them. If only I had my phone at the ready, I could have enjoyed the video replay for years to come.

He found me in the kitchen, rustling up the cats' dinner. "A person could break a leg trying not to step on them," he said.

I set their dinner bowls on the floor. "Maybe if a person didn't take it for granted I'd be home, he wouldn't have been in such a hurry to get past them." I took Sashki's food to the powder room, where he was waiting, and closed the door.

Travis had followed me, probably curious about where I was headed with the bowl of food. "Isn't he going to want out of there?"

"My mother and he worked it out years ago. He'll yowl when he's finished eating and wishes to rejoin his subjects."

He grinned. "Do you think you might be spoiling him a bit?"

"He's not just any cat; he was my mom's familiar," I said, daring to remind him about the family business. "Now, march yourself into the living room. You owe me some news."

It was growing dark earlier these days, and I begrudged autumn every single minute of the waning light. The living room was already bathed in twilight shadows. Before sitting down, I closed the blinds and turned on the two lamps that gave the room a warm, rosy glow. Travis waited until I was settled on the couch before sitting down beside me. Right beside me. Don't read into it, I told myself. "Okay," I said, "I'm ready to be wowed."

"Apparently, if folks in New Camel own firearms, they prefer rifles and shotguns over handguns."

"What do you mean?"

"Rifles and shotguns don't have to be registered in this state, except in New York City. Only handguns do."

"That makes sense," I said after a moment's thought. "My guess is that handguns are used mostly for protection in your home. We have a low crime rate up here. Most people feel safe, or at least they used to. Is that your big news?" I felt cheated.

He glossed over my question to ask me another. "How many forty-five-caliber handguns do you think there are in this town?"

"I don't know, ten?"

"Twenty," he said. "And by the way, that's pretty low when you take into account the size of New Camel with its outlying areas." I shrugged, still waiting to be impressed. Travis sounded like he was just warming up. "How many of those are owned by people you probably know?"

"Travis, please, enough with the twenty questions."

"All right. The answer is two."

"I know who owns one of them," I said with a little smirk, enjoying turning the tables on him. I could see that I'd surprised him. At that moment, Sashkatu started yowling for his freedom, so I went to his rescue. He followed me back into the living room. I reclaimed my seat beside Travis. He used his steps up onto the couch and then scrambled the rest of the way to his perch on the top. The couch bore the marks of hundreds of such treks, the fabric pulled in tufts and loops by his claws. Morgana had made peace with the damage back when he first started to decline, declaring that he was far more valuable than any piece of fabric. No one mentioned it again.

"Who do you know?" Travis asked once we were all settled.

"Patrick Griffin. I had a chat with Zach today. His friend, Chris, told him his dad has one. He didn't know the caliber, but I'm guessing it's a forty-five."

Travis laughed. "Way to steal my thunder. But do you know who owns the other one?" I shook my head. "Rusty, the curmudgeonly janitor."

It was my turn to be surprised and excited. "That's it then. Either he or Patrick killed John Doe."

"Not necessarily," he said. "Regardless of the law, a lot of people buy handguns on the black market. Cash on the spot. No permit needed. No background checks."

My heart sank to somewhere in the vicinity of my knees. One step forward, three steps back. "Of course, that would have been way too easy. Where do we go from here?"

"Since we can't investigate names we don't have, I say we take another look at the two we do have. When you interviewed Rusty and Patrick, you were totally focused on Amanda's death. It's possible you dismissed information because it didn't fit her case. Now that we have a second murder, I want to interview them again."

"You mean both of us together, right?"

He shook his head. "I think I should conduct the interviews this time. Maybe it will shake up our suspects."

"They might not let you in the door," I pointed out.

"I'm a lot more charming and sly than you may think."

"I guess we'll find out soon enough," I said, feeling like he was kidnapping my investigation. I told myself that was absurd. We were partners, and he was only trying to help close both cases. One thing nagged at me. "But even if one of them did kill John Doe," I said, "we're no closer to finding the creep who dug that knife into Amanda's throat. And I have to tell you, finding justice for her is a lot more personal to me."

Before Travis could respond, his phone rang with the rousing theme from Star Wars. I'd heard it often enough to know it was his boss. Travis's side of the conversation was limited to "yes," "no," and "on my way."

"Sorry," he said to me, already on his feet and heading for the door. "Talk soon."

I stayed where I was, staring at the blank TV screen, my mind just as blank. Maybe Sashkatu sensed how unsettled I felt because he made his way along the top of the couch until he reached me. Using my shoulder as a step, he climbed down into my lap and curled into a comforting ball of fur.

Chapter 32

Sashkatu slept close to me all night. When I changed position, he did as well, never more than a wisp of fur away. In spite of his valiant efforts, my spirits were still sagging in the morning. The thought of spending the day in Abracadabra was usually enough to get my engine revving. That plus a decent cup of coffee. But with no tour buses scheduled, Mondays are generally slow in the magick trade. I could go in a bit late and use the extra time at home to try teleporting myself, I suggested to my reflection as I was combing my hair.

I'd been dying to give it a try ever since Merlin translated the spell for an easy landing. Maybe dying wasn't the best word choice, given the inherent dangers of the activity. My reflection didn't have any advice or misgivings about the idea, but then she rarely does. So it was decided by me, myself, and I that now was as good a time as any to give it a whirl. If nothing else, having a plan pulled me out of my doldrums.

I chose the kitchen again for my trial run. I had teleported objects from there to the upstairs bathroom without mishap several times. Why mess with success? I made sure the bathroom door was closed to keep cats from wandering into the target area, and I took Bronwen's advice about doing a practice run. This time I used a plain drinking glass. When it disappeared, I ran upstairs to see if it was waiting in the bathroom. I found it on the floor, none the worse for its brief trip. All systems were "go," as NASA liked to say.

I took my seat at the kitchen table, my anxiety like a churning bubble machine in my chest and stomach. It took quite some time for me to calm and center myself before I could even begin the process. When I finally reached that Zen-like state, I drew on the energy from each cell in my body. I said the ancient spell and envisioned myself leaping over time and space to a gentle landing in the bathroom. I felt myself quivering like the objects before they disappeared. I struggled to maintain my concentration and block out thoughts of what might happen if I lost control in the middle of my passage.

I was reaching the hard limits of my energy when I finally became weightless, as light and insubstantial as a snowflake. And then I was sitting on the bathroom floor. I'd made it. I felt fine, but I checked my body for bruises or bleeding anyway. I appeared to be unscathed by my journey. For the last part of my evaluation, I stood up and peered in the mirror. My reflection stared back at me for the second time that morning; nothing had changed. I breathed a sigh of relief and promptly collapsed onto the floor.

I didn't regain consciousness for two hours by my watch. And when I did, I felt like I'd partied too hard. My only experience with alcohol had been one beer my freshman year of college, but that was enough to convince me that Morgana and Bronwen were right. Wildes must never drink. They warned me that even a tiny amount of alcohol could fry the special circuitry in our brains and cause mutations to the unique parts of our DNA and RNA. That one rebellious beer nearly cost me my magickal powers and possibly my life.

I sat up, feeling like a rag doll with most of its stuffing torn out. Standing would have to wait. At least the haze in my head was starting to dissipate.

"You'll be fine," Bronwen said, her cloud popping out of the ether all white and fluffy with a grandmotherly glow. "You just need to strengthen yourself before you try that again. It's clearly a lot more difficult than teleporting objects." I was happy to hear her voice and have the reassurance of her company. "If your mother or I had been fortunate enough to have your gift, we would be better able to instruct you in its proper uses and pitfalls."

"Any suggestions gladly accepted," I said.

"I'm afraid my advice hasn't changed. You need to build up your psychic muscle, so to speak."

"If all the telekinesis and teleportation I've been practicing aren't enough, I don't know what is," I said, sounding peevish, a little girl wanting her grandmother to fix the problem. Exhaustion was making me vulnerable and cranky.

"It may be that your concept of enough in this matter simply isn't," she said.

I could tell her patience was slipping. As warm and loving as she was, she never could put up with whining. But then I didn't have much tolerance for it myself. "I guess I have some work to do," I said, feeling stronger by dint of trying to sound that way.

"That's more like it, my dear girl." There was a definite smile in her tone. Without another word, she winked away.

* * * *

I didn't make it into work for another hour, and when I did, Tilly swooped in from her shop. She had been busy with a client who begged for a reading the moment Tilly opened her door. The woman had gone to a psychic fair over the weekend and was desperate for reassurance that she wasn't actually going to have another baby at the age of sixty-two.

"She wasn't, was she?" I couldn't help asking.

"Of course not," Tilly said. "The poor girl was so grateful; she gave me a fifty-dollar tip for accommodating her. But I didn't come in here to tell you that. I was concerned about your tardiness." I gave her an abbreviated version of my morning. "That's worrisome," she said, her brow furrowed. "You didn't have the energy to return to your starting point?"

I shook my head.

"Very worrisome, indeed," she repeated. "Caution must be your watchword. Caution above all else. I could not bear to lose you too. I know it sounds selfish, but that's the truth of it." She grabbed me into a hug and didn't seem to be in any rush to release me until Merlin came in like the town crier, spreading the word that the pumpkin muffins might be burning.

The rest of the day was a typical Monday, and given the morning's adventure, I was grateful for it. I caught up on paying bills and on reordering the products I don't brew or concoct myself, like candles and incense, healing stones, and our signature tote bags. Through trial and error, Morgana and Bronwen had discovered that if a magick shop was to succeed in the twenty-first century, it not only had to look like an old magick shop in the eye of the customer but also had to keep up with current trends.

From the outside, Abracadabra had fit the bill down through the centuries. But inside, the inventory had changed over time. Tourists now made up the majority of the customers, and they expected more than dried plants and herbs with strange names. Witches and warlocks could roll their eyes until they fell back into their skulls, but our shop had survived since the days of the French and Indian Wars. We were clearly doing something right.

* * * *

Travis called as I was arming the security system in the shop. "Breaking news," he said with the gravitas of a news anchor with important information to impart.

I stopped and reset the system. There was no way I could ignore such an alert. Sashkatu, who'd been leading the way to the back door, grumbled and gave me a weary, what-now look over his shoulder. Travis's teaser won hands down.

"You have my attention," I said, holding up one finger to show the cat I'd be with him in a minute.

"Brace yourself," he said dramatically. "The bullet that killed John Doe didn't come from any of the registered guns in the area."

I was stunned into silence.

"You still there?" he asked.

"I'm here. Are you sure? How did you find out?"

"I figured the results of the tests should be in by now. I was in Watkins Glen anyway, so I stopped at the precinct to see if I could talk Duggan into revealing them."

"He told you?" That didn't sound like the Duggan I knew.

"No, of course not," Travis said. "In fact, he was in a particularly belligerent mood. But I took my time leaving the building, which is when I overheard two cops discussing the results."

"Then the gun could have come from anywhere," I said, frustrated. "Isn't there a national gun registry the police can access?"

"Every state has its own laws governing firearms."

"At this rate we're never going to solve the John Doe murder. For that matter, did the police ever find the knife that killed Amanda?"

"No, but on the off chance that her killer threw the knife into the marsh, they've let the Waverly crew go back to dredging. There's a CSI team on the scene in case there's anything else hidden in there. For all anyone knows, criminals have been tossing bodies and evidence into that marsh from time immemorial."

Until now, I'd never given much thought to all the cold cases stored away and forgotten. "I'm not going to let Amanda's death become just another unsolved case," I said with more vehemence than I intended. "John Doe's either, for that matter. They deserve better. This town deserves better."

"We're not going to let that happen," Travis said, his voice like a warm arm around my shoulders.

Chapter 33

I was standing in the open doorway of my shop, looking for something to distract me. I hadn't been able to settle into any productive work, since opening. My mind was stuck on an early morning text from Travis, in which he said he hoped to drop in on Rusty and Patrick before the end of the day. I texted him back, asking why he was still going now that we knew their guns were clean.

In the name of efficiency, he called me to explain. "When you have no leads to follow, you create some," he said. "I have nothing to lose by talking to them. Rusty and Patrick probably know other gun enthusiasts. Maybe one of them or one of their friends heard a rumor or saw something suspect."

I wished him good luck. But waiting for news was a lesson in patience, and I was failing it.

Lolly appeared in her doorway, looking up and down the street as though she were expecting someone. She waved when she saw me and crossed over to chat.

"Who are you looking for?" I asked.

"A group of women who were supposed to arrive here at eleven," she said, checking her watch. "I hope they didn't get lost."

"Women you know?"

"Not yet, although I did speak to Frieda last week. She's sort of an unofficial leader of the group. Since they've never been to New Camel before, she wanted to make sure the shops that interest them would be open. She told me they've all lost spouses to one thing or another, in her case it was 'younger-than-springtime Jessica,' as she put it. They get together to knit and crochet. It's a nifty idea when you think about it," Lolly said. "A support group with exercise to keep their fingers nimble." She sounded a little wistful, though she already had a plate that was so full it was often overflowing.

"Nifty," I said. Lolly was the only person I knew who still used the word that harkened back to the beatniks of the late fifties and the hippies of the sixties.

"I'm sure they'll be going to Busy Fingers," I said. The shop, on the other side of Main Street, close to the site for the Waverly Hotel, was one of the town's top draws. When I was little, I loved going in there to see the skeins of yarn in every color and shade I could imagine. They filled the wall behind the counter, a cubby hole for each color.

"According to Frieda, it's the main reason they're making the trek. That and my chocolate," Lolly added, beaming.

"I didn't get a call from them, but I'm not surprised. They don't sound like a good fit for a magick shop."

"Don't be so sure. On paper, a magick shop might put some folks off, but once they see Abracadabra, they have to be charmed enough to take a peep."

"It has happened before," I said, trying to think positively. And today was a good day for it. I could have used the distraction as much as the business.

"I'll talk up your shop to them," Lolly said. "I'll tell them they can't leave town without visiting the famous magick shop that's been here for four hundred years."

"I'll have to give you a commission," I said with a laugh, knowing she was as good as her word. I didn't know a soul in New Camel who didn't love Lolly. Honesty and chocolate were a hard combination to beat.

Two sedans, one white and the other a light blue, came slowly around the curve in the road, entering Main Street at our end of town.

"That's probably them now," Lolly said, excusing herself to scoot back to her shop.

Rather than make a U-turn, the drivers parked in front of Abracadabra. Seven women emerged from the cars, sprightly enough in spite of their ages. The majority appeared to be in their late seventies, but there were definitely a couple on the far side of eighty. Without a glance in my direction, they made a beeline for the chocolate shop.

I went back in to tidy up in case Lolly's propaganda was successful. There wasn't much to tidy, though. I kept the shop neat as a pin, the way my mother and grandmother had. So I realigned books on a shelf and straightened the framed portrait of my great-great-grandmother, Gwent Wilde. It took all of two minutes. I cleaned out Sashkatu's water dish and refilled it. When the phone rang, I grabbed it, hoping it was Travis, but the caller asked me to take a survey. I told him I didn't have time. He promised it wouldn't take long. I explained the meaning of no time; said I was sorry, though I'm not sure why; and hung up.

Twenty minutes later, the door chimes jingled, and one of the ladies in Frieda's group marched in. Her hair was several shades of gray, from charcoal in the back to salt and salt-and-pepper on the sides to a snowy white framing her face. Her only makeup was a dash of red lipstick. She was wearing floral capris with a T-shirt that matched the bold pink in them. In one hand, she was holding a quilted purse and, in the other, a white paper bag from Lolly's shop.

Before I had a chance to welcome her, she came to me, holding out her hand. "I'm Frieda," she said, introducing herself in a hearty voice.

"Kailyn," I said, glad to retrieve my hand from her iron grip.

"What a tantalizing store you have." Her gaze flitted around the shop as she spoke. "Are you a witch? Oops, I apologize. Ever since menopause I don't seem to have any filters."

"I'm sure some people might call me a witch," I said wryly, "but I prefer sorcerer."

Frieda giggled. "Good one. Mind if I browse on my own? I can't stand salespeople hovering over me. Sorry."

"It's actually refreshing to hear the truth. Of course you can browse solo. Come to me if you have any questions."

"I like you," Frieda declared.

The chimes pealed several times in quick succession as three more of her group arrived. Within ten minutes, all but one of the women were circulating through my shop, calling for each other to "come look" at this treasure or that oddity. They all had questions, many of them the same, so Frieda took charge. She told everyone to gather near the counter. In no time, I was answering questions from the entire group without having to keep repeating myself. I explained the skin-care line, gave them an overview of the natural remedies, and taught them the difference between white magick and black.

After fifteen minutes, Frieda announced that they had another fifteen to buy what they wanted before they were moving on. The women took off in different directions, baskets in hand, like participants in a scavenger hunt vying for a prize.

Frieda was the first one back to the counter with her goodies. "I noticed that one member of your group is missing," I said as I rang up her purchase.

"Ruth," she said. "She's afraid of her shadow. Always has been. What can you do?"

"I could give her a spell to build her self-confidence."

"Ah, and there's the rub," Frieda replied. "She'd be too afraid to try it."

I handed her the credit card receipt and a pen with which to sign it. I let go of the pen a second before she had it firmly in her grasp. We juggled it between us for a few seconds before it fell into the narrow space where the counter was separating from its backing.

"I'm sorry," Frieda said, leaning on the counter to peer into the crevice. "Maybe I can get it out with a coat hanger. I'm really good with a coat hanger."

"It's not a big deal," I assured her. "I've been meaning to have that fixed." I plucked another pen off my desk and made sure she had it in her hand before I let go. I rang up the five other purchases, thanking each woman for her patronage. Even if they lived too far away to come back anytime soon, word of mouth accounted for a lot of my business.

After they left, I went through the shop, straightening up. There were only a few items in the wrong places. Frieda's group was more thoughtful than most customers. I was about to poke my head into Tilly's shop to get the name of her handyman when a thought struck me, parading through my mind in glaring neon letters. How had Travis and I not realized it sooner? The counter would have to wait a while longer to be fixed. I grabbed my purse, set the alarm, and raced out the back door.

Chapter 34

I called Travis as I dashed home to get my car. His phone went straight to voice mail. I told myself not to worry. He must have turned if off so it wouldn't interrupt his interviews with Rusty or Patrick, but I wasn't very convincing. I ran up the driveway, clicked my car open, slid under the steering wheel, and fired the engine. I backed into the street and slammed on the brakes. I had no idea where to go first. What would I do if I were in Travis's position? I'd start with Rusty, who lived farther away, and then hit Patrick's shop on my way home. Of course Travis lived in Brooklyn, but I was certain he'd head for my place so we could strategize. I couldn't waste any more time second-guessing myself. I might already be too late. No, no more negative thoughts. I shook my head hard enough to cause whiplash and put the car in Drive. Rusty's house it was.

It seemed like every slow driver on the road had conspired to detain me. The ten-minute trip took twenty, my belated epiphany playing over and over in my head. "I have another one right here," I'd told Frieda when the pen fell into the crevice. "Another one right here." The bullet didn't come from the .45s that were tested. But what if Rusty or Patrick had another gun, a black-market gun, bought for the sole purpose of murder? The police might not think about searching for a second weapon when the owner of the registered gun had obeyed the law to the letter. I recognized that there could be other people with black-market .45s in our area, but as Travis had pointed out, you eliminate the ones you know before you start knocking on every other door in town, which was next to impossible anyway without benefit of a detective's shield.

I kept trying Travis's number as I drove. Still no answer. I jerked the car to a stop in front of Rusty's Cape Cod and looked around. His pickup was in the driveway. Travis's car was nowhere to be seen. I ran up to the front door and rang the bell. I heard it chime inside.

"What do you want?" Rusty yelled without opening the door. He must have seen me through the peephole, or he would have asked, "Who's there?" His naked hostility made me think he'd already had a visit from Travis or was possibly holding a gun to Travis's head during our little exchange.

"It's just me, Kailyn," I said to remind him he'd known me forever. I tried to sound childlike and harmless. Nothing to worry about from me.

Rusty wasn't impressed. "Like I said, what do you want?"

"Can I come in? I only need two minutes of your time."

"Go away." Someone innocent might have added, "Or I'll call the police."

"I want to help you, Rusty." Silence from beyond the door. "Together we can come up with a plan." I didn't like lying, but if there could be such a thing as gray magick, why not gray lies for when the truth just wouldn't do? "Rusty?" Still nothing. I didn't dare leave until I'd at least established that Travis was not being held captive there. I was about to circle the house on the off chance that Rusty had forgotten to close the blinds when the door swung open and I was face-to-face with the janitor, only the screen door between us. His skin was a mottled red, his eyes sunken in dark circles. Grief over Amanda or the stress of being a suspect or both?

He regarded me warily. "You're not coming in. You can talk to me from out there."

"Okay," I said, listening hard for any sound that could mean Rusty wasn't alone in the house. "Has Travis Anderson come by to see you today?"

"What's it to you?"

"It's just that he's a reporter, and if he doesn't show up for work, the police and the media will be all over the place looking for him."

"Yeah, so?"

"I'm afraid for you. If his boss knows he came to see you..."

"I didn't do anything to him. Why can't you all just leave me alone?" He started to close the door on me.

"Rusty, wait. I've given this a lot of thought. If you were somehow involved in John Doe's death, I'm sure you had a good, solid reason." I didn't mention Amanda, afraid the implication would be like throwing a lit match into gasoline. "We have to make sure you present your side of it in the best possible light. And it's extremely important for you to stay out of trouble while the investigation is ongoing."

"I didn't hurt anybody," he said. "Go away." He sounded like a broken man. It was hard to tell through the screen door, but I thought I saw the reflection of tears in his eyes. This was the Rusty I remembered from my childhood—all bluff and bluster.

I found myself believing he was innocent. I hoped I wasn't wrong. I hoped he wasn't one terrific actor. I told him I'd be in touch and got back in my car. I drove straight to Patrick's store, breaking every speed limit. I pulled to the curb and parked directly behind Travis's car. I'd found him. But I didn't know if he was alive or dead.

I took the steps up to the porch, where Patrick and I had shared some delicious lunches. He'd lived in New Camel for as long as I could remember and was still married to his high school sweetheart. By all appearances, he was a great father to Chris, even if some would take exception to the skeet and target shooting. The Patrick I knew was too smart to risk losing his family and the life he'd built for any reason. But prisons were full of smart people who'd done exactly that and lost it all.

The shades in the store were drawn. I couldn't remember if he always lowered them against the late-afternoon sun. It was one of the million things you see on a daily basis but don't absorb. Like white noise. I turned the doorknob, but it wouldn't budge. My heart, already on a hair trigger, leaped to attention. Don't panic, I told myself. As old as the knob was, the mechanism might simply be stuck. But what if Patrick had locked it on purpose? I seemed determined to panic. I rapped on the glass part of the door until my knuckles hurt. I shouted Travis's name. I put my ear to the door but didn't hear anything. If there were innocent explanations, they eluded me.

I considered opening the door with the spell I'd adlibbed to escape the abandoned candle shop. But Patrick was probably in there, and he'd find out a lock couldn't stop me. I'd forfeit an important weapon in my arsenal. I couldn't stand there dithering either. Travis's life could be hanging in the balance. I centered my focus on the doorknob and was halfway through the first recitation when Patrick opened the door.

"Kailyn," he said, looking surprised to see me. "Are you all right?" He didn't wait for me to reply before adding, "I didn't hear you at first because I was in my office. I'm locking up early to take Chris to the dentist; my wife is down with a bug." His words were hurried, and he already had on a down vest. He looked like someone rushing off to pick up his son.

I'd raced down there loaded for bear, and it took me a moment to readjust my approach. "I...I saw Travis Anderson's car out front," I sputtered. "His mother called me when he didn't answer his cell. His father was in a bad accident." Patrick seemed to be buying the story, or his eyebrows had knit together with a good imitation of concern.

"Travis is in my office. I'll take you right back there," he said with an appropriate touch of urgency. First, he reached around me to relock the front door. "Closing up for that dental appointment," he reminded me when he saw the questioning look on my face. "Travis was in the area," Patrick said as he led the way to his office, "so he stopped in for a few minutes."

He made it sound as if Travis was an old friend who dropped by on a regular basis, but Travis had never mentioned that he knew the antiques dealer. This was all wrong. I knew it in my gut. I had to get out of there and call the police. But Patrick had relocked the door, and I wouldn't make it through even one recitation of the spell before he'd be on me. Even so, it was my only option. No one else knew where we were. I'd considered running into Tea and Empathy to tell Tilly, but she was in the middle of a session, and I didn't want to interrupt or frazzle her. If she lost focus, her readings tended to be subpar. With the clarity of hindsight, I realized I should have told Elise. Now there was no one to raise an alarm or mount a rescue.

Patrick glanced over his shoulder, no doubt checking to see if I was still following him, and caught me assessing the distance to the front door. He whirled around and grabbed my arm. "You're not going anywhere," he said, dragging me the last few yards to the closed office door. He pulled his key ring from his pants pocket and unlocked it. Who locks in a friend? On the other hand, there was no reason to lock Travis in if he was already dead. My heart lightened with hope.

Patrick threw the door open, revealing a large, expensively appointed office dominated by a heavy desk with intricate carvings. Travis was sitting in a back corner of the room, his hands bound with cord that lashed him to the back of the chair. His mouth was covered with packing tape. When he saw me in the doorway, his shoulders slumped.

"You wanted to see Travis," Patrick said when I hesitated in the doorway. "In you go." He ground the business end of a gun into my back as encouragement. I hadn't seen the gun before. He must have had it tucked into the back of his pants under the down vest. It was probably the black-market .45. "Go ahead, tell him about his father's accident," he said, pushing me into the room.

Travis's eyes sought mine for confirmation. I had to relieve his mind. "There was no accident," I admitted.

"Just like I thought," Patrick said. "Go sit in the chair in front of the desk." He must have seen enough TV and films to know he should keep Travis and me apart or we might try to untie each other bonds.

When I was seated, he grabbed the ball of cord off his desk and started tying me up the way he had Travis. I realized he didn't have enough hands to tie me and hold onto the gun. He must have set it on the floor at his feet. I had no way to reach it, but maybe with telekinesis I could draw it to me.

"Don't try anything," he warned me. He must have been feeling vulnerable matching wits with a sorcerer. "I can have it back in my hand and kill you both in five seconds flat."

I'd already come to that conclusion myself. "I guess that's the gun you used to kill John Doe," I said, "but for the life of me, I can't figure out why." I knew I shouldn't be baiting him, but I was as angry and curious as I was afraid. I glanced over at Travis. His eyes wide, he was shaking his head at me, begging me to leave bad enough alone.

Patrick's response was to slap packing tape over my mouth, rip it off with what felt like ten layers of skin, and reposition it with a slap to secure it. Message received. He wasn't a fan of smart-ass remarks. In spite of everything, I was having trouble accepting that this was the same man I'd known all my life and not some evil twin or alter ego.

He sat on the edge of his desk staring at us and chewing on his lip as if trying to figure out what to do next. "Sit tight," he said, chuckling at his pun.

He locked the door behind him, making me wonder if he knew more about my abilities than I imagined. I had no idea how long he'd be gone, but I had to assume this would be our only chance to get away. My last effort to teleport myself had proved I wasn't strong enough yet. I'd been lucky my cell structure hadn't come apart halfway through it. And that was under ideal circumstances. Here it would have to be my last resort.

With our unknown deadline ticking down, I remembered that Morgana had created a spell to untangle her necklaces that were always getting knotted together. It might work with the cords binding our hands. I did my best to adapt it to our current needs and recited it three times in my head since saying it aloud wasn't an option:

Let loose the knots.
Free all tangles.
Release all bonds
That bind us here.

The cords should have fallen from around our hands, but nothing was happening to mine. My back was to Travis, but I had to assume that if it worked on him, he'd already be busy untying me. This was a bad time to be striking out. What had I done wrong? I ran through the words again scrutinizing each one. I finally seized on the only thing that could possibly be off. If it didn't work now—no, it had to work now, I told the doubting voice in my head.

Let loose the knots.

Free all tangles.
Release all bonds
That bind me here.

The cords loosened and fell away, freeing me from the chair. I jumped up and ran over to Travis, whose eyes were wide with amazement and a spark of hope. Standing behind his chair, I wrapped my arms around his chest and recited the spell again, changing the word me to him. The second the cords fell away, he was on his feet, peeling the tape off his mouth. He tried to remove my tape gently, but we didn't have the time to finesse it. I pushed his hand away and pulled it off myself. Raw skin was a small price to pay for my life. But without more traditional weapons, we were a long way from being safe.

Chapter 35

Travis and I made our way quietly over to the door to listen for any noise that meant Patrick was still in the shop. I decided if we didn't hear anything for five minutes, I would attempt to open it. At first there was complete silence beyond the door, but just as I was starting to recite the spell, a heavy door creaked open and slammed shut. The dialogue that ensued was conducted in harshly whispered words I couldn't make out. I looked at Travis to see if he understood any of their exchange, but he shook his head. It occurred to me that the second man could have been Patrick's accomplice in the John Doe murder and any number of other crimes we weren't yet aware of. In any case, it was difficult not to be disheartened. With two of them to defeat, our odds of surviving dropped substantially.

The dialogue came to an abrupt end, after which there was the unmistakable sound of rubber-soled shoes approaching the office. There was no point in going back to our chairs. Patrick would immediately notice that we were no longer bound.

"We need something we can use as a weapon," Travis whispered. The footsteps were coming closer. We were nearly out of options. He picked up the chair where he'd been tied, struggling under its weight and bulk. He carried it across the room to the hinged side of the door, where he'd be hidden when it was opened. There was no time for me to rummage through the desk for scissors or a letter opener. Instead, I focused on my chair and gathered my telekinetic energy.

The key was inserted into the lock, the doorknob turned, and the door swung open. Patrick hesitated in the doorway as he took in the fact that we were free. A boy Zach's age pushed past him to see why he'd stopped. Travis remained hidden. At the exact moment when they passed the door and would be able to see him, he hefted the chair over his head. Both were in my sights too. I unleashed my energy, sending the chair careening across the floor with so much force that it slammed into their legs, knocking them down like bowling pins.

As they fell, Travis brought his chair crashing down on their heads, the force cracking off three of its wooden legs. They were conscious but dazed. Travis and I made a mad dash for the door. I was able to skirt them safely. Travis wasn't so lucky. Patrick grabbed his ankle, twisting it at a horrible angle and bringing him down so hard I cringed.

"Run. Get out of here," Travis shouted at me, but it was already too late.

Patrick was on his feet, gun in hand. He jammed the barrel into Travis's temple. "You take one more step, witch, and he's dead."

The teen hauled himself off the floor, holding his knee. "Dad...stop!" he cried. "I told you...no more."

Patrick wheeled on his son. "Shut up. Just shut up and let me handle this!" He turned to me. I was frozen in the limbo of the doorway. I wanted to go for help, but I didn't want to leave Travis. Besides, even if I did make a run for it, Patrick might shoot me in the back and then shoot Travis. He really couldn't afford to let either of us live.

"I will kill your reporter friend," he said to me, enunciating each word with a hostility that chilled me. This was not Patrick. This was a rabid distortion of the man.

"He's bluffing, Kailyn," Travis said, breathless with pain. I knew Patrick wasn't bluffing. A man who already committed murder once, and possibly twice, had little to lose by killing again. Travis was just playing the odds, hoping that if I ran, I might have a chance. I think we both knew that staying was an absolute death sentence.

"She's stupid but loyal," Patrick said when I stayed where I was. "I've got to give her that. Chris, bring her back in here."

"Dad, please," he begged as he took my arm and led me in. When I first heard the boy's reluctance to be involved, I entertained the slim hope that we might be able to coax him over to our side. Now it seemed that objecting was as far as he would go.

Patrick ordered Travis to get up. I watched his face crumple in pain. He must have wanted to scream, but he didn't make a sound. I couldn't stand there and watch him struggle on his own. Patrick be damned. I went to Travis and draped his arm over my shoulder to take the weight off his injured foot.

"You're a regular Florence Nightingale," Patrick said with a nasty curl to his upper lip. "Not to worry. He won't be in pain much longer. Both of you, over to that wall."

He was pointing at the wall opposite the door, the wall farthest from the front of the shop and the people walking by. I helped Travis walk haltingly across to it. It was slow-going, which gave me a chance to think. In spite of our dismal circumstances, my brain was working furiously, unwilling to accept defeat. Telekinesis was out until I had a chance to rest and recharge my energy. I didn't know any spells that could actually change someone's mind. The one I'd used on Devon worked for mere seconds. With Travis's injury, we wouldn't even make it to the door.

I once asked Bronwen about spells that can more permanently change a person's mind. I was told, in no uncertain terms, that such a spell would be black magick and she never wanted to hear me speak of such things again. My grandmother was rarely stern with me, which made her reply that much more powerful. If that kind of spell was out of bounds, I had no doubt that causing someone to have a stroke or heart attack, suffer blindness, or become paralyzed were black magick of the darkest kind. All I had left to work with were words.

"I don't want to do this," Patrick said reasonably. "Kailyn, why did you have to start meddling in things that don't involve you? I enjoyed our lunchtime conversations. Of course, now I see that you were just trying to build a case against me. Look, I'll do you a favor and make this quick. No point in prolonging the inevitable."

Travis leaned back against the wall and put his other arm around my waist to draw me closer. At least we'd go down together. Patrick raised the gun and sighted down the barrel. I watched his finger move to the trigger.

"No more! It ends now." Chris screamed, his voice shrill and shaking as he jumped in front of the gun. His injured knee buckled under him, but he shifted his weight and managed to stay upright.

Patrick's face was white. "Idiot! I could have killed you."

Chris burst into tears. "Maybe that would have been better. This was all my fault anyway."

"Don't you ever say those words again. You were heroic. You saved your mother."

"Why couldn't you just call the police and let it go then and there?"

"You think it would have been that easy?" Patrick said. "You're so young and naive. Let me teach you about the law. If someone breaks into your house and threatens you or your family, you are within your rights to shoot him, even kill him. But if that person is running away, he's no longer a threat to you. If you shoot him, then you're guilty of manslaughter or possibly murder. And if you shoot him in the back, like you did, you can't even claim he was coming back at you." Patrick was so focused on his son he seemed to have forgotten about us. If he hadn't been blocking the path to the door, I might have made a run for it. But who was I kidding? I would never have left Travis to die alone.

"So you got home around that time and decided to get rid of the body by throwing it in the marsh," Travis said, summing up for him,

Patrick sneered. "Brilliant deduction, Sherlock."

"It wasn't a bad idea," Travis said equitably, "until Waverly came along to drain the marsh."

I figured he was trying to draw out the time before our execution in the hope the cavalry might still arrive. Although I'd run out of optimism, a talking Patrick was preferable to a shooting Patrick, so I dove right in. "What I don't understand is that the bullet didn't come from your gun."

"The kid never had time—" Patrick stopped abruptly. "That's it. We're not doing a Q and A here."

"How about a last request?" Travis tried. "You have nothing to lose. If you're going to kill us, we won't be able to tell anyone else."

To my surprise, he seemed to be considering the request.

"Yeah, why not? Dead men tell no tales. Besides, venting is supposed to be cathartic. That day, when Chris came home from school, he found the front door wide open. We never leave the door open, so he got suspicious. He went around the house, looking in the windows to see what was going on. When he got to the kitchen window, he saw this bum, this vagrant, holding a gun to his mother's head. He was so furious he came through the back door like gangbusters and rushed the creep. They struggled over the gun, and Chris got it away from him."

"The guy ran," Travis said, filling in the blanks, "and Chris was so stoked on adrenaline that he went after him and shot him with his own gun."

"But I didn't kill Mrs. Boswell," Chris piped up. "She was one of my favorite teachers."

"No," I said as all the pieces fell into place in my mind, "your father did. Amanda was going to vote in favor of the hotel, which meant the body would be dredged up. Your father pretended to be in favor of the hotel, too, so he could take her place on the board. Once he was there, he had a convenient epiphany about conserving wetlands and voted against it."

"All that effort," Travis said, "and the proposal passed anyway. It must have made you nuts, Patrick."

I knew immediately he'd pushed Patrick too far. Like Jekyll morphing into Hyde, a storm gathered in his face. His jaw clenched, and his brow lowered, casting his eyes into deep shadows.

"Nuts enough to do what needs to be done here," he said. "I should have taken care of you two sooner, when you first started snooping around."

He turned to Chris. "Go home. Get out of here. I'll deal with you later."

If there was any chance of getting the boy's help, it was now. "Chris," I called out as he limped to the doorway. "You know this is wrong. We've never done anything to you or your family. My nephew Zach is your friend." Zach wasn't technically my nephew, but this was not the time to worry about semantics. "How will you be able to look him in the eye again? How will you ever forgive yourself or your father if you don't stand up for what you know is right?"

"Shut your trap!" Patrick shouted at me. "One more peep out of either of you, just one, and I'll drag out your deaths until you beg me to end it."

Chris was crying, tears streaming down his face. "No more killing," he pleaded.

"Home," Patrick ordered him. "Your mother must be wondering where we are. Don't you ever forget that you owe your allegiance to your family and only your family."

Chris avoided looking at Travis and me as he shambled out of the room. Moments later I heard the rear door open and slam closed, extinguishing my last hope.

Patrick looked rattled. He paced the width of the office, back and forth, back and forth. Having Chris break ranks with him seemed to be eroding his confidence, maybe pushing him to question what he was doing. He stopped across from us. "No more stalling," he muttered as if giving himself a pep talk. He assumed a shooting stance again, legs apart for stability, both hands on the gun to steady his aim.

"How does your wife feel about what's happened?" Travis asked. He didn't give up easily.

"I told you before, no more questions." The James Bond theme erupted, making all of us jump. Patrick pulled his phone out of his shirt pocket. "What is it?" he asked tightly.

I could only hear his side of the conversation, but that was enough to make me sure the caller was his wife.

"No, nothing's wrong," he said, glaring at us like we were to blame for all his troubles. "He's not home yet?" Patrick looked at his watch. "He should be there any minute. He was helping me finish up. Stop nagging me. I'll be home as soon as I take care of a few things." He clicked off the call and shoved the phone back in his pocket. Had it been an old landline, he probably would have slammed the receiver down.

I figured his wife had to know about John Doe. But did she also know Patrick had murdered Amanda? Had she condoned it to protect her son?

The rear door creaked open and slammed shut again. For a moment, I entertained the hope that the police had figured things out and come to our rescue. I would have paid good money to see Duggan's bulldog face appear in the office doorway. But the police wouldn't have announced themselves by letting the door slam behind them. So I wasn't surprised when Chris hobbled back into the office. He'd stopped crying, but the tracks of his tears had dried on his cheeks like scars.

"I see you've come to your senses." Patrick sounded vindicated and relieved.

"I have," he said firmly. "I'm tired of the secrets and the lies. You said it had to be this way if we wanted to keep our family from being destroyed. Well guess what, Dad? My life's become a living hell. So have yours and Mom's. You never used to fight, but you fight all the time now. You're just too proud and stubborn to admit I'm right."

Patrick's eyes burned like a fever. He strode over to his son and slapped him hard across the cheek, leaving a hand-shaped welt. "I did what I had to do—for all our sakes."

Chris stood his ground, his voice strong, his eyes leveled at his father. "Why can't you see that everything you were afraid would happen has happened anyway? I can't be part of this anymore. You raised me to be a good person. How can you expect me to change just like that? From now on, I'm doing things my way, and maybe I'll be able to sleep again."

"And exactly what is your way? Patrick asked. "Turning yourself over to the police so they can lock you away in some hellhole until you're an old man?" He batted away a yellow jacket that was circling his head. "Because that's what the justice system is going to do with you."

"That's my choice to make."

"You're fifteen. You're not old enough to have a choice."

"Then stop me. You go ahead and try to stop me."

I didn't know how this father/son confrontation was going to end, but for the moment Travis and I weren't the focus. Travis shook his head and put his finger to his lips—a reminder to stay out of it. Patrick was still holding the gun.

"Okay, Son," the antiques dealer said condescendingly, "tell me what you want to do."

I didn't know if he was regrouping to fight anew or had suddenly decided to follow his son's lead. From what I'd seen so far, I wasn't betting on a new and improved Patrick.

"I'm going down to the police station to turn myself in," Chris said. "But first I want you to release these two."

"If I do that, they'll also go straight to the police to press charges against me."

"Yeah," Chris said, "I'd be shocked if they didn't. But that's the least of your problems."

Patrick stood there, staring into the distance like he was working things out in his mind. "All right," he said. He turned calmly to his son and slammed the hilt of his gun into the boy's head. The impact resounded in the room like a crack of thunder. Chris's eyes widened in surprise before he wilted and went down in a heap.

I was so stunned I gasped. Beside me, Travis groaned and slid down the wall onto the floor. If a father could inflict that kind of pain on his son, we didn't stand a chance.

Patrick turned to us and ordered Travis back on his feet to die like a man. I was trying to help him up when Patrick screamed in pain, slapping at his neck. The wasp must have finally struck. I couldn't work up any sympathy. In fact, I was glad it was a yellow jacket. They didn't die after stinging, a fact soon corroborated by Patrick's encore of screams. A second wasp had entered the fray. Patrick dropped his gun in a frantic attempt to cover his head with his arms, only to have them stung repeatedly too.

I whispered to Travis to sit very still. Wasps are aggressive. Any sudden movement could make us the next targets.

Unable to take the insect's assault, Patrick finally turned tail and ran out of the office and then the building, judging by the sound of the door slamming after him. Unfortunately, the wasps stayed behind with us. I suggested we crawl slowly to the door. It seemed like the most practical solution since Travis couldn't walk anyway. We had gone no more than six feet when we heard the implausible sound of giggling behind us. Bewildered, we turned around to find Tilly and Merlin, flushed with victory, grinning back at us.

Chapter 36

It was past closing time when Tilly, Merlin and I returned to our shops. I knew the cats were waiting for dinner. I walked in, expecting a cool welcome from Sashkatu, but he must have known on a primal level about my brush with death. He immediately leaped from his windowsill onto the desk, from there to the counter, and almost into my arms. His internal compass wasn't as accurate these days. I had to pluck him out of the air before he overshot me and came in for a bone-jarring landing on the hardwood. Safe in my arms, he gave the tip of my nose a lick. He'd never been much of a licker, so I was pretty sure it was a thank-you for having his back. He planted his front paws on my chest and stared into my eyes for several seconds as if to satisfy himself that I hadn't sustained any serious injuries of either the physical or metaphysical kind.

I took him home, where I was greeted by an angry chorus of yowls for my tardiness. Sashkatu gave me a look that seemed to say, "Peasants, what can you do?" Tilly called later that evening to invite me to tea at noon the next day to celebrate the fact that Travis and I were alive and mostly well. I could tell from her voice that she was still beaming with pride over the part she and Merlin played in our rescue. At the time, it had taken me a few seconds to wrap my traumatized head around the fact that they were the wasps who'd zeroed in on Patrick and saved the day. I suspected Travis would be grappling with the idea for a lot longer, given that his acceptance of even basic magick was a work in progress.

After Patrick had run out of his shop, I'd called 911 to tell the police that Amanda's and John Doe's killers could most likely be found at home or at the hospital. I also requested an ambulance for Travis, who needed to be seen by an orthopedist, and Chris, who was still unconscious on the floor.

Duggan caught up with Patrick in the ER and arrested him. He called me back with grudging thanks for the tip and to demand an interview with me. I played the trauma card, asking him to give me until the next morning. To my surprise, he agreed. I must have sounded even worse than I felt.

I crawled into bed early and fell asleep the second my head hit the pillow. But I must have been fighting Patrick all night. The next morning I was hopelessly tangled in the sheets, and there wasn't a cat in sight. Even Sashkatu had abandoned me for more serene sleeping quarters.

I decided to give myself the whole day off. I was due to meet Duggan at the local precinct at ten, after which there was Tilly's tea. My aunt had closed her shop for the day as well. Pumped from her adventure, she hadn't been able to sleep. After tossing and turning, she finally gave up and started baking at 4 a.m., first at home and later in the shop. When Sashki and I walked in through the connecting door, the air was so heavy with the layered smells of her baking that I could almost taste it. In fact, Sashkatu kept sticking his tiny pink tongue out as if he were tasting it.

The tea tables were small, accommodating two people comfortably or squeezing three. For this event, Tilly clustered three of the tables together so there would be plenty of room for the five of us and all the goodies she'd whipped up. Merlin was already seated, waiting eagerly for the starting gun.

"Not a morsel, until everyone's here," Tilly reminded him in a lilting tone, clearly too happy to scold him.

When she turned away from him to greet me, I saw him filch a chocolate truffle and pop it into his mouth. I gave him a conspiratorial wink.

I offered to help Tilly if there was more to be done, but she insisted she had it under control, so I sat down beside Merlin. Sashkatu staked out a spot at his feet, because he was Merlin, after all, as well as the person most likely to drop food. Elise arrived five minutes later. She told me not to get up. Instead, she gave my shoulder a loving squeeze and kissed the top of my head. Since Merlin was next to me, she kissed his head as well, causing him to blush, which embarrassed him more.

According to Tilly, when she invited Elise, she simply said that Travis and I had found the killer. With a teaser like that how could anyone resist? Couple it with one of Tilly's elaborate teas and most people would clear their calendars in an instant.

Tilly came out of the kitchen, holding two piping-hot ornate English teapots and set them on their trivets before embracing her. At that moment, Travis knocked on the door. Elise ran to let him in. He had a soft cast on his left foot and crutches under his arms. He greeted everyone with a general "Hey" because making the rounds to deliver personal hellos was clearly more than he could manage. He had some difficulty maneuvering into the chair on the other side of me. When he finally made it, he dropped the crutches with a grunt of relief.

"Sorry I'm late. Turns out there's a bit of a learning curve with crutches. The doc said it was easier for people who learned to use them as kids. Apparently, breaking bones as a child has its benefits, though I doubt you could convince my mother of that."

Tilly brought out the customary tiny tea sandwiches and some man-sized fare with roast beef for Travis and Merlin. For the second course, there were the scones with clotted cream and raspberry jam, my personal favorite, and, finally, mini pastries and buttery cookies dipped in chocolate. Tilly had outdone herself—not an easy accomplishment.

She poured the first round of tea and held up her cup to make a toast. "I'm ever so grateful we are all together today. I daresay it might have been a very different sort of gathering. But I don't want to dwell on that. I want to rejoice. To us, may we continue to gather in good health and celebration for many years to come!"

We lifted our cups and echoed her sentiments with a hearty "amen." Then we dug in. I could have sworn I wasn't hungry until my first bite of the moist raisin-walnut bread spread with cinnamon cream cheese. No one uttered a word for the first five minutes of indulging, but then the questions started coming.

Travis suggested he tell the story up to the part where I arrived at the antique shop and then I could tell the rest, with him adding anything I forgot. Our little audience listened silently, except for the slurping and lip-smacking coming from Merlin. At the end of our tale, Travis and I applauded the cavalry who had literally flown in to save us.

"Wait a minute," Elise said, "if Fletcher and Dwayne Davies weren't involved in Amanda's death, why did Dwayne disappear?"

I shrugged. "That's still a mystery. His poor mother has been going through hell since the day he dropped out of sight."

"I have the answer," Travis piped up, "but you have to promise not to breathe a word of this until after the evening news, or I'll be looking for a new job."

Tilly, Elise and I all promised. Merlin didn't seem to be listening, but he promised nonetheless when Tilly gave him a well-placed kick in the shin.

"Okay," Travis said, "it appears that Dwayne and the accountant at Winterland had been cooking the books long enough to embezzle a couple million. They must have figured their luck wouldn't hold forever, and it was time to make tracks."

"For a smart businessman, it's hard to believe Fletcher didn't realize what was going on a lot sooner," I said.

"The men were flying under his radar, so to speak. Stealing small amounts over a long period, banking on the fact that Fletcher was running so many enterprises that he wouldn't miss what amounted to pocket change in his world. When Fletcher caught on, he sent his henchmen to take them out. They caught up with Dwayne in Aruba and the accountant in Morocco and eliminated them on the spot."

"Did the FBI trace their deaths back to Fletcher?" Elise asked.

"Yeah, right," Travis said with a wry smile. "That man knows whose pockets to line."

"I have a bit of news too," I said, swallowing my last bite of scone. "When I was leaving my interview with Duggan this morning, Curtis was hauling in Alan Boswell. He was all disheveled and had his hands cuffed behind him. He was looking down like he wished the ground would open up and swallow him. Curtis whispered to me that he'd stopped Alan for driving under the influence, and there were drugs in plain sight on the passenger seat."

"That part about the ground opening up—I can arrange it, if you'd like," Merlin offered, selecting a miniature éclair. Tilly and I wasted no time making it clear that he would pay a steep price if he did any such thing.

"You'd think Alan would consider what he's doing to his daughter," Elise said. "Everyone knows about the wild parties till all hours, the prostitutes, and drugs."

"What a sleaze, I said. They should lock him up and throw away the key." I poured myself another cup of tea and took a sip. "You know who I feel sorry for in this whole mess?" No one ventured a guess. "Rusty Higgins. His only crime was unrequited love."

"What about painting those awful things on your fence?" Tilly asked. "And trying to run us off the road with his truck?"

"Duggan told me it was all Patrick. He'd been trying to run me out of town even before the Waverly Corporation floated the idea of building in the marsh. He was afraid I'd figure it out."

"That makes him smarter than I thought," Tilly said.

We all looked at her, puzzled.

"Patrick actually believes in the power of magick. He was smart enough to fear it would take him down."

I laughed. "But I doubt he ever imagined it would be in the form of wasps."

"You gave me the idea," Tilly said, "when you told me about the fly on Fletcher's wall."

"How did you two get inside?" Travis asked.

"We almost didn't," Tilly said soberly. "We missed our first two chances, when Chris arrived and again when he ran out in tears, because Merlin the Magnificent was busy pollinating hydrangea."

"One should assume all the characteristics of a species when transformed into it," he said indignantly. "Besides, one should always repay nature for its gifts."

"As I was saying," Tilly went on, "when I saw Chris coming back, I shoved Merlin out of a big blue flower, and we made it into the building with him by the skin of our teeth."

"We didn't have teeth," Merlin muttered.

"Fine, but I nearly lost a wing in the process," Tilly reminded him, "and I had no idea how that might translate when I returned to my human form. Fortunately, I don't seem to have suffered any deficit."

"How did you know where we were?" I asked her, in part to stop their bickering.

"I was in the middle of a reading for a bride-to-be when she vanished from my mind and I saw Patrick holding a gun on you and Travis. I felt your fear as if it were my own. I jumped up and told the young woman I had to save my niece's life. I promised her another reading, gratis."

"You don't usually get visions of the family," I said. "You didn't even foresee the accident that killed Morgana and Bronwen."

"My best guess is that you were meant to survive and I was near enough to save you."

Merlin cleared his throat pointedly. "Do I not receive any credit at all?"

"Thank you, Merlin," I said, giving his arm an affectionate squeeze.

"No question about it," Travis added. "You and Tilly are the reason we're alive today."

That seemed to satisfy the wizard—that and the last cookie he snatched off the plate Tilly was removing. Elise and I got up to help clear the table. Merlin complained of continued exhaustion from his heroic feats of the previous day and went back to Tilly's house to stretch out on the couch and watch TV.

Tilly laughed. "More like exhaustion from eating everything in sight."

Travis thumped his way to the kitchen doorway and thanked Tilly for the tea. "Now I'm going to get out of here before I break something or trip someone with these crutches."

I walked him to the door. "I want to apologize for not asking you to stay at my house last night," I said. "I could have helped you manage with the cast and crutches. I wasn't thinking straight."

"No need to apologize. There's nothing quite like the threat of imminent death to scramble the old neurons."

"In any case, you're welcome to stay tonight," I said, "and for as long as you need my help."

Travis searched my face as if he was looking for the exact meaning of my words. "Thanks," he said finally, "but can I get a rain check?"

"Sure," I said, more disappointed than I'd anticipated.

"I'm standing in for the anchor on the news tomorrow morning. National exposure. You don't pass up an opportunity like that, or you may not get another one."

"You're driving back to the city now?"

"Yeah, it's a good thing Patrick didn't break my driving foot."

We said good-bye. I held the door for him and watched him make his way to his car parked in front of my shop. He really was awful with the crutches.

* * * *

At dinnertime I was still too stuffed from the tea feast to think about food. At eight o'clock I decided on ice cream. I was on the couch, making my way through a dish of vanilla when my mother and grandmother popped in from the hereafter. Thankfully their clouds were aglow with a cheerful pink light.

"Please tell me you eat other things than ice cream," my mother said by way of a greeting.

I didn't take offense. It was just my mother being motherly. I'd learned that death didn't eradicate such concerns. At another time the remark might have irritated me, but having come perilously close to my own mortality, it was nice to be reminded of her love and the knowledge I'd be with her again someday, as long as that day didn't come anytime soon.

"We brought her up right, Morgana," Bronwen said patiently. "Trust in that. Besides, that's not the reason we're here." I waited for the sparks to fly. But Morgana didn't get annoyed with her. Both of them were on their best behavior. This really was a special night.

"We missed you at Tilly's," my mother said. "We want you to know we're proud of the way you handled yourself and kept your wits about you during your captivity by that horrid man."

A spark of lightning flashed in Bronwen's cloud. "To think I once liked visiting his shop."

"If not for Tilly and Merlin, it would not have gone as well," I said.

"Rest assured that we thanked and praised them both," Bronwen said. "Your aunt Tilly has become quite the daring one. I never would have thought it possible. Perhaps she merely needed to lose the coverage of our protective wings."

"One more thing as long as we're here," Morgana said. "We know your progress with teleportation has been slow and frustrating. But remember, it's a rare ability that's occurred only once before in our line. One day it will be worth all the work," I told them I had no intention of abandoning my efforts, which made their clouds glow more brightly.

They were bidding me farewell when the doorbell rang. I shooed them off and went to see who was at my door at that hour. The peephole showed me a distorted view of Travis. I yanked the door open. "What happened?"

"It seems the anchor made a miraculous recovery. Since I'm due back here tomorrow afternoon, I turned around. The only problem is that I checked out of my hotel room, and they've already given it away. Some big festival over in the Glen tomorrow. I hope your invitation still stands?"

"Of course," I said. "Come in."

"I just have to grab my bag from the car."

"I'll get it. I've seen you trying to walk with those crutches and you need both hands." I left him in the foyer and went out to his car, parked behind mine in the driveway. When I wheeled the overnight case into the house, I found Travis leaning back against the wall, his crutches on the floor and his face a scary shade of white. Oh no, I never looked back to make sure Morgana and Bronwen were gone before opening the door.

"What's wrong?" I asked with great reluctance.

Travis swallowed hard, his eyes fixed on the spot where their clouds had been. "I...I think I just met the rest of your family."

Don't miss the next delightful Abracadabra mystery by Sharon Pape

MAGICK RUN AMOK

Coming soon from Lyrical Press, an imprint of Kensington Publishing Corp.

Turn the page to enjoy an intriguing excerpt . . .

Chapter 1

"I'm going to be a pariah. A pariah!" Tilly wailed. "People will avoid me like I've got the plague." She'd come into Abracadabra through the door that connected her shop to mine. Since it was not yet nine o'clock, she found me at my desk behind the counter paying bills online. She shuffled up to me in ancient slippers she refused to replace because the soft last had stretched to accommodate her bunions and arthritic toes. Merlin was right behind her, like an odd shadow.

"Nonsense, Matillda" he said sternly. "There is naught to be concerned about. On that I stake my substantial reputation. You will never become a nasty little fish with sharp teeth! Besides, were it to happen, I would immediately change you back to your dear self. Kailyn, please tell her that. She refuses to take my word for it."

"Pariah, not piranha, you old fool," Tilly muttered. "As if I don't have enough to deal with right now." She turned to me. "What am I to do?"

"Why are you worried about becoming a pariah? I asked, figuring she was back to her original plaint. "Everyone in town loves you."

"They won't once they realize I'm the angel of death," she replied miserably.

"Hold on; you want to catch me up?"

"I had a premonition about yet another murder." Her voice trembled as if with pent-up tears. "First, I stumble across Jim Harkens's body, then Amanda's, and now this new murder—well, mentally anyway."

"What did this premonition tell you?" I asked, coming from behind the counter.

"Just that someone else would be killed."

"No images of the victim, the location, the time of the murder?"

She shook her head.

"Aunt Tilly," I said, "please sit down and listen to me." Tilly settled into the chair I kept there for bored husbands and exhausted shoppers. "You have things a little muddled. First of all, I'm the one who tripped over Jim Harkens; you fell on top of me."

She perked up. "You're right! You found him."

"Second, both you and Beverly discovered Amanda at the same time. And this premonition of yours is probably nothing more than a...a hunch, a bad dream, a figment of your imagination. It could be just another glitch in our magick."

"What a blessing you are," Tilly said, popping out of the chair as if she were reborn. She pulled me to her and hugged the air right out of my lungs. "I'm off to bake some of your favorite linzer tarts," she chirped. "Traditional raspberry or tangy apricot?"

"I believe I'd like some traditional," I said.

"Never mind. I'll make both."

"I am in your debt as well," Merlin whispered before following her back to Tea and Empathy. He graced me with the modified bow he'd adopted in deference to his age and a growing tendency to fall on his face if he attempted a deeper one.

Sashkatu had been watching us from his private loge on the window ledge. He rose, stretching languidly before he descended his custom-built steps, and accompanied the wizard back to Tilly's place, the home of fine aromas and finer tastes.

When I looked at my watch, it was ten past nine. I hurried to open the shop for business. Bronwen and Morgana would have frowned at my lack of punctuality, regardless of no one beating down my door in urgent need of a cure or a spell. My progenitors agreed on very little, but on this subject they were united. I could only hope they hadn't noticed, but, of course, they had. My grandmother's cloud of energy popped out of the ether first, my mother's a moment later. Both were calm and white. Maybe I'd be spared a lecture after all.

My grandmother Bronwen spoke first. "You did an admirable job of quieting your aunt's fears," she said, "but there is something you need to know."

I was pretty sure I didn't want to know what she was about to tell me.

"At least a few of our ancestors were remarkably talented at predicting death."

And there it was—exactly the sort of thing I didn't want to hear. "Did they have the ability from the time they were young, or did it come on later in life?" I asked, looking for a loophole to crawl through.

"I believe it's happened both ways," Morgana said, dashing my hopes.

"But this premonition was very vague," I pointed out. "For all we know, it wasn't a premonition at all." I felt like I was pleading my case before a panel of judges.

"The details may fill in over time," Bronwen said, "or not."

I was rooting hard for the "or not."

"If it doesn't come to pass this time, can we assume she doesn't have the ability?"

"That would be nice," my mother said, "but I'm afraid it's not that simple."

Of course not. Why would it be? "I don't suppose there's any way to turn off or blunt this particular talent?"

"None I've ever heard of," Bronwen said, "but I'll ask around."

Ask around? Was there a bartender or a manicurist beyond the veil who knew things? A guy on a street corner who could get you information for a price? Before I could ask what she meant, Morgana said they were being summoned and promptly vanished.

"Don't forget that punctuality is a sign of respect for your customers," Bronwen snuck in, her voice trailing behind her as she, too, winked away.

While waiting for customers, I finished paying my bills and caught up on some dusting, trying not to dwell on the havoc my aunt's nascent ability could cause in our lives. I wasn't successful until the bells above the door jingled to announce the day's first customer. She looked to be about thirty, petite and pretty enough to forego makeup and still turn a man's head. She seemed to be blown into the shop by a cold gust of wind, along with the last of the shriveled oak leaves that skittered across the hardwood floor. She had to put some weight into closing the door behind her, as if the wind were pushing back.

"It's awful out there," she said, shuddering in a jacket that was more suited to early October than November.

"Welcome," I said. "It's the sun that tricks you into thinking it's a nice day to be outside. Are you from around here?"

"Sort of," she extended her hand. "I'm Jane Oliver."

"Kailyn Wilde," I replied, briefly putting my hand in hers. It was overly formal for a shopkeeper and a customer, but hey, I'd been taught the customer was always right.

"To answer your question," she continued, "I moved to Watkins Glen two years ago. I guess by now I should know what the weather's like this time of year, but I go from the garage where I live to the garage where I work and hardly ever poke my head outside."

"What brings you to New Camel today?" I asked.

"Your shop. I'm on a mission to find a good moisturizer, and everyone raves about your products."

"Word of mouth is our best advertisement," I said. It was nice to hear that a customer made the trip to town specifically to visit Abracadabra. In many instances, my shop was an afterthought, a let's-peek-into-the-magick-shop idea after the tourist had already bought pounds of candy at Lolly's, skeins of wool at Busy Fingers, or lunch and a shake at The Soda Jerk. My mother had been pragmatic about it. For her commerce was commerce no matter how it came about. But I got a kick from knowing the shop was the primary reason someone came into our town.

"Let me show you where to find the moisturizers," I said, leading the way to the second aisle. I pointed out a shelf at eye level. "There are quite a few, so take your time. Feel free to ask questions."

"Thanks." Jane sniffed the air. "Where is that incredible smell coming from?" She was turning in a circle, trying to pinpoint the source. "Do you have a bakery in here too?"

I laughed. "It's coming from next door. The owner is a not only a renowned psychic but also an incredible pastry chef. You can have a glimpse into your future and then enjoy an authentic English tea."

"The tea sounds great," she said, "but I don't believe in psychics or any of that paranormal stuff. I'm a scientist from the bottom of my feet to the top of my head."

I pasted on a smile, and in the politest of tones, I reminded Jane that she was standing in a magick shop.

"I know," she said. "It's a cute gimmick."

"Are you sure it's just a gimmick?" I was baiting her, but I couldn't help myself.

"Of course. Not even the Great Houdini was capable of real magic."

"But you're willing to believe my products are somehow better than others, or you wouldn't be here."

"You've hit upon more successful formulas than anyone else in the industry, and I've seen proof of it on friends and colleagues."

I would have loved to demonstrate some levitation or a little telekinesis and watch her jaw drop to the floor. But she would probably chalk it up to a clever trick, the way Travis had the first time I disobeyed the rules. So I left her to browse on her own and marched myself out of the aisle and up to the front of the shop, before I did something hat warranted another visit from my dearly departed.

When Jane came up to the counter a few minutes later, she was holding two jars. "I can't decide which would be better for me."

I pointed to the one in her left hand. "That one is better for really dry skin." I would have loved to add a spell that made hairy warts grow wherever the cream touched her, but I behaved myself. Jane charged the purchase and went on her way, blissfully unaware how lucky she was that my family never dabbled in black magick.

Only two more customers stopped in during the morning, locals who needed health-related items. One was desperate for a lip balm that would actually work for her kids, and the other bought my last bottle of cough medicine for her husband, an early victim of the flu. I wasn't aware I'd run through my entire stock of cough medicine until she pointed it out. The slow morning instantly turned into a boon, giving me time to whip up more of the three different formulas I sold.

It had been a whole lot easier to keep up with demand and still run the front of the shop when my mother and grandmother were alive to share the workload. But I found that if I left the storeroom door open and didn't listen to music, I could easily hear the bells marking someone's entrance. That worked well for simple formulas. The more complicated ones required me to add ingredients at specific times in the process or complete the recipe without interruption. I had to leave those for afterhours. It made for longer workdays and a glower of cats unhappy about their delayed dinner hour, but I didn't collapse from the longer day, and they didn't starve from waiting an extra hour or two to eat. If it wasn't an elegant solution, it was at least an equitable one.

Fortunately I had all the ingredients I needed on hand. The basic honey, lemon, coconut oil mixture was number one on the hit parade. It always sold out first. The thyme tea only appealed to those who enjoyed the flavor of the herb, but those who did were rabid in their devotion. The ginger peppermint syrup was favored by people who preferred a little zip to the taste of their medicine. They were all somewhat effective in easing coughs. The game changer was the addition of the spell my mother created decades earlier. It drew its strength from the power of three. It required three candles, three oils—myrrh, mint and sandalwood—and three pieces of quartz. I anointed each of the candles and quartz pieces with each of the three oils. Then I placed a candle and a piece of quartz together at each point of an imaginary triangle with three equal sides. The words of the spell were deceptively simple, but repeating them three times imbued them with power if the practitioner came from the right bloodline.

Magick mend and candle burn.

Illness leave and health return.

I printed out the labels and was applying them to the bottles when I checked the time and realized I was late. I ran out of the storeroom, set the I'll Be Back clock to one thirty, put it in the window, and bundled myself into my down coat, gloves, and scarf for the two-block walk. No amount of weather was going to discourage me from meeting Travis for lunch. As I hurried to The Soda Jerk, I saw other shopkeepers using the quiet day to switch out the Halloween decorations in their windows for images of turkeys, cornucopias, and pilgrims. My family always steered clear of decorating our shop for holidays, believing that magick isn't seasonal.

I wasn't surprised to find The Soda Jerk less than half full. Folks who didn't need to leave the warmth of their snug homes hunkered down on days as raw as this one. I looked around to see if Travis was waiting at a table. He was usually punctual, but this time I'd beat him there even though I was five minutes late.

I didn't know any of the other patrons, but I could tell by their uniforms they were deliverymen, cable guys, and one lone mail carrier. For those who worked outside year-round, a warm restaurant was a welcome refuge from the cold.

The wait-staff at The Soda Jerk was back to its post-summer numbers, one busboy and the two waitresses I'd known all my life. Margie spotted me first and whisked me off to her section, which was fine with me. Her counterpart was often brusque and stingy with a smile.

"There are only two people you'd come out for in this weather," Margie said, seating me at a booth away from the draft of the door. "Who is it today: Elise or Travis?"

"Travis," I said with a grin. "I'll bet you know all the secrets in this town, don't you?"

"Who me?" she said with a wink. "How about I whip you up a cup of hot cocoa?"

"You twisted my arm, though to be honest, it didn't take much twisting."

"One cocoa, double whipped cream coming up."

Travis arrived as Margie was setting the cup in front of me. She must have seen his eyes widen at the sight of it. "Can I get you one too, Mr. TV?"

He slid into the booth across from me, looking harried. "Another time. I'll stick to coffee, thanks. Mind if we order right away?" he asked me before Margie could leave.

"No, sure." I knew the menu by heart anyway. "Grilled cheese and tomato soup combo."

Travis handed back the unopened menus. "Make it two." He always engaged in a little banter with Margie, but today he was all business. It derailed me for a moment.

"I'll put a rush on it." Margie said. She'd waitressed enough years that she could read people and situations better than most psychologists.

"What's wrong?" I asked after she left.

"A colleague of mine is missing."

"Oh, Travis, I'm so sorry. Are you two very close?"

"I've known him since high school."

"I'm sure his family must have notified the police."

"He has no family. Besides, the police won't act on a missing person's report for an adult until they've been gone for at least forty-eight hours."

"That's crazy."

"Not really. Can you imagine what it would be like if you could call the police and send them searching for everyone who's late arriving somewhere or isn't answering their cell? There's a fine line between protecting people and keeping tabs on them."

"I guess I didn't think of it that way." But I was still far from convinced that forty-eight hours was a reasonable amount of time to wait.

Travis's coffee arrived by busboy. While he was adding sweetener, I took a sip of my cocoa. When I looked up again, he was smiling.

"A white moustache is a great look for you."

I grabbed my napkin and wiped it off. "Way to win a girl over with compliments." The moment of levity felt good, but it couldn't last beneath the cloud of Travis's concern. "You're certain this colleague is missing?" I asked.

"I am. If you knew him, you'd understand. He digs for stories that might be better left unearthed. Stories that can get him killed. And he has a bad habit of trusting the wrong people. This wouldn't be the first time he's needed to be rescued."

"We needed a little rescuing ourselves not too long ago," I said, reminding him of our last case. "Things aren't always as dire and hopeless as they seem."

"But we had a secret weapon; he doesn't."

"You mean my family?" There was a time when the idea of real magick had sent him running from me and now my family had become his secret weapon. Talk about zero to sixty in a flash.

Margie arrived with our lunches, gooey cheese and steaming soup. "Enjoy," she said, off to the mailman who was beckoning her.

I took a bite of my sandwich, Travis took two, polishing off half of his. "When did you start looking for your friend?" I asked.

"Six p.m. yesterday," he said between spoonsful of soup. "We were supposed to meet for an early dinner in Watkins Glen. He never showed. Doesn't answer his cell."

"Have you slept or eaten since then?"

"I catnapped in my car for an hour or two this morning. And I had a couple of donuts and lots of coffee." He looked up and met my eyes. "I'm fine. Believe me. I've survived on less." He checked his watch and stuffed the last of the sandwich into his mouth.

"I understand if you want to leave," I said. "Lunch is on me. Just, please, don't choke on it."

He gulped down the coffee and reached across the table for my hand. He turned it over and planted a lingering kiss on my palm. As kisses go, it was a lot more effective than I would have thought.

"I'll call you."

"You'd better," I said, "or I'll have to go searching for you."

About the Author

Sharon Pape launched her delightful Abracadabra mystery series with *Magick & Mayhem* and plans many more adventures starring Kailyn Wilde and her fellow characters. Sharon is also the author of the popular Portrait of Crime and Crystal Shop mystery series. She started writing stories in first grade and never looked back. She studied French and Spanish literature in college and went on to teach both languages on the secondary level.

After being diagnosed with and treated for breast cancer in 1992, Sharon became a Reach to Recovery peer support volunteer for the American Cancer Society. She went on to become the coordinator of the program on Long Island. She and her surgeon created a nonprofit organization called Lean On Me to provide peer support and information to newly diagnosed women and men.

After turning her attention back to writing, Sharon has shared her storytelling skills with thousands of fans. She lives with her husband on Long Island, New York, near her grown children. She loves reading, writing, and providing day care for her grand-dogs. Visit her at www.sharonpape.com.

CPSIA information can be obtained
at www.ICGtesting.com
Printed in the USA
LVOW11s1459271017
554034LV00001B/123/P